LOVING SUMMER

The Summer Twins — Book One

DEBRA ST JAMES

Loving Summer | The Summer Twins — Book One

Website: www.debrastjamesbooks.com

Email: debrastjamesbooks@gmail.com

Published by: Debra St James Author

Edited by: Double AA Author Services

Formatted by: Debra St James Author

ISBN: 978-0-6450483-1-5 (Paperback)

ISBN: 978-0-6450483-0-8 (Ebook)

-inspiration-

This story was inspired by the lyrics ...
—> *Only Heart by John Mayer* <—

ONE

-oliver-

[fifteen months prior]

"Fuck, this humidity might kill me! Explain to me why I couldn't send a large donation again this quarter, rather than spend five days in this shitty hell hole?"

The people here have been great and appreciative of our work, but I don't like to be away from my business for this length of time. Plus, the humidity and bugs have been driving me to despair. I can barely see a smooth area of skin on my arms and legs from all the fucking bites.

"I want you to be seen as a compassionate human being, as opposed to the dick people think you are! Plus, you had no choice but to come since I organized this little jaunt behind your back." Jase claps me on the back, as he smiles and laughs.

It's true. Most people think I'm an asshole because I'm solely focused on making my company the best it can be. I don't dedicate any effort into building relationships with people outside of business —why bother with people? They hurt you and let you down. My business has never disappointed me, cheated on me, or broken my trust. It makes sense to invest all of my time there. I don't care that people think I'm an asshole because of that. Being perceived as a dick helps keep people from trying to get close to me—that's a win in my book. My singular focus has made me successful beyond my expectations and that's why, at thirty-two, I could retire and play golf for the rest of my days.

Fuck that, though.

Besides the fact that I hate golf, I thrive on the excitement of closing multi-million dollar deals for my clients—it makes waking up in the morning worth my while.

"C'mon Olly, you've only got another twenty-four hours to play nice with others, then you can go back to living your lonely life far above the rest of us mere peasants. You can do it, man!"

"My life isn't lonely. I've got plenty of willing women lining up to keep me company," I scoff. "Can you say the same?"

"Nope. Can't say that I do." He shakes his head in disappointment. "I spend my time with family and friends, because I don't want 'plenty of women'; I want that one special lady." He actually holds his hand over his heart and looks off into space when he says, 'that one special lady.' What a sap. He's naïve if he believes in that happily ever after bullshit.

"Ah yes, that elusive 'special lady.' Don't go down that path man, you'll only end up broken-hearted and destroyed."

Been there, done that. I thought I'd found that 'special lady'— turned out she only wanted my money and the social status that came with dating me. When someone higher up the corporate ladder came along, she ditched me real quick. I won't be making that fucking mistake ever again. The women I see agree to my terms, which satisfies my needs and keeps them at the distance all women should be kept. They know it's only a physical arrangement most of the time. Occasionally, I'll invite a woman to attend a business function with me, which also benefits her by increasing her public profile.

"Whatever, Olly. Not all women are heartless bitches."

Yeah, I've heard that before, too. This is a regular discussion for us. He's still single and I'm still safe.

It's finally time to shower and get some food after working another ten-hour day. The extreme heat and humidity is sucking the life right out of my body. Even though I honestly didn't want to come here, I have a sense of satisfaction seeing our hard work coming to fruition. It feels fucking fantastic to know I helped build a school, with my bare hands, for this underprivileged community. That I've contributed to helping make some kid's future better. With an education, who knows where life will take them? That's a fucking unbelievable thought. I'll never admit it to Jase, though. I don't want to give him the satisfaction of thinking he made the right call—it would go to his head.

I know school saved my life. It was my one constant. The one thing I could focus on and pour my energy into. My singular focus on doing my best in school led to my eventual success and earned me the scholarship I desperately needed to get into college so I could follow my dream. Without school to focus my energy, I don't know where I'd be today.

According to Bob and Ella, the couple who birthed the idea of this project, a couple of volunteer teachers from the States will arrive tomorrow. Apparently, one of them has won a ton of awards in her field and will work with the local teachers to help them establish a suitable curriculum for the elementary-aged students; while the second teacher will help establish the curriculum for the middle and senior students. Which is why we need to complete the building tomorrow. There isn't much left to do. We should finish the construction by tomorrow afternoon, then we'll head back to our real lives tomorrow night. It's been fucking exhausting working on this project *and* keeping on top of everything back home. For now, I'll enjoy a cold beer while I catch up on work emails. Then I need to get a decent night's sleep, ready to start all over again at the ass crack of dawn tomorrow.

"Pass me those nails, man."

"How about a 'please'? Pass me those nails, please?" Jase calls out over his shoulder with a smile on his face. I'm not sure how I've worked with him these past five years, since he's such a sarcastic bastard. Luckily for him, he's the best assistant I've ever had, and I don't have to worry about offending him. He's easy-going, efficient, organized, wicked smart, and manages to keep up with me, if not occasionally knowing what I need before I do. I'd never tell him that.

"Pass the fucking nails! I'm nearly done with this window."

"Sure thing, boss. Here ya go. It would be nice if you said 'please' occasionally."

"Hey, less of the boss thing. You know I don't want anyone else here knowing who I really am. It's bad enough that Bob and Ella know. I only agreed to do this if we kept it on the down-low. Unlike you, I don't care if everyone thinks I'm an asshole. The only thing that matters is taking people's investments and making them a shit ton of money."

"I get where you're coming from, even though I think you're wrong. You pay me the big bucks to watch out for you. Remember?"

Turning to take the nails from Jase, I spot a striking woman walking toward us with a duffle on wheels. She's genuinely struggling with it on the uneven terrain and if I weren't struck dumb, I'd offer to help. She's wearing tiny denim shorts, which show off a stunning set of shapely legs which end in a pair of battered red Converse. Raising my eyes to skim the rest of her exquisite body, I see she's wearing a tank, which shows the ideal amount of cleavage.

Woah! If I can see the tops of those sensational tits, that means every other asshole can, too.

I scan the area, noticing she's garnered quite a bit of attention, that I'm not happy about, from the other men working on site. Her fiery red hair, tied in some sort of intricate braid, has fallen over her shoulder. I don't think I've ever seen hair that color before; it's like the sunset at the end of a scorching hot day. Even though she's finding it tough to maneuver her duffle, she's got the biggest smile and her big blue eyes are sparkling like some kind of fairytale princess.

She's like sunshine streaming through gloomy gray clouds.

No wonder every guy in a five-mile radius is checking her out. She's the quintessential girl next door, except she's stunning.

"Put your tongue back in your mouth, boss! You're making a scene." Jase points out with a laugh.

Shit, I didn't realize I'd been staring at the woman. "Fuck off."

Jase moves toward her, helping with her duffle and situating it on the veranda.

She stops right in front of us as I'm glaring at Jase and gives us an award-winning smile. "Hey there! I'm pretty sure I'm in the right place. I'm supposed to meet Bob and Ella at one, but I think I'm a bit early. Are they around?" She looks around expectantly, as if they're going to walk out of the building at any second. "Oh sorry, I'm excited and forgot my manners. My name's Kate."

She's obviously nervous because all of that comes out in a rush. Her nose, dotted in freckles, scrunches up as she thrusts out her delicate hand for me to shake, but Jase steps in before me, greeting her with a friendly smile—*asshole*. I scowl at him, but he ignores me, moving into her space.

"Hey, nice to meet you, Kate," he raises his chin, giving her a friendly smile. "Bob and Ella stepped away for a bit, but they'll be back shortly. I'm Jase, and this is Oliver."

He's so damn polite, making me appear more of an asshole because I haven't said a word.

"Hi, nice to meet you guys. How long have you been working on the construction? I'm excited to start and can't wait to see what I'll be working with. This is such an incredible opportunity."

She's almost bouncing on her toes. Far too sweet for the likes of my cynical ass, but I'll be damned if I can stop thinking about getting my hands and mouth on her sweet body.

"Are you one of the teachers who'll be working with the local staff to help them set up?" I finally ask as I step into her space, forcing Jase back a step.

"I sure am! I'm a kindergarten teacher back home. I'm spending part of my summer break here to help Bob and Ella get the elementary part of the school established. It's going to differ vastly from anything I've ever done before, but I love a challenge and you know, kids are kids, no matter where they live," she says with a shrug.

Yep, sweet as honey, this one. I wonder if she tastes as sweet?

"How long have you guys been here?"

"Jase and I have been here for five days. We're on our way home late tonight. We need to return to the real world and our actual jobs." But damn, I wish I were staying longer, so I could see this woman naked. To pull that long, fiery-colored braid of hers back, allowing me to lick up her slender neck, trail my hands along all that smooth ivory skin encasing those shapely legs which I could wrap around—

"Oh yeah. What do you guys do for work? Are you in construction back home?"

Her question jolts me from my thoughts of having her for a night and drags me back into the conversation.

"I work for this—" Jase starts, pointing towards me.

"Nope. We work in corporate investments." I cut Jase off before he opens his big mouth and outs me as his boss. He looks at me as if I've lost my mind.

He knew the deal.

"Oh wow. I bet this was quite an experience for the two of you."

Her eyes keep wandering down my body. I took off my shirt because it's fucking hot. I work hard for my body; I certainly don't mind that she can't keep her eyes to herself.

Jase smirks at me. "Yeah, we're used to suits and ties and temperature-controlled offices. It's been a wake-up call. I'm going to appreciate the luxuries of using my own shower, sleeping in a comfortable bed, and not sweating bullets all day." *I hear ya, brother.*

He winks at Kate.

Fucking winks!

The bastard thinks he's so fucking smooth with the ladies.

She laughs.

Fucking laughs at him, but she's still looking at my chest.

I run my hand down my body to adjust my shorts and sure

enough, her eyes follow the path. I haven't taken my eyes off her and when she finally looks up and notices I've caught her ogling me; she swallows hard and blushes.

Now that's what I'm talking about! That's the reaction I want from her. To have a woman look at me like I'm a piece of meat as opposed to a walking credit card is something else. Most women know who I am, which means they only look at me for what I can give them, not for the man I am.

It's rather refreshing.

TWO

-kate-

OH MY!

How embarrassing. He caught me ogling his impressive body.

Wait, is that an eight pack? Is that even a thing? He's beautifully defined; he's even got that awesome V thing, pointing to the promised land that hot guys have. I thought only guys on the covers of my favorite reading material had that. Oh, and Chris Hemsworth. *So hot!* And that sexy trail of dark hair leading down into his shorts, like a trail of graham cracker crumbs, guiding me to a house of candy. My thoughts are rambling like crazy. He's a lot to take in.

I've been here five minutes and I've already embarrassed myself. *Keep up the good work, Kate!* But there's something about him besides a hot body. He seems very intense, and he gives me the impression that he is laser focused when he finds something or someone that he wants.

When I was walking toward the building, I saw these two men working. It was like discovering my very own hot guy club as their muscles pulled and stretched as they hammered and lifted the timber. Both men have the same height and build; one with darker hair, one lighter. The one with lighter hair is, dare I say, almost pretty. But for some unknown reason, my eyes keep moving back to the dark-haired one called Oliver.

A tall, slim, middle-aged man with weathered skin and a graying ponytail and a stout, but attractive blonde woman with an enormous smile approach from the side of the building, saving me from myself. I'm guessing they might be the people I need to check in with. I've been communicating with them via email for the past several months but have never met them in person. Bob and Ella founded the non-profit organization called *Schools for Everyone* since retiring from teaching. In the past eight years, they've helped two other communities like this one. They help to secure the funding and volunteers to build schools in remote communities all over the world. They'll stay with the project until it's self-sufficient before moving onto their next one. I didn't want to miss the opportunity to work with such an inspirational couple. Helping them work with this small island community in the middle of the Java Sea is a dream come true.

"Hey, you must be Kate. I'm Bob and this is Ella. It's lovely to meet you in person, finally."

He steps in for a hug, closely followed by Ella. Oh, I love that. I'm also a hugger. I hear a growl behind me and turn my head. Jase is smiling as he pats Oliver on the back in a reassuring fashion. Oliver's eyebrows slash low over his mesmerizing green eyes while his mouth forms a firm, straight line. He's scowling at me as if I've broken his favorite toy.

"I see you've already met Oliver and Jase."

"It's great to meet you both and yes, we were just introducing ourselves. It looks like they've done remarkable work here," I say as I gesture to the building behind us. "I'm a little early, but I was too excited to go to the hotel first. "I'm a little early. I was too excited to go to the hotel first. I hope you don't mind that I asked the driver to bring me straight here from the airport."

Ella smiles, taking hold of my hand. "Not at all. We're grateful you could give up your valuable time to help us with this project.

You sounded perfect in your application for this volunteer position. We feel incredibly fortunate to have you onboard." A blush rises from my chest in response to her words. I hope I don't disappoint them.

"How about we show you around and then we'll deliver you to the hotel to settle in? We can chat about the plan for the coming weeks over drinks," Bob suggests as he picks up my duffle like it weighs nothing. *Ugh, it felt like it weighed a ton to me.*

"That sounds great. I've got a rough plan ready for you guys and the local teachers to look at. I can't wait to get started." Rubbing my hands together, I turn toward Jase and Oliver. "Bye, Jase. Bye, Oliver. Perhaps I'll see you later?"

Oliver observes me as though he's studying an exhibit. "Doubtful. Once we've finished here, we'll be heading out late tonight."

His stare and body language are freaking full on. I've never experienced anything as intense before. I feel as though I'm about to combust from the potency alone and he hasn't laid a single finger on me.

"Ohh-kay then. I guess a big thank you is in order for all of your hard work."

Leaning in, I give Jase a hug goodbye. Oliver's watching me like a hawk. Maybe Jase is his boyfriend, and he doesn't like other people touching him? When I step across to hug Oliver, I'm unsure if it's such a good idea, but I don't want to appear rude. I don't know what it is about him that says, 'stay away from me', but draws me to him in equal measure. As I wrap my arms around Oliver's large body, there's a shift, something I can't explain. I realize my mistake instantly. His torso is naked, which means I'm touching his glorious, bronzed skin. He's so hard and *so* … male and smells so good and *so* … male.

Ugh, Kate. Get it together.

He takes a few beats to reciprocate the hug, but when he does, his large hands engulf my back. He's much bigger than I am, but I like it. I love feeling tiny and feminine in his embrace. His body relaxes slightly, and he sucks in a breath.

Did he smell me?

As I reluctantly step away, I'm a little dizzy, a little off-balance, and I take a second to get my bearings—wow, he certainly has a powerful effect on me.

Luckily, he's leaving today because I don't need any distractions. It's important to me to do the best job I can for Bob and Ella, as well as the teachers and children who need this school.

I'm about to leave the hotel bar after my meeting with Bob and Ella when Oliver steps through the double doors. He looks as though he's had a shower—something I desperately need. He's looking around the bar as though he's searching for someone. I scan the room. Maybe he's looking for his friend, but I didn't see him here unless he snuck in when I was in the ladies. His eyes eventually land on me and if I'm not mistaken, his posture relaxes somewhat, as if he's found what he was looking for. He moves forward, making it into my space within five strides.

"Kate."

"Oliver. I didn't expect to see you here. I thought you were leaving."

"We are. Not until later. I thought I'd have a quiet drink before heading to the airport."

"Oh, that sounds like a great idea. I'm a nervous flyer, so a drink usually calms me down and stops me from stressing out as the plane takes off from solid ground. I would prefer to travel overseas without leaving the ground." There I go again, rambling like a complete fool. *When will I learn to temper what I say?*

He huffs out a laugh as he places his hands in the pockets of his shorts. Perhaps he doesn't mind my rambling all that much.

"That sounds like a fair approach. Would you like to join me for a drink?" He gestures toward the table I was about to leave.

"Uh, oh." Well, his invitation is unexpected. I figured he'd be having a drink with his friend. "Uhm. I can keep you company while you wait for Jase."

"I'm not waiting for Jase. I *was* hoping to catch you."

Huh! I'm not sure what to make of that. I guess it's only one drink and he'll be gone in a few hours. I'll never have to see him again, which means he won't become a distraction I don't need.

"Uh, sure. That sounds … *nice?*" My acceptance of his invitation isn't convincing. He gestures for me to sit. His tanned forearms and the display of sexy veins draw my eyes as he leans on the back of the opposite chair.

"What would you like to drink?" My eyes snap back up to his. *Damn.* He caught me staring again.

I would normally stick to soda because I've got an early morning tomorrow, but I think I'll need something stronger while I'm with Oliver. "Uh, a sweet white wine would be great. Thanks." I grab my purse to give him some money, but he waves it away, then heads to the bar. He returns with a glass of wine for me and a beer for himself.

We each take a drink, and the cool liquid soothes my nerves and my dry throat. He takes the opportunity to observe me, making me self-conscious of my messy braid, bare face, and travel-creased clothes. After twenty-four hours of travel, I went straight from the airport to meet Bob and Ella. Plus, I've been sitting here for the last three hours, so I'm certain I don't look or smell very fresh.

"What made you volunteer to travel half-way around the world to help Bob and Ella build this school?"

I guess we're going to skip the usual small talk about the weather. "I'm a teacher back home. My greatest joy comes from helping people, kids in particular. When I saw this opportunity advertised in an education newsletter, I knew I had to apply. Working to build a school from the ground up was a challenge I couldn't pass up. I knew I had to get involved. There was no other option for me." I take another large gulp of wine to shut myself up. "How about you? What made you volunteer?"

He shakes his head. "Not what, but who. Jase signed us onto the project without telling me. He arrived at my place last week, packed my bag, and drove me to the airport—explaining the plan on the way. I was pissed at him at first." He runs his hands through his thick hair. "I don't like taking time away from my work, let alone a full week. It took me a few days to calm down enough to realize this is a worthwhile project." He takes a sip of beer and I watch his Adam's apple move up and down. "I'm glad he did it now. It's been genuinely satisfying to watch the structure grow from a pile of materials into useable buildings." He huffs out a laugh. "Don't tell him I said that, though. It'll go to his head." I laugh with him.

"Wow. How did he manage to get you off work for a week without you knowing?"

"I don't actually know. Sometimes I think that man can work miracles." He seems to have a great deal of respect for Jase.

We chat for over an hour and another round of drinks. The day of travel has finally caught up with me and I can't hold in the yawn that's been trying to escape for the last twenty minutes.

"You must be tired. I'll walk you up to your room. You need to rest and I need to pack, ready for my flight."

"Thanks. It was nice to chat with you."

"It's been my pleasure." He pulls out my chair, guiding me from the bar with his hand resting on the small of my back. The heat and electricity from his barely there contact are completely new to me.

Stopping at my door, I lean forward to hug Oliver in thanks. He's quicker to reciprocate this time. It seems as if he squeezes me a little tighter and holds on a little longer, and I definitely hear him take a deep breath close to my hair. Stepping back from his large body, I put some much-needed space between us.

"Thanks again, Oliver. And thanks for everything you and Jase did for the school." I tuck my hands in my back pockets, searching for the key to my room. His eyes have dropped to my boobs. *Ugh!* "Have a safe trip home."

"No problem. Good luck with the setup."

"Thanks." I turn to unlock my door, and as I step inside, Oliver stops me with his hand on my forearm. My skin practically sizzles where his calloused hand touches me.

"Be careful, Kate. Make sure you always keep your door locked. Okay? A striking woman like yourself needs to be careful." The furrow in his brow tells me he's deadly serious about my safety.

"Uh, sure. Thanks again. Bye." Did he just call *me* striking? That's laughable, especially how I look at the moment.

"Bye." I watch him turn away, tucking his hands in his shorts as he walks down the passage toward the other end of the hotel.

Well, that was crazy!

THREE

-oliver-

[present]

I spot Jase walking past my doorway, carrying a stack of files. "Jase, have you got those updates I requested this morning?"

He stops and leans on my doorframe. "Sure thing, Boss, I'll bring them by in a sec. Did you hear from the private investigator you hired to find Kate? Not that it's weird or stalker-ish that you've hired someone to find her." He smirks at me—*asshole!*

"I saw something I wanted and I'm working toward getting it. If you've got a problem with that, you're working for the wrong fucking guy."

"I don't have a problem with it—you talk about her as though she's some kind of commodity. She didn't come across as the type of woman you usually spend time with and probably won't go for your usual arrangement."

I shrug. "Probably not, but she's worth pursuing. I know she's not like the usual women I spend time with, but there was something about her that intrigued me. I don't need you to be my fucking conscience." The woman hasn't left my thoughts. That's why I hired a PI to find her last week.

"Well, that's something, I guess." Jase rolls his eyes at me. "I'll get those updates for you."

"I need them ASAP." I turn back toward my computer, effectively dismissing him.

I'm unsure what it was about Kate that woke something inside me—she sparked my interest beyond wanting to meet my physical needs. After spending less than two hours in her company, I could tell there was an innate goodness about her I honestly shouldn't taint, but fuck me, I can't stop thinking about her. I'm compelled to find out exactly what it was about her that caused such a profound reaction in me. Not only is she sexy as fuck, but she's obviously intelligent, compassionate, and brave. I need my fucking PI to hurry and find her. How hard can it be?

"Here ya go, the updates you requested. They look pretty good to my untrained eye." He drops the papers on the corner of my desk and pushes them toward me.

His untrained eye is bullshit. He doesn't give himself enough credit for his knowledge across this field. If he says they look pretty good, I'm certain they do, in fact, look pretty good.

"Thanks. This quarter is looking pretty spectacular at this point. Can you get Mike on the phone for me? I want an update on his search."

"Sure thing."

As Jase leaves my office, I scan the updates for this past quarter and I can't help being impressed with what my team and I have achieved for our clients. We're making them a shit ton of money, which is exactly the way I like it.

My phone buzzes with the internal line from Jase's desk. "Mike's on line one for you."

I press the button to connect to Mike and get straight to the point. "Hey, Mike. Have you found Kate?"

"I'm getting close to finding her. I managed to get in touch with Bob and Ella to find out her surname, but they wouldn't budge. They were protective of her privacy."

I had already called Bob and Ella asking the same thing; hoping that my substantial funding toward their project would get me the information I wanted, but they wouldn't share any details. They even reminded me how protective I am of my identity.

"I've got a contact inside the airline that flew to the area that day. He ran a search for a Kate on all flights heading to that community, and what do you know? He found Kate and her surname. Her name is Kate Summer. I traced the origin of her flight back to our very own international airport. Which means she's possibly a local girl."

Well, fuck me, she's probably been under my nose all this time.

"There are actually two women named Kate Summer living in this city. It's too complicated to figure out which school she might work at because there are over seventy kindergartens within the city. It will be easier to locate them via their driver's license."

"How long will it take for you to get their identification for me?"

"I need to get in touch with my contact. I hope to have something for you within the next few hours. As soon as I do, I'll bring it directly to you."

"Good. See you soon."

"No problem."

The conversation with Mike leaves me frustrated. Even a few more hours of waiting to find out who she is feels too long. She's been a regular guest in my thoughts since I met her on that school veranda. Sharing a couple of drinks and a brief conversation with her in the hotel bar fifteen months ago left me wanting more. I never spend this much time dedicated to thinking about one woman. I've got to find her and spend a night with her. That way I can see she's not everything I've built her up to be in my mind. I haven't been able to spend time with another woman since meeting her because she's fucking invaded my every thought.

Kate Summer—even her fucking name is like sunshine.

Watch out, Kate. I'm coming for you.

Jase interrupts my musing. With his shoulder leaning against my doorframe, he's the epitome of a laid-back guy—everything I'm not. I'm unsure how we work so well together, but we do. He stares at me with a smile on his pretty-boy face, as though he's trying to work out where my head's at. Good luck buddy, because I don't even fucking know at this point.

"You ready to work on *The Parkerville Project* this weekend?"

"Yep. That's why I've been working later than usual every night this week, to free up my weekend to do my civic duty for your latest attempt at making me appear less of a dick."

Even though I've been giving him a hard time about working on this project, I *am* looking forward to helping with the makeover of the latest acquisition for *The Parkerville Project*. They do sensational work with kids who need to be removed from abusive or neglectful homes. In the past, I only threw money at these projects, but Jase is determined to improve my image, meaning my money alone isn't good enough—I have to give them my time as well. At least it's only a weekend this time, as opposed to the seven days I spent working and traveling the year before last—taking me away from my work for far too long.

"You know they're doing great work for the kids—kids whose upbringing isn't that dissimilar to yours." He raises a blond eyebrow as a form of punctuation.

I made the mistake of sharing my history with Jase a couple of years ago and now he loves to use it to guilt me into working with organizations like *Parkerville*. Generally, I don't mind offering financial assistance, however, my time is another matter. I need all of my focus on my business. I don't need any distractions or anything else eating up my time, except maybe Kate—for a night, or maybe two.

"Anyway, I'm heading out. Do you need anything before I go?" He presses away from the doorframe.

"Nope, I'm good. I'll finish reviewing this data and then I'm heading home myself."

I drop my head back down to the document I'm looking at, dismissing him.

"I'm catching up with some college buddies for drinks at Brady's Pub. See you at the house on Winchester Street at eight a.m. sharp."

"Sure. Don't drink too much. I don't want to be holding up your hungover ass all day."

He laughs at me, waving over his shoulder as he retreats. Sometimes I envy the lightness he has with his easy smiles and ready laughs. That he has time to spend socializing for the fun of it, not just for business purposes. Then I remember that I'm safer keeping everyone at arm's length. Though I may have a problem with that if I ever find Kate. I have a feeling I won't want any space between us —at all.

The buzz of my alarm wakes me at five. Even though it's Saturday, I want to get my workout in before heading to the project site. I dress in my workout shorts and hit my home gym—having a dedicated room with the equipment I need saves me time. Plus, I can avoid dealing with people. It's leg day and I'm working up quite a sweat as I lift and pull, stretch and strain to the sound of *Praise You* and *Best of You* pumping over the bluetooth system. While I'm working my body, I run through what needs to be done before I leave for the Winchester Street property. I need to go downstairs to my office after breakfast, to double-check some figures from the data I was reviewing last night. By the time I've finished my workout, it's almost six and I head to the kitchen, collecting the ingredients to make myself a high-protein breakfast. After showering, I dress in shorts and an old college t-shirt for comfort and ease of movement. I'm not sure what I'll be doing today, a bit of this and a bit of that I expect.

I still haven't heard from Mike. I've been calling since last night and all I get is his fucking voicemail. Snatching up my wallet, phone, and keys, I slam the door as I step out of my penthouse. Making my way to the subway aiming to get to the property for the eight a.m. start, I try Mike again. *Still no fucking answer!* Being early on a Saturday, the subway isn't too crowded and will probably be even less so when I make this ride again tomorrow. Once I clear the subway, I try calling Mike again with the same result. I run my hand through my hair and study the people around me going about their normal business.

I wonder if she uses this subway?

Have our paths crossed over the last fifteen months and I didn't notice? Nah. I would have definitely noticed *her*.

Arriving at my destination, I take in the property we're working on this weekend. The goal is to make it as warm and inviting for the kids as possible. This is where they'll stay after being removed from an unsatisfactory family situation, while the Department of Children's Services locates more suitable family members, or approved foster families to take the kids in and care for them. I'm impressed with the space out front of the property, which would be great for a game of basketball. There's something therapeutic about bouncing a ball and taking shots to center the mind and make any confusion settle. The house isn't very appealing, but by the end of the weekend, I'm sure it will be more suitable for its intended purpose.

I freeze mid-step as I spot Jase hugging a woman with the same striking fiery hair as Kate. Now I'm fucking imagining her wherever I go. I think I'm in trouble.

Good ol' Jase is at it again; already chatting up the ladies and making friends. He notices me over her shoulder and says something to her while motioning me over. She turns and I see her face for the first time. I feel as though I've been sucker punched in the gut—all the breath leaves my lungs in a rush.

It's her!

My Kate!

Fuck, when did I start thinking of her as mine?

For some reason, it feels right to think of her in that way. As she takes in my determined strides toward them, her eyes widen and she swallows hard while she takes a step away from Jase—*good girl*. I increase my pace and make it to them in a few long strides.

Jase nods to me with the biggest shit-eating grin I think I've ever seen. "Morning, Olly. Remember Kate from our stint building the school a while back?"

As if he needs to remind me.

"Morning, Jase. Kate." I step into her space and look her square in the eyes. I want her to know she has my sole attention. "Of course I remember Kate. I always remember a beautiful woman."

She's wearing something similar to what she wore the first time I saw her. I'm gratified to find she truly is as stunning as I remembered. If she looks this good with no makeup, that gorgeous hair back in a simple ponytail, shorts, tank, and those battered red Converse; imagine how she looks when she's trying.

"I bet you say that to all the women you meet. I'm far from beautiful," she says as she rolls her eyes.

That attitude of hers is going to have to change.

"I was telling Jase how much I enjoyed working with the teachers to create a curriculum for the kids in the community where we met. They were open to some new hands-on ideas for the kids and using the latest open-ended learning techniques designed to encourage self-learning and allow the child to learn and develop at their own rate." She's gesticulating like it's an Olympic sport and her stunning blue eyes are sparkling with absolute joy—it's fucking spectacular to watch. "Oh my gosh, sorry. There I go, getting carried away. I can't seem to help myself."

I can't believe she's apologizing for being passionate about her work. I wait until I've got her eyes on me. "It's all good, Kate. It's something special to listen to someone dedicated to and passionate about the work they do."

Her shoulders drop, and the worry disappears from her eyes. I feel ten feet tall that I could easily take away her obvious worry.

Suddenly, some tall, blond-haired, man-bun-wearing guy comes up behind her, wrapping his arms around her waist, lifting her off her feet. She startles, letting out a surprised squeal, while the dick behind her laughs. Without intentional thought, my fists clench and my body prepares to fight. The adrenaline begins to pump, increasing my heart rate and my breaths. All I can see is this guy holding *My* Kate and a red haze takes over my vision. I'm ready to kill this motherfucker! The guy next to him, who's built like a linebacker, steps toward me with a 'don't fuck with me' expression on his face.

Yeah, well, don't fuck with me either, man.

He lets her down. Landing on her feet, Kate spins around, punching him on the arm, laughing the entire time. "Oh my gosh, Toby, don't do that! You scared the crap outta me." Kate presses up onto her toes to hug him, all the while smiling her award-winning smile.

He returns her smile and hug readily—a clear familiarity between them. I quickly scan her hands and notice she doesn't wear any rings, nor is there any sign that she's worn a ring for a long period. He doesn't show any signs of a ring either, only wearing leather bands around his wrist. But this guy must be a boyfriend to be so familiar, which pisses me the fuck off.

She turns to us while holding onto his arm with a gigantic smile. "This is my brother, Toby. I wasn't sure if he was going to make it because he's been extremely busy lately." She gestures to the other guy. "This is his, uh … friend, Shane." Turning to her brother she says, "I'm ecstatic you could make it. I've missed you beyond measure." She steps across to hug Shane. "Hey, Shane. This is Jase, and this is Oliver."

My hands release and my body relaxes, coming out of fight mode. Jase glares at me, telling me I'm acting like an asshole, but I don't fucking care.

Toby kisses her forehead. "You know I'll always try to support your causes if I can. I'm happy to get dirty for a couple of days renovating if it makes you happy, Squirt." He acknowledges Jase and I with a nod over her head.

"Hey, don't call me Squirt. I'm the big sister, remember?" She seems affronted by the nickname, but Toby obviously thinks it's hilarious.

"You may be older than me." He looks over at us. "By four and a half minutes, but I'm much bigger than you. Squirt."

Ah, twins! They have different color hair, but their eyes are the same shade of blue. Shane laughs as Toby quickly dodges the next swing from his spunky sister. He must be used to their antics. Clearly, the fiery-colored hair reflects her feisty personality. She *is*, hands down, a lethal combination. The siblings obviously have a lot of love for each other, which makes me think about my own lack of siblings. Jase is probably the closest thing I have to a brother.

Sarah, the head coordinator of this renovation for *The Parkerville Project*, interrupts my musing. She gains everyone's attention, thanks us all for donating our time, and *The CornerStone Foundation* for funding the project. Jase winks at me, nudging his shoulder against mine—*obvious much?* I know I don't need to worry. I'm pretty much anonymous. The only person associated with *The Parkerville Project* who knows who I am is Marcus Trainor, the CEO. Sarah then allocates tasks to people working in pairs. To ready the floors for sanding and polishing, she gives Jase and I the job of removing all the old, dirty carpets and cracked linoleum, which are in great condition. I find I'm constantly on alert for any glimpse I can get of Kate as we work through each room, lifting the disgusting flooring, which must have been here since the house was first constructed.

FOUR

-kate-

TOBY, SHANE, AND I HAVE THE DELIGHTFUL JOB OF STRIPPING THE
bathroom and separate toilet ready for new tiling, a basin, a
combined bath and shower, and toilet to be installed tomorrow.
Toby, Shane, and I chat and laugh our way through the morning as
we demolish the small spaces, but the company and the work aren't
enough to distract me from Oliver. It disappointed me when I saw
Jase on his own this morning, and I was undeniably relieved when
he mentioned Oliver was on his way. I can't believe I actually get to
see him again. He's been a regular starring feature in my thoughts
over the past year and a bit, even though I spent less than two hours
with the man. I thought my mind had made him into someone
more spectacular than he was in real life, but he literally is a twelve
on the Richter scale of hotness! Which is great for my eye candy
today and tomorrow, but no chance someone as handsome as him
would be interested in someone as plain as me.

I mean, I know I'm not ugly, but I'm certainly nothing to write
home about. When he said he 'always remembers a beautiful
woman', I knew he was being kind, as it was so far from the truth, it
wasn't funny. My attraction to him is strong, though. I'm going to
need to work hard to hide my natural reaction.

As we work to clear out the bathroom and toilet, I find I'm on alert for any glimpse I can get of Oliver while chatting with Toby and Shane. He was intense again this morning and his muscles looked fantastic in his college t-shirt, which looked soft and comfortable. I wonder what it would be like to spend a night with him, then get up and throw that shirt on? I bet my body would feel fantastic after a night in his bed.

I'm entirely focused on my daydream that I almost tip the wheelbarrow over in the front yard, losing the load. When I look up to determine what stopped the fall, I'm greeted with intense green eyes looking at me as if they can see what I was thinking. Oops, that would *not* be a good thing. The heat from my blush rises all the way up from my chest until it heats my cheeks. I wish my complexion wasn't so fair. Every time I feel the slightest bit embarrassed, everyone immediately knows. I may as well hold a banner over my head with an announcement.

"Oh, sorry. I nearly lost my load all over you!" I say without thinking as I work to rebalance the wheelbarrow.

His eyes widen, and crinkles form around the edges as his lips press together. "You can lose your load over me anytime you like, Sunshine."

My blush gets hotter. I must look ridiculous by this point, as I realize how my words sounded and the way he threw them right back at me. Surely he's not flirting with someone like me? I'm at a loss how to respond, totally thrown by his candor and how easy it was for him to respond in a sexy way.

"Go to dinner with me tonight," he says in a rush, contradicting his normal confidence and catching me off guard with his demand. It *was* a demand, right? It certainly didn't sound like a question.

Who does that?

"Uh," I stammer out like a fool, working quickly to gather my wits. "You didn't really ask me. It seemed like you were demanding I join you for dinner tonight." I narrow my eyes. "Besides, I have a date, which means I can't go to dinner with you. Even if you asked nicely." Digging into confidence I don't feel, I raise a single brow at the man.

If you could call my plans tonight a date—I'm not sure why I referred to my evening in that way. I spend my Saturday afternoons, which often turn into evenings, at another house associated with *The Parkerville Project*. I hang out with kids waiting for new, safer living arrangements. We usually bake, learn some new recipes, watch movies, make popcorn, play games, and generally do stuff to distract them from the unfairness of their life. Some of the kids have had horrendous experiences and they're still very young. Too young! It breaks my heart. I love that I'm able to spend time with them, giving them some positive, happy experiences. I'm privileged to be able to show them not all adults are bad, and there are people who care.

His eyes narrow and his dark eyebrows form slashes over those tantalizing green orbs. "I rarely 'ask' anyone to join me for dinner. Women usually ask me." He looks positively dumbfounded—*cocky much!*

Well, that just lowered his rating on the Richter scale of hotness.

"Sorry to disappoint you, but I'm too busy most nights to be asking random guys out to dinner." Not that he's totally random, but I'm gonna go with that. "Between work, family, and other obligations, I have little free time."

I collect my wheelbarrow and begin moving away when he stops me with his hand on my arm, reminding me of the last time we met.

"What about tomorrow night?"

I can't believe he's asking *me* out to dinner. It sounds as though he has plenty of offers from other women. Why waste his time and energy on me? I'm a mess. I'm pretty sure I still have glitter in my hair from yesterday's craft activity. "Sorry, but I'm expected at my parent's home for dinner tomorrow night. I'm looking forward to it because Toby's finally back in town; which hasn't happened in months."

He runs his hand through his hair. I'm guessing he's used to women asking *him* out and he's not used to someone saying 'no' to him. He finally releases me so I can empty my wheelbarrow and get back to the guys for the next load. I miss the pressure of his hand on my arm and I kick myself for being disappointed in having to say no. I don't need some hot guy thinking he can play games with me. He'll probably ask me out and then stand me up, or cancel at the last minute, for the fun of it. I know guys like him aren't genuinely interested in girls like me. I already learned that lesson when Michael made a big deal about asking me to senior prom in front of everyone, only to never show up. When I turned up on my own, he was dancing with Samantha Riley. I was proud of myself for holding my head up high and semi-enjoying the dance with my friends.

He steps in, taking over the wheelbarrow handles. "Here, I'll do this. Since your brother and his friend are such wimps, they let the woman do the heavy lifting."

I'm pretty sure my eyebrows are at my hairline. I can't believe he implied I can't do manual labor because I'm a woman. Oh, now it's on! I cross my arms, narrow my eyes, shore up my feet, and ready for battle.

"Uh, what did you say?" I tilt my head to the side. "It sounded like you think I'm incapable of handling manual labor because of my gender?" I pause for a moment. "I sincerely hope I've misunderstood you." His eyes have dropped to my boobs—*ugh!* "My eyes are up here, Mr. Macho."

I wait until he makes eye contact, but his demeanor is not one of contrition for being called out for sexism, it's more … *animalistic.*

He smirks at me and I'm ashamed to say the action causes tingles in my nether regions.

"Oh, I'm certain you are more than capable of handling manual labor, but you shouldn't have to. It's my job to watch out for you and make your life as easy as possible."

I drop my hands to my sides. *Whaat?* What does he mean, 'his job'? This guy is intense. He doesn't have any type of relationship with me—doesn't even know me. He walks away with the wheelbarrow, dumping the load, then returns it to me and walks inside without another word. I glance up, noticing Toby leaning against the porch, and I recognize the concern on his face. He must have seen what happened.

As I get closer to him, he takes the wheelbarrow from me and nudges my shoulder with his elbow. "What was that all about?"

"Nothing. Oliver was asking me out to dinner, but I'm not interested in being made a fool. I turned him down. And then he started being all macho, implying I'm too weak to push the wheelbarrow!" Shrugging my shoulders, I walk toward the bathroom we're working on.

"How do you know he would make a fool out of you? He looked pretty interested from where I was standing, *and* he looked frustrated when he walked away from you. He was probably trying to help you out. You weren't overreacting, were you?"

"I may have overreacted a little," I say sheepishly. I do have a tendency to overcompensate for my stature when I'm surrounded by giants. "But look at me." I wait for him to look at me, not just look, but study me closely. "Now look at him. Guys that look like him don't go out with girls that look like me. We both know that."

"You're gorgeous, Sis! Any guy would be proud and consider himself lucky to be with you. It's not only the way you look on the outside, you're gorgeous on the inside, too. You have the biggest, most generous heart of anyone I've ever known, bar Mom."

"Aww Toby, *you* have to say that. You're my brother."

I give him the biggest hug, pressing up onto my toes to kiss his cheek. Geez, I always forget how tall he's become. I still remember him before he went through puberty. He had to stand on the step Mom kept in the kitchen to reach the 'sometimes' treats on the top shelf in the pantry.

Holding my shoulders, he pushes me away. "No, I don't, Kate. You are one of the special angels put on this earth to make it a better place for the rest of us. People can't help but see your goodness shining out of you."

"Oh, stop!" I playfully hit his arm. "You're gonna make me cry and we'll never get this work finished."

Toby's eyes widen as he retreats from me, holding his hands up in surrender—he can't handle Mom or me being upset. We all get back to work, clearing out the bathroom and toilet within the set time allocated. I'm impressed with our achievement. I wasn't sure we'd get everything done. Things seem to be going smoothly with the renovation up to this point. Everyone is on target and ready for the next phase tomorrow. It's exciting to see these people willing to give up their precious weekend to help the kids who will call this place home for however short or long they stay.

By four I'm exhausted and sore, but I need to haul ass home, shower, and then head over to Lloyd Avenue to spend my evening with a bunch of nine-, ten-, and eleven-year-olds. We'll be making dinner and watching the latest Avengers movie tonight. I don't mind, I'll be getting my fill of all my Chris's; you know Hemsworth, Evans, and Pratt—a girl certainly can't complain. I hear my name being called as I walk across the front yard. Turning around, I find Oliver jogging over to me. He still looks more than handsome, while I probably look like I've been spat out of a tornado—*as usual.*

"Are you sure you can't cancel your date tonight and go out to dinner with me?" He tucks his hands in his pockets.

What? For all he knows, I've got a boyfriend taking me out for a romantic dinner and he's still asking me out. Who does he think he is? "Yeah, I'm sure. Thanks for checking! Enjoy your evening and I'll see you tomorrow." No matter how rude I think he's being, I don't have it in me to be rude back to him or call him out for being inappropriate. Waving goodbye, I spin around to keep on my way.

He steps around in front of me again, preventing my retreat. "Can I give you my number? In case you change your mind."

Geez, he's persistent. "I can take your number, but I won't be changing my mind. My date tonight is important to me and canceling at the last minute is not who I am. Enjoy your evening and I'll see you tomorrow." I can't be any more clear than that.

He holds out his hand, gesturing for my phone. I roll my eyes and place my ancient phone in his large hand. He fiddles around, inputting his number, and then I hear an alert from his pocket. The sneaky so and so must have sent himself a message from my phone. He hands it back with a sheepish smile and a nod. "My loss. Your boyfriend is one lucky son of a bitch. I hope he appreciates what he has." He begins to walk backward, away from me. "See you in the morning, Kate."

The way he says my name, the disappointment in his voice, along with something that sounded a lot like respect, almost makes me correct his assumption. Almost. But I don't.

It's better this way.

FIVE

-kate-

I GET TO THE LLOYD AVENUE HOUSE RIGHT ON TIME AND AM greeted at the door by Roman. He has his arms open wide, ready for a hug. He's on duty tonight, like every Saturday, making him the legal guardian for this shift. I love working with him because he's such a warm person and understands my penchant for hugs! As I walk inside, the kids come rushing forward with cheers, high fives, hugs, and the biggest smiles on the planet. These kids don't trust easily and it's the greatest honor that they've given their trust to me.

The kids love our big nights in as much as I do. I would never think of canceling our plans—this time with them is especially important in building their safety net and confidence. They need to know they can rely on someone; that someone cares enough to want to spend time with them on the regular. Often, they haven't ever had those types of important connections with the adults in their life. Normally, I would have been here much earlier and we would have baked a cake, or cookies, or something equally bad for my hips. The kids understood I had to come later today because of the work we needed to do at the new house.

We make a simple fried rice dish and heat some ready-made spring rolls for dinner. The kids demolish it in record time while they fill me in on their week. We make popcorn with a generous amount of M&Ms in readiness for our movie and find our regular positions in the living room. Sammy, the youngest of the bunch, snuggles into my side, while Evelyn and Ivy take up the rest of the couch. The boys grab their pillows and make themselves comfortable on the floor. I'm battling to keep my eyes open after working hard today.

Once the movie's over, I say goodbye and hug each of the kids and Roman tight, with the promise of returning next Saturday. When I arrive home, I go straight to bed, but sleep doesn't come easy, because my mind won't stop replaying all of my interactions with Oliver today.

I sort of feel bad that he thinks I have a boyfriend. Maybe I'll set him straight tomorrow? Maybe I won't? Him thinking I have a boyfriend might be the one thing I need to keep him away.

Ugh, go to sleep Kate!

-oliver-

OKAY, I'M OFFICIALLY A STALKER NOW. I'M NOT PROUD OF MY actions but I couldn't fucking stop myself from following her yesterday afternoon—my feet seemed to move of their own volition. Positives from the situation, though: I have her number; I know where she lives, and I've seen her boyfriend. He seems a little old for her, not sure what the fuck is going on there. *Perhaps she has daddy issues or some shit?* Once I get my hands on her, I can sort that out. She won't even remember her own name, let alone his. From what I saw yesterday, I think she's careful with her money—from her worn-out shoes, ancient phone, and the older model car parked out front of her small detached home. Everything suggests she's not caught up on material things, which adds to her attractiveness in my eyes.

I move through my regular morning routine before heading over to Winchester Street. I paid attention to how she asked for her coffee yesterday, so I stop at the local coffee shop to order Kate and myself a coffee. Hopefully, the gesture will earn me at least a smile. I felt like a dick yesterday when she thought I was implying she's weak. As if anyone could possibly think of her as weak or incapable. She traveled half-way around the world on her own, to a remote island community to work with strangers. Yesterday, she bashed the shit out of the bathroom and toilet as she demolished everything ready for the new install. Anyone can see she's strong beneath all those smiles, sparkling eyes, and bouncy steps.

Jase spots me with two cups of coffee and steps forward to take a cup. I scowl at him, turning my body to block his access. "It's not for you, asshole."

He laughs at me and nudges my arm. "Good morning to you, too. I'm guessing it's for Kate?" He gestures toward one of the cups.

I nod.

"I'm hurt! I work with you for over six years. You know Kate for five minutes and you bring her coffee? Not once have you ever brought me coffee." He puts on a puppy dog face as he holds his hand over his heart, which I'm sure has some effect on other people, but does nothing for me.

"Fuck off! I'm trying to make amends. I think I was a dick to her yesterday."

He huffs out a laugh. "Oh, I'm sure you were. What did you do?"

"I'm pretty sure I implied she wasn't capable of doing any manual labor. That she's weak."

His eyebrows shoot up as his eyes widen. "Oh shit! Yeah, you were definitely a dick to her. I think you'll possibly need more than a cup of coffee to get in her good graces, man." He pats me on my back, then crouches down to retie his shoelaces. He looks back up at me. "You could offer to take her out to dinner or something."

"I tried yesterday. She blew me off for a date with her boyfriend last night, and apparently, she has dinner with her family tonight." I'm still recovering from the sting of her rejection yesterday. She's lucky I like a challenge.

Jase looks dumbfounded as he responds with a smirk. "Ah, the great Oliver Stone has had his first taste of rejection from a beautiful woman. Ouch! That must have hurt, man."

"There's always a first time for everything. I'm guessing you're pretty used to being rejected, huh?" I smirk at my longtime friend and colleague, enjoying our no-holds-barred banter. There aren't many people in my life that I can be relaxed with and have a bit of easy back and forth.

He laughs at me. "Touché, man. I'm going to get a cup of coffee, since you didn't get one for me."

As he walks away, I spot Kate, Toby, and Shane walking my way. When Toby sees me, he gives a chin lift and bends toward Kate to say something. She looks up and our eyes connect. My body relaxes, even though I didn't realize I was carrying tension across my shoulders. I move toward them, passing Kate the coffee I bought for her. She takes it even though she's clearly confused.

"Morning. I wanted to apologize for being a dick yesterday when I implied you weren't capable of doing manual labor. I figured coffee would be a good start. I hope I remembered how you like it." I give her my best smile. The one that usually helps me to get what I want.

Toby and Shane snicker, while that adorable blush I love rises to pinken Kate's cheeks.

"Good morning to you, too." She raises her cup toward me. "Thank you, but you didn't need to go to any trouble for me. Although, great coffee makes it easier to start my day."

She gives me that dazzling smile I've quickly become addicted to. It was the reward I was hoping for—not bad for a three-dollar investment. Without warning, she steps into me and embraces me. Her warm body presses against mine, and I inhale her subtle jasmine scent and savor having her body this close to mine. She's everything I never expected or even knew existed in this world. After a beat I return her embrace, careful not to spill my coffee on her, and bring her in closer to my body. We fit perfectly, and if I have my way, she's going to be spending a lot of time with my arms around her, protecting her from everything that might take that smile off her exquisite face. She releases me and I'm pretty sure I growl as she steps back.

I don't remember making the conscious decision, but she's quickly moved from someone I want to fuck for a night or two to someone I want to get to know. I glance up and find Toby and Jase looking at me with two distinctly different expressions. Jase's lips are tipped up, barely holding back a laugh, while Toby looks as though he wants to go all big brother on me. Shane looks indifferent.

Kate takes a sip of her coffee and her eyes cut across to me. "Mmm. This is perfect. Thanks again."

"You're welcome. Maybe you can allow me to apologize properly by having dinner with me tonight?" I try again because I don't give up when I want something. It works in business, I don't see why it shouldn't work here.

"Uh, I told you yesterday I have dinner with my family tonight. I don't want to miss it. It's been months since we've had Toby home." She looks at her brother with such love and adoration, and wraps her arm around his, pressing the side of her body against him in affection. "Mom's excited to have the four of us together again."

Toby clears his throat. "Mom probably wouldn't mind a couple of extras. She always makes too much food for the four of us. I could call her and check if you like, Squirt?"

"No, I don't—"

I cut Kate off, so she can't deny me again. "I'd appreciate that, man. Thanks." This will be a step in the right direction in my quest to get to know her better.

"Sure, I'll give Mom a call now. Jase, you want to come, too?"

I give Jase a look, telegraphing he better fucking decline the offer. He shakes his head, laughing under his breath at me.

"Thanks, but I'm busy tonight. Plus, I need a break from Olly before I have to see his ugly mug at work tomorrow." Patting me on the back, he walks away to speak with some of the other volunteers. As Toby steps away to call his mom, I step closer to a stunned-looking Kate.

"I'm not sure what's happened." She looks around as if searching for an answer. "Why would you want to come to dinner with my family? You don't know me, and I don't expect any more of an apology for yesterday than the coffee you've already given me today. Not that I even expected that." Her eyes widen as that phenomenal blush rises from her chest. I wonder how far down that blush goes? I bet her tits are spectacular when they're flushed that soft pink color.

I ensure I'm in her personal space; partly because I enjoy being close to her, and partly because I don't want her to misunderstand what I'm about to say. Looking down into her denim-blue eyes, I tell her what I want in no uncertain terms. "I *want* to get to know you, Kate. I want to know who you are, what you like, how you behave around your family. I want to know everything about you. How you taste. How far that blush travels beneath your clothes. How your skin feels under my touch. *Ev-er-y-thing.*"

She swallows hard and looks down at those red shoes she always seems to wear. The blush on her chest, neck, and cheeks heightens as her breaths quicken. The pulse point at the base of her delicate neck pounds out a fast rhythm. She's not as unaffected by me as she portrays. Toby returns, interrupting the moment with a slap on my back. He looks at his sister. "Mom said she'd love to have your friend over for dinner, Sis." He turns back to me. "She said Kate's friends are always welcome and they never need an invitation." He smirks. *Good to know.*

Sarah gains everyone's attention and shares the progress made yesterday. There are only a few of us who were here yesterday, alongside some fresh faces today. The new men and women have the skills we were lacking yesterday. The prep work had to be completed, ready for them to lay tile, install the plumbing, and sand the timber floors. Today, Kate, Toby, Shane, Jase, and I will paint while the skilled workers do their work. We're lucky the fall weather is in our favor because a small group will work outside to get the yard presentable, as well as painting the exterior of the house. Bright, sunny colors were chosen to make the house as appealing as possible for the kids who will call this place home, however temporary that might be. Tomorrow will see the installation of new blinds on all the windows, a security system complete with cameras, and all new appliances for the kitchen and laundry. On Tuesday, new furniture will be delivered to outfit the house, making it suitable for up to six kids to stay with a paid live-in counselor, who acts as their guardian while the kids are under his or her care. Volunteers are also welcome to spend time with the kids, but I'm not sure how often that happens or even if anyone gives their time regularly.

We all get to work and I catch Kate's eyes on me more than once over the course of the day. We all talk and the others mess around to make the tedious work more fun. Shane's quiet, but Kate, Toby, and Jase find it easier to relax and joke around. I have a tendency to become singularly focused on a task and want to keep working until it's complete. The messing around does my head in a bit, but hearing Kate laugh and seeing her smile overrides my annoyance. With her easy smiles and laughs, she is without a doubt like summer and sunshine.

I'm counting down the hours until we've finished here; I'm ready to learn more about her. As we near the end of the day, Toby gives me his parent's address and tells me what time I should arrive for dinner. It's not all that far from here, but I'll have to cross town to shower and change, then drive back in time for dinner.

SEVEN

-kate-

We all say goodbye and I give Jase a hug because I probably won't see him again any time soon. He and my brother have hit it off; perhaps they'll stay in touch. I may see him here and there, I suppose. Toby usually finds it difficult to make genuine friends because of his fame. Actually, come to think of it, everyone's been really respectful this weekend. I've noticed a few glances and a couple of the younger people discreetly asked for a selfie, but they more or less left him alone.

I can't believe my brother, the jerk, invited Oliver for dinner tonight. He's going to be so dead when I get him alone. I could text Oliver and tell him not to come. After all, he gave me his phone number, and encouraged me to contact him. My fingers hover over a new text message, but it feels rude to ask him not to come. I'm many things, but I'm not a rude person. I never set out with the intention of purposely hurting or offending anybody. I'll stand up for myself, or someone else I think isn't being treated properly, but I certainly won't do anything to upset another person on purpose. I guess I can manage to sit through one meal with the guy.

When I arrive home, I decide to check on my neighbor, Margie, before going inside. I like to check on her every couple of days because she's elderly and lives alone. Her husband passed away five years ago before I moved in, and her older sister passed away last year. Unfortunately, Margie couldn't have children, which means she doesn't have anyone to check on her. She's a lot of fun and the best neighbor a girl could have. I think she lost her filter over the years because she says whatever she's thinking. I don't think I've ever met anyone as straightforward as her. Plus, it doesn't hurt that she bakes delicious pies. I cook dinner for her a couple of nights each week to make sure she eats properly. Otherwise, I think she would eat canned soup or toast every night because she can't be bothered to cook for herself anymore.

I knock on her door and hear her shuffling toward it, then I hear the locks release. She opens the door with a smile and hug, ready for me—our usual greeting.

"Hey, Katie-girl. You look like shit." She holds me at arm's length and checks me out from head to toe.

A laugh bursts from me. "Of course I look like shit. I've been renovating that house I was telling you about."

"Oh, that's right. How'd it go?"

"We got everything done. It's ready for the finishing touches, then the kids can move in." As tired as I feel, I also feel accomplished. "Anyway, I've gotta go. I'm having dinner with Mom, Dad, and Toby tonight." We say our goodbyes and I head to my place to shower and get ready.

While I'm in the shower, Oliver's words run through my mind—him wanting to get to know me, that he wanted to know how I tasted, and how I felt. Oh my gosh; I think I almost combusted from his words in his rich baritone. Heat from my blush works its way up my body thinking about how his proximity and words made me feel. I don't know how I'll make it through dinner if he comes at me like that again. I shave and scrub my body, using my favorite jasmine-scented shampoo and conditioner to clean all the paint from my long hair. Heading into my bedroom, I plan in my head what I might wear to dinner. I've felt grimy all weekend. I think I'll wear my cute yellow midi skater dress with the square neckline, fitted bodice, and flared skirt that finishes an inch below my knees. I dry my hair, leaving it loose down my back, and apply a light amount of makeup. After all, it is *only* dinner with my family … and Oliver. I tie on my red micro-suede wedges that I saved for ages to buy, and I'm on my way.

EIGHT

-kate-
_____

ARRIVING AT MOM AND DAD'S, THERE'S AN UNFAMILIAR CAR PARKED
in the driveway, which must belong to Oliver. It looks very expensive
to me, not that I know much about cars, only that they get you from
one place to another, and you need to maintain them. I walk up the
wooden steps to the front porch, where I can hear voices coming
from inside. Opening the screen door, I call out as I enter, "Hey,
Mom. Hey, Dad."

Mom comes out from the kitchen with her arms open wide, a
huge smile on her face, and a sparkle in her blue eyes which match
mine. She embraces me tightly, as though she hasn't seen me for
months; when, in reality, I was here last Sunday for dinner.

"Hey, Katie-girl. I missed you." She kisses my cheek.

I giggle. "Aww, Mom, I saw you last Sunday for dinner and
we've talked on the phone almost every day."

I glance over her shoulder while we're hugging, and see Oliver
standing in the doorway, looking edible in worn jeans, a fresh t-shirt,
and black Converse that are in much better condition than mine.
What I wouldn't give to be able to afford a new pair of Chucks. I
have to be careful with my money, because I'm trying to pay my

mortgage down as quickly as I can. He's looking at us as though he's studying a science experiment with the earnestness I've come to expect from him.

"Hey, Oliver. I see you beat me here and you've already met my mom."

I step forward to hug him in welcome, steeling myself for the impact touching him has on me. I try to step back quickly, but he squeezes me closer, engulfing me in his warmth and masculine scent.

"Hey, Kate. Yeah, I've met your beautiful mom," he smiles at her, "and your dad, before he left with Toby and Shane to buy more beer." Mom's looking between us as if she has a secret. He leans around the doorway, bringing out a large floral arrangement. "These are for you."

I've never been gifted flowers this lovely before. They're full of yellows, reds, and oranges. They remind me of a warm summer's day.

"He also gave me a bunch. Isn't he positively thoughtful?" Mom's gushing like a giddy schoolgirl. "Your mom brought you up right, Oliver." Oliver's face blanches, then smooths quickly as Mom walks back into the kitchen to continue dinner preparations, patting his arm gently as she passes.

"Thank you. They're beautiful." I tuck my hair behind my ear. "You don't need to keep buying me stuff to apologize. I've already accepted your apology for yesterday. It's all good." I touch his arm to ensure I get my point across. "I promise."

"The flowers have nothing to do with my behavior yesterday. I bought them because you remind me of summer and sunshine and the flowers made me think of you." He places his hands in his pockets, carelessly shrugging. "I wanted you to have them." He looks me up and down, in an appraising manner. "You're absolutely edible in that dress. I won't be able to take my eyes off you over dinner. Your dad's going to want my head on a spike."

I roll my eyes and huff out a laugh. "There you go again, being polite. You can stop. It's unnecessary."

Dad, Toby, and Shane stride inside, saving me from Oliver's directness. Dad greets me with a giant bear hug, followed by a kiss on my forehead. He then offers Oliver a beer.

Oliver's phone rings. Checking the display, he looks at me apologetically. "I'm sorry. I need to take this. I won't be long." He steps onto the back porch to take the call, while we all move into the kitchen to catch up on the adventures my 'famous' brother has had over these past months on tour. He's a singer-songwriter, and he's extremely talented—we're all very proud of him. Mom's a music teacher, which means we've always had music in the house. I can't hold a tune, but singing came naturally to Toby. Now he's famous and spends half of the year touring and performing to packed stadiums. Shane sees more of him than we do because he's with him twenty-four seven. He's like another brother to me. Shane's been Toby's best friend since school, before he became his bodyguard a few years ago. Oliver steps inside, obviously finished with his call, which took almost thirty minutes.

"C'mon you lot, dinner's ready. Let's move this to the table," Mom calls out to us.

Mom's made her delicious pot roast with all the trimmings. We all work together to help carry the plethora of dishes to the table. Mom and Dad sit at either end of the table, with Toby and Shane on Dad's left, and me and Oliver on his right. I fight for a full, steady breath sitting this close to him. After we've all settled with plates full of food, Dad starts peppering Oliver with questions.

"So, Oliver, what do you do for a living?"

Oh gawd, here we go!

"Dad, I'm sure Oliver didn't come to dinner to be put through the third degree." I give him my 'please stop' face.

Oliver presses his thigh against mine beneath the table and my skin buzzes at the contact. "No, it's alright," he says to me, then looks back to Dad. "I work in corporate investments. I've been doing it since I left college."

"I hope you're not after Kate's money to invest because she puts all of her hard-earned money into paying down her mortgage."

Earth, open up and swallow me whole, please. Could this be any more embarrassing?

"Dad, I'm sure Oliver doesn't want *my* money or anything else of mine. He works in 'corporate investments'. I'm guessing that would involve working with businesses, rather than individuals? Am I right?"

"Squirt, I beg to differ." He smirks. "He wanted a dinner date with you. He certainly *wants* something from you." Toby winks at me, as though he's in on some big secret, while Shane snickers. *I think I've just turned as red as a beetroot!*

Oliver coughs and looks at Toby and Shane as though he's trying to contain a smile. Then he looks at me with pride, as if it's miraculous I figured out what he does for a living. "One hundred percent." Looking back at Dad, he says, "Sir, I would never take your daughter's money, even if I worked in small investments. She's completely safe with me. I'm not here to take advantage of her, in *any* way."

Oh, well, that's a shame. I can think of some ways I wouldn't mind being taken advantage of. Oh my gosh, stop it, Kate!

"That's good to hear, Son." Dad seems pleased with Oliver's answer.

Toby pipes up, with a smirk on his face. "The work must pay pretty well, because that's a sweet ride you've got parked out front. I only took a quick peek. What is it?"

Oliver clears his throat, looking a little uncomfortable as he answers Toby, "It's an Aston Martin Vanquish. It's been a dream of mine to own an Aston Martin since I was younger. It's magnificent to drive. I could take you for a ride after dinner."

"That'd be awesome; as long as I get to drive." Toby winks at me as he cracks his knuckles. Shane shakes his head at Toby's antics. He's always been quiet, but more so since he returned from service.

Oliver presses his thigh against mine under the table again and I swear my leg catches fire. I gulp down some water, attempting to calm myself, causing myself to choke. Oliver immediately rubs my back to ease my discomfort, but that makes me even more flustered, making my situation worse.

Will this dinner ever end?

It's Mom's turn to carry on with the inquisition. "Where do you live, Oliver?"

His hand, still resting on the back of my chair, twists a lock of my hair as he answers her. "Uh, I live in the city close to work. It makes more sense with the long hours required for my job. I don't get many opportunities to drive my car, because the office is close to home."

"Oh, that's convenient for you. You can roll out of bed and go to work." She chuckles.

"Something like that, I guess." He seems happy enough to answer their questions and looks at me as though he's waiting for me to ask him something.

Instead of asking him a question, I tell my family, "Oliver and I met briefly when I went overseas to help set up the new school. Do you remember?"

Everyone around the table nods, encouraging me to go on. "Oliver and his friend, Jase, were finishing up the construction of the school so I could work with the local elementary teachers. They did an extraordinary job."

"Oh, you sound just like our Katie-girl. She's always helping someone, trying to make the world a better place." She looks at me with such pride. "We wish she would slow down a little and give herself some time to meet a nice man and settle down."

Just kill me now!

My mother did not just say that in front of Oliver. I appreciate that he's trying his best to keep his laughter contained. He's got quite the sparkle in his eyes. I can't even complain about Mom when she's produced such a spectacular reaction from him. He looks different when he relaxes and smiles—I'm not sure my defenses can withstand a relaxed and happy Oliver.

I decide it's time to change the subject. "How's Nan doing on her Alaskan cruise?"

Dad puts down his knife and fork. "She's having loads of fun, so we haven't had regular contact with her." He turns, speaking to Oliver. "My mom is currently living it up on a Royal

Caribbean Cruise as she explores Alaska. She was very excited because the ship she's on has an observation pod which rises out of the top of the upper deck. Apparently, it rotates three hundred and sixty degrees to give a spectacular view of the area."

"We named our Katie-girl after David's mom. It turns out she has the same sense of adventure as her nan." Mom looks at me full of love. This, categorically, is my safe place; here with my family, in the home where I grew up.

Dinner settles down. The questions slow and the discussion turns to lighter, more general topics, suitable for the dinner table. We clear away from dinner and Mom serves home-made apple turnovers with ice cream for dessert. She makes the creamiest ice cream you'll ever have, and I can't help but moan in appreciation. Oliver's head snaps my way and the potency and heat in his eyes takes my breath away.

Oh my! Could it be possible that he *does* honestly think I'm beautiful, and they're not only words? He's had some part of his body touching mine throughout dinner.

Once dessert is finished, Toby, Shane, Oliver, and I clear the table and wash the dishes. We've told Oliver repeatedly that he doesn't need to help, but he insists on doing his share. After we've finished, he invites Dad, Toby, and Shane to take a drive in his 'sweet' ride as Toby calls it, leaving Mom and me alone for a while. Mom makes us hot chocolate and we move into the family room, getting comfortable on the couch.

She wastes no time going straight for the kill. "Oliver's a hand-some young man. He seems very taken with you."

I roll my eyes. "Don't start, Mom. Toby invited him here for dinner—not me. He's being polite." I take a sip of my hot choco-late. "And yes, he's a very good looking man. That's why I know for certain he would *never* be interested in someone like me. He could have any woman he wants. He told me yesterday he has women asking him to dinner *all* the time."

Repeating the words he said yesterday makes me sick to my stomach. I don't understand why he's wasting his Sunday evening here with my family, when he could have dinner with any gorgeous woman he wanted.

Mom looks positively livid. "What do you mean, 'someone like you'? You are such a kind soul, Kate, and beautiful, and intelligent to boot. You are quite a catch for *any* man. I'm not sure where you got the idea that you're not a beautiful woman?"

Shrugging, I study my drink, avoiding her gaze; hiding further behind the curtain of my hair. "If I was as great as you say, Brandon wouldn't have cheated on me. He wouldn't have gone behind my back with Crystal, now, would he? Not to mention every single boyfriend I've ever had. They've always left me for someone prettier. Someone more 'interesting'." Brandon broke me when he cheated with my best friend. It was out of the blue and completely unexpected. There were never the sparks I experience when I stand next to Oliver, but I thought we were happy.

"He was an idiot! Your father and I never warmed to him. Plus, it's his loss and your gain that he let you go. Not all men are as stupid as Brandon and those other boys, Katie-girl." She glides her hand down my hair, then slides my loose hair behind my shoulder. "Don't let those boys from your past keep hurting you. Promise me you'll open your heart to the possibility of love." She moves closer to me, wrapping me in a hug I didn't realize I needed.

The guys walk inside, and Oliver's gaze immediately snaps to me in Mom's arms. His eyebrows slash down over his arresting eyes as he moves straight for me. "Everything okay?"

I nod, not wanting him to press me further. Mom gets up to make them each a hot chocolate, carrying the sweet drinks into the family room.

Toby turns toward me. "You spent last night with the kids over at the Lloyd Avenue house, right? How are they?"

Oops, busted!

Oliver's head swings toward me. His narrowed eyes making me feel guilty for my half-truth yesterday.

"They were great. They were beyond excited to see me. We made fried rice and spring rolls, which they demolished. Then we had popcorn with M&Ms, while we watched the latest Avengers movie. I struggled to keep my eyes open, though. I was pretty tired after the work we did yesterday."

"Did Kate tell you she spends some time every weekend with a group of kids in one of *The Parkerville Project's* share homes? She adores those kids." Dad doesn't realize the trouble he's dropped me in. In fact, he doesn't seem to notice the icy vibe coming off Oliver in waves.

"No, she didn't tell me. She told me she had a date last night. But I bet those kids think they're the luckiest kids on the planet when Kate turns up." He looks disappointed. It curls around in my tummy, making me feel terrible for my subterfuge.

We finish our drinks. "Thank you very much for inviting me to dinner. I'd better head home and allow you guys some time to catch up." He stands. "Dinner was delicious. Thank you, Mrs. Summer."

Mom gives him a giant hug, rubbing her hands up and down his back like she does when she's hugging us goodbye. Dad shakes his hand and pats him on the back. "You're welcome anytime. You don't need an invitation."

Whaaat? Really? Where's the family loyalty?

Oliver turns toward me. "Would you mind walking me out?"

I know this is going to be all kinds of tense—it's like I'm walking to the gallows! As we're walking, his big, warm hand settles at the small of my back, guiding me along. That small amount of contact sends my body into alert mode and tingles race up my spine.

As we stand beside his car, he rubs the back of his neck. *When did that action become sexy?* Slowly, he raises his head, looking at me in his usual way. "Want to explain to me why you lied about having a date last night?"

Here we go. "Uh, nope! To me, it's a date. I don't cancel on those kids unless I have a prior engagement I've planned ahead of time. I would *never* cancel on them at the last minute unless I was sick. They've had enough disappointment and flakey people in their life. I refuse to be another adult who lets them down."

How dare he be upset I didn't change my plans to suit him—the nerve!

He moves into my space; he seems to like being close. "Fair

enough. But you could have said what you were doing. I feel you purposely let me think you were going on a date with a boyfriend. Is there a reason you wanted to shut me down, beautiful girl?"

Uh, geez, he's direct. "Um, see, that would be why. You keep saying things that are definitely out of the realm of what could possibly be true. I *know* you must be playing with me—"

He moves even closer, if that's possible, interrupting me. "You can stop right there, Sunshine. Each time I've called you beautiful, you act like I'm lying. Beautiful isn't a strong enough word for how I see you, so that attitude of yours is going to have to change. I won't tolerate you disrespecting yourself like that."

Aaand there go my knees. Is that even physically possible for words to make your knees collapse out from under you?

This guy is smooth. Luckily, I won't see him again, or I would have to be super careful.

"Now, when can I see you again? Tonight made me want to get to know you even more."

Gently gripping my chin, he directs me to look into his eyes, which I was desperately trying to avoid. His track around my face, checking my eyes and pausing on my mouth—I swear, I stop breathing. I'm going to pass out at his feet at this rate. Which would not be sexy—*at all*. I want him to kiss me, but I don't want him to kiss me at the same time. I can't get my head on straight around him. He leans in, sliding his bristly cheek across my smooth one and brushes his full lips across my mouth. He pulls back ever-so-slightly to check my eyes again. I'm not sure what he's looking for.

Swallowing, I attempt to get my words out straight. "As I said yesterday, I'm pretty busy with work, my family, and other obligations. I rarely get time to catch up with friends or simply eat lunch at work; I'm *that* busy. I honestly don't have time for anything else." I manage to whisper.

He's studying me like I'm an expensive artwork. He must see what he needs because he nods and gently brushes my lips with his again. Then he steps away from me. "I'll text you, Kate. Eventually, I'll wear you down, and you'll agree to a date with me."

I'm not sure why he wants to 'wear' me down when he, apparently, 'has women asking *him* to dinner'. He steps away from me, and I miss his body heat immediately. Walking around his car, he gets in smoothly and drives away, leaving me to stand in the driveway wondering what on earth just happened, and why on earth it just happened to me.

NINE

-oliver-

THE FIRST THING I DO MONDAY MORNING IS CONTACT MIKE. I FILL him in on the events of the weekend and inform him I no longer require his services to find Kate. He thanked me for my business and told me to expect his invoice.

I'm hanging up the phone from Mike when Jase stops in my doorway. "You've met the parents already, huh? Must be serious." He raises his eyebrows at me and chuckles. Sometimes he can be worse than an old lady.

"I'm not about to let an opportunity pass me by. I don't do it with my business and I won't do it with something that I want as badly as I want that woman."

"Yeah, but meeting the folks is a bit much, don't you think?" He stuffs his hands in his trouser pockets, his brows furrowed.

"Nothing's too much for her. Now, if you've finished sharing your thoughts, which I never asked for, get back to work. I've got shit to do." Like message my girl.

He holds his hands up in surrender. "No problem, Boss."

As soon as he's gone, I pull my out phone to message Kate.

Me: Good morning Sunshine

Sunshine: Good morning to you too

Me: Thanks for letting me crash dinner with your family

Sunshine: It wasn't left up to me now was it?

Me: I guess not

Me: Can I see you again?

Sunshine: I'm pretty busy atm

Me: I'll let it go

Me: For now

Sunshine: Gee, thanks

Me: Enjoy your day

Sunshine: You too

I need to check in with the rehab center, looking after my father. I pick up my phone to make the call.

"Good morning. Welcome to *Square One*. My name is Doris. How may I help you?"

"Hi, Doris. It's Oliver Stone. I'm calling for my check-in with Dr. Wyatt."

"Oh hello, Mr. Stone. I'll check if he's available. Please wait one moment."

On-hold music fills the line while I wait to connect with the doctor working with my father.

Dr. Wyatt's deep baritone reaches across the line to me. "Hello, Oliver. Nice to hear from you."

"Hello, Dr. Wyatt. It's that time of the week again. How has my father's week been?"

"He's had a tough week. He's been rather difficult, threatening the staff and demanding to be released. You realize we can't keep him here against his will?"

He goes through highs and lows; refusing to attend the therapy sessions and giving the staff a hard time, then being the model inpatient and impressing the hell out of everyone on staff.

"Yeah, I understand. But he's not mentally stable to be out on his own. Are you able to assess his mental health and ensure his long-term habit hasn't created some type of mental health issue?"

"We're already in the process of assessing your father's mental health. There's no point in him kicking his addictions, leaving the center, and then being left undiagnosed and untreated for something else. We need to be sure he can stay clean and function successfully in society, or else all the hard work will be for naught."

I'm happier knowing they're on top of things. It was a tough road getting him into the rehab center.

"Your father still carries a great deal of guilt about the accident which claimed your mom's life. His behavior has been his coping mechanism, *and* his punishment."

My father lost the will to live after Mom was killed in a car accident. Mom and Dad had been out celebrating their wedding anniversary—I was seven years old and home with the babysitter. He must have had a few drinks and decided he was okay to drive. Nobody knows what caused the accident, but he drove off the road and skidded sideways into an enormous tree. Mom's side of the car was annihilated, killing her instantly. My father woke in the hospital five days later and was charged with her death because he had a high blood-alcohol level at the time of the accident. He was sent to prison for six years. When he was finally released, he spent all his time drinking and escaping into drugs.

"I know he feels that way. I also know I lost both parents that night. First, because he was sentenced to time in prison for his actions, then later because he couldn't keep his shit together." I struggle to keep the anger out of my voice, but I'm certain Dr. Wyatt can hear it.

I was sent to live with a family of strangers while my father was in the hospital because there were no other family members to take care of me. Eventually, I ended up in a foster home with a decent family, but I always felt like an outsider. I didn't make life easy for them, getting into trouble on the regular and shutting them out. I was only with them for a couple of years, because they decided I was too much trouble and sent me back to the shelter. Over the years, I was placed with five different families until I aged out of the system. None of the families were terrible. They just didn't know how to deal with a closed-off, troubled kid. I rejected any type of bond or affection and only communicated when absolutely necessary—I'm more or less still like that. I hide it better now.

"I could have easily blamed him for everything, but I didn't and I still don't. A relationship with my father is very important to me. He's all I have left. I purposely sought him out to build a relationship, but he makes it difficult with his addictions. He chooses that path instead of a path with me, his only son."

A couple of months ago, he hit rock bottom. He had passed out in an alley and was badly beaten within an inch of his life. The hospital contacted me when they found my business card in his pocket. From there, I finally got him into rehab. It's the best place in this city with a high success rate. I only hope he can rebuild some semblance of a life, because I truly miss him.

"Oliver, I understand and I hear what you're saying. He's been in the cycle a long time, fighting the guilt over losing your mother *and* failing you. He's trying his hardest to become the man he needs to be. But you have to remember, this has been his life for the past twenty-five years. It's a difficult cycle to break."

"I get it. Truly I do. I'm just feeling frustrated."

"That's understandable. You must feel you're doing all the work. Making all the effort. But let me assure you. Your father is working his ass off in here." He pauses for a bit. "Why don't you come in for a visit soon? We can all sit and chat. Maybe clear the air a little."

"That sounds good, Dr. Wyatt. I'll get my assistant to set it up in my calendar."

"Good. Good. I'll look forward to it."

Disconnecting the call, I slump back into my chair, running my hands through my hair. Looking out my windows, not seeing the view, I wonder if I'll ever have a positive, healthy relationship with my father.

As I move through my workday, responding to emails, making phone calls, and speaking with clients, my thoughts keep returning to Kate and the way she looked after everyone on the worksite over the weekend. Not only did she manage her own work, but she was also always checking in on everyone else, getting them bottled water, and offering an extra pair of hands to anyone who needed the help.

I wonder who looks after her?

I can't stop thinking about the sweet taste of her soft lips—the hot chocolate and my sweet, sweet Kate. I kept the kiss light, even though everything in my body wanted to devour her, taste her tongue, and experience her desire.

Her dad and brother questioned my intentions toward Kate during our drive. I told them as clearly as I possibly could that I want Kate in my life, and I will do everything in my power to make it happen. I think they were as surprised by my declaration as I was. I'm at a loss to work out at what point my intentions moved from one or two nights to wanting Kate as a permanent fixture in my life. It's so far removed from every relationship, or lack thereof, I've had with women throughout my adult life to date.

I only hope I can be worthy of her goodness.

TEN

-kate-

THE WEEKEND GAVE ME A LOT TO THINK ABOUT. I DON'T THINK I'VE ever met anyone like Oliver. He's way out of my league and extremely overwhelming. There's no way I could keep the interest of a guy like him. I can't even keep the interest of a normal man for more than a few months before they look for someone prettier and more interesting.

It surprised me when he messaged this morning. I don't know what type of game he thinks he's playing with me, but I've learned my lesson in the past. I'm nobody's fool. The best thing I can do is steer clear of him. I'm sure he'll get bored and move on sooner rather than later, or else he *may* tempt me to give him a chance.

The school day goes by and I drive home. I'm cooking dinner for Margie and me tonight. Washing up, I get out the ingredients I need to get started. From memory, I make our dinner because I've made this dish several times before, then plate it up to take next door. I knock on Margie's door and when she answers with her big grin; I hand her the dish.

"Hi, Margie. How was your day? Anything exciting happen down our street?" She often sits on her small porch, watching the comings and goings of our quiet street.

"Hey, Kate. Oh, you know, Pete down the street was chasing Joe's dog out of his garden, and cursing up a storm while he was doing it. Nothing new!" She laughs. She loves watching the antics of the old guys who live down the street—they keep her entertained regularly.

"Anyway, enjoy your dinner before it gets cold. Have a great night, and I'll see you tomorrow." I give her a careful hug, so as not to disturb the plate of food, then go back to my place to eat my dinner before it gets cold. Afterward, I plan on having a hot bath and getting lost in my new book by one of my favorite authors.

Soaking in the tub with my new book, I can't help compare Oliver to the hero in the story. The hero is rather bossy and seamlessly takes charge of the heroine's life before she realizes what's happening. I think Oliver would definitely be like that if the person he was with didn't put some clear boundaries in place. I lay my head back, recalling last night when he held my chin and touched his lips to mine. He was gentle and respectful—sweet. I take it further in my mind, and I can almost feel his hands running over my body, down my hips, and across my soft tummy. My body heats, my breasts become heavy; my breaths quicken, and the blooming of my arousal makes itself known. How easy it would be to touch myself and release the pressure, but I don't want to condition my body to respond to him. I get out of the tub and dry off , then head to bed.

After another restless night's sleep, I go to work to start a new day.

It's Saturday morning, and I'm busy catching up on laundry and other chores around my house, dancing to my favorite playlist, when I receive a message. When I see it's from Oliver, butterflies erupt in my stomach. We've chatted via text every day these past two weeks and I've come to look forward to seeing his name on my screen.

Oliver: How's my beautiful Kate this morning?

Oh my! He's pulled out the big guns straight up. Let's have some fun.

Me: Who's this? I think you have the wrong number
Oliver: Don't who's this me! You know exactly who this is and I definitely have the correct number
Oliver: Answer me
Oliver: How is MY BEAUTIFUL Kate this morning?

Oh-kay! No fun to be had here. He sounds pissed.

Me: I'm great. How are you today?
Oliver: I'm feeling pretty good myself. What are you doing today?
Me: I'm catching up on laundry and other exciting chores around the house before I spend the afternoon and evening with the kids at Lloyd Ave
Oliver: What about tomorrow?
Me: I've got prep work to do for school next week and then dinner with my family
Oliver: Can you spare an hour to catch up for lunch?

Oh geez, what can I say? I've blown him off a heap already, and he's been incredibly sweet with his texts every day. That he hasn't given up already makes me less inclined to say no, and I guess he *is* only asking for an hour.

Me: I guess I can spare an hour for lunch. Where would you like to meet?
Oliver: I'll pick you up at 1

No, no, no. That's not okay. I'm worried if I give him an inch, he'll take a mile, and if he drives, then I won't be able to leave when I'm ready.

Me: I insist that I'll meet you there or we won't meet at all
Oliver: Damn Sunshine, you make my life difficult

Me: Sorry (not really) *shrugging emoji*

Oliver: No need to be sorry. I wanted to do the right thing and pick you up, like a gentleman. Maybe someday you'll let me do that?

Me: Maybe

Oliver: How about we meet at Pier 7 at 1?

Oliver: Does that suit you?

Me: Sounds great. See you tomorrow

Oliver: See you tomorrow, Sunshine

Why does it feel like I've agreed to something that's going to be life-changing? I realize I'm smiling even though I swore I wouldn't give him a chance.

ELEVEN

-oliver-

I'M PACING AT THE ENTRANCE OF PIER 7, WHERE THERE ARE several restaurants, casual cafés, and bars, waiting for Kate to arrive. It's been two weeks since I've laid eyes on her and I'm balancing on a knife's edge, waiting for her to get here. It's 1:25, meaning she's late—what if she's changed her mind and doesn't show? I run my fingers through my hair. I can't believe she's got me this worked up. She's got me acting like an inexperienced teenage boy. I check my phone for any messages, only to find work-related emails which can wait. The realization that I'm happy to put work on hold for an afternoon hits me hard and fast, but I want to give Kate all of my attention. Hopefully, she enjoys her time with me and doesn't notice the time, giving me the opportunity to spend longer than the designated hour with her. Raising my head, I see her walking quickly toward me. She's breathtaking in a pair of light skinny jeans worn at the knees, and a navy boat-necked t-shirt, with those battered red Converse on her feet. Her hair is tied up, but blowing in the wind and as she spots me, her eyes light up while an enchanting smile settles on her face.

I hope I get to keep her.

She's everything good in this world. I walk toward her with long strides, eating up the distance as quickly as possible. She stops abruptly as I reach her, looking up at me.

"Hi," she says looking up at me, with a small smile. Stepping up on her toes, she gives me what I've been needing for the past two weeks—a hug.

It's so simple, but I feel like I can breathe again.

Having her in my arms is like a balm to soothe my soul.

"Hey." I return with a smile of my own, looking into her sparkling blue eyes. We seem to stand like that; caught up in each other for several moments as everything around us falls away, then she steps back, breaking the spell. She tucks her hands in her back pockets, thrusting her tits out for my perusal. I'm doing my best to be a gentleman and keep my eyes locked on hers, though. *Go me!*

"I'm sorry I'm late. My car stalled in the middle of an intersection, and it took a lot of persuasion on my part to convince the old girl to start again," she tells me as she huffs out a nervous laugh. "I wasn't sure if you'd still be here."

"I'm not going anywhere, Sunshine. I thought you'd changed *your* mind." I run my hand through my hair. "I don't like the sound of what happened, though. That could have been a dangerous situation. Does your car break down often?"

I'm already planning what to do about the old sedan she drives. She needs something safer, more reliable. I'm certain it will cause an argument with her, though—she's such an independent firecracker.

Looking up at me, she responds, "Occasionally. It's happening more often as she gets older, but she was my first car, so I'll nurse her through. The car's special to me, because she belonged to my nan." She shrugs.

Hmm, I won't be able to get rid of the car, but I would be happier if it had a complete overhaul. "Fair enough. C'mon, let's get something to eat. What are you in the mood for?"

I take her hand in my larger one and we move down the pier, over the water, toward the eateries. I like how her hand feels in mine —*natural*—as though we were made to fit together. Glancing down at our joined hands, I notice she doesn't have those long, fake nails some women seem to covet. Kate's are a practical length, with a pale pink polish.

She looks around thoughtfully, tapping her first finger against her luscious bottom lip that I'm dying to bite. "I love the food at *Declan's Diner*. Mind if we go in there?" She turns to me with a hopeful expression.

The place is an institution on the pier, serving diners for the last eighty years. "Sure, let's go."

Still holding her hand, I lead her across the pier, quite pleased that she hasn't pulled away—that's a win in my book. We step onto the worn black-and-white checkered linoleum tiled floor, our eyes needing to adjust to coming inside so we can see properly. The first thing that hits us as we enter are the delicious aromas of fish and chips, burgers, kebabs, and whatever else the guys are cooking. The second thing is the heat from all the fryers and grills. I don't get down here very often, but it's always busy because the food is fantastic and comes out fast. We both take a few minutes to study the menu boards, deciding on our preferences. Kate orders a Greek lamb salad wrap with an iced tea, while I order the burger, fries, and a root beer. We sit at a chrome and red 1950s-style table, making general small talk about the pier and tourists while we wait for our number to be called. We opt for a table outside on the pier, allowing us to people watch as we enjoy our food.

As Kate unwraps her lunch, she looks at me as though she wants to say something. I nod, motioning for her to tell me what she's thinking.

"Thanks for lunch."

I put my hand on hers to pause her. "I sense a 'but' coming in here, and I know I won't like it, but go on."

"You're right, there is a 'but'. I was happy to pay for my lunch. I can't keep accepting your generosity—it makes me very uncomfortable. It's not like you're my boyfriend or anything." I growl under my breath, and her eyes widen. "I didn't mean you *should* be my boyfriend or anything like that. Oh my gosh, can the earth open up and swallow me now? I can't believe I said that! How embarrassing!"

She's adorable in her embarrassment—her natural blush rising, while her hands cover her face. I gently remove them from her face. "Don't hide from me, Sunshine. I told you last time I want to get to know you. *Everything* about you. Remember?"

She looks properly chastised. "Yeah, I remember," she responds quietly while looking down at her food, avoiding my eyes.

I don't like that our date has taken this negative turn. "Tell me about what you did with the kids this weekend."

Immediately her shoulders go back, she sits up straighter, her face lights up, and the smile I love adorns her alluring face.

"It might be easier to tell you what we didn't do over the course of the afternoon and evening." She giggles. "I'm pretty sure the kids spend all week thinking up stuff for us to do; recipes to try, movies to watch, and games to play. We spent ages taking turns competing against each other, playing racing games with Luigi and Mario on their console. Those kids are crazy good. I'm pretty sure I spent most of my races falling off the side of the track." She shakes her head and laughs at herself. "But I'm sure you don't want to hear me wax poetic about hanging out with a bunch of pre-teens."

"I absolutely do. I enjoy watching you light up when you talk about things you're passionate about. I actually find it pretty sexy— who knew?" I finish with a smile to put her at ease. And the blush is back! I mentally congratulate myself, because I love that fucking blush.

We finish eating and decide to walk along the pier, taking in the scenery and other people as we go. We stop here and there to take a closer look at items for sale at the cottage craft stalls, which were set up for the Sunday market. Kate seems to be more comfortable with me, chatting freely about different crafts her mom started and gave up over the years.

The fall weather is perfect, with a soft warm breeze, making the entire experience exceptional. I even notice Kate hasn't bothered to check the time, and I've snagged more than an hour with her. "Would you like—"

"Hey, Kate! I thought that was you." She freezes on the spot and I know from the stiffness in her body and the pinched look on her face, this won't be good. The guy is shorter than me and a little pudgy around the middle. He's standing with his arm around a boney blonde woman, who's looking at Kate like she's covered in mud, and me as though I'm a juicy steak she's dying to devour. He looks over at me, pointing his finger. "Hey, I know you, you're Oliver Stone." I stiffen and prepare for Kate to pull away from me. He'd better not blow my chance with her. "What are you doing here with someone like Kate? Surely you can do better than her, man?"

What the fuck did he just say?

My blood's boiling, and my free hand tightens into a fist, ready to knock this motherfucker out.

Kate attempts to pull her hand from mine, dropping her face toward the decking. "Uh … hi, Brandon. Hi, Crystal." She looks up at me with wide eyes, then glances around us quickly. "I've got to go." She breaks free from my hold, turning to walk away briskly.

I'm torn whether to follow Kate or to put this dick in his place. The second option wins out, and I turn back to dick face. I stand to my full height, taking the few steps needed to get into his space. My clenched fists, the pissed off look on my face, and the tick in my jaw *should* make me appear menacing. "What. The. Fuck. Did you just say about Kate? Surely I misheard you."

This guy must be as dense as a brick when he smirks at me. "Nah, man, you can do better than her. You're *the* Oliver Stone!"

It's not even a conscious decision when I raise my arm back to swing. My fist collects him on the jaw, he falls flat on his ass in the middle of the pier. I leave him there, taking long, quick strides, attempting to catch up with Kate. It's not easy because a crowd gathered around us, and I have to weave in and out of groups of people. I can't see her anywhere; she's fucking disappeared. I head toward the parking lot to search for her car, but it's not there.

She's gone! *Fuck!*

TWELVE

-oliver-

I QUICKLY CLIMB IN MY CAR AND DRIVE TOWARD KATE'S HOUSE, which is going to be fucking awkward to explain, since she never told me where she lives. I'm not sure how I'll explain, but I don't care at this point. I need to see her and find out what that was all about; but above all, I need to make sure she's alright. She's at her front door, about to step inside, when I pull into her driveway behind her car. She must hear my car pull up because she turns around. Turning off the engine, I step out of my car, and even from this distance, I can see she's been crying. She stays locked in position, fidgeting with the hem of her t-shirt as I walk toward her.

"I'm sorry I left like that. I was having a great time with you, but Brandon's right. You can do much better than a girl like me—"

I'm not having this; I step up to her, getting as close to her body as I can. Cutting her off, I lift her chin gently to ensure she can see my face clearly. Then I kiss those luscious lips that I haven't been able to stop thinking about; she takes a beat to respond. Slowly, I pull back to study her eyes, checking I haven't overstepped, but it doesn't seem as if she wants me to stop. I cup her face in my hands, using my thumbs to wipe her tears away as I move in to kiss her lips again. I start gently, enjoying the warmth of her lips, then I use my

tongue to taste her—the iced tea she drank at lunch, and the salti-
ness of her tears are at the forefront. Her dainty hands hold on to
my hips as I press in to deepen the kiss, encouraging her to open up
and let me in. She does, and it's the best feeling. I sense the importance of her allowing me to taste her like this. Fire licks up my spine
as our tongues tangle in a sensual kiss, breathing each other's air,
and learning each other's taste. We kiss for long minutes, and she
finally gives in. I capture her sigh. The chemistry between us is
beautifully exquisite. I slow down and soften the kiss, finishing with
a light peck to her swollen lips. I press my forehead to hers. If I
don't stop now, we'll be at risk of being charged with indecent expo-
sure. Her eyes open slowly as she takes a deep breath, giving me a
timid smile.

"I've been wanting to kiss you since I first met you on that
stinking hot veranda fifteen months ago, and I was *not* disappointed." She huffs out a laugh as her cheeks turn pink. I notice the
curtain drop into place at the neighbor's window and chuckle to
myself. Nudging her nose with mine, I whisper, "I'm going to want
to do that a lot. Probably a lot more than that, too."

She smiles broadly and I feel ten feet tall that I could do that for
her. "I can't believe you kissed me on my porch after what just
happened. This isn't my life. I'm not the girl hot guys chase after
and kiss!" She looks up at me. "I guess you want an explanation,
huh?"

I didn't miss the fact that she referred to me as a 'hot guy'.
Perhaps I *do* have a chance here. "Whenever you're ready to talk
about it, I'll be ready to listen. Now, are you going to invite me
inside?"

Her eyes widen, as if she can't believe I would want to be invited
inside her home. "Uh, I don't think that would be a good idea after
what's happened."

She attempts to put space between us, but I don't allow her.
"Truthfully, you *can* do better than a girl like me, Oliver. I'm not
much of anything and you're … well," she waves her hand up and
down, gesturing to me. "You're *you*."

"I'm not following you, Kate. You're going to have to explain it better." I *know* I'm not going to like what she's about to say. She's going to demean herself in my presence yet again, and that's going to piss me the fuck off.

"Oh, come on!" She huffs out, slapping the side of her thighs. "Don't pretend you don't see the disparities between you and me. Judging by your car, you're clearly a successful guy. You're confident and exceptionally good looking. You told me yourself, you have women asking *you* to dinner. You seem to be intelligent and you're kind and thoughtful—if not a little overwhelming." I'm not sure what I've done for her to assume I'm kind and thoughtful. I wouldn't use either term to describe myself. She takes a step back, straightens her spine, presses her shoulders back, and looks me directly in the eye—she's ready for battle. "I can't keep a boyfriend from straying. I'm average looking at best. I'm a simple kindergarten teacher and spend my free time with my eighty-five-year-old neighbor and a group of prepubescent kids. Is that clear enough for you?" She finishes with wide eyes and a sassy head shake.

Yep, she fucking pissed me off!

I cup her face in my hands, my thumbs resting on her delicate cheekbones, while my fingers slide to the back of her head, cradling it more gently than the anger boiling inside me should allow. Backing her up against her front screen door, I tilt her face up to mine, slamming my mouth down onto hers. I give her everything I've got, pressing my body as close as I possibly can. She has to feel my growing cock, hard as stone, behind my zipper. She has to feel what she does to me. She can't go anywhere while I've got her like this and eventually relaxes, giving in to me and our off-the-charts chemistry. She melts against me, wrapping her arms around my neck, pulling me down—as if she wants us to join as much as I do. I pull back gently after a long while, placing light, delicate kisses against her swollen lips and the tip of her nose. I wait until she opens her eyes. "You've pissed me off, Kate. I told you before, I won't tolerate you disrespecting yourself. Let me tell you the dispari- ties I see between you and me." Using my fingers, I hold her chin so I don't lose her focus. "I see a woman who has the biggest heart of anyone I've ever met. Who gives her time freely to make the world a better place for others without asking for anything for herself. My heart is closed off, and I guard my time as though it's buried fucking treasure—I wasn't sure I had a heart until I met you. I see an intelligent woman with a truckload of patience to work with kindergarten children, day in and day out. I see a caring and thoughtful neighbor, who freely gives her time to make sure she's okay. Me, on the other hand. I only focus on myself and my work. I see an absolutely stunning woman with the most ravishing set of legs I've ever seen, a miracle of a smile, because it allows me to breathe, and a great set of tits that I can't wait to get my hands and mouth on." She laughs at my last comment, which is exactly what I wanted. "Surely you can feel what you do to me." I press my hard length against her belly. "I've never, in my life, had such a visceral reaction to a woman. The chemistry between us is palpable and I would like the opportunity to explore it with you. But you have to trust that what I'm saying is real and stop doubting me or denying this connection we have." She seems stuck for words, so I lay one more gentle kiss on her and take a reluctant step back. "I won't insist on an invitation inside this afternoon." I tuck a lock of hair behind her ear. "Be warned. I'm not giving up on you and the idea of us. Enjoy your family dinner tonight, Sunshine. Say 'hi' to your mom and dad, as well as Toby from me."

I do one of the most difficult things in my life—I walk away. She needs time to come to terms with everything I've said. I only hope she makes the right decision—to cooperate because I'm not giving up.

THIRTEEN

-kate-

STANDING, IF YOU CAN CALL IT THAT, AGAINST MY FRONT SCREEN door in a daze, I realize I've *never* been kissed like that. Full of passion and desire. The need between us was like an independent living organism. My heart is still beating a million miles a minute, and I'm dizzy from the lack of air entering my lungs. I am absolutely floored by what happened; the things he said.

Brandon completely embarrassed me when he told Oliver he could do better than me. The afternoon had been going exceptionally well. I was thinking my issues were stupid before Brandon flayed me open, reminding me Oliver *is* totally out of my league. I wanted to make myself as small as possible, and escape as quickly as I could before Oliver realized it was true—that he was wasting his time with me.

I hear the locks next door disengage and Margie steps out of her front door. She fans herself. "My God, girl. Who was that and tell me where I can get one?"

Aaand that does it. I burst into laughter and she joins in. Our laughter eventually slows, turning into girly giggles when she nudges me with her elbow. "That kiss was movie-worthy. I could feel the heat and steam from inside. You need to hold on to a man who knows how to kiss like that. Believe me, men like that are few and far between these days. They're all pansy asses who don't want to mess up their hair or manicure."

Ha! She's spot on there. I experience more chemistry standing next to Oliver than I've ever felt, even in the most passionate of moments, with any of my exes.

"Can you imagine what he's like between the sheets … or against the wall … or in the shower?" Margie sighs.

My blush rises, thinking about her witnessing the hot kisses we shared on my front porch, and that she's thinking about Oliver and sex.

I put my hands on my hips and deadpan. "Were you spying on me, Margie?"

"Absolutely, I gotta get my thrills from somewhere, Love!" She has not one ounce of shame in her game. It's exactly why I love her. We smile at each other as she winks at me. "So, tell me all about that hot hunk of man."

"Well, you probably won't see him around again. He's way out of my league—"

Margie holds up her hand in the universal sign of stop, inter-rupting me. "Stop right there! There was no 'out of my league' from where I was watching. You two are stunning together, and the chem-istry was off the charts. He would be lucky to catch and keep a young woman like you. Mark my words, I'll be seeing him around here quite often."

"But—" I try to explain, but she cuts me off again with a slash of her arm.

"No 'buts' about it. Now go inside and get ready to visit with your family for dinner. Make sure you say 'hello' to everyone for me."

Margie gives me a stern glare and tight hug, then heads inside, engaging the locks. I guess that's that then.

FOURTEEN

-oliver-

I'M ATTEMPTING TO WORK, WHEN JASE WALKS INTO MY OFFICE, AND makes himself comfortable in the chair opposite my desk. He looks as if he wants to sit and chat for a while, but I'm too discombobulated to carry on any kind of meaningful discussion this morning. He's slouched back in the chair with his right ankle resting on his left knee, looking at me—waiting me out.

I raise my brows. "Okay, I'll bite. What's up?"

"That's what I want to know. You don't seem your usual self. You look a little, shall I say, disheveled." He waves his hand around in my general direction. "You've missed your nine-thirty check-in with *Square One* for your father, and I've had a call from a guy named Brandon. He's threatening to sue your ass for his fractured jaw."

I glance at the time, realizing he's right—*fuck!* Kate's got my head in such a spin. I barely slept last night, and I can't seem to focus—on anything. I've never experienced these kinds of feelings for a woman before. Jase drops his leg. He places both feet on the floor and leans forward, resting his elbows on his knees.

"Talk to me, Oliver. What's going on?"

I huff out a breath. "It's Kate."

His posture straightens, and that relaxed air about him is gone. "Is she alright? Nothing bad has happened to her?"

I wave him off. "No, nothing like that. Unless you count her dick of, I'm assuming, an ex-boyfriend humiliating her in front of me." Thinking about it has a red haze entering my periphery, my fists clenching, ready to fight.

"What do you mean?"

"I finally got Kate to agree to go on a date with me yesterday afternoon." Nodding, he smirks while gesturing for me to continue. "We were having a brilliant afternoon. It felt surprisingly natural, as though we're in sync. Then this guy approaches Kate—Brandon." I raise my eyebrows. "When he sees she's with me, he says, 'What are you doing here with someone like Kate? Surely you can do better than her, man?'. She shuts down, right then and there."

"What the fuck?" Jase looks as though he wants a piece of the bastard as well. "I hope you set him straight as well as punched him in the jaw. Any guy would be lucky to have a woman like Kate." Glaring at him, I tense. I don't want him to consider that he should be with Kate, but I'm also relieved that he thinks highly of her. He raises his hands in surrender. "Hey. Calm down, I don't mean I'm interested. I *know* she's all yours."

Relaxing back in my chair, I run my hand down my face. "Damn right I set him straight. He deserved what I gave him and more. The lawyers can deal with his slimy ass." I almost smile—it felt good to knock that asshole on his ass in front of his current girlfriend.

"Good, glad to hear it. I would have done the same. I'm guessing things are moving forward with you two, then?"

Shaking my head, I peer down at my desk, gathering my thoughts. Looking back up at Jase, I take a deep breath. "I don't know. By the time I decked the guy and went after Kate, she was gone. I turned up at her house, catching her before she got inside. She thinks she's not good enough for me." I poke my chest with my thumb, shaking my head. "She thinks *I* can do much better than her. That she's not beautiful enough to be with someone who looks like me." My blood boils all over again.

"That ex must have done a number on her. She's going to need you to show her how wrong she is; help her rebuild that self-confidence." He looks at me as if to check if I'm up for the job. "What are you going to do?"

"First of all, I kissed the shit out of her and told her she wasn't to disrespect herself like that ever again."

Jase snickers.

"Then I laid my cards on the table." I run my hand down my face. "I've never been this invested in spending time with a woman that isn't only about sex. I want to get to know her and soak in all her goodness. I told her I wanted to be with her, and I would consider myself very lucky if she would give me a chance. Then I left her to think about it." I pause, looking out of the floor to ceiling window. Jase allows me the time. "I have to hope she makes the choice to let me in, and gives this thing between us a chance to grow."

"It sounds like you did the right thing. She'll come around."

"I hope so."

But I'm not convinced.

"Can you find the closest coffee shop to Northwood Elementary? Place a recurring order for every Monday to Friday to be delivered to Kate Summer in the Kindergarten. Make sure she gets a large skinny latte, with a vanilla shot, in a reusable cup, with some type of pastry each day. Make sure the pastry isn't the same two days in a row unless she shows a preference for a particular type. Then make sure they let me know which pastries she prefers."

He makes a note on his tablet. "Sure, boss. But you don't think that's a little excessive? You might scare her off."

"She told me she's too busy to eat lunch most days. I don't think it's excessive at all. I plan to look after her and make her realize she needs me in her life. This week we'll start with coffee. Next week we'll be including lunch. I need to find out if she has any allergies. Actually, make sure they deliver the coffee before school starts. She probably can't have hot drinks once the students enter the room."

"I'll get right on that, but don't say I didn't warn you when this bites you in the ass, and she tells you to leave her alone." He shrugs. "I'll also contact your lawyer about Brandon."

"Thanks, Jase. Appreciate it. Now get out and let me get back to work. Next thing I know, you'll want to paint my nails and braid my hair." My lips lift in a half smile.

He huffs out a laugh. "You wish."

He offers me the bird over his shoulder as he leaves my office, and I can't help but laugh.

I haven't heard from Kate for almost forty-eight hours when my phone buzzes around twelve-thirty. As I reach for it, I see it's from Kate. A true smile breaks and I can't open my phone quick enough. This is exactly what I was hoping for.

> **Sunshine:** Thanks for my coffee and pastry this morning. This is the first chance I've had to respond. But please stop buying me things. I don't need it
>
> **Me:** You're more than welcome and I'm not going to stop looking after you. You need someone to take care of you and I'm going to show you I'm that man

A few minutes pass and I figure the conversation is over.

> **Sunshine:** Woah! Slow your roll, big guy. I'm not some little woman who needs a big strapping man to take care of me. I've been doing fine this long, and I'm certain I'll continue to do fine all on my little ol' lonesome

Fuuuck! I went too far, and I didn't mean it like that. But hey, I raise my brow at the phone. She said I'm a 'big strapping man'. I'm happy with that.

> **Me:** I didn't mean it like that. I know you are a highly capable

woman. Please let me make it up to you. Can I take you out to
dinner tonight?

Sunshine: It's all good. You don't need to make anything up
to me

She totally ignored my dinner invitation. What's it going to take
to get this woman on a proper date? I hope I haven't fucked my
chances before I even get started.

Sunshine: I also, uh, wanted to apologize for my breakdown on
Sunday. I'm sorry you had to witness my self-loathing and I'm
rather embarrassed

Oh Sunshine, you have nothing to be embarrassed about.

Me: You have nothing to be embarrassed about. I hope I made it
abundantly clear I want to get to know you, Kate. Spend time with
you. See where this chemistry might lead

I've never felt this way about a woman, and as much as it shocks
me, I like it. There's quite a wait for her next message to come
through.

Sunshine: I think I would like that very much

Yes! It's like I've won the lottery. I abruptly stand from my chair,
knocking it back as I throw my fist in the air to celebrate.

I finally get my head back in the game and get back to work.
We've got a big quarter coming up, and I need to prep for a meeting
tomorrow with my senior staff to ensure we're all on the same page.

FIFTEEN

-kate-

OH, THAT MAN. HE'S CERTAINLY DIFFERENT FROM ANY MAN I'VE ever encountered before. The girl took me aback when she arrived from *Coffee and Cookies* with *my* coffee order. When she told me someone had phoned an order in yesterday to be delivered to me—I didn't understand what she was talking about. I rarely buy take away coffee or a pastry, because I'm watching every penny. When I asked her who placed the order, she smiled at me and said his name was Oliver. She asked me to tell her if I liked the pastry she had selected for me, presented my coffee in a reusable coffee cup, and left. As I took a sip, I couldn't resist closing my eyes while I absorbed the rich flavor and aroma—no wonder they're considered the best coffee place around.

I spent the morning walking on clouds because it made me feel special to have someone pay attention to how I like my coffee, and then organize to have it delivered to me at work. Even Emma, my friend, and the first-grade teacher in the class next door noticed. She said I looked even more energized than I usually do. When Jack pulled Sue-Anne's hair, I was still floating in the clouds. But then I messaged to thank him for the coffee, and it all went to shit! He comes across as a bit of a caveman—a sweet and thoughtful cave-man, but a caveman all the same.

I wonder if he would be that bossy in the bedroom? Aaand there goes my blush again!

After a restless night's sleep, I drive to work, mentally preparing for a new day. When I arrive, the girl from *Coffee and Cookies* is waiting by my classroom door with another cup of coffee and an interest-ing-looking pastry. I'm going to put on ten pounds at this rate. I never eat this type of food regularly. Sure, once in a while, but certainly not two days in a row.

"Morning, I'm guessing this is from Oliver?"

"Good morning to you too!" She has such a cheerful demeanor for this time of the day. "Bingo! Oliver strikes again. Let me know if you like the pastry. It's a new creation of mine. Have a great day!"

She collects the cup from yesterday, waving as she leaves. I can't help but sigh at his kind gesture, but I don't want to encourage him to keep spending money on me. These types of expenses add up without you realizing it. Before you know it, you've spent twenty dollars here and thirty dollars there, and then you can't make your mortgage payment. I get out my phone and shoot Oliver a quick message before the kids arrive.

Me: Good morning Oliver. Thank you once again for my coffee and pastry. I appreciate your kind and thoughtful gesture, but I must insist you stop. It truly is unnecessary. I hope you have a great day
Oliver: Good morning, Sunshine. You are more than welcome for the coffee and pastry. Enjoy them and think of me. Have a productive day

Oh, I surely will be thinking of him. How can I stop? I hope I'm not appearing ungrateful for my delicious treats, but I'm not used to having a man spoil me without expecting something in return. I drink my coffee, made exactly how I like it, and eat the delicious chocolate-filled pastry, finishing in time to greet my energetic students. As I greet each child, I can't clear my head of thoughts of a hot, green-eyed bossy man named Oliver.

Each morning, I'm greeted in the same way—coffee with a pastry. I won't fit into any of my clothes at this rate. I've started sharing the pastries with Emma—I figure I'll be eating fewer calories that way. Each day, I send him a thank you text which also asks him kindly to cease and desist. On Friday afternoon, I receive a text out of the blue.

> **Oliver:** Good afternoon Sunshine. Do you have anything that you're allergic to?
>
> **Me:** Why?
>
> **Oliver:** I wanted to check and make sure I'm keeping you safe
>
> **Me:** You need to worry about that. I can keep myself safe. Thank you for checking in though
>
> **Oliver:** Do you have any allergies? Answer, or I'll keep texting you until you tell me anyway. Your choice!
>
> **Me:** Geez, you're one persistent dude! No, I don't have any allergies. Happy?
>
> **Oliver:** Unbelievably so

Well, that was weird. He's too much! I don't know what to make of him. Honestly, I don't. I've never experienced anyone like him before.

SIXTEEN

-oliver-

It's been ten days since I've laid eyes on Kate. Ten days too long for my liking. If I want to make any headway with her, I'm going to have to push forward, because I know she won't come to me.

Me: Can I see you tonight?

Perhaps I'm being pushy, but I need to have her in my arms again—and soon.

Sunshine: I can't tonight. I'm cooking dinner for Margie. I try to cook for her a couple of nights each week to make sure she eats properly

Why is that not a surprise? From what I can tell, she's always looking out for everybody else.

Me: I can bring Chinese, or whatever you like
Me: Enough for the three of us

I sit, staring at my phone like a teen, impatiently waiting for her response, which doesn't come. Maybe I pushed too hard, too fast. I need to slow down and tread gently with this woman, or I may scare her off. My phone vibrates as I turn toward my computer. I pick it up as if I'm an addict, receiving the message I was hoping for.

Sunshine: Sorry I took a while to respond. I had to check with Margie. That would be great. Margie and I love Chinese. We'll see you at 7

Aaand, touchdown!

Me: See you soon Sunshine. Get home safely

Well, this is interesting. I don't think I've ever left the office before seven and I need to order dinner, pick it up, and get to her place at seven.

"Trinity Fox has dealt with Brandon." Jase announces as he steps through my office door.

Turning his way, I raise an eyebrow. "Good. I like how she works. Swift and sharp."

He nods. "Yeah. She threatened to sue him for public embarrassment and humiliation. He backed down straight away."

I huff out a breath. "Of course he did. Goes to show how weak and insipid the fucker obviously is."

"Yeah." He thumbs over his shoulder. "I'm off to grab lunch. Do you want me to bring anything back for you?"

"I could go for a sandwich. Use the card."

SEVENTEEN

-kate-

IT'S FOUR BY THE TIME I WALK OUT TO MY CAR TO DRIVE HOME. I can't believe Oliver's coming to have dinner with Margie and me tonight. I'm not sure whether I'm more excited or more nervous about having him in my space.

I stayed to display the giant shapes the children put together from our shape hunt today. We wandered around the school, identifying the different shapes the children could see in the built and natural environment. They took photos of the different shapes with their tablets, then I printed them on the school printer. The students then sorted them into categories of images of the same shape. We took it one step further, making a giant shape using the shapes in each category. It was great fun and now the kids are determined to identify shapes everywhere they go. I live for that stuff. The best part of teaching kindergarten is watching the students grow and develop confidence in their skills and knowledge over the course of the year. I love developing a bond with them and watching them grow as learners.

As I look down at my yellow blouse covered in green paint and glue from our craft activity this afternoon, I frown. I don't want him to see me in such a mess. I desperately need to have a shower and change before Oliver arrives.

I pile all of my gear in the back seat of my car and climb in, so I can be on my way. Nothing happens when I turn the key. I pump the gas a few times, then turn the key again. Instead of nothing, I get an enormous bang and a heap of gray smoke pours out of the engine bay.

Crap! Now what do I do?

I scramble out of my car, working quickly to collect all the files I loaded in. The I step as far away as I can—just in case it explodes. Okay, I'm probably being dramatic, but as smoke keeps pouring out of the engine, I feel justified in my position to stay clear. I guess I better call a tow. This is annoying. I was hoping to pay a little extra off my mortgage this month. This wasn't an expense I budgeted for, but it has to be fixed—how else will I get to and from work?

Reaching into my bag, I pull out my phone. As I navigate my way to the phone app, my phone rings. It's Oliver. I quickly press to accept the call. "Hey, Oliver. How was your day? Are you still planning on coming for dinner tonight?"

All of that comes out in a rush. I'm sure I sound like a madwoman who might miss out on her fix. Which I might, thanks to my car.

His rich laugh comes across the line. "Hey, Sunshine. Of course, I'm still coming for dinner. I was calling to find out if you needed me to pick up anything else on my way?"

He's incredibly kind.

"No thanks, just bring yourself, and dinner, of course. I'm having some car trouble. I'm hoping to make it home on time. I was about to call a tow to come and get my car. Then I'll need to work out a way to get home."

"Where are you? I'll organize my mechanic to come and pick up your car. I can come and take you home."

Oh geez, I'm pretty sure the mechanic he uses for that fancy car of his would be out of my budget.

"No, that's okay. I'll sort it out. I've got a mechanic I use, so I'll get in touch with him. He's my friend's brother. I trust him. But I wouldn't say no to a ride home if it's not too much trouble? I'm still at school."

I'm holding my breath, hoping he'll be happy to swing out of his way to take me home.

"Of course. I'll get there as quickly as I can. Text me the contact details of the mechanic you use, and I'll organize the tow for you. You go back into the building and wait for me."

Gosh, he's bossy, but I think it's because he wants to help.

"Okay, I'll text it to you now. Hopefully, the tow truck can get here at the same time you do. That way, we won't have to wait around. Thanks, Oliver. I truly appreciate your help. See you soon."

"No problem, Sunshine. Happy to help you out any time you need. I'll see you soon."

He disconnects the call, and I carry all my files back inside the building. Lucky for me, the cleaners are still around and the school's still open.

EIGHTEEN

-oliver-

THIS IS THE SECOND TIME SHE'S HAD CAR TROUBLE SINCE I'VE known her. Once the number comes through, I call her mechanic. It rings several times and I'm about to call my mechanic, when someone finally answers.

"Stanfield Auto Repairs. This is Max. How can I help you?"

"Hi, Max. My name is Oliver Stone. My girlfriend's car has broken down and needs a tow. Can you pick it up now?"

"Sure. Where is it?"

"Northwood Elementary. Do you know it?"

"Yeah. My sister's a teacher there."

"I need you to do me a favor. She keeps having trouble with the car. I want the entire vehicle stripped and everything mechanical replaced."

He whistles. "That'll mean the only original parts of the car will be the body and the interior."

"Yep. That way, I can rest assured the car is safe and reliable. The car is special to her. It belonged to her nan."

"I have to be honest with you. It's probably going to be more expensive to complete this work than it would be to buy her a new one."

I huff out a sigh. I guessed as much. "She's attached to the damn thing, so this is how it has to be. You need to keep it between us and invoice her for something inexpensive to explain the smoke."

"Okay. I can keep it between us. But it's going to take a fair bit longer to do the work you're asking for than a simple fix."

"I'm sure you can come up with some excuse. It's important that she feels she's dealing with her own problems."

"No problem. I'll work something out. I'll see you at the school."

I arrive at Kate's school at the same time as the tow truck. She steps out of the building, loaded down with her bags of files for work. Striding forward quickly, I press a kiss to her forehead as I take some of the load. I've never seen her in her work clothes. She looks adorable wearing red ballet flats, a black-and-white striped skirt, and a yellow blouse with green splotches … of … is that paint? I have the distinct feeling that Kate loves red shoes. Each and every pair of shoes I've seen her wear are red. I brush a kiss across her lips in greeting and her shoulders drop. I guarantee she's worried about the expense associated with getting her car repaired.

I brush a lock of hair that's come free from her braid behind her ear, but it's stiff … is that … glue? She's adorably messy after her day at work, and I'm working hard to hold back a smile.

"Hey."

She looks up at me, eyebrows drawn tight. "Hey. Thanks for coming to pick me up, and organizing a tow."

"No problem. I'm always happy to help."

Together, we walk toward the tow truck, which is parked next to Kate's car. I reach my hand forward. "Hi, I'm Oliver. I spoke with you on the phone."

He nods in greeting, shaking my hand. "Max."

Kate steps forward. "Hi, Max. Thanks for coming out quickly. Do you have time in your schedule to work on my car? I'm going to need it fixed pretty quickly because I need to get to and from work."

"Yeah, of course, Kate. It'll probably take a few days, though. You might have to rent a car or borrow one from a friend. I used to offer courtesy cars, but the insurance on them was too much for my business."

"Oh, thanks. Yeah, I'll work out something. Can you please call me when you work out what's wrong, as well as an estimate of the cost and time it's going to take?"

Max looks across at me, then back to Kate. "Sure, sure. No problem. I can do that. I'll most likely call you tomorrow afternoon; once I investigate the issue."

She tucks a lock of hair behind her ear. "Thanks, I really appreciate your help."

He nods and moves toward her car. "Have you got everything you need out of here?"

"Uh, yeah. It's good to go," Kate responds, moving forward to hand Max her car key.

I tuck Kate in close to my body as Max loads her car onto the tow truck. When he's done, we watch him drive away. Kate slumps against me, releasing a long sigh. I kiss the top of her head and she looks up at me. "Thanks for coming to my rescue. I hope it's not going to cost an arm and a leg to fix my car."

I squeeze her shoulder. "You didn't need to be rescued." I pull away to study her tense face. "Come on, we'll load your stuff into my car and get going."

We load Kate's work gear into my car and make our way to her place. I have to drive back to my office to tie up some loose ends for an overseas client—work I need to finish before I can leave for the day.

I arrive at Kate's place at ten minutes past with several bags of Chinese food from my favorite restaurant. Considering the way my afternoon went, I did well with time. I chose several dishes because I wasn't sure what Kate and Margie like. I figure they can survive on what's left over for the rest of the week. Her front door is open, with the screen door closed. I can hear her talking with another woman.

"I told you I would see that young man again. You've got to listen to me. I know my stuff!"

I'm guessing that's Margie.

"I know what you said. I guess I need to let go of my apprehension and trust in what he's showing me. He's genuinely sweet and thoughtful, if not a little overwhelming and intense."

I can hear silverware and crockery clanking; they must be setting the table for dinner. I take the cue to knock on the screen door. Kate comes to the door wearing yoga pants, a loose t-shirt draped off one shoulder, showing smooth creamy skin, interrupted by a red bra strap. Her feet are bare, with red polish on her toes. I could get used to coming home and having her greet me at the door in such a comfortable state. Her hair's wet; she must have washed the glue out of it.

"Hey, you're right on time. I wasn't sure if you could even get here on time after I messed up your afternoon. Traffic can be hectic at this time of the day."

I think she's nervous. She's barely taken a breath. She unlocks and opens the screen door. Standing to the side, she allows me to enter her home. I want to greet her with a kiss, but I don't want to push my luck as I spy her neighbor standing off to the side, observing us with a cheeky smile on her face.

As I pass Kate, her delicate jasmine scent fills my senses and I want to soak it all in.

"It's unusual for me to be out of the office while it's still daylight." I turn toward Margie. "You must be Margie, I'm Oliver. It's nice to meet you."

I step in to shake her hand, but she knocks it out of the way, hugging me. My body's stiff, unused to being hugged in a platonic way. Tonight should be interesting. I'm desperate to spend any time I can with Kate. I wasn't going to miss this opportunity, but having a friendly dinner with strangers is out of my comfort zone. This is the second dinner I'll have sat through with people I don't know, just to spend time with this woman.

"Kate and I are huggers! None of this shaking hands business."

As she releases me, she squeezes my biceps and gives Kate what she thinks is a covert nod and a wink. Kate blushes in response. I love that fucking blush.

We get situated at Kate's small dining table, dishing up our plates of food. At first, we're all quiet, taking in the delicious aromas and flavors.

Margie swallows down a bite of food, then places her fork on the side of her plate. She studies me intently for a moment. Then, with a serious expression on her face, she asks, "Tell me, Oliver. What are your intentions with my girl, Kate?"

Kate spits out the water she just drank in utter shock. "Margie! I can't believe you asked that. Do you have no filter at all?" She looks mortified, which I find charming. The blush I love is creeping up her neck, burning her cheeks, as she attempts to wipe up her mess.

Margie laughs, hitting the table with an open palm. "Oh God girl, settle down. I was having a joke with Oliver. He doesn't mind."

Kate turns to me and mouths, "I'm so sorry." Then she gives Margie a death glare, filled with obvious underlying affection for the woman.

Placing my palm on Kate's forearm, I gain her attention while speaking to Margie. "My intentions are simple. I want to spend time with Kate. I want to get to know her. I want to know *everything* about her. I want to care for her, and have her in my life for as long as possible."

I feel as though I've repeatedly had to make my intentions clear. I don't mind. It makes me happy to know she's surrounded by people who care for and love her fiercely. Margie seems satisfied with my answer as she nods and smiles, looking lovingly at Kate. Kate still looks unsure of my intentions, and well, I'm a bit surprised myself by the overwhelming desire I have to get to know her. Not only on a physical level, but on an emotional one as well. We move on, making small talk about each of our days, and the happenings down their street.

Kate relays the afternoon's ordeal to Margie. Without hesitation, Margie offers to loan Kate her car, which she barely drives anymore, because of failing eyesight. The tightness in Kate's body releases with a solution to her transportation problems. I offered to rent a car for her, but she's a stubborn, independent woman—so very different from any other woman I've encountered. Kate surely knows I have more money than she does, yet she refuses to allow me to help her out.

We finish the meal and Margie excuses herself to go home. I offer to walk her to her door and she accepts; hugging Kate goodbye.

At her door, Margie turns to me. "Please don't hurt my girl. She has such a kind heart and a generous soul."

"You needn't worry, Margie. I have absolutely zero interest in hurting Kate. I can see exactly how much she has to offer, and I selfishly want it. I want it all, and I want it all from Kate. Now that I've met her, nobody else will do."

She hugs me, patting my cheek, then steps inside to lock up for the evening.

I let myself back into Kate's home, which is as sunny as she is. Comfortable furniture with colorful cushions, rugs, and prints fill the space, making it feel joyful, warm, and welcoming. The exact opposite of my cold, clinical penthouse.

She's already cleared the table and is currently standing at the sink, washing the dishes. Her ass looks fantastic in her yoga pants and I can't stop myself from needing to touch her any longer. I move in close behind her; the front of my body pressing against her back. She pauses what she's doing, turning her face to the side, allowing her to see me. Placing my hands on either side of her body, I box her in. Moving in, I place gentle kisses and nips along her exposed shoulder, up her slender neck, finally reaching her soft lips —something I've been desperate to do all evening. The plate drops into the water with a splash, and I swallow her sigh. It's as though she's been waiting for me to touch her, to kiss her.

NINETEEN

-kate-

My God. *Finally!* From the minute he walked into my home and I smelled his woodsy masculine scent, I've wanted him to kiss me. To touch me. To show me he meant everything he said to me after the pier.

When I saw him in his suit, I'm pretty sure I stopped breathing —holy hotness! I've always been a sucker for a guy in a suit, but Oliver takes it to the next level. I figured it couldn't get any better, but he took off his jacket, undid his tie, and rolled up his sleeves.

I may have had heart palpitations.

The hotness level skyrocketed one thousand percent—it was as though all my arm porn fantasies came to life, right before my very eyes. Now, as his warm, muscular body presses against mine, I want to turn around and absorb every inch of him.

As he kisses me, the rasp of his short beard is delicious against the sensitive skin on my shoulder. The delicate kisses make me feel like I'm precious to him. Losing my grip on the plate I'm washing, it drops into the sink, and I tilt my head, giving him better access to my neck. His kisses heat my blood and goosebumps cover my flesh.

I can't go another minute without touching him.

Turning around, I lift my arms around his neck to pull him

closer. I'm so lost in him I forget my hands are wet, running them through his thick hair, which he doesn't seem to mind. Wrapping his arms tighter around me, he squeezes me as close as he can to his body, deepening our kiss. Our tongues mingle, mixing our tastes, and our breaths.

It feels astonishingly right—I want to keep doing this forever.

He moves his hands to my waist, picking me up as though I weigh nothing, and places me on the counter next to the sink. Nudging my legs apart, he positions his hips in the space he's created. Without breaking the kiss, I wrap my legs around him, pulling him in as close to me as possible. He grumbles, thrusting his hips forward, connecting with my most sensitive area. He makes me aware of the pulsing need I have to feel him in the most primal way. I can't miss the hardness in his pants, separated from me by two layers of thin fabric. The kiss is spectacular and continues for what seems like hours.

Hands groping, mouths joined, sighs, and moans filling the air. This is the most erotic experience I've had to date. I'm experiencing more than a physical connection with this man. He somehow reaches into my soul.

The muscles of his back and arms are so hard, so strong beneath my hands. My heartbeat is out of control and with my chest touching Oliver's, I can feel his is the same. We gradually pull away from each other to catch our breath and I bury my face in Oliver's neck, suddenly feeling shy. He gently cradles either side of my face, his thumbs resting on my cheekbones, his fingers in my hair. Tilting my head back carefully, he kisses my forehead. He seems to like cupping my face in his hands. I like it, too; it makes me feel cherished.

"I've been wanting to do that since I left here ten days ago. The thought of never being able to see you, or kiss you, or touch you again was too much for me, Kate. I couldn't concentrate at work; even Jase was worried about me. Please trust in what I say and what I show you. Don't let the assholes of your past ruin something that could be mind-blowing between us."

Oh my heart, he's being incredibly vulnerable.

"I've *never* felt this way about a woman before, Kate. It's also new and scary for me." He drops his forehead back to mine.

"Believe me when I say I've wanted those kisses as well. I've been thinking about what you said. I'm going to do my very best to move forward and let the hurt from my past relationships go." *I only hope I can do what I say.* "I might mess up sometimes, or feel inadequate, but know I am working on it. I'm ready to trust in what you say, and the things you do that show me you care."

He uses his hold on my face to angle my lips for another heartfelt kiss. This kiss is hungrier, more demanding. If he keeps kissing me like this, I may never gain full control of my brain again.

He pulls away, kissing the tip of my nose. "If I don't stop now, I may not stop at all. I don't want to push you, Kate. I want to do this the right way. You're worth more than just a couple of nights."

We eventually finish cleaning up from dinner and Oliver reluctantly leaves me to the rest of my evening.

TWENTY

-oliver-

As I'm analyzing stock options for a client when I get a call from Kate's mechanic.

"Hey, Max, what've you got for me?" I ask, my pen at the ready to record any information I need.

"Hey, Mr. Stone. I can get everything I need over the next two days. It will probably take about a week to put the car back together. That's working as quickly as possible. I'm a sole operator."

"No problem. Sounds good. Now, what are you going to tell Kate?" It may be deceitful to organize this behind her back and not tell her what's happening, but her car has been unreliable and I'm not comfortable with her driving a vehicle that could potentially leave her in a dangerous situation.

"I'm going to tell her coolant was entering the combustion chamber, and I needed to drain it out to change the hose. A low-cost fix will be $150, including the tow. I'll tell her I have to order in the hose, which will take about a week, to allow for the additional time."

"Sounds good, Max. Thanks for the call. Let me know if you have any issues and I'll sort them out. Talk soon."

"Yeah, bye."

Over the next several hours, I meet with a new client and speak with existing clients over the phone. I like to keep them up-to-date with changes to their investment portfolio, before following up with a formal email.

My phone buzzes with several messages from Kate.

Sunshine: Hey

Sunshine: Max called

Sunshine: My car's only going to cost $150 for the repair and the tow *relieved face emoji*

Me: Hey

Me: That's not too bad, you've got to feel relieved

Sunshine: But I'll be without my car for a bit over a week

Me: Margie won't mind how long you use her car

Sunshine: I guess, I just don't like being a bother

Me: I doubt Margie thinks you're a bother

Sunshine: I hope not

Me: Have a great afternoon with your students

Sunshine: Thanks. I hope you have a productive afternoon too

I want to spend a day with Kate hiking in the woods before the weather makes getting outdoors difficult. I'm not sure if Kate is much of an outdoor person. I enjoy getting out and about in nature to center myself after being cooped up in an office all day, every day. It helps to reduce my stress levels, and improve my mood and productivity. I've got some important meetings coming up and I want to be functioning at my best. I think spending the day with Kate, hiking in the woods, would be the best possible way to get me there.

She usually spends her Saturday morning catching up on chores around the house. This is a perfect time to call her to organize a date for Sunday.

"Hey, Oliver." Her voice soothes something deep inside of me.

"Hi, Sunshine. How's things?"

"Great. I'm catching up on my usual Saturday chores. How about you?"

"Great. I was hoping I could take you out hiking tomorrow." I hold my breath, waiting for her rejection.

"Oh, I'd love that. I haven't been out for a good walk in ages." I release the breath I was holding with a whoosh. I'm surprised since she's been resistant to spend time with me. We organize the details and I disconnect the call with a wide smile.

Waking up Sunday morning, I still have the smile on my face in anticipation of spending the day with Kate, in one of my favorite places. I move through a shorter workout because I'll be walking today. After my shower, I eat a protein-rich breakfast, and I'm on my way; stopping only to pick up some healthy snacks and bottled water for our hike.

When I arrive at Kate's tidy home, I find her waiting on the small porch wearing those yoga pants that drive me wild, carrying her own backpack. Her hair's in a braid over one shoulder, reminding me of the first time I met her. Exiting my car, I remind myself that I'm going to behave like a gentleman and open the door for her; however, I trap her between the side of my car and my body without cognition. I know I've caught her by surprise, and when her mouth opens on a gasp, I take advantage, capturing her lips in a desperate kiss. My cock grows, preparing to be inside her. It hasn't got the memo that I'm taking my time with this beguiling woman.

Gentling the kiss, I pull back, finally greeting the woman who has stolen my every thought since I met her, and is rapidly stealing my heart. "Hey."

Her eyes open slowly, a shy smile touching her lips. Dilated pupils greet me and it's satisfying to know she's as turned on as I am.

"Hey." Her swollen lips spread into a proper smile. She looks ravishing.

I release her and situate her in my car so we can drive toward the outer limits of the city, where we'll spend our day hiking in the woods among the towering redwood and sequoia trees. Kate tells me all about her latest adventures with the kids from the shelter, and I find I have nothing of value to share. I'm happy to listen. I don't want to talk about work—I don't want Kate to know I actually own the company. Not yet, anyway.

Climbing out of the car, I draw in a breath—the air feels fresher, cleaner. We collect our gear, and holding hands, we trek toward the park entrance. From here, we can choose from a variety of walks, ranging from thirty to ninety minutes. We opt for the longer trail and head off, stopping now and then to admire the trees or an amazing view. I take every opportunity to touch Kate with my hands and mouth, planting kisses on various parts of her exposed skin. The day is perfection.

TWENTY-ONE

-kate-

TODAY HAS BEEN PERFECT. OLIVER'S BEEN SUPREMELY ATTENTIVE, and it's been wonderful to see him relaxed. He clearly enjoys spending time in nature, which is something I also enjoy. The weather will change soon, making today a great opportunity to experience an outdoor adventure before we're no longer able.

Mom and Dad have a church event tonight, so they've canceled our family dinner.

I turn to him. "Would you like to stay for din—?"

"I'd love to." He cuts in before I can finish the invitation.

I chuckle at his eagerness. "I didn't tell you what we'd be having for dinner."

"Don't care what we eat, as long as I'm spending time with you." Aaand cue the melting heart.

"I've got the fixings for home-made burgers. We could sit on my small back deck to enjoy them as the sun goes down."

He reaches across, taking my hand and placing it on his firm thigh. "You don't need to sell it to me, Kate. If you're there. I'm there. End of story."

Once we arrive home, we work together to prepare our burgers and then sit on my small back deck to enjoy them as the sun sets.

We seem to always find something to talk about, but don't necessarily need to fill all the silences. I'm just as comfortable sitting quietly next to him as I am when we're chatting. It's as if we've known each other for much longer than we actually have.

After the sun's gone down, it's too cool to stay outside. Once again, we work together to clean up our mess and move to my couch. Oliver looks huge on my tiny two-seater, but that works in my favor. While Oliver sits on one cushion, I sit to the side of him, with my back against the arm, tucking my legs up. He takes hold of one of my feet and begins to rub it absentmindedly. It feels fantastic after spending the day walking. He switches to my other foot and I sink further into the couch, my body thoroughly relaxed—which I find entirely weird this soon after meeting him. We talk softly about this and that; the music we each like; whether we prefer the beach or the river—we both love the riverside. We talk about how we developed our passion for the work each of us does as I get sleepier and sleepier—my eyes drooping low.

Waking to my alarm and the sun streaming through my window, I bolt upright, disoriented. I don't remember getting into bed. The first thing I realize is that I'm still wearing my clothes from yesterday. Getting up quickly, I move through my house to find Oliver missing. My heart sinks with an instant pang of disappointment. I can't fathom what he thought of me falling asleep on him and having to put me to bed last night. Between that and him seeing me covered in paint, with glue dried in my hair during the week, he must surely be second-guessing his choice to pursue me.

I set my embarrassment aside and start getting ready for my day. Oliver even thought to put my phone on charge last night, before locking my house to keep me safe. Unplugging it, I spot messages from him.

Oliver: I didn't want to wake you. You looked peaceful, absolutely captivating. Have a great day Sunshine. I'll talk with you soon

Oliver: Thanks for spending the day with me

Oh, my heart! He seems too good to be true.

Me: Good morning. Thanks for putting me to bed. I'm sorry I fell asleep on you last night
Me: Maybe I can make it up to you tonight?

I hope I'm not being too pushy.

I drive to work, beginning my day, hoping that I'll see Oliver later. As I greet my students at the door and check in with them, I know my smile is a little brighter and my mood a little lighter. We go through our morning routine of puzzles, counting, and songs to get our bodies moving. The joy and happiness on their little faces fills my heart to overflowing. During the first break of the day, I check my phone and am disappointed with the messages I've received.

Oliver: I'm honored you fell asleep in my presence. Please don't ever apologize
Oliver: I'm sorry, I have a business dinner tonight which will probably run very late

I try to put the disappointment to the back of my mind, moving on with story time and our fine motor group activities. At lunch, the school office clerk knocks on my classroom door with an impressive floral arrangement from *Blooms and Balloons*.

"These were just delivered for you. You are one lucky girl because these are absolutely lovely."

"Thank you for bringing them down."

"No problem, Kate. Enjoy!"

Emma must have seen the delivery come past her classroom because she comes in to investigate as the school officer leaves. "That is one of the most stunning floral arrangements I think I've ever seen. Do you know who they might be from? Is there a note?"

I look through the arrangement to find a card tucked inside a baby pink envelope. I open it.

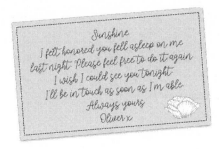

Emma's giddy as she reads over my shoulder. "Swoon. Who is this Oliver? You've been holding out on me."

I take a minute to catch my breath, reigning in my disappointment over not seeing Oliver tonight. The gesture of flowers is unexpected, and so … Oliver. I quickly explain how I met Oliver. That it's all very new, and how determined he's been to establish a relationship with me. I tell her about my fears that he's way out of my league and one day, I'll have my heart broken by him when he eventually wakes up and realizes this. She swoons at the appropriate times and chastises me for my self-doubt, then hugs me and tells me to 'go for it'.

I shoot a quick text to Oliver.

Me: Thank you for the impressive flowers

I attach an image of the arrangement.

Me: I'm disappointed I can't see you tonight, but I understand about prior engagements. Good luck with your business dinner
Me: I'll be thinking of you x

TWENTY-TWO

-oliver-

READING KATE'S MESSAGES, I'M NOT SURE I'VE EVER HAD ANYONE wish me luck for a meeting. It's assumed I've got it in the bag—that I don't need luck. Kate's working-class background and down-to-earth nature are refreshing for someone like me; surrounded by people who are all about money, status, and what I can do for them.

Jase pokes his head inside my office, interrupting my musing.

"Oh, I almost forgot. I've set up the lunch deliveries for Kate, as per your request. They'll rotate through various wraps, salads, soups, and subs during the week."

"Thanks, Jase. Appreciate it."

Apart from my sweet messages from Kate, this morning has been an absolute shit show. The meeting with my senior staff went well over the allocated time. If we don't nail these contracts next quarter, we could lose out on more than $375 million. I'm not prepared to lose that sort of money because my staff can't get their heads out of their asses. I made it clear I won't tolerate any sloppy work or anyone who drops the ball. Jase was giving me the 'calm down' look, but I was too worked up to care.

After putting Kate to bed last night and leaving her to sleep *alone*, I drove home and spent the night tossing and turning to thoughts of her. How her body felt in my arms as I carried her to bed, her gentle sigh as I placed her down on the soft mattress and covered her with blankets. I've decided I need her in my bed. I don't want to leave her—ever. I organized a flower delivery from *Blooms and Balloons*, because I wanted to make her smile, even though I won't have the opportunity to see it today.

Returning to work, I prep for the meeting I have tonight with a new overseas client. I'm completely engrossed in my work, so I startle when my phone buzzes. I look at the time, noticing it's three-thirty, which makes me hope it's a message from my girl. I pick up my phone and breathe a sigh of relief—it's Kate.

> **Sunshine:** Hey. I wanted to thank you for my coffee and pastry this morning, followed by a delicious chicken and salad wrap for lunch. Even though I appreciate your very thoughtful and generous gesture, you don't have to go to so much trouble for me
>
> **Me:** Hey Sunshine. You are more than welcome for the food. I enjoy taking care of you

Fuck! There I go again, making it sound like she can't look after herself.

> **Me:** I KNOW you can take care of yourself, but I want to take care of you too
>
> **Sunshine:** You're lucky you qualified your statement. I was about to send you a not very nice message big guy

I chuckle at her sass.

The rest of the day passes by in a mash-up of emails, meetings, and phone calls before I need to leave for my business meeting. After work, I make my way upstairs to shower and change, all the while thinking I'd rather be getting ready to spend the evening with Kate. Last night, sitting on her couch was the most relaxed I've been for … well … I can't remember the last time I felt that relaxed and comfortable. The kisses we shared and the intimacy of sitting and talking with her are things I've never experienced with a woman before, even though I have been in a long-term relationship. Since that relationship ended, I've never taken the time to get to know a woman, but with her, I want to know everything. I crave considerably more than just a physical release when I'm with her. I'm inexplicably drawn to the woman and the goodness inside of her.

When I arrive at the hotel, I allow the valet to park my car and I make my way inside to meet my overseas guest. The hostess greets me, guiding me through the compact restaurant to my table. The restaurant is particularly exclusive. There are only a dozen tables, with rich golden chairs, matching the gold inlay on the walls, and the decadent chandeliers hanging overhead. I wish, once again, I was sitting on Kate's couch, rubbing her feet and learning more about her, rather than meeting Lena Rhinecourt. She took over her father's mining conglomerate when he passed five years ago. She's a force to be reckoned with, and if I can impress her tonight, I'll close a $500 million investment deal over the next four years. I'm getting comfortable when the hostess approaches with Lena.

I stand to greet her. "Good evening, Ms. Rhinecourt. It's good to finally meet you in person." I hold out my hand to greet her. She's about my age, if I could guess, and most would say she's classically beautiful. Kate is significantly more attractive, in my opinion.

"Oh, don't Ms. Rhinecourt me. Lena, please. It makes me sound old." She takes my hand, shaking it while moving in to reach up and kiss my cheek, taking me by surprise. I don't give or receive affection from people with whom I have a business relationship—*ever*.

We sit, and the sommelier efficiently takes our drink orders. We begin by making generalized small talk about her trip, how long she's staying, and what she hopes to see and do while Stateside. Her Australian accent and terminology make for interesting conversation. We order our meals and conversation turns toward our business for the evening. The award-winning, Michelin-star chef, brings out our meals, outlining the flavors and textures we can expect to experience.

As the meal progresses, Lena is constantly touching my arm and leaning into my body. I'm not ignorant. I know she's flirting, but I *never* mix business with pleasure, and I'm certainly not interested now I have Kate in my life. I would never do anything to jeopardize my chance with her.

Lena excuses herself to visit the bathroom, and I spot a familiar man looking pissed as he walks toward me. It takes a second or two to place him, but when I do, I stand to greet him.

"Hey, Toby, good to see you." I hold out my hand, which he ignores, looking at me like I'm shit under his shoe.

"I'd like to say the same, but I can't. This is exactly what Kate was worried about. She's had her share of assholes who think it's okay to step out on her. She doesn't deserve another one." I'm taken aback by his assumption. "I knew who you were from the get-go, but I figured I'd give you the benefit of the doubt. You seemed like you were genuine when we spoke. That's why I didn't tell you to fuck off and leave her alone. But I'm going to say it now—fuck off and leave Kate alone. If you can't keep it in your pants and be faithful to her, you don't deserve her." His posture, along with the tick in his jaw, alerts me to how angry he is.

He thinks I'm fucking around behind his sister's back. *As if that would ever happen.* "I'm not stepping out on your sister. This is a business dinner. I would prefer to be sitting on your sister's couch, rather than sitting in this stuffy restaurant with a woman I have zero interest in, apart from the multi-million dollar deal I'm hoping to close tonight."

"It looked pretty damn cozy from where I was sitting." He gestures to a table close by, where a group of men dressed in casual business suits sit talking and drinking. His friend, Shane, is among them.

"Well, you've got the wrong idea. I would never cheat on your sister. I know how special she is, and I would never do anything to jeopardize my chance with her. I'm not letting her go any time soon. You need to get used to seeing me around, Toby."

He must recognize the sincerity and determination in my face.

"Make sure you keep it that way." He steps away, walking back to his companions.

Fuck! I wonder if Kate knows who I am? I don't get the impression she does. I'm agitated now and finding it hard to still my body. I take a moment to check my phone and calm myself down, noticing it's after ten. When Lena returns to the table, I'm ready to conclude this initial meeting and follow up in the office tomorrow.

Lena moves in close to me. "Is everything okay? You seem deep in thought."

"Yeah, everything's great. I think we've covered everything we need to this evening. We can tease out the minor details tomorrow in the office at our nine a.m. meeting. Did you want to order anything else, or shall we call it a night?"

"Oh, we can have a nightcap in my room." She rests her hand on my arm once again, her voice huskier. "If you know what I mean?"

"Sorry Lena, but I need to leave. I'm hoping to catch my girl-friend before she turns in for the night." Best I cut Lena off at the pass, letting her know my interest clearly lies elsewhere.

"We could make it quick. She would never have to know."

She's too close to me, her breast now pressing against my arm. Her heavy perfume and red glossy lips are too much and I crave the natural scent and perfect soft pink lips of Kate. "Ah, you see, *I* would know. She's everything to me, and I'm not prepared to do anything to jeopardize my relationship. It would be best if we say goodnight now. I'll see you tomorrow morning in my office to continue our business discussion." That was clear.

Lena pouts at me like a child. "Oh, that's too bad. I hope she appreciates how faithful you are to her. I'll see you in the morning."

"Would you like me to walk you up to your room?"

She waves me off. "No, that's fine. Go visit your girl."

"I'll send a car to collect you in the morning. Enjoy the remainder of your evening."

We both stand and as I make the move to shake hands, she steps into me, kissing my cheek and whispering in my ear, "Your girl is one very lucky lady."

Lena steps back, hurrying away. When I glance up, Toby's watching me with distrust. I give him a chin lift as I leave the restaurant. He's going to have to learn to trust me with his sister.

I drive toward Kate's house without conscious thought; when I thought about 'catching' Kate before she turned in for the night, I was only going to send her a text. I had no intention of actually going to her. I know it will be almost eleven when I get there and probably too late, but I would feel better knowing I'm close to her.

At this point, I get the impression I'm more invested in this relationship than Kate is, but I think it's because she doesn't trust my intentions. I have to show her she can trust me and that I'm in it for the long term. I pull into her driveway where her car would normally be, which I would prefer to replace, but know the gesture wouldn't be welcomed. I shake my head.

I don't think Kate realizes who I am. I don't want to tell her, because I know it will give her another reason not to believe my interest in her. She already thinks I'm out of her league. If she knows I'm a billionaire, she won't come near me with a ten-foot pole—and isn't that fucking ironic. For once, I meet a woman who garners my full interest, and she wouldn't want to have anything to do with me, *because* of my money, and who I am. I need her completely invested in our relationship before I tell her. I only hope her brother doesn't out me before I get the chance.

I'm unsure how long I sit in my car in her driveway—it's probably a bit stalker-ish, to be honest, but I can't bring myself to leave. Maybe she's still awake.

Me: Hey, how was your evening?
Me: Are you awake?
Sunshine: Hey
Sunshine: I am now, my messages woke me up
Me: Sorry, I had to see you
Sunshine: What do you mean?
Me: I'm parked in your driveway

Me: If it's too late, I can leave

I see the dots bouncing as if Kate's responding, then they disappear. The lights come on inside, and she appears at the open door, waving me inside. I let out a breath in relief. She's such a good person. She should have told me to 'fuck off'. I'm out of my car and at her front door before I know I'm moving.

Stepping inside, I kick the door closed with my foot as I grab Kate's delectable ass, lifting her to press her against the wall. Her shapely legs wrap around my hips as I crash my lips against hers. We're lost in the kiss and everything around us falls away. Her fingers dig into my scalp as her hot pussy grinds against my engorged cock. Being within five feet of her makes my cock hard. I've got no hope of keeping it under control when she's actually touching me. Miraculously, I slow the kiss and press my lips gently to the tip of her nose. "I missed you, Kate."

She pulls back further, looking into my eyes. "You saw me last night." She looks truly puzzled by my statement.

"It's been too long for me. Thinking I wouldn't see you tonight felt interminable. The whole day, in meetings and on phone calls, you were always on my mind."

Her eyes soften, her body melding further into mine as she moves forward to kiss me again. This is the first time Kate's initiated a kiss between us, and it feels like a monumental step forward. We kiss for minutes, maybe hours—time makes little sense when I'm like this with her. Slowly, she pulls back, gifting me a shy smile. I take in her sleepy state—messy hair, sleepy eyes, a white tank that hides nothing, and her sexy red boy shorts.

"I should say I'm sorry I woke you, but truthfully, I'm not. Pretty sure that makes me an asshole." I shrug, taking her mouth in another scorching kiss.

She pulls away, biting her bottom lip. "You want to come to bed with me?"

My wide eyes must convey my shock because she quickly corrects herself.

"To sleep. I'm not ready for anything else—yet." She looks away briefly then turns back to me. "Is that okay?"

"It's more than okay. I'm happy to go at your pace, Sunshine."

I sound like a lovesick pussy.

"I'm grateful for the trust you're giving me. I didn't come here expecting anything from you. This has been more than I expected. I would love to sleep with you, but I'll have to leave early because I have a conference call with an overseas market early tomorrow."

Her radiant smile lights her entire face. "Then take me to bed. Down the hall, first door on the right."

She holds on like a koala, with her arms around my neck and her legs around my hips, my hands where they belong—on her ass. I carry her to her bedroom; turning off the lights as we go. Carefully, I lay her on the bed and she scoots back, covering herself—which is disappointing.

Without taking my eyes off her, I remove my tie and jacket, placing them neatly over a chair in the corner of her room. Her eyes follow every movement, encouraging me to take my time to undress for her enjoyment. Next to go are my shoes and socks. I stand, slowly unbuttoning my shirt, when she climbs out of bed, moving into my space to take over. I feel as though I've hit a home run when she willingly puts her hands on me to undo my shirt buttons, pulling my shirttails out of my pants. She removes it slowly, sliding it off my shoulders and carefully draping it over my jacket. Then she turns her focus to my belt. She must recognize what she's done to me because she sucks in a quick breath and her sexy blush starts moving up from her chest. My cock is fucking hard, and it's more than obvious in my pants. She removes my belt with shaking hands, undoing my pants and letting them drop to the floor. As she bends down to pick them up, I get an unexpected view down her tank at her stunning tits. I can't wait to get my hands and mouth on those beauties. She folds my pants along the creases, draping them on the chair, then guides me to her bed. Facing each other—her hand on my neck, fingers playing with the hair at my nape—we quietly study each other while my hand rests on her hip as my thumb draws circles over her soft skin.

I tuck a lock of hair behind her ear, looking into her eyes. "You are incredibly striking. You take my breath away and yet when I'm with you, I feel like I can finally breathe."

I kiss the tip of her nose, guiding her to turn over, allowing me to hold her while we sleep. I wrap my body around hers and decide I never want to let her go. The calm and peace she brings me is something money can't buy. All the other shit and noise in my head disappears when I'm with her. I'm not sure I'll ever be able to explain to her what she gives to me. "Goodnight, Sunshine," I whisper into her hair.

TWENTY-THREE

-kate-

I TRY TO SLEEP, BUT MY BODY WON'T SHUT DOWN. HE'S exceptionally thoughtful and genuine with his actions. His breaths deepen as his body relaxes, so I take the opportunity to turn over and study him in the darkness. I can barely make out his relaxed features in the limited amount of light creeping through the gaps of my bedroom curtains. It's surreal to study at him like this. He looks very different in sleep; relaxed—more boyish. He must feel as though he has a great deal of pressure on him when he's awake because he always looks formidable.

When he was undressing, I couldn't help myself. I had to get my hands on his body, which is to die for. I can't believe I invited him to spend the night in my bed, which he readily accepted, knowing I wasn't ready for sex. He suddenly rolls onto his back—which scares the crap outta me, and I almost fall off the bed. Yeah, that would be awesome. He wakes up to find me on my ass on the floor.

The sheet has slipped down, allowing me to appreciate all those sexy abs, as well as the tantalizing trail of dark hair which leads to the promised land—if the substantial bulge in his pants is anything to go by. I almost don't want to go to sleep and waste this uninterrupted time to study him, but it's probably a little creepy to perve on him while he's sleeping. As hard as I try to stay awake, my eyes droop, and sleep takes me, knowing that I'll be waking up to an empty bed in the morning.

I wake to my alarm and a furnace of hard muscle at my back. My body's on fire from the heat of Oliver's body, and I'm instantly aware of his impressive erection pressing into my backside. My heart races with surprise that he's still here and I'm worried he's overslept. Attempting to roll over, I struggle to move with the way he has me pinned to his body. His large hand cradles my breast, while his leg drapes over my thigh, tangling between my calves—no wonder I'm roasting.

He kisses the back of my head. "Good morning, Sunshine." He's got the sexiest, raspy morning voice I've ever heard. *Swoon!*

I turn my head to look at him. "Good morning, hot stuff!"

He smiles and laughs, kissing the tip of my nose. "'Hot stuff' huh? I'll take that."

"Hot stuff, because you feel like a furnace. I've never known anyone to be as hot as you while they slept."

His body stiffens behind me, and a grumble emanates from his throat.

"Please don't remind me first thing in the day that some other asshole has shared your bed. The reminder will put me in a bad mood."

Uh oh. When I said that, my previous boyfriends didn't enter my mind. I mean, is Oliver even my boyfriend? I don't know what this is with him. He says he wants to get to know me and spend time with me, but what does that mean for a guy like him?

"I can hear you thinking."

He relaxes a little, placing kisses on the back of my head and shoulder. Oliver loosens his hold, releasing me slightly, allowing me to maneuver my body to face him. He immediately goes in for a morning kiss, which is alarming, since I have yet to brush my teeth. He's very convincing, and I relax into the best good morning kiss

I've ever received. I slowly pull away and connect with his eyes, noticing the various shades of green—ranging from the color of fern leaves to a deep emerald within the flecks—colors I've not noticed before, because I'm always trying to avoid them. "I figured you would be gone by now, since you had a conference call this morning."

"I've already dealt with my conference call. I wasn't ready to leave you, so I climbed back into bed. I must have dozed back to sleep, which never happens. Usually, once I'm awake, I'm up and ready to go for the day. You make me want to stay in bed."

He nuzzles my neck, sliding his hand along my hip toward the small of my back. I notice he's being respectful now he's awake.

"I do have to get up and go, though. I have a nine a.m. follow-up meeting with my client from last night."

I feel terrible now because I didn't even ask him how his business dinner went. What sort of person am I?

"How was your dinner meeting? Do you think it was successful?"

He looks surprised I've asked him about his meeting. Doesn't he have anyone interested in him and his life?

"It went pretty well. We'll sign the contract today, and we'll work hard to make the initial investment multiply over the next four years."

He looks away from me, takes a breath, and then turns back to me. "I saw Toby at the restaurant. He got the wrong idea and told me to leave you alone if I couldn't be faithful to you."

Why would Toby think Oliver was being unfaithful? My mouth drops open as the light bulb goes off in my mind. I assumed his business dinner was with a man; I never gave it a second thought. My muscles tense and tighten as I consider the possibility he may have crossed a line. Toby must have seen something he didn't like to approach him like that. How intimate was this dinner? Trying to pull away so I can get out of bed and away from him is pointless as he tightens his hold.

"It was a *business* dinner. She flirted a bit, but I set her straight that I have a girlfriend."

I draw in a sharp breath, my eyes widening. I'm surprised he referred to me as his girlfriend.

He keeps talking, oblivious to my inner thoughts. "I didn't lead her on in any way because I'm not interested in anyone but you."

He moves forward, kissing me gently, teasing my mouth open to allow him entry. His kisses are drugging, exceedingly exquisite, and delicious.

I *never* want to stop kissing him.

My body responds to him readily—my nipples pebble and my sex is hot and wet. My body's hot and my breaths labored. His arousal is obvious through the thin fabric of his boxer briefs, and it would be oh so easy to surrender to our chemistry, but I actually need to get ready for work and so does he.

We gently separate as though it's the most painful experience for both of us.

"I wish it was the weekend and we could stay in bed all day," he grumbles. "I never feel like skipping out on work." He looks at me pointedly, as if it's my fault.

The ironic thing is, I would skip out on work today if it meant spending the day with him. Pressing his lips to the tip of my nose, he rolls out of bed, pulling me up with him. Dragging me in close, he kisses my forehead. Then he releases me so he can get dressed. I immediately mourn the loss of his body against mine, along with losing the visual perfection of his form. His muscles dance under his bronzed skin as he dresses quickly. We say goodbye with lingering kisses that I never want to end. He leaves to drive across town to get ready for work.

I drift through my morning routine in a daze and before I know it, I'm at work, ready to greet my delightful students for another day.

TWENTY-FOUR

-oliver-

THESE PAST FEW DAYS HAVE GONE BY IN A BLUR OF MEETINGS, LATE-night kisses with Kate, and early mornings to get back to my pent-house to start the day all over again.

I'm more than hooked on this girl and am happy to burn the midnight oil to see her for brief moments before we both crash for the night. I want to spend every waking minute with her and if I could bring her into the office with me, I would most definitely do so.

I need to come clean with her soon, but I'm still not convinced she's as invested in our relationship as I am. I'm not sure what it'll take to make her fall as deep as I already am. I need her to be tied to me, to ensure she won't walk away when I tell her.

Kate finally gets a call from Max that her car is ready to be collected from the mechanic and I receive the invoice for services rendered. I was right, it would have been cheaper to buy her a brand new car. But seeing the excitement on her face when we collect her nan's car —the dollars simply don't matter.

TWENTY-FIVE

-kate-

OVER THE LAST TWO WEEKS, OLIVER AND I HAVE SETTLED INTO A routine of sorts. He sleeps at my place more often than he sleeps at his own, and it almost feels … *domestic*. I love having him in my space, seeing him relaxed in sports shorts and a tank, or dressed casually in jeans, or impeccably dressed in his superbly fitted suits. Some nights he doesn't get to my place until after ten, and I realize how much time his work takes away from his personal life. I thought I was busy, but he dedicates an excessive amount of time to his job —I hope his boss appreciates his dedication. It doesn't matter how late he arrives, or how exhausted he seems, he always checks in with me about my day, my students, the kids at the shelter, my family, and even Margie. I've spoken to him about his long hours, but he brushes it off as a busy time of the year, with the quarter coming to a close, and preparations underway for the new one.

One thing that gives me pause: he's never invited me to his place, and he never talks about friends or family. He seems very isolated with his work. Jase, his colleague, is the only person he speaks about.

This morning, he said he's going to try to get home in time to have a meal with me, so I've made a chicken and mushroom risotto —his favorite.

I've showered, washed my hair, blown it out, shaved, and scrubbed my entire body because tonight I'm ready to take our relationship to the next level. I'm wearing my sexiest red underwear beneath my lacy black dress. It has the cutest cap sleeves with a fitted bodice and flared skirt, landing slightly above my knees. On my feet, I'm wearing my favorite red wedges. I hope it has the desired effect because I'm pretty sure I trust him with my heart and my soul, and now I'm ready to trust him with my body.

I even bought a box of condoms to be prepared.

I'm nervous though because I get the impression he's a lot more sexually experienced than I am. I mean, it's not like I'm a virgin or anything like that. It's the expertise of and confidence in his kisses and touches which set my body on fire to the point I could explode. The real thing is going to be something I know I've never experienced before. I hope I'm able to keep him satisfied enough that he doesn't stray or get bored and move on, like my previous boyfriends.

As I add the final touches to my small dining table, making sure everything is perfect for tonight, a flash of light through my curtains signals his arrival.

It's showtime. I can do this. I can be sexy. I can seduce my man.

The knock on my door interrupts my pep talk. My heart thumps as if it's trying to escape my chest. Opening the door, I'm locked in place by Oliver's arresting green eyes and a smile that seems to come more easily these days. I blatantly roam his body with my eyes. He's wearing his most comfortable pair of jeans, which shows off the definition of his strong thighs and firm ass, matched with a college t-shirt, fitting his torso like a glove. He's holding a gift box, which I'm guessing is for me, because he often brings me little treats and treasures he thinks I might like. I've given up trying to stop him because he likes to spoil me. When my eyes finally make it back up to his, he's checking me out from head to toe, and the heat in his eyes tells me he also likes what he sees.

"Hey, Sunshine. You look edible. It must be my lucky day." He steps into my space, grasping one hip firmly. "I feel a little under-dressed." Leaning forward, he gives me a spectacular kiss, making my heart race and my mind dizzy. "Am I unaware of a special occasion?"

"Nope. I wanted to dress nice for you, since you only ever see me in my lounging-around-the-house clothes, or messy from work. But you're right, today might be your lucky day if you play your cards right." I give him a wink, closing the door behind him. I'm digging deep, attempting to appear more confident than I really am. When he reaches the main living room, his eyebrows rise as he notices I've set the table, complete with flowers and candles. He gifts me a grin and then must remember the gift he has for me.

"Here, this is for you," he says as he passes me the box.

"You don't have to keep bringing me gifts. I'm just happy to spend time with you."

I can't quite decipher his expression. Maybe it's disbelief? Has he never had anyone *want* to spend time with him? If that's the case, then I'm truly sad for him.

Opening the box, I'm surprised to see a brand new pair of red Converse shoes, like my battered pair. He bought these for me. I can't believe it. I've wanted, no needed, a new pair for such a long time, but I always seem to have something else I need to buy or repair. I launch myself into his arms.

"Thank you. My shoes were close to dying on me."

I hold on to each side of his face to cover him with kisses while he bands his arms around my waist and holds me off the floor. Oliver holds me tight to his body as he laughs at my antics. His whole face changes dramatically when he smiles and laughs.

Watching me while I admire my new shoes, he simply says, "I know. I could see the rubber sole is almost worn all the way through."

This is the thing; as busy as he is, he's super observant and notices every little thing about me. Last week, he bought me new pillows because he could see that I was struggling to fluff up my old pillows to my liking. The other day, he bought Margie a pair of binoculars, because she was complaining she couldn't properly spy on Pete and Joe down the street. Needless to say, Margie thinks Oliver's definitely a keeper. I agree, but there's a small voice in the back of my mind which is still holding me back a little.

"Well, thank you, kind sir. I appreciate your thoughtfulness. I'm going to take such good care of these. That way they'll last ages." I stroke them as I would a kitten.

After placing them in the box carefully, I invite Oliver to sit down at the table and start serving our dinner.

He looks surprised as I place his plate in front of him. "Is this what I think it is?"

"Depends. What do you think it is?" I smirk.

In a playful way, which is unlike Oliver, he smacks his lips together, rubbing his hands. "Chicken and mushroom risotto. My favorite meal."

"Ding, ding, ding! Ladies and gentlemen, we have a winner. He guessed correctly," I announce, applauding like a crazy loon, while he laughs at my game show host impersonation. I'm glad he could recognize the dish and I didn't mess it up.

"It really *is* my lucky day. What have I done to deserve such special treatment?"

"I figured … well, you're always spoiling me; it was time to spoil you for a change. You've been very generous and extremely patient with me—I thought you deserved some special attention."

Leaning forward, I gesture for him to meet me halfway. Our lips meet in a sweet, delicate kiss. His hand moves to the back of my head and he quickly takes control—deepening the kiss until I'm lost and breathless. Our kisses get better every time, and I can imagine the combustion that will erupt between us later tonight. I have to press my thighs together to control the tingles spreading through my nether regions.

Eventually, we eat our meal, chatting about our day. He praises my cooking thoroughly, making it clear how much he enjoyed the risotto I prepared for him. Wait until he gets a taste of the chocolate brownie I've made for dessert.

After we clean up from dinner, we move across to my couch, each with a glass of wine. Whenever we end up here, I inevitably end up straddling his lap; it's his preferred position, but I'm uncomfortable initiating the sitting arrangement. Usually, I'll start out sitting on my own cushion, and Oliver situates me where he wants me—but tonight, I want to take the lead. I want to show him I'm ready for more. I'm nervous I'm going to make a fool of myself and he's finally going to realize he's wasting his time. I wait for him to sit and get comfortable. Then I make my move, hoping I look somewhat sexy.

TWENTY-SIX

-oliver-

My beautiful Kate seems a little nervous tonight; she hasn't stopped fidgeting and I get the sense tonight's important to her for some reason. These last couple of weeks have been out of this world for me. I feel as though I'm coming *home* at the end of each day, not just going to a cold, empty apartment. She's always telling me I give her too many things—that I spoil her—but she's the one who's given me more than I've ever had.

Kate can't seem to decide where to sit—my preference is always on my lap. I can study her eyes while we talk and take all the kisses I want with the close proximity of our lips. She finally seems to decide, surprising me by sitting on my lap.

This is a big deal for her … for both of us. She's showing me a level of trust she hasn't shown me before. I'm honored and humbled by her actions. She places her forearms on my shoulders; her slender fingers caress the back of my neck, fidgeting with the hair at my nape. Wrapping my arms around her lower back, I draw her closer, resting her pussy against my hard cock. I'm dying to get inside her, but I promised to go at her pace, and I'm bound and determined to keep my word—even if it kills me. I gently tip her chin up with my forefinger, to ensure eye contact, as my other hand moves down to cup her delectable ass.

"Tell me what's worrying you, Sunshine."

She sighs, shifting her head in an attempt to look away from me, but I gently guide her eyes back to mine.

"Um, I'm a bit nervous and might be out of my depth and, well, I'm not very confident and I'll probably be terrible at it—"

I cut her off before she can go any further. "Woah, slow down, Sunshine. Take a breath with me."

Drawing in a deep breath, I nod for her to mimic my actions, which she does. She closes those beguiling denim eyes for a few seconds, and when she opens them, I can see her resolve.

"Thanks for that. I needed to calm down a bit. Geez, anyone would think I'm a virgin, with the way I'm acting."

She giggles, and a grumble emanates from deep within me. I don't like to be reminded that some other asshole has been inside her, especially since I haven't—*yet*. I have to physically stop my hand from tightening on her lush ass.

"Anyway." She takes another deep breath. "I have a surprise for you. Uh, it's probably easier if I show you."

Gracefully, she climbs off my lap, stepping into her bedroom, and returning with her hands tucked behind her back and a coy smile on her enchanting face.

"You didn't have to get me anything. You've already spoiled me a whole lot with your sexy outfit and my favorite dinner."

She moves closer, bringing an empty hand out from behind her back, closely followed by her other hand, balancing a small box … *of condoms!*

My eyes widen and my cock jumps in anticipation.

Is this what I think it means—is it hopefully my lucky day?

Words escape me at this moment.

"Uhm … we don't have to do—"

I'm on my feet, crowding her space before she can get the next word out of her delectable mouth that I've pictured around my cock more times than I care to admit. She's looking at the floor and I know she's misinterpreted my surprise and silence.

I lift her chin, holding her eyes with mine. "Is this what I think it means, Kate? Are you ready to let me worship your luscious body the way it should be worshipped? Are you going to let me taste you, caress you, feel your body beneath mine? Take my body inside yours?"

She opens her mouth and closes it again as her eyes widen and her cheeks flush. She nods her head, but that's not good enough for me.

"I need your words, Sunshine. Tell me what you want."

"Uhm, yeah ... all of that. I want all of that with you. Please, Oliver," she breathes.

"Once I've been inside you, you *will* be mine forever. There's no going back, Kate. You'd better be certain this is what you want."

I bend forward without wasting a second, lifting her onto my shoulder in a fireman's hold, carrying her to the bedroom, while she giggles and squirms. Once inside, I slide her slowly down my body, ensuring she can feel how hard I am, then I take her mouth in a heartfelt kiss. Cupping her face in both of my hands, I direct and deepen the kiss exactly how I want it. She melts against me and her heart beats a rapid tattoo against my chest to match my own. I slowly drag my kisses down her neck and across her collarbone, but her dress only allows me to go so far.

"I'm going to worship your exquisite body, Kate. You're going to feel everything I do to you for days. I hope you're ready for me, Sunshine."

"I'm pretty sure I was ready the first time I laid eyes on your naked chest in front of the school." She bites her bottom lip as though she's said too much.

I'm stunned she felt the same way I did. It seems we've been on the same page all along. I pull back to study her guileless eyes. Cupping her face in my large hands, I confess with a whisper, "Me too, Sunshine, me too." Releasing her, I step back slightly, encouraging her to turn around. I collect her silky hair in one hand and gently place it over her shoulder, draping it over her breast. Caressing down her exposed neck and shoulder, I place my fingers on her zip. "Is this okay?" I don't want to move too fast in case she changes her mind.

"Of course." Comes her breathy reply. Slowly, I slide the zipper down, exposing ivory skin and the lacy red band of her bra.

Could this get any better?

I have to take a deep breath to compose myself, or I'm going to ruin my pants like a sixteen-year-old virgin.

"As much as I love you in this sexy dress, it's gotta go."

While peppering kisses along her neck, I smooth my hands up the silky skin of her spine, sliding them across to her shoulders and slipping the lace dress from her arms. She tilts her head to give me better access to her neck, allowing me to press soft kisses from behind her ear to her shoulder. Slowly, I turn her around. She's holding her dress in place, preventing it from falling. Her body language suggests she's on board with what's happening, but maybe her mind isn't quite there yet.

I search her heavy-lidded eyes and ask, "Is this still okay with you, Sunshine?"

She releases a long breath. Locking her eyes on mine, she releases her dress, dropping it to the floor, creating an inky puddle of fabric around her red shoes. It takes every ounce of self-control to keep looking at her face. All I want is to look down and study her curvy body, wrapped in red lace, finally on display for my perusal. Holding out my hand, I help her step out of her dress, taking the opportunity to run my eyes slowly from her face, down her slender neck to her irresistible tits, encased in red lace. The limited amount of blood left in my brain makes its way to my cock. I remind myself to slow down. My eyes scan her soft stomach to her matching lace panties, and further still, down her shapely legs, to the sexy red laces wrapped around her ankles. The groan that I've been holding back escapes, and I adjust my pants, attempting to release the pressure of the zipper against my painfully engorged cock.

She is my every wet dream come to life.

"I knew you were beautiful. But, Kate, 'beautiful' isn't strong enough to describe you. You're exquisite. I'm one lucky man. I'm going to show you exactly how lucky I feel to have you trust me with your body."

"I'm the lucky one here, Oliver. I hope I don't disappoint you." She blushes, and it begins from her tits, rising quickly and painting every inch of her alluring creamy skin up to her cheeks.

"There is no way to disappoint me, Kate. This experience is already one hundred times better than anything I've experienced before. We're going to be combustible. I know this because when we kiss, it's like nothing I've ever felt."

I move in. Using my teeth, I gently bite and pull her bottom lip, moving in to take her mouth fully, tasting every crevice and sharing every breath. Her hands move up to the hem of my t-shirt, attempting to slide it up my body. I take over, dragging it over my head with a grip on the back of my collar. Tossing it to the floor, we move straight back into the kiss. I flick the clasp of her bra with one hand to release it and gently slide the straps from her shoulders, letting it join the rest of our clothes on the floor. Sliding my hands around her ribs, I glide my thumbs along the underside of her heaving breasts. Her body trembles. Not from the cold, but from desire.

I feel the same, Sunshine.

I'm torn between continuing to kiss her lips and pulling away to admire her breasts. The need to see her tits wins out, and I pull back to soak in my fill. They're firm and full, with peachy-colored nipples drawn tight into peaks.

"I've been dying to see these beauties, and they were definitely worth the wait."

Cupping them in my large hands, I drop my head, taking one globe into my mouth. We both groan simultaneously. If she only ever let me do this to her, I would be a happy man. She tastes like sunshine and I know I'm going to become addicted to her flavor. With a shuddering sigh, her hands move to the back of my head, holding me in place—as if I was going to move anytime soon. Moving across, I pay equal attention to her other breast—*because I'm fair like that.*

She moves her hands to my belt buckle and manages to get it

undone, then works to undo my button and zipper. The pressure releases from my cock and the relief is instant, until her hand grips my rock-hard shaft through my boxer briefs, sending whatever blood was left in my body to my engorged cock. She gasps as I grow impossibly larger under her touch. Her eyes widen and I'm unable to hold my groan. My jeans slide down my legs, getting stuck on my shoes. She pulls away, her tits swaying as she drops to her knees to untie my laces and remove my shoes and socks. The sight of her on her knees in front of me causes my cock to jump, leaking precum from the eager slit. I know once I get inside her, I'm going to fucking embarrass myself, shooting my load before we even get started. Stepping out of my jeans, I hold out my hands to pull her back up, then grab hold of her perfect ass to lift her; encouraging her to wrap her legs around my hips.

I whisper into her ear, "I'm going to fuck you so good that you become addicted to my cock. No other cock will ever satisfy you like mine will."

Her entire body shivers in response to my promise.

All we have between us are her lace panties and my cotton boxer briefs. She's grinding down on me and the heat of her pussy makes my cock weep. I take the few steps needed to her bed and slowly lower her as she holds onto me. I explore her curves and valleys, wrapped in the silky skin of her body until I reach her panties. Dipping my thumbs inside the waistband, I begin removing them. Once she catches on to what I'm doing, she releases her legs and lifts her ass, making it easier to slide the garment off. She's naked, except for her sexy as fuck shoes I've decided to leave on for now. Her hands find the waistband of my boxer briefs as she attempts to remove them, but my cock makes it difficult. I remove them, freeing myself from the constricting material.

Caging her beneath me, with my forearms on either side of her head, I lean down to take her mouth—I need to own her, mark her. I could kiss Kate's mouth for eternity, but I've got other areas on my mind tonight.

"I need to taste your hot pussy."

Her muscles lock and her entire body freezes.

"Oh, you don't have to do that. That's okay, I'm pretty sure I'm wet enough for you to slide right in," she whispers as she blushes. I lose her eyes as she turns her head away from me. Well, that won't fucking do. *At all.*

Using my fingers, I direct her eyes back to mine. "I know I don't have to, but I've been dying to taste your pussy for weeks, if not months. It's what I intend to do. You'll learn soon enough when I make my mind up about something, I'm solely focused on it until I get it."

Her body tenses further at my words and she attempts to wriggle out from under me.

"Uh, uh, uh, what's wrong, Kate?"

I hold her in place. If she wants to stop, I'll fucking stop. It'll kill me, but I'll stop.

"Um, nothing."

"It's not nothing. Something I said put the brakes on and I want to know what's going on."

She shores up her resolve before she finally speaks.

"I guess I'm worried. Once you get what you want from me, I mean like physically, you'll probably move on to someone new. Someone better. Someone more suited to you. I'm not sure I'm cut out for that, to be honest. Maybe I didn't think this through properly."

Pulling back, I look at her fully and I'm guessing I look as pissed as I feel, by the way she's attempting to put space between us. Shaking my head, I take a breath to calm myself because a pissed off dude in her bed is not what she needs right now. Obviously, I haven't been clear enough with her.

"Let me make this crystal clear. You won't be able to get rid of me, even if *you want* to end this relationship. I've decided that … You. Are. Mine. I'm not going anywhere. If I could knock you up and marry you tomorrow to lock you down, that's exactly what I'd do. I can't explain to you what being with you gives to me. It's not a material thing, it's nothing money can buy. When I'm with you, I experience peace for the first time—the noise in my mind quiets. When I come here at the end of each day, I'm coming *home*. You give that to me, Kate. I'm not a stupid man. I know a good thing when I see it—you're that good thing for me. You give me a whole lot more than the shitty pillows and shoes I've given you. Believe in what I say, what I show you."

Her body relaxes beneath mine. Her eyes softening, becoming glassy as if she's holding back tears. She gives me a tentative smile, then leans forward to take my mouth in a kiss that blows my mind and almost has me blowing my load.

I slowly pull back to check on her. "Are we all good?"

She nods at me. "Yeah, we're all good. Now, where were we before my stupid insecurities got in the way?"

"I was about to taste your hot pussy. No more interruptions. I need to focus."

She giggles, then spreads her legs wider for me. "Go ahead, be my guest." She winks.

Smirking at her, I slowly make my way down her neck, kissing and sucking lightly, biting gently, soothing with my tongue. My hands blaze a path down her body, caressing her tits and stomach, following diligently with my mouth. I'm singularly focused on getting to the promised land between her thighs. I don't know how many nights I've imagined having my head between Kate's legs, but this is more than even I could conjure up in my wildest fantasies.

Moving down, I settle my shoulders between her silky thighs, situating my head in the ideal position. My hands cradle her perfect ass once I place her thighs over my shoulders. I take in her exquisite pussy—impeccably groomed—swollen, wet pink lips are the perfect sight, waiting for my kisses. I move in, rubbing my nose along her pussy lips, inhaling her scent—which is all woman—then flick my tongue out for my first taste of perfection.

Yes. I knew she would be my favorite flavor.

Her sighs and soft moans are music to my ears. She's enjoying my kisses, but I want to drive her wild. I want to push her to let go. I up my game, biting gently and licking her pussy as though it's the last time I'll ever have her like this. Her hands hold on to my head with a vice-like grip and her body pumps with my rhythm. She's getting close to her first release. Putting pressure on her clit with my thumb, I insert my middle finger into her tight opening, until I find her g-spot. Her channel is fucking tight and hot and my cock is dripping against my stomach in anticipation. Massaging both areas rhythmically, I add another finger, making her channel tighten. Her body convulses as she reverently whispers my name over and over. I smile against her pussy, feeling like a king. Her body comes down from the high as I slow my fingers and mouth. I gently remove them and wipe my face then move back up her body with teasing kisses and gentle caresses.

"That was better than any fantasy I could have possibly dreamed up. Watching you come undone was breathtaking."

"I didn't know it could be like that. That was out of this world." She whispers through her harsh pants, her tits heaving up and down.

"I haven't even begun, Kate. We've got all night, and I know I'm going to want to do that again and again. You're addictive."

Kate grasps my face in both hands and kisses me enthusiastically, attempting to roll me onto my back. I roll, taking her with me, so she straddles my lower stomach. My need to get inside her is growing more insistent by the second. I'm working hard to control my instincts to take over and hammer my way inside what I now know is a sensational pussy. The importance of allowing Kate to take some of the lead, helping her gain her confidence, helps to calm me a little. She licks her lips as her eyes peruse my body. She moves in and starts kissing, biting, and licking down my torso; paying extra attention to my nipples and abs.

"Your body is a work of art, Oliver. I can't believe I'm the lucky woman who gets to be up close and personal with it."

She sighs, her warm breath on my body driving me crazy. I have to stop her though because if she gets near my cock, it'll be game over and I desperately want to be inside her when that happens.

"It's all yours, Sunshine, but I need to be inside you when I come. I want that tight pussy of yours strangling my cock."

She sits up, straddling my thighs, then reaches over for the box of condoms. Opening the box to remove one, she rips it open with her teeth and rolls it down my length. I don't even try to contain the groan fighting for release at the sensation of her hands working the condom slowly over my shaft, ensuring it's firmly in place. My skin is on fire and my heart thuds out an uneven rhythm.

She moves forward, rising as she holds my cock, swiping it back and forth along her pussy lips. She finally notches the head at her opening and slides down, painfully slowly. We both groan at the sensation of my length making contact with her pussy walls for the first time. I watch my cock disappear inside her body, looking up at her. Her head has fallen back, her slender neck elongated. Sitting up, I suck on her pulse point, then move upwards to take her lips, thrusting my tongue inside to dance with hers.

"I was wrong before. Now. Now I've come home. Your pussy is heaven. So tight. So … hot." Her walls tighten—she likes that.

Sliding my hands up Kate's back, I grip the top of her shoulders to keep her still for a beat, while I revel in the sensation of finally being inside her, giving her time to adjust to my size. She begins to undulate her hips, letting me know she's ready. Thrusting up gently, I fully seat my cock inside and Kate takes that as a sign to start moving in earnest. She rocks back and forth, adding a swivel of her hips, which is going to work me over too quickly. I want this to last as long as possible. She needs to come before I can let go. I roll her onto her back and, rising on my forearms, I take her mouth as I cage her in, building a rhythm to drive her to the brink.

"That's right, let me fuck this tight pussy," I pant in her ear.

She moans as her walls tighten around my cock—her body loves my dirty mouth.

"So good, Oliver. Please don't stop."

"I'm never stopping, Sunshine."

Her walls tremble—she's close now.

Sitting back on my haunches, I lift her ass with one hand, while my other works over her clit. I take her in; tits bouncing with my thrusts, skin red and blotchy from exertion, her head thrown back, eyes closed—she's a stunning sight. It doesn't take long to push her over the edge. Calling out my name on a long moan, her body tightens around my cock as her release overtakes her.

Now I can let loose, pumping my cock harder through her

orgasm feels sensational as her walls convulse around my length. My balls tighten up, and my release explodes out of me as I see stars. It seems to go on forever, triggering a second, smaller release for Kate. My hips gradually slow and I lower my lips to Kate's in a languid kiss. With our hearts racing, our skin slick from exertion, we both take a minute to catch our breath.

I know I'll never be the same.

Kate's the first to break the silence. "Wow."

"Wow's right."

Kissing her nose, the apples of her cheeks, and her forehead, I touch my forehead to hers; our eyes connect and hold. The soul-deep connection I feel with her in this moment is extraordinary. The connection I've had with her from the first moment I laid eyes on her only grows deeper and more powerful.

"I'm lost for words. Give me a minute to gather my thoughts."

She giggles, causing her pussy to tighten, reminding me I'm still inside her.

I don't want to leave the warm cocoon of her body.

Reluctantly, I pull out to sort out the condom. We're going to have to talk about birth control because I don't want this latex between us. Walking into her bathroom, I ditch the condom and wet a small towel to tend Kate's pussy. I meant to be more gentle our first time together. Once we connected, I lost my mind and my body took over. As I'm wiping gently between her legs, a shy smile forms on her face.

"I'm sorry. I meant to be more gentle with you. I lost my head and got carried away," I murmur, looking at her swollen lips and the beard rash on her tits while I wipe. Call me an animal, but my chest swells with a sense of pride when I see the marks I've left on her perfect skin.

She smirks at me. "You can lose your head with me any time you like if that's the result."

Oh, she's getting sassy now. I like this side of her. I take the wet cloth back to the bathroom, then I make my way through her home, locking up, and turning off lights. Snuggling under the covers with my girl, I think about how tonight took an unexpected turn.

"I can honestly say I'm going to want to do that again and again. As many times as you'll allow me the privilege."

"I think we might be on the same page with that idea." She snuggles down, resting her cheek on my chest. Her breaths deepen, her body sinks into the mattress, and I know she's close to sleep, if not already there. I follow Kate into a peaceful sleep.

I wake Kate in the middle of the night with my mouth on her pussy for round two, and she wakes me in the morning with her luscious lips wrapped around my cock. A perfect start to my Saturday morning. I only wish I didn't have to get out of bed and go to work.

I startle when I hear the elevator open on this floor because I'm deep in the zone. I'm the only person in the office, so I get up from my desk to investigate who's about. Stepping out of my office, I'm surprised to see Sonia, my ex, strutting toward me like she owns the fucking place. I haven't seen or heard from her in over four years. She left me via text message. Apparently, she'd 'fallen in love with someone else'. I later discovered who she was madly in love with— Robert Sinclair, hotelier and worth more than I was. I've since overtaken his financial worth twice over.

She's wearing the tallest spiked heels I've ever seen with the shortest skirt, which looks more like a belt, paired with a low-cut blouse, showing more breast than it covers. Her lips are painted scarlet, to match the long talons on the tips of her fingers, and I'm surprised she can open her eyes with her heavy-looking eyelashes and thick makeup. She's dressed more like a hooker than a high-society lady. As she looks forward, she notices me standing in my office doorway. Her botoxed lips spread in an enormous fake smile and she adds more sway to her non-existent hips. She's had a lot of work done. The rest of her face looks frozen in place.

Tucking my hands into my trouser pockets, I stand to my full height. "What the fuck are you doing here, Sonia?" The scowl on my face should be enough of a deterrent, yet she moves into my space to hug me; forcing me to take a step back to prevent her touch from reaching my body. Her arms drop to her sides and she fakes a disappointed pout, which looks fucking ridiculous on a grown-ass woman.

"That's no way to greet the love of your life, Oliver." She steps forward, and I stay rooted to the spot. Is she fucking delusional? "You're ignoring my calls and texts. I decided we needed to talk, in person."

I huff out a laugh of disbelief. "Love of your life? Have you hit your fucking head?" I snarl. "It was a long time ago I felt anything other than malevolence for you." I study her closely and I can't see what it was I thought I loved about her. What I thought was love back then was nothing compared to how I feel about Kate now. What Kate and I have is authentic and unconditional. What I had with Sonia was convenient and shallow. "I've come to realize that what we had was a shitty excuse for a relationship. I'm not interested in anything you think you have to offer."

She manages a look of surprise, which is miraculous with the amount of work she's had done. "Oh, Oliver." Placing her hand on her chest. "I didn't realize how much I hurt you back then to cause you to still be angry with me now. I was stupid. What can I say?" She flicks her platinum hair over her shoulder, attempting to appear contrite. "I made a dreadful mistake. I've missed you terribly over the years, and I'll do anything you ask to win back your love and trust."

I cross my arms, narrowing my eyes in suspicion. "Don't waste your time. As I said, I'm not fucking interested." She reaches forward, attempting to place her hand on my arm, but I step back again. "Don't fucking touch me. Now leave my building before I call security to drag your scrawny ass out of here."

She sighs as if she's negotiating with a five-year-old child. "Okay, Oliver. I'll leave for now. But I'll show you how much I love you and what I'm willing to do to win you back. I'll remind you how good we were together." She turns, walking back to the elevator, looking over her shoulder to see if I'm watching her walk away—which I am, to make sure she fucking leaves. She smirks and adds more sway to her hips in a bid to look sexy. Rolling my eyes, I wait for her to enter the elevator. When the doors close, I step back into my office to call security, ensuring they escort her out of the building and ban her entry in the future.

I attempt to get my head focused on the account I'm working on, but I can't shake the foreboding feeling that Sonia's going to become a problem. I need to see Kate. She'll settle me.

TWENTY-SEVEN

-kate-

I COULD BARELY WALK THE MORNING AFTER OUR FIRST NIGHT together last week. It was as though the dam had burst, and now that we had broken the barrier, we couldn't stop ourselves. I think we've christened every surface in my little house over this past week with the amount of sex we've had. Oliver's certainly not one for predictable sex, and you'll never hear me complaining about that.

I can't help but reminisce about last Saturday after we'd had sex for the first time.

He arrived right after I got home from spending the evening with the kids. Prowling toward me with determination written all over his face, he thrust out paperwork I hadn't noticed he was holding in front of me. I took the papers gingerly from his hand and looked them over. It surprised me he was showing me test results for any STDs. Then he looked me straight in the eye. "I need to be bare inside you, Kate. Please tell me you're clean and on some form of birth control," he said in a low tone.

To say it shocked me was an understatement—it took me

several seconds to recover enough to respond. I think he was expecting me to reject his request by the way his face fell. Even though I was totally embarrassed, I made sure to make clear eye contact.

In a handful of minutes, I'd explained I was already on the pill to regulate my periods. I told him I was stringent about taking them every day at the same time. And while I didn't have paperwork on hand to assure him I was clean, I embarrassingly confessed how I had to get checked for STDs after I discovered Brandon's infidelity. I also quietly confessed that I hadn't been with anyone since then. His expression, at the news that it had been some time for me, was rather comical.

He blew out the biggest breath, picked me up, and carried me to my bedroom. Then he spent hours ravishing my body. I wasn't sure how I was going to walk the next morning, which was an unnecessary concern, because we spent most of the day in bed.

Breaking out of my recollection, I take a minute to calm myself, then change into my gardening clothes. The weather is holding out nicely today, and I want to tidy up the front of Margie's yard as well as mine before winter settles in.

Margie has a handful of various-sized pumpkins on her front porch with a couple of lanterns ready for Thanksgiving. Ever since I've lived next door, she has always done a simple display on her front porch. It's adorable she's still doing that type of thing at her age. She's going to spend Thanksgiving with my family again this year. My nan and Margie are heaps of fun when they're together. I wonder if Oliver has any plans this year, or if he would like to spend the day with my family?

As I work through the two yards, Margie keeps me hydrated with cool refreshments and my energy levels up with fresh fruit snacks. The weeds are everywhere, and several of the bushes need a prune. I need to keep moving if I'm going to get finished and cleaned up before it's time to visit my favorite kids. Oliver parks his car behind mine when I'm about three-quarters through the task. I wasn't expecting him back this soon. He never comes over until after I'm home from seeing the kids.

I stand from my crouched position and move forward to greet him with a hug, careful not to touch his suit with my grubby gardening gloves. "This is a pleasant surprise."

"Sorry if I'm intruding. I needed to see you."

I pull back to study him. The tightness around his eyes and in his posture suggests something's wrong. "Are you okay?"

"I feel better now that I have you in my arms." He leans forward, laying a gentle kiss on the tip of my nose, then kisses my lips. "Can we talk? There's something I need to tell you."

Biting my lip, I guide him to sit on the front step of my porch as I remove my gloves. "Sure."

"I need to share something from my past. Something I was trying to ignore, but it seems it won't go away so easily." Oliver grasps my hands in both of his. Looking down at where we're joined, he tells me about his ex, Sonia.

He purges everything about their relationship and how it ended. Oliver tells me about her visit to his office today, as well as the text messages and phone calls which started about a month ago. He'd been ignoring her in the hopes she would lose interest and leave him alone. What he fails to see is that he's such a great guy, it's not possible for any woman to lose interest in him easily.

"She needs help, Oliver. Her behavior seems desperate."

"She's not my problem, Kate. I don't want to have anything to do with her. She's toxic, and I don't want her anywhere near me, or you, for that matter."

"Just because *you* don't want her around doesn't mean she'll stop. I think you need to be careful. Perhaps you need to sit down with her and discuss where you're at now. That you've moved on." I glance across the road. The thought that he may have a secret wish to rekindle what they once had strikes me out of nowhere. "I mean, you have moved on, right?"

He looks at me as if he doesn't understand what I'm asking.

"There's no part of you … deep down, that doesn't want to try again?" Oliver stands up abruptly, running his hand through his hair. He paces away from me and then back again, then pulls me up to stand in front of him. "Maybe it would work—"

Taking my hands in his again, he cuts me off with his firm response, "Unequivocally no. There is not one ounce of anything I feel toward that woman, but distrust and loathing."

"If it's been so long since you've seen her, why do you think she's coming back for you now? What's changed for her?"

"I don't know." He breaks eye contact with me, as though he can't bear to tell me the next words. "I know my bank balance is healthier than it was back then."

He must be reasonably high up in the company he works for, which means he probably earns a pretty good income. I guess that's appealing to some women, and it seems like Sonia is a woman who is attracted to someone's bank balance rather than the actual person.

"What are you going to do?"

"I'm going to keep ignoring her. She'll get bored and move on to some other schmuck." Typical man, thinking he can bury his head in the sand and the problem will go away.

We stand quietly, secure in each other's presence, allowing time for our conversation to settle between us. I don't like thinking about her coming after him. What if he changes his mind and decides she's more suited?

Pulling away, I explain I need to finish the yard work so I can get to the kids on time this afternoon. He offers to help, and we work together to finish the pruning and clean up the mess. We shower together, which remains platonic, because I started my period this morning. I told Oliver, so he didn't waste his time coming here tonight, since I don't feel comfortable having sex during my period. He insisted he'd still be sleeping in my bed with me tonight. He made it clear that, although the sex is magnificent, our relationship is more than that to him. As we dress, I have second thoughts about leaving Oliver on his own while I visit with the kids, but I don't want to flake out on them.

"Will you be okay if I spend a few hours with the kids?"

"Of course. I'm going back into the office to finish some more stock analysis for a couple of my clients. I'll meet you back here later." He gently tucks a lock of my hair behind my ear.

"You work too much, Oliver. You should speak to your boss about his expectations and your workload."

He waves off my suggestion. "Nah. It's okay. It's not always like this."

I reach up on my tiptoes to kiss his bristly cheek. "I worry about you."

His face softens, and he slouches a little. "Do you have any idea how long it's been since someone worried about me?"

"No."

"A very long time. Not since I was a boy, Kate."

Tears sting the back of my eyes and I'm unable to swallow past the lump in my throat. My heart's breaking into a million tiny pieces for this man. "Oh, Oliver. You've got me now. I care about you and I'll worry about you." I'm not one hundred percent clear about Oliver's childhood, because he doesn't talk about it, but I get a sense he was very lonely and isolated growing up.

His large hands cup each side of my face as he moves in to devour my lips. This kiss is different from any other we've shared thus far. It's full of passion … and something else I can't quite place. It's deeper, reaching down into my soul, and it's so very Oliver.

We part ways, and I spend the afternoon shooting hoops with the kids. We make pumpkin pie cupcakes ready for dessert, and turkey subs for dinner, in recognition of Thanksgiving later in the week. After dinner cleanup, we play various card games, where Jack and Blake lead the kids in a competitive showdown. I bought each of the kids a new journal from the discount shop, and we spend time thinking about and writing what we are each grateful for while enjoying our delicious cupcakes. I'm astounded when each of them easily lists things they are grateful for. Even in their current situation. It's a testament to Roman's dedication to these kids.

When I arrive home, Oliver's waiting for me with a tub of my favorite ice cream, a block of chocolate, and a heating pad, in case of discomfort. I fall asleep with him snuggled behind me, massaging the cramps that started late this afternoon.

As we're getting ready to leave for our Thanksgiving dinner with my family, hummingbirds take over my stomach. I think I'd better give Oliver a heads up about Mom. Every time I speak with her, she gives me the third degree about him. Every Sunday, she gets annoyed with me because I haven't brought him over for dinner again. She's got her heart set on him sticking around.

"Uh, just a heads up. Mom's been trying to get the inside information on our relationship. Be prepared for the third degree. It'll probably be worse than last time."

He laughs. "It wasn't that bad. I had a great time with your family. I loved how your dad was watching out for you." He raises a brow. "You know your dad and brother asked me what my intentions were when we went for a drive after dinner?"

Oh my gosh, my family is too much sometimes!

I look at him in shock. I'm certain I'm as red as a tomato as my blush rises with my embarrassment. "Seriously? I'm really sorry." My family has the best of intentions, but geez, it's embarrassing.

He huffs out a laugh, shaking his head. "No need to apologize, Kate." He moves into my space, his body heat warming my front. "I set them straight. They know exactly what my intentions toward you are. They were satisfied with my response."

I look at him closely, dying to ask what he said, but I also don't want to know, because I think it will make me even more anxious about our relationship. I like how it's growing organically at this point.

We pile into Oliver's fancy car after I collect Margie. I have to sit in the cramped back seat because it's too difficult for Margie to climb through the front door opening. I'm not sure how my dad, brother, and Shane fit in here. We arrive after stopping to buy flowers for Mom and Nan, as well as beer for Dad, Toby, and Shane at Oliver's insistence.

He quickly exits the car while I take a deep breath, attempting to calm myself. It'll be different this time; they're going to be able to see it all over my face—I've fallen for him. Oliver helps Margie out of the car while I wait in the backseat, then he helps me. The three of us walk to the front door, where I knock and enter without waiting for an invitation—which is customary in my parents' home, calling out my hellos, to let them know we've arrived. Mom comes rushing out of the kitchen with her arms open wide, ready to hug me as though she hasn't seen me in months.

"Oh, my Katie-girl, it's fantastic to see you. I missed you this week." She gushes as she envelopes me in her arms and kisses my cheek.

I roll my eyes. "You saw me last Sunday, and we've spoken and texted every day." This is a regular conversation for us.

Oliver's smiling at us, and I don't know if he has people around him to greet him like this. Not that I know for sure, because he doesn't talk about his family. I take my family for granted, and I'm realizing I should appreciate them more. Not everyone is as lucky as I am. Mom moves on to greet Oliver and Margie. Dad and Nan step in from the back deck, moving forward to greet us with the same exuberance.

Mom decorated the house in her usual Thanksgiving style. A range of small, but different-sized pumpkins and candles decorate the center of the table and the silverware is set in cute hessian bags, with fall leaf decorations. On the fireplace is a wreath with the word 'FAMILY' made of wooden blocks, surrounded by photographs of our family, including the little boy who lived with us for two weeks when Toby and I were one.

TWENTY-EIGHT

-oliver-

I step forward to give Kate's mom and nan their flowers and the beer to her dad. "These are a thank you for letting me crash your Thanksgiving dinner."

Mrs. Summer hugs me. "The flowers are beautiful, but unnecessary. We're thrilled you could join us." Mr. Summer gives me a hearty pat on the shoulder, in thanks for the beer as his wife releases me.

Kate's nan looks me up and down, testing the muscles at my bicep. "Who's this hunk joining us for Thanksgiving?"

Oh yeah, she's as spunky as Kate and reminds me of Margie. I bet the two of them are trouble when they get together. I struggle to keep my smile at bay.

"Nan, this is Oliver. He's a ... a ..." Kate looks unsure how to introduce me, which just won't fucking do—*at all!*

I reach out my hand to introduce myself properly. "I'm Kate's boyfriend. It's a pleasure to finally meet you."

I feel better now. I've clearly stated our relationship. I glance around to see smug smiles on Mr. and Mrs. Summer's faces. Kate's nan slaps my hand away, coming in for a tight hug. A very tight, lingering hug. She's smaller than Kate, but she's deceptively strong for a woman her age.

"Really, Katie-girl? You didn't think to mention you were seeing someone. Especially someone this handsome." She winks at me. I see how it is. She's teasing Kate.

Kate looks mortified. I've let the cat out of the bag, but her family needed to know I'm in Kate's life, and I plan to be around for a long time.

Kate stutters, "Oh, well … its early days yet, Nan. I didn't want to jinx it." She gives me a small smile, tucking her hair behind her ear.

Toby and Shane arrive, interrupting the discussion with warm hugs and pats on the back. He narrows his eyes at me as he shakes my hand—hard—in greeting.

"Dinner's ready." Mrs. Summer calls and we move into the dining room to sit in the same seats as last time, with Kate's nan between her son and Margie. Kate's mom has gone all out with a traditional Thanksgiving meal and decorations.

We take turns around the table to give our thanks. Kate's mom sounds choked up when it's her turn. "I would like to give thanks for my family and the good fortune we have to have a roof over our heads, food on our table, and an abundance of people to love. I also give thanks for Oliver coming into our lives, and I pray he's happy, healthy, safe, and loved."

My breath catches, and my heartbeat quickens with a feeling I can't describe at being included in this close-knit family. "Thank you for including me, Mrs. Summer."

Her hand goes to her throat, and her eyes widen slightly and she releases an embarrassed giggle. "Oh, Oliver, I'm sorry. I didn't think." She looks across at her husband for help. "Of course you're included in our family."

Kate's dad clears his throat, looking back at his wife. Kate's hand settles on my thigh, and I get the impression that I've misinterpreted Mrs. Summer's prayer.

"We, uh, actually had a little boy live with us for two weeks when the twins were only a year old. His name was, uh, probably still is, Oliver. Every prayer I've made since then has always included my hope that he's okay. I didn't consider the confusion it would cause. I'm very sorry." She looks quite embarrassed.

"Oh, that's okay. I made an assumption."

"You know, you actually look like a grown-up version of him, to be honest. He was seven at the time and was such a sad, quiet little boy; which was understandable. He'd just lost his mom, and his dad was in a coma in the hospital. He only ever smiled when he was with Kate." She looks at Kate with a half-smile. "He used to dote on her. We were heartbroken when he left us to go back to his father. We have his photo on our mantel."

My heart's beating a million miles a minute. I'm worried it's going to beat its way out of my chest. Surely she's not talking about me. I remember being picked up from home by a man, and staying with him, his wife, and their two babies.

That would have to be some coincidence.

Kate squeezes my thigh, breaking me from my confused memories, and I release the breath I must have been holding. Her face is pinched tight in concern. While my mind is stumbling around in confusion, I miss Kate's mom and dad serving the turkey and passing the various dishes around the table.

After the initial silence, as everyone tucks into the tasty Thanksgiving meal, discussion begins around the table—everyone catching up on each other's lives. It was like this the first time I joined them for dinner; these people genuinely love each other and are interested in what's going on in each other's lives. I'm finding it difficult to stay focused; my thoughts stuck on the possibility that I lived with this family. After Mom died and Dad ended up in jail, I never had this—these deep family connections. I'm unpracticed in this type of situation, but I want to soak up all the genuine love surrounding me.

Kate's nan pipes up, "So, Kate." She looks pointedly at her namesake. "A boyfriend, huh? When did this happen? Am I the last to know?" She looks accusingly around the table.

Margie chuckles under her breath. "It's always the quiet ones you've gotta watch, Kate. You know that."

Kate blushes, while I smirk and slide my hand over to rest on her thigh.

Mrs. Summer speaks up, "Uh, no, Mom, we all found out at the same time tonight. But I'm not surprised by this fresh development. I could tell we would see more of Oliver after the last time he was here for dinner." She looks at me, giving me a motherly smile as she taps me gently on the arm. Mr. Summer and Toby nod simultaneously in agreement with Kate's mom. "I knew he was taken with our Katie-girl." She gives Kate a look that tells her, 'see, I told you he was interested'.

I'm happy they're on board with our relationship. I clear my throat. "You're right Mrs. Summer, I am very taken with your daughter. I'm hoping to join your family dinners for many years to come if you'll have me."

Kate's jaw drops open, her eyes widening, and that adorable blush I love is tinging her cheeks. She probably can't believe I made such a bold statement in front of her family, but it's essential they know how important Kate is to me. I squeeze her knee in reassurance, while Kate's nan and Margie snicker, nudging each other as they wink at me across the table.

Mr. Summer clears his throat and says, "You're welcome here, as long as you treat Kate with the respect she deserves."

Kate's nan mumbles something which sounds suspiciously like, 'not too much respect, I hope'. Causing her and Margie to burst into giggles again. Kate must catch it too, because her blush intensifies while I wink at the octogenarians across from me, which they return with interest.

"Yes sir, that's my plan."

He smiles at me with approval, and I'm satisfied with the result of this conversation. I take pity on Kate, changing the subject to ask Kate's nan about her Alaskan cruise. She spends the rest of our meal telling us all about her adventures. We clean up and Mrs. Summer brings out three different pies to choose from for dessert, which go down a treat. Apparently, Toby's favorite is pumpkin, Kate's is pecan, while Mrs. Summer always likes to have apple pie on hand. I get the sense Kate's mom enjoys feeding her family and any extras that may show up.

"The meal was delicious, Mrs. Summer. Thank you for allowing me to gate crash."

"You're always welcome."

While eating dessert, Kate's mom asks Toby, "So, how did your dinner meeting go with the music executives? You said nothing had been finalized yet, but have you heard any more?"

"Oh yeah, I did. They've offered me a contract to record a new album, and take it on tour throughout the country. I'm pretty stoked about it because I have a bunch of new songs rumbling around in my head."

Hugs, congratulations, and cheers go up all around the table. I feel as though I've missed something important. I turn to Kate with questions clearly written all over my face.

She looks at me with a raised eyebrow. "Toby Summer. *The* Toby Summer." She looks at me as if the name should mean something to me. I'm shaking my head in the negative. At this stage, everyone's gaping at me.

"I'm offended you don't know who I am," Toby says with a smirk and twinkle in his eye, hinting that he's truly not upset.

"He's been number one on the charts six times in the past three years. How can you not know of him?" Kate says, totally dumbfounded.

I shrug. "I'm sorry. I don't follow music all that much. I listen to whatever's on in the car when I'm driving. Which isn't very often."

Kate pulls out her phone, pulling up a popular music app, selects a playlist, then presses the play icon. Music plays and I *do* recognize it. This song was played to death about six months ago. What a relief. "Oh, I know this one."

Everyone seems to release a collective breath, as if relieved I'm not a complete moron.

"I'm guessing this is you."

Toby nods.

"Sorry. I didn't make the connection. I've heard this song a heap, but didn't know the artist's name."

"It's cool, man. Don't stress. Kate thinks everyone on the planet should automatically know who I am." He winks at Kate and pats me on the shoulder as he walks behind me, taking his dishes to the kitchen sink.

While cleaning up, Shane walks into the kitchen as Toby sidles up closer to Kate. "Hey Kate, can I have your opinion about something?"

"Sure, Tobes. What's up?"

We stop what we're doing to give him our full attention.

"Uh well, an old classmate from high school reached out to me on social media. He wanted to let me know our high school graduating year is having their ten-year reunion. I'm guessing they couldn't find you, because you don't have any social media accounts. They also asked me to let you know about it. I'm not sure I should go. What do you think?"

He's running his hand through his almost shoulder-length hair —he seems nervous, unsure. Not sure why, if he's as famous as I've gathered from the previous conversation.

"I know you didn't have a great time in high school. You felt as though you didn't belong, but look at you now. You should definitely go. Show all those jocks who gave you a hard time how successful and confident you are now." She wiggles her eyebrows. "You never know, Cassia Phillips might be there." She nudges his arm with her shoulder because she's too short to reach his shoulder to nudge. "We'll go together. I would love to see what the bitchy girls are like now and if those too-big-for-their-boots-jocks still think they're all that."

He huffs out a laugh and Shane smirks. "Oh yeah, Cassia. She was gorgeous … and smart … and sweet … and kind." He's got this wistful, faraway expression on his face as he's talking about this girl. I'm confused because I thought Shane was his boyfriend. "She tried her best to include me, but I was too damn awkward around her for my own good because I was crushing on her hard. Then she started going out with 'Jake the Jock', breaking my heart." He shakes his head. "What if they're still together? I'm not sure I'm up for it."

Kate wraps her arms around his waist in comfort, looking up at him. "You play to audiences of tens of thousands of people. Millions of people listen to your songs. You *can* walk into a high school reunion with a bunch of nobodies from high school." She squeezes him extra hard. "You've gotta go. You need to show them they didn't win. They didn't crush your spirit. You succeeded despite them. You *will* walk in to the reunion with the same confidence you have when you walk on stage in front of all your fans. Shane and I will be with you for moral support." Shane nods in agreement. The guy never seems to say much.

"I'll think about it. Thanks, Squirt." He shrugs, and she pinches the side of his stomach in retaliation for calling her Squirt. I'm man enough to admit I'm envious of their relationship. I've never had that sibling bond. I wonder if my parents would have had more children?

We move into the family room, and I purposely wander over to the mantel to study the photographs on display. I've been itching to look throughout the meal but didn't think it appropriate to leave the table. I find the photo I'm looking for.

My heart speeds up. I feel dizzy, and I'm struggling to breathe.

I can't believe what I'm seeing.

This can't be real.

It's got to be some cosmic joke.

Kate's arms wrap around my torso from behind and she notices what I'm looking at.

"That's the boy Mom was telling you about." She leans forward, studying the photograph closely. "Huh. She's right, you could be a grown-up version of him. What a weird coincidence." She squeezes me tight. "Are you ready to leave?" I feel utterly discombobulated and can only nod in response.

We call it a night, saying goodnight to Kate's family and drive back to her house. We see Margie safely inside, then we spend the night tangled in her sheets, making love until late, when we both eventually collapse, exhausted. As Kate sleeps, I study her closely. I can't believe she's the little girl I used to hold in my arms. I remember the powerful draw I had to her then and maybe it explains why this is my favorite place in the world to be.

Deciding to call it a day, I drive to Kate's place for the evening. She's still with the kids, but I might check on Margie to see if she wants to share dinner with me. I enjoy spending time with her; she's such a quirky old duck. Once I arrive, I dump my briefcase and step next door to check if Margie's eaten yet. The light shining through the side window lets me know she's home, so I knock on her door and wait for her to answer. After several knocks without an answer, I peer through the side window and see Margie's foot poking out from behind the couch.

My heart pounds in my chest as my adrenaline rushes through my system. I try her front door, but it's locked. I know Kate has a key, so I race back inside, finding it on the hook in the kitchen. I grab it and my phone, rushing back to Margie's.

I hope she's okay.

Unlocking Margie's door is difficult because my hand is shaking like crazy, but I eventually get it open. Moving swiftly to where she's laying, being careful not to jostle her, I check for a pulse; I find it present, but it feels weak. She's unresponsive to my touch. "Margie. Margie, it's me, Oliver." Still no response, so I immediately call for an ambulance, giving them the address and the limited information I have about Margie. She's got a lot of blood on her face and her glasses are askew, so I carefully remove them.

Looking around, I notice the tipped over dining chair and broken bulb on the floor nearby—she must have been trying to change the light bulb. Using the blanket draped over the back of the couch, I cover her body, trying to keep her warm. I sweep up the broken glass, get a clean cloth from her bathroom to put pressure on the wound, which is still oozing blood.

I sit beside her, holding her hand, and speak to her softly. It's in this moment that I realize how much Margie has come to mean to me. She's been extremely kind and welcoming and she means the world to Kate. I'm going to do everything I can to ensure she's looked after and fully recovers. As I'm about to stroke her hair away from her face, her eyelids flutter open slowly as she lets out a low, pained moan of discomfort.

"Margie. Stay still, help's on the way. It looks like you've had a fall." She's clearly disoriented and confused. Her eyelids flutter closed again.

"Margie, if you can hear me, stay awake. Help is on the way. Stay with me, Margie." She battles to open her eyes again. She shakes her head slowly back and forth, obviously causing herself pain if the tight expression on her aged face is any indication. I'm doing my best to stay calm, but my heart's pounding like it's going to burst right out of my chest.

"Stay still, Margie. Okay. I'm here. Everything's going to be okay." She moans again, attempting to lift her hand to her head, which is covered in blood. I gently clasp her hand and lay it back by her side, holding it still as I hear sirens blaring down the street.

Doors open and slam closed, then footsteps sound on the front porch. A voice calls out to announce their arrival, checking they're in the right place.

"Come in." I call out and two paramedics enter. I move out of the way, allowing them to help Margie without me impeding their work. They rattle off a steady stream of questions, of which I can only answer a few, explaining who I am and how I found her. I have no idea how long she had been on the floor, or what happened. I've made an assumption based on what I found. They carefully lift her onto a gurney, situating her in the back of the ambulance. I collect my wallet, locking both houses, and jump in with them. When we get to the hospital, I'll let Kate know what happened. I don't want to upset her while she's with the kids.

The ambulance arrives at the hospital and Margie's surrounded by a flurry of activity. Margie's wheeled down a corridor, and I'm bombarded with what seems like endless questions I can't answer. Questions about what happened, her medical history, health insurance information, and payment information. I don't know if Margie has insurance.

"Look, I'll pay for anything and everything she requires to ensure a full recovery. Just look after her, and make sure she gets the very best treatment. Do everything you can for her. I want the best doctors and the top medical treatments and support for her recovery."

The administrator is surprised, especially since I only just finished explaining my relationship to Margie. "Okay, Sir. I'll need you to complete this paperwork." I'm frustrated that the hospital's focus seems to be on the money, rather than Margie's care.

"No problem." I'm determined to help Margie in any way I can. What's the point of having money, especially the obscene amount I have, if I don't use it to help make the lives of the people around me better? It's been a long time since I've had people around me I truly care about. In the short amount of time I've known Margie, I've grown to care for her very much.

I complete the horrendous amount of paperwork involved in paying for any additional care and hand it back to the woman behind the counter. "Can this remain between us? I don't want Margie, or anyone else, to know I'm paying any additional costs for her care. I'm happy to offer a large donation to the hospital to keep it between us."

"Sure. I'll put a note on the file."

"Thank you, I would appreciate that. Now, where do I go to be with Margie?"

"Head through those doors. You'll need to wait to be called back." She gestures toward a set of doors on the opposite side of the room.

I walk through to the emergency waiting room and directly approach the clerk at admissions. He dismisses me immediately because I have no familial relationship with Margie. I sit and wait, impatiently. Kate is due home shortly and will probably worry because I was supposed to be waiting for her.

My phone buzzes in my pocket. I quickly collect my thoughts and answer.

"Hey, I'm home. Your car's in the driveway, but you're not here. Where are you? Are you okay?" Her words are rushed, panicked.

I run my hand through my hair; I don't want to tell her what's happened. "I'm okay, but Margie's been brought to Mercy Vale

General Hospital by ambulance. I'm at the hospital, but they won't let me through to her, because I'm not family."

Silence greets me on the other end. "Kate. Kate. You there?"

"What happened? Is she going to be okay? Oh my gosh, I need to get to the hospital. Now!"

"I'll call an Uber for you. I don't want you driving while you're upset. Stay put."

I quickly put Kate on speakerphone, pulling up the app on my phone, I book her a ride. I let her know her Uber is fifteen minutes away.

"What happened?"

I explain how I found Margie, and that I called 9-1-1 to get her help. We end the call as her ride arrives, and all I can do is sit and wait.

Forty-five minutes later, Kate bursts through the emergency entrance doors, frantic. I quickly move toward her, engulfing her in my arms; drawing her into my body and kissing the top of her head. She sinks into me, releasing the tears she must have been holding at bay. We find comfort in each other's embrace for several moments, then she pulls herself together and peers up at me. Searching each other's face, she gives me a small nod, letting me know she's okay. We move together, as a unit, toward the administration desk.

The clerk seems distracted by whatever he's looking at on his computer screen. "Welcome to Mercy Vale. How may I help you?"

Kate steps forward. "Hi, my neighbor, Margie Watson, was recently brought in. She suffered a fall at home. My boyfriend, Oliver, called 9-1-1, and an ambulance came and brought her here."

"Are you family?" he asks.

"Uh, um, no I'm not. I'm pretty sure I'm listed as her emergency contact person because her husband has passed and she has no children or other family. Can you please tell me what's happening? If she's okay, at least?"

He turns back to his computer, typing some information. He reads quietly for a few minutes. His eyes rise to us, then back to his screen. "Ah, here we go. Margaret Watson." He looks up at Kate. "And what's your name?"

"My name is Kate Summer. I'm Margie's neighbor. I watch out for her, checking on her regularly." She grips my hand tighter.

He looks back at the screen and nods. "Yes, I have you listed here. Walk through those double doors, down the corridor, and follow the signs to the emergency ward."

"Thank you."

We don't waste another minute. We rush down the corridor, following the signs to emergency where we're greeted by another desk. Kate goes through the process of identifying herself again and we're sent through, finally, to see Margie. She looks every one of her eighty-five years. Her skin is gray, and she looks frail in the hospital bed; very different to the Margie I've come to know and adore.

Kate moves straight to her bedside, taking her hand carefully, avoiding the IV attached to the back. I pull a chair closer to the side of the bed, encouraging Kate to sit down while still holding Margie's small hand.

"Oh Margie. What did you do to yourself?" Kate sniffles and I realize she has tears tracking down her cheeks. I stroke her back, offering comfort in the only way I can right now. We sit quietly, side by side, for some time. The only sounds are the beeping of monitors and other various noises throughout the ward. I'm unsure how much time passes, but after what seems like hours, a nurse opens the curtain to enter our cubicle.

"Oh, good evening. I didn't realize anyone was in here. My name is Adele. I'm looking after Margaret this evening." She moves efficiently around Margie, checking tubes, recording information, and assessing the drip of the IV line.

"How's Margie? Do you know what's wrong? Will she be okay?" Kate's questions come tumbling out in rapid-fire. The nurse smiles gently at her.

"The doctor in charge of Margaret should be in shortly. She'll be able to answer any questions you have." She finishes up her checks, tells us there are snack machines at the end of the corridor, and leaves after returning the curtain to its closed position.

We sit and wait. And wait. And wait some more.

I get up to pace because I can't sit in the chair and do nothing. Even though the pacing is a waste of energy, my body needs to move. Kate's head has dropped to Margie's bed and her breathing has evened out; she's utterly exhausted.

The curtain opens without warning, and a tired-looking woman in a white coat enters the cubicle. She looks up from her tablet, noticing Kate and me with Margie. Kate stirs, sitting up carefully to avoid disturbing Margie.

"Hello, my name is Dr. Fieldman. I'm Margaret's doctor while she's here with us in the ED."

"Margie. She likes to be called Margie. She says Margaret sounds too formal for her liking," Kate firmly states. "What's wrong with her Dr. Fieldman?" I move to stand beside Kate as she stands, holding her close to my side.

The doctor studies us carefully. "Are you family?"

"No. We're not. I'm her neighbor. I'm also her emergency contact because she has no living relatives. My name is Kate, and this is my boyfriend, Oliver."

The doctor checks something on her tablet, then looks at Margie and turns back at us. "It seems the fall Margie had was quite nasty. She's broken her hip, and has a contusion to her forehead, as well as bruising to her face caused by her glasses." A gasp escapes Kate, so I tug her in tighter to my body. "We're going to take her in for a CT scan to check she hasn't got a bleed on her brain. Assuming it's clear, we have organized an orthopedic surgeon to replace Margie's hip in a few hours."

The doctor leaves, and we're left waiting again. The time feels interminable in this small room with the monotonous beeping of machines. An hour later, an orderly arrives to take Margie for a CT scan. Kate looks absolutely shattered, so I wrap her in my arms, kissing the top of her head.

"C'mon, Sunshine. Let's get something to eat. Then we'll wait for word." I guide her out of the ward and the hospital. We cross the road to a late-night deli, which seems to be the only place open at this time of night. While we've been in the hospital, night has fallen and everyone has gone home. It's quiet in the deli, meaning they take quickly our order and served efficiently. The staff here are probably used to having to work quickly for the medical staff who must frequent this place.

We take a seat at a table next to the windows. Kate's shoulders slump forward, her eyes glassy.

"I don't know what I'll do if Margie's not okay."

I reach across to grasp her hand. "She'll be okay. They're doing everything they can for her, and we'll be her support as she recovers." Kate nods, drawing a shuddering breath.

We eat quickly, then purchase coffee to take back with us. We settle in the waiting room on the ward and wait to hear from Margie's doctor.

TWENTY-NINE

-kate-

OLIVER AND I MUST HAVE DOZED OFF BECAUSE WE BOTH WAKE WITH a start when the doctor clears her throat. We stand quickly, with hopeful faces, for good news.

"How is she, Doctor?"

"The CT showed no internal cerebral bleed, so we've stitched up the wound. The surgery went well. The orthopedic surgeon successfully replaced her hip, and she's currently being settled into her room. A nurse will collect you once she's stabilized." She refers to her tablet. "She'll be in room 318. Margaret won't be conscious for some time." She glances between both of us. "I would recommend going home. Get a good night's sleep and come back late tomorrow to check on her progress."

I turn to Oliver. "I'm not leaving her. She's got nobody else, and I won't leave her to face this alone." Oliver nods in agreement as his eyebrows draw tight. He looks exhausted. I know Margie has grown to mean the world to him in the short time he's known her. He's as worried about her as I am.

"Maybe we should wait to see Margie, then go home to have a shower and some sleep before coming back tomorrow." He looks at his watch. "Uh, later today, since she'll be unconscious."

I nod. Even though I don't want to leave Margie, I know it doesn't make logical sense to stay. "Okay." He leans forward, kissing my forehead. He wraps his arm around my shoulder and tugs me close to his warm body.

The doctor acknowledges our decision, leaving us to wait for the nurse to collect us. After what seems like hours, we're led to Margie's room. When I lay my eyes on her, I swear I feel my heart breaking. I'm not sure my knees can hold me up. She has a bandage covering her head and the bruising on her face is more pronounced than before. She's got wires, an IV, and a bag collecting fluids attached to her body—she looks unnaturally still among the loudly beeping machines. I cover my mouth to hold back a sob and find myself pressed into Oliver's hard chest. One hand cups the back of my head, while the other caresses gently up and down my back.

"Shhh, shhh. She's going to be okay. I promise." His confidence comforts me and I nod into his chest. "C'mon, let's say goodnight and we'll come back later. Okay?"

I say goodnight to Margie, gently placing a kiss on her paper-thin cheek. Oliver guides me out of the hospital to a waiting car to take us home.

Once we're back at my place, he starts the shower. As the steam builds in the bathroom, he strips us both naked and guides me carefully under the water, where he washes my hair and body with gentle care and affection in silence. Even though he's exhausted, he takes charge, knowing I'm incapable of looking after myself. He dries us both, tucking us into bed after ensuring the house is secure. He pulls me close to his body, kisses the top of my head, and encourages me to get some sleep. I'm absolutely wiped out; it doesn't take long for me to fall asleep.

Slowly, I wake to the sun streaming into my bedroom and the smell of bacon wafting in from my kitchen. I stretch out, rolling onto my side, and tuck my hands under my cheek as I look out of my bedroom window. I take a few minutes to remember the events of yesterday and last night, mentally preparing myself to face what's to come. I roll out of bed and step into my bathroom, brushing my teeth, and taking care of business. I head to the kitchen, ready to see my guy.

Oliver's standing in my kitchen in his boxer briefs and one of my aprons. The sight is comical and sexy at the same time. His back muscles shift and roll as he turns the bacon and stirs the scrambled eggs. His butt cheeks squeeze and shift in the most delicious way. Stepping into the kitchen, I press my front to his back, wrapping my hands around his middle and placing a kiss between his shoulder blades. He's tremendously warm and strong and has quickly become my home. I turn my head, pressing my cheek against his back. "Morning." I'm beyond thankful for this strong man.

He turns his head to gaze over his shoulder at me. "Good morning, Sunshine. How did you sleep?"

I release him, allowing him to turn around. He shuts off the burners on the cooktop and turns to engulf me in the biggest hug, then he lowers his face to take my mouth in a searing kiss. Thank goodness I brushed my teeth before finding him in the kitchen.

"What's all this?" I ask, giving him a genuine smile of appreciation.

"I thought I would surprise you with a cooked breakfast. I figured we'd spend most of the day at the hospital, and it would be a good idea to start with a solid meal." He kisses the tip of my nose. "I called the hospital to check on Margie, but they won't tell me anything, because I'm not family."

I can see the worry he has for Margie, as well as the care and concern he has for me. "Thank you for everything you did for Margie yesterday. I'm not sure what would have happened if you hadn't been there."

"I'm not happy about finding her the way I did, but I'm glad it was me and not you." I nod, attempting to push down my worry.

We eat the delicious breakfast Oliver prepared and get ready to drive back to the hospital. As we're walking down the corridor toward Margie's room, Mom and Dad are coming out. They must have stopped by to check on her for themselves after I messaged them earlier. We all hug in greeting. If they're surprised to see Oliver here, they don't show it.

"Oh Katie-girl, it's such a shock to see Margie that quiet and still. Just the other day, she was giggling up a storm at our dining table." She holds me tight in comfort because she knows how strong my bond is with Margie. "If there's anything we can do to help, please call us anytime."

"Thanks, Mom. I've got to go to work tomorrow. Would you mind checking in on her? Then I'll come by straight from school."

"Of course. I was going to come back tomorrow anyway because I don't have any classes on Monday. Dad can come on Tuesday because he doesn't have any face-to-face appointments. Wednesday, we'll have to work something out. Maybe Toby could stop by?" She brushes my hair away from my face and cups my chin. "We'll work it out together. She won't be alone for long. Okay?"

I nod, giving Mom an appreciative smile. "Thanks, Mom. You are honestly the best." We hug once more before they leave.

Oliver and I step into Margie's room to the regular beeps of the heart monitor, and my heart skips in my chest. I feel helpless to do anything. She still hasn't woken. As we sit in the sterile room, Oliver and I take comfort from each other, holding hands in a comfortable sort of silence. Having him here beside me gives me a sense of strength, and that everything will be okay.

The nurse breezes into the room, focused on his patient, not noticing us in the room. "Good morning, Margaret. How are you feeling today, lovely lady?" When he looks up and sees us watching him, his step stutters as his eyes land on Oliver. He gives him an appraising once over, then turns toward me with a wink, mouthing, 'lucky lady'. I can't help but laugh. "Hi, I'm Stephen. Margaret's day nurse."

I smile. "Hi, Stephen. I'm Kate, and this is my boyfriend, Oliver." It still feels surreal when I think of Oliver as my boyfriend. "It's nice to meet you. How's Margie?" Oliver nods in greeting.

"Oh, the pleasure's all mine." He fusses around Margie,

checking her vitals and recording the information. "Margaret's been a dream to look after. We had a lovely chat earlier this morning."

I'm surprised. I didn't think she had woken up yet. "Did she wake up?"

"Oh no. But I always chat with my patients as if they're fully lucid. I believe it helps them to stay connected with us." He's busy swapping out the bag for Margie's IV when he looks over at us. "You should fill her in on what you guys have been up to. Just as you normally would when you see her."

"I never even thought of that. Thanks, Stephen. By the way, she prefers to be called Margie." I smile at Oliver, proceeding to tell her about the delicious breakfast he surprised me with this morning.

Stephen interrupts, "Oh my! A man that handsome and cooks as well. You've done mighty well for yourself, Kate." He looks over at Oliver. "I don't suppose you happen to have a brother?"

Where I would have expected Oliver to be offended, he huffs out a laugh and shakes his head. "I'm sorry. No, I don't."

"Ah, such a shame." He finishes his work, and as he's preparing to leave, he tells us Dr. Jackson will stop by shortly.

Oliver and I chat with Margie about our plans, and I tell her about my afternoon and evening with the kids. I can't believe it was less than twenty-four hours ago. I make sure to include every detail. Oliver listens intently, and I notice his smile comes easily when it comes to the kids. I must remember to ask if he's allowed to visit. Oliver leaves to buy coffee and snacks, and I find a cloth to wipe over Margie's face, neck, and arms. As I'm gently massaging her feet, Oliver returns with coffee and pastries from the diner across the road. He kisses my forehead, then places the items on the table. "Margie's lucky to have you in her life." He kisses the tip of my nose. "So am I, for that matter." This man melts my heart.

Dr. Jackson enters the room, breaking our moment. He glances up at us from his tablet. "Good afternoon, I'm Dr. Jackson. I'll be looking after Margaret during her stay."

Oliver acknowledges the doctor with a nod and introduces us. I love how he's stepping back, allowing me to take the lead.

"Good afternoon, Dr. Jackson. How is Margie's recovery progressing?"

"Things are progressing as we would expect." He looks at Margie and back at us. "Margie will probably experience some discomfort from her head wound and facial bruising, and her hip will be sore. As soon as she's able, we'll get her to walk."

"That seems fast to get her back on her feet after such major surgery." I'm shocked. I figured she would have to stay off her feet for quite some time.

"Patients have more positive results after a hip replacement if we get them up and moving as quickly as possible. She'll need to follow a detailed recovery program with our physiotherapists over the next several weeks, tapering off until Margie is looking after her body on her own. She'll need to keep up with regular, gentle exercise to ensure she looks after herself and her new hip."

"Thank you, Doctor. Do you have any idea when Margie will wake? I would like to be here when she wakes up." Oliver rubs his warm hand up and down my back in a show of support.

"I can't give an exact time, but we'll aim to start reducing her medication around this time tomorrow. It usually takes some time before the patient starts to come around, but this varies from person to person." Dr. Jackson taps his tablet, then moves around to check the machines and drip.

"Thanks, Doctor. I'll come straight from school tomorrow. My mom is going to come during the day to keep Margie company."

"No problem. I'll see you tomorrow." He nods, leaving the room.

"Well, everything sounds positive so far, Kate. I think Margie's in expert hands with Dr. Jackson." He gestures to the seat and I sit down so he can pass my coffee and pastry to me. He gets his own, sitting in the uncomfortable hospital chair beside me.

We sit for another couple of hours on the uncomfortable chairs. Oliver suggests we go home for the night; I love the sound of that ... 'home'. I can't imagine he would want to live in my tiny place when he probably has a fancy apartment in the city—not that I've ever been there. I can't believe I'm thinking about Oliver living with me.

It's not that far-fetched though, because he's pretty much living with me already—even though we haven't spoken about it. He spends every night at my place, and I can't remember what it was like to *not* have him in my space. We stop to order food for dinner and then drive home.

When I arrive at the hospital after work, Oliver's already sitting in the chair beside Margie's bed, his laptop balanced on his thighs. My step falters because I assumed Oliver would be too busy at work to be here on a workday. I take a minute or two, to observe him quietly while he's working.

"Are you going to come in, or are you going to perv on me all afternoon?" He looks up, giving me a half-smile, then he stands and places his laptop on his chair. We both move forward at the same time, crashing our bodies and mouths together as if we haven't seen each other for weeks, not hours.

I look into his emerald eyes. "How is she? Has Dr. Jackson been by yet?"

"He came by about half an hour ago to reduce the medicine. It has to be reduced gradually over the next couple of hours." He tucks a lock of hair behind my ear. "So, we sit and wait." He pulls a chair across next to his, gesturing for me to sit down.

"Sorry. I didn't even say hello." I was focused on Margie, and I let my manners slip. "So, hey."

He looks at me in that blistering way he always does and smiles. "Hey."

"How was your day?" I return his smile.

"It's better now. How was yours?"

"Okay, I guess. I found it difficult to focus on the kids. How long have you been here?"

"I came after my meeting finished at one. I figure I can work as easily from here as I can in the office. But I do need to step out to make a phone call. Will you be okay for a bit?"

"Sure. Go do what you need to do. I'll catch Margie up on my day." He bends down to kiss the tip of my nose, then leaves the room.

Not long after, Stephen comes into the room to adjust Margie's medicine again. "Hey, Kate. How's your day been?"

"Hey, Stephen. Good to see you again. My day will be better when my friend wakes up. Have you had a good day?"

"It's certainly been a busy day. We need one more reduction in Margie's meds. Then we should begin to see some changes. Where's that hunk of man of yours?"

I smile because Stephen has certainly made his thoughts on Oliver plain. "He had to step out to make a call for work. He'll be back shortly."

We make general chitchat about his day and mine, then he moves on to check his next patient. I'm in the process of telling Margie all about Emma's latest attempt at dating when Oliver steps back into the room with a sandwich and hot chocolate for me.

Kissing me on the forehead, he passes the items over. "I figured we'd be here until late, and you probably haven't eaten since lunch."

My heart goes all soft and gooey. "You're always looking after me. Thank you." I unwrap my sandwich at the same time he unwraps his. "How did your phone call go?"

He studies me for several seconds. "You know, I've never had anyone in my life, outside of work, check in on me and how I'm going with my work the way you do." He glances out of the small window and then back to me with a smile. "I find I like it. The normality of it feels ... domestic. I've never had that before. Thank you, Sunshine." He leans forward and skims his lips lightly across mine, then leans back to take a bite of his sandwich. I'm sad that he's not experienced that normality.

"What about when you were engaged to Sonia? Surely you talked about your days with each other?" I don't enjoy thinking about her with Oliver. Apart from what she could get from him, I don't think she was genuine in her affection. Which breaks my heart, because he was going to settle for that type of relationship, and he is worth a whole lot more.

"She was only interested in spending my hard-earned money on her various treatments, outfits, and luncheons. She was never interested in me as a person, only what I could give her, closely followed by the size of my cock." He looks contrite when mentioning their intimate relationship. "I was hurt and angry when she left me eight weeks before our wedding to be with someone with a larger bank account. Now, though, I could kiss the ground on which she walks in gratitude for her leaving me. I believe I dodged a bullet there." He looks at me, studying my face closely. "If I was in a miserable, superficial relationship with her, I would have missed out on meeting you. The best thing that has ever happened to me in my life." He reaches across and grasps my hand, kissing the back of it gently, reverently.

"Oh, Oliver. Maybe we should send her a thank you gift." I giggle. "I'm exceptionally lucky to have you in my life. I can't believe I made it so difficult for you in the beginning. You never gave up on me, and I'll be forever grateful."

"Perhaps I should send her on a vacation. That way, she'd stop bothering me." He says it evenly, but I'm on automatic alert.

"What do you mean?"

He realizes his faux pas and attempts to backtrack. "Oh, nothing. Don't worry about it."

"I *do* worry about it, Oliver. I care about you. I don't want you dealing with her on your own. Can I help?" He sighs explains she's still harassing him. He's quick to tell me he's done nothing to encourage her or lead her to believe there's any chance of reconciliation, and I believe him.

I'm about to respond when Stephen comes waltzing into the room to complete the final adjustment on Margie's medicine. He says we should start noticing some activity soon.

Once he leaves the room, I turn toward Oliver. "I think you should let the police know. She's pretty much stalking you."

He huffs out a laugh. "Yeah, I can imagine how that would go. 'Officer, my ex keeps contacting me and showed up at my office.' They would laugh it off and tell me to grow a new set of balls. I don't think the police would take it as seriously as they would if I were a woman, being stalked by a man."

Margie lets out a soft groan, attempting to lift her hand, but can't because of the IV attached there. I quickly move closer, holding her hand still. "Margie. You're okay. Stop moving, we'll get the doctor for you." I keep soothing her, while Oliver goes to find Stephen or Dr. Jackson.

Oliver bursts back through the door with Stephen hot on his heels. He comes straight to me, placing his warm hand on my lower back in comfort. Stephen checks the machines attached to Margie. Margie moans again. This time Stephen reassures her she's okay. He records some information on her file, tells us it will take a little while for her to wake completely, and moves toward the door. Apparently, Dr. Jackson will be by shortly.

We pull our chairs closer to the bed, putting our conversation on hold, while we both watch Margie closely. I feel her squeeze my hand. Looking across to Oliver, I can tell he noticed, which doesn't surprise me. He doesn't miss much.

He smiles, nodding back at me. "She'll be back with us in no time."

I breathe a sigh of relief, nodding. We sit quietly by Margie's side. It's getting dark outside when I feel another squeeze, and Margie releases another groan. Watching her face closely, she opens her eyes slowly, as her head moves back and forth on the starchy pillow.

"Margie. We're here. Whenever you're ready, you can wake up," I whisper reassuringly. Coaxing her to come back to us. We dim the lights, ensuring they're not uncomfortable for her when she opens her eyes fully.

She moans in response, opening and closing her eyes several times. It takes a little while for her to keep them open to look at us.

"Wh— What happened? Where am I?" She attempts to sit up, but Oliver quickly scoots around to the other side of the bed, gently pressing her shoulders back down.

"Stay still Margie. The doctor will be in soon," Oliver whispers to her.

"Margie. You're in the hospital. You fell off the chair when you were trying to change your light bulb." I'm furious with her. I've told her I'll change her bulbs, but she's stubbornly independent.

I give her a sip of the water we've had waiting for when she woke up. "Sip slowly, Margie. Not too much."

Dr. Jackson enters the room. "How's my patient?"

"If you're talking to me, young man, I have the headache from hell, and my body feels like death warmed up." I smile to myself because it's good to know she's still got her attitude.

"To be expected after the nasty fall you experienced. We can give you something for the pain. Can you tell me, one to ten, one being very little pain, to ten being unbearable pain, what would you rate your pain level at?"

"Probably close to a nine."

"Okay, I'll get the nurse to administer some pain medicine. Do you remember how you fell?"

"I climbed up on a dining chair, so I could change the light bulb in my living room. I guess I must have lost my balance. Then I don't remember anything else."

"Okay, Margie. You bumped your head pretty badly. When you came in, your forehead was bleeding profusely, probably because of your blood thinners. You also broke your hip, which we've replaced. You'll have several weeks of physical therapy to get back to your level of mobility before the fall. But I see nothing to stop you from gaining full mobility." The doctor looks across at us and smiles. "You've got some pretty great people here who I'm sure will be more than happy to help you. I'll tell the nurse about your pain meds so we can help you feel more comfortable."

Soon after the doctor leaves, Stephen comes in with a bright smile. He chats to Margie the whole time as if they're best friends while administering pain medicine. After a few minutes, Margie's face and shoulders relax. I guess the medicine is working—thank goodness.

We sit with Margie for a while. "You kids should go home. I need my beauty sleep and you're keeping me up."

I head straight to the hospital after school to visit Margie, finding Oliver already there, the same as yesterday. He's been worried about her. I stand in the doorway to watch them for a moment with Dr. Jackson. Margie looks much brighter today; her cheeks have more color, and the sparkle is returning to her eyes.

"Thanks, Doctor. I'm not sure how I'm going to pay for all the extra help I'll need. I don't have health insurance."

"The hospital registrar told me the hospital can cover everything you need. Apparently, you fit a particular criterion, Margie. Don't worry about the cost. It's all covered," Oliver tells her.

"Oh, that's wonderful. Thank you so much, Doctor. Such a worry has been taken off my mind."

"You concentrate on getting well." Dr. Jackson leaves the room, and I step inside to join them.

We visit with Margie, updating her on what's been happening since Saturday. I also take the opportunity to chastise her for attempting to change her light bulb, which she brushes off as only Margie can.

Oliver and I have spent this past week going back and forth to the hospital to visit Margie. The constant back and forth and worry is taking its toll. We're both exhausted. It will be a relief when she comes home. The hospital has organized for a nurse to visit Margie at home twice each day, to help her shower and ensure she's able to complete everyday tasks safely. Oliver organized a temporary ramp to be installed in the morning before Margie's due home. I've had to let the kids know I won't be able to visit them this week, because I need to be available for Margie. They were downright sweet, making her get-well cards for her mantle and funny videos for her to watch.

It's finally Friday, and as I leave the school building, I inhale a deep breath. I need to visit Margie before I give her place a quick clean, ready for her return home tomorrow.

THIRTY

-kate-

MARGIE'S EXCITED TO BE GOING HOME TOMORROW. OLIVER AND I
have warned her repeatedly that she's to follow the doctor's orders
to the letter. After a couple of hours, Oliver and I make our way
home. While I clean Margie's place to make sure it's ready for her
return, Oliver cooks me breakfast for dinner as a treat. He's been
my rock throughout this past week, and I'm not sure how well I
would have kept myself together without him by my side.

"I'll clean up. You have a hot shower to wash away the week."

I press up on my toes to land a kiss on his cheek. "Thank you."
He smacks my ass playfully as I head for the shower. When I return
to the living room, he has two glasses of wine waiting. He truly
makes my heart sing. Never in a million years would I have expected
the man I met all those months ago, across the other side of the
world, to have such a soft and gooey center.

I position myself on his lap, playing with the hair at the nape of
his neck. His hands tighten on my hips and I lean in to lay a delicate
kiss on his full lips. I pull back enough, allowing me to see his lumi-
nous emerald irises, whispering, "Thank you for taking care of
Margie, and especially for taking such good care of me." I lean

forward, pressing my forehead to his. "I'm incredibly lucky to have you."

His hand comes up to cup the back of my head as he directs my mouth to his in a deep, sensual kiss; expressing all of our gratitude, our connection, our deep feelings for one another. "I'm the lucky one, Kate."

I feel as if, maybe, I'm falling in love with this man. No, not maybe. Definitely.

He passes my wine, collecting his own, as we talk over what the next week will look like in terms of Margie's care.

After another glass of wine, we fall into bed, loving each other's bodies into exhaustion. I fall asleep, listening to Oliver's rhythmic heartbeat beneath my cheek. His powerful arms wound around my body, keeping me bound to him—*as if I would ever want to leave.*

The weekend passes by in a blur. Between bringing Margie home and helping her out with her steady stream of visitors—including Pete and Joe from down the street—I feel like I've been in a time warp. It's Monday morning already, time to start the school week again. I don't feel rested, and I can't help the worry I have about leaving Margie home alone.

As soon as I see the smiling faces of my students, my spirits lift exponentially. We have a great day together reading stories, singing songs, creating towers, and practicing our balancing skills. I high-five each child as they leave for the day, and then collapse in a heap on my chair.

Collecting my things together quickly, I leave earlier than usual. I'll do my work while sitting with Margie; I need to get home and check she's okay. I walk out of the building, amid shocked faces I'm leaving on time, for once.

Over the course of the week, Oliver and I spend our days working, and our evenings with Margie, before falling into bed, wrapped around each other's bodies, exhausted.

THIRTY-ONE

-oliver-

I ARRIVE LATE TO KATE'S ON FRIDAY EVENING BECAUSE MY MEETING with a new investor ran long. I also needed to collect some fresh clothes from my penthouse for the next couple of days. I don't like being away from Kate any longer than I absolutely need to. The meeting seemed to take longer than necessary, and for some reason, I was compelled to search for the photograph I had carried with me throughout my childhood. I hadn't thought about the picture in years, but I made sure to always keep it safe as I moved from home to home. It's a photograph of me sitting on a couch, holding a baby girl with a baby boy sitting next to me. My expression as I look down at the baby girl is one of pure adoration. That baby is Kate, and the other baby is Toby. It's like a punch to the gut; all the air in my body whooshes out, leaving me dizzy and off-balance. Sitting on the edge of my bed, I attempt to regain my composure. I'm unsure what to do with this revelation. Telling Kate means revealing my shitty background, and I'm not certain I'm ready. At this point, I'm keeping more secrets from the woman I'm definitely falling in love with than I'm sharing.

Kate greets me at the door with a gorgeous smile on her face, and I settle now that I'm back in her orbit. Knowing what I know

now, it explains the feelings she evoked in me from the moment I laid eyes on her. The familiarity and the instant connection I felt with her. The calmness I find with her—only ever with her. She throws her body at mine as though she hasn't seen me for weeks, kissing me as if it's the last time we'll ever be together.

"I'm ridiculously happy you're home."

Home.

Now that's something I haven't had since I was a boy. I would love to make a permanent home with Kate. At the moment, all of my belongings are in my penthouse. I only bring over what I need to get through to the next day or so. I want to change that, but now's not the time.

"I've got some great news for you." She tugs me inside, directing me to sit on her tiny couch. She straddles my lap—just the way I like it.

I grab her ass, pulling her closer. "Yeah? What is it?"

Her smile grows wider, if that's even possible. "Well, I asked Roman to check if it would be okay for you to come with me sometimes when I visit the kids. He had to get permission from the higher-ups, but I think it was just a formality." She's bursting at the seams in her excitement. "He messaged me tonight. They've cleared you to volunteer at the shelter with me." I'm truly shocked and I'm incapable of responding straight away. "If you want to, of course. No pressure!" She must think my lack of response means I don't want to.

I grasp her face, ensuring she can't turn away. "Of course I want to come with you. I'm surprised you're willing to open up that part of your life to share with me." I whisper, kissing her nose and her forehead. I press my forehead to hers—locking eyes—meadows to sky. "That you want me to be with you means the world to me, Kate. Thank you." This is a giant step forward in our relationship. Kate's showing me a level of trust and openness that terrified her in the beginning—I'm a fucking fortunate man. Maybe I'll be able to tell her who I am sooner than I thought.

She strokes the hair at the nape of my neck, which feels fucking fantastic. "Let's go to bed." She stands, pulling me up with her. I check the house is locked, turning off the lights, and join my ravishing girlfriend in bed. Wrapping my body around hers, our bodies come together naturally. Loving, joining, combining, fucking until we fall asleep together, just as I hope we do for the rest of our days.

"Morning, Sunshine," I whisper, in between peppering kisses along her exposed neck.

"Morning." She sighs while tilting her head to give me better access to her smooth neck. "I was going to bring you breakfast in bed."

"I would rather have you in bed. I don't like waking up without you." I nuzzle her neck, and spin her around to face me.

She gives me a shy smile, her natural blush rising from her tits. "Yeah?"

"Yeah." I move in, taking her mouth in a good morning kiss to begin my day the way I like. Though I'd prefer more bodily contact. Our bodies respond instantly, taking Kate's control to separate us, so we can eat the breakfast she's prepared while it's still hot.

I want to speak with Kate about our living arrangements, and forging forward with a life together, but I'm not convinced she's ready. There's still a lot about me she doesn't know. It wouldn't be fair to move forward without her knowing all of my secrets. I'll have to maintain my patience for a while longer. While she collects another load of laundry, I step next door to check on Margie.

She's looking fantastic after her ordeal as she shuffles toward the front door with a walking frame. She's only been home for one week, and she's getting around remarkably well for an eighty-five-year-old woman, who recently had a hip replacement.

"Well, hello, young man." She opens the screen door, welcoming me inside.

I give her the hug I've become accustomed to giving and receiving since meeting Kate. "How are you feeling, Margie? You're looking fit as a fiddle."

She brushes off the compliment with a wave of her hand, offering me a cup of tea, which I gratefully accept. I find I enjoy Margie's company—she's like the grandmother I never had.

"How are you and Kate going? You've been busy looking after me since my fall and subsequent stay in the hospital." She leans forward, patting my arm. "I honestly appreciate all that you two have done for me these past weeks."

"You're more than welcome, Margie. We'll always keep an eye on you." I pause, ensuring I have her undivided attention when I say, "But no more climbing up on chairs. I'll change any bulbs in the future." She tries to interrupt, but I stop her. "Don't be stubborn. Kate was beside herself with worry … and so was I. I don't want to go through that again. Understood?" My expression must deliver my message clearly, because Margie looks properly chastised.

She gives me a firm nod. "Understood."

"Good. Now, how's the physical therapy going? You seem to be getting around well."

Margie tells me all about her therapy and the lovely nurse who stops by to make sure she's showered. They installed a couple of grab rails in her shower and toilet to make them safer. I'm exceedingly pleased with the attention the health workers are giving to Margie's care. I'll need to give them a personal bonus. Of course, Margie and Kate think the hospital organized the home visits, and I'm hoping to keep it that way. We finish up our tea and I head back to Kate's place.

She's sitting at her small dining room table, working on her dated laptop. She says I work too hard, but she puts in a lot of additional time outside of school hours to provide the students in her class with every possible opportunity. Stepping behind her, I lean down and tug her braid to the side so I can kiss her neck. Then I gently pull her hair back further to raise her face toward mine. Leaning forward, I kiss her lips. "Come on, Sunshine. It's time we got ready to visit your kids."

THIRTY-TWO

-kate-

I'M NERVOUS AND EXCITED TO BE INTRODUCING OLIVER TO ROMAN and the kids. I didn't give them any warning that Oliver was visiting today. I wasn't certain if he would be interested in coming along, and I didn't want to disappoint them. They don't need any more disappointment in their lives. It made me beyond happy when he readily accepted my invitation.

Roman opens the door with his usual smile, his arms open wide in readiness for a hug. I step in as I normally do to receive one of his enormous bear hugs. Roman's a big guy, making his hugs all-encompassing. Oliver grumbles behind me. When I turn around, I'm surprised to see the possessive way he's watching our exchange. The kids come out from wherever they've been to greet me, stopping dead in their tracks when they see I have company. I pull away from Roman, stepping back to grasp Oliver's hand. "Everyone, this is Oliver. My boyfriend." It feels unreal to introduce him as *my* boyfriend. "Oliver, this is Roman, Pete, Evelyn, Ivy, Blake, Jack, and Sammy." I gesture to each person as I introduce them.

Oliver steps forward, shaking Roman's hand, and waving to the kids. "Hey everyone. Thanks for letting me crash your big night in."

He receives a series of "no worries man" and "no problem" as we step further into the home. It's been two weeks since I've seen the kids, so our catch up is energetic, to put it mildly. We traipse into the backyard to shoot hoops while the kids update me on school and friends. Oliver's great with them, joining the game, making it four on four—girls versus boys. A whole heap of smack talk is going down at the moment, and Blake's constantly posturing into Oliver's space. The girls grow bored shooting hoops, so we move inside to paint our nails and do fancy braids in our hair.

The girls giggle like crazy as we settle down for mini makeovers. Ivy's the first one brave enough to ask about Oliver. "So … Kate, what does Oliver do for a living?"

I'm not surprised Ivy asks about his job. She's all about job security and earning buckets of money once she's able. Her dream is to become a CEO of a Fortune 500 company. With the way she reads everything she can get her hands on, and her negotiation skills with the other kids in the house, I'm positive she'll fulfill her dream.

"He works in corporate investments. Probably an industry that would interest you. He drives a pretty nice car and lives in an apartment in the city. I'm guessing the job pays reasonably well." I wink at her.

"Do you think he would let me follow him around for work experience?" she asks excitedly. I don't know too many eleven-year-old girls already planning out their work experience.

"I'm pretty sure he would. You might have to wait until you're a little older, though." She claps her hands together excitedly, racing to her room to get her journal, which is full of tips and secrets for business success.

"Are you going to marry him?" Evelyn questions. She always shows all her feelings clearly, and she looks worried.

"I don't know. We haven't been dating all that long. Why do you look worried?" I rub my hand up and down her back, attempting to soothe her.

She looks at the other girls. "If you marry him, you'll probably stop coming here, and you'll have babies, and you won't want to spend time with us anymore."

The other girls are nodding in agreement. I'm shocked they're thinking that far ahead. I pull them all in for a hug. "My life may change, but I will always make sure I am in each of your lives forever. You can't get rid of me that easily, no matter where my life takes me, or your life takes you. You can always count on me. I promise."

The girls seem satisfied with my answer for now and relax. We finish our mini-makeovers, making general chit chat about favorite nail colors and hairstyles. We hear the boys stomping in through the back door and know our girl time is about to come to an abrupt end.

Oliver's herding the boys through to the bathroom to wash up before touching anything food-related. He winks at me as he passes, making my heart melt. He's come a long way from the guy complaining about interruptions to his work life. Roman, Oliver, and I settle the kids with an afternoon snack, a brownie slice they made after dinner last night, and glasses of milk. Blake situates himself between me and Oliver at the table. I look over his head to find Oliver attempting to hold back a laugh.

We decide to take the kids to the local park before getting ready for dinner. Oliver and I bring up the rear. Blake hangs back, being very obvious in his attempt to keep Oliver and I separated.

All afternoon and evening, through afternoon tea, the park, dinner, and games, Blake is like our very own personal wedge. As we're leaving, everyone cheerfully says their goodbyes to both Oliver and me, with wishes for a great week. Everyone except Blake, who's worn a constant frown today. Midway down the path at the front of the house, Oliver pulls me to a stop.

"You know, Blake's got the biggest crush on you. He was posturing up to me the entire time we were playing basketball. I felt as though I was being interrogated by him all afternoon." He laughs, pulling me forward, planting a gentle kiss against my forehead. I feel his smile as his warm lips press against my skin. He seems carefree. I think spending time with the kids was good for him. I know I always feel great after being in their company.

"I don't think so. He's only watching out for me. He's making sure you're good enough to date me." I poke my tongue out at him.

"Evelyn was worried we'd get married and have babies. The girls were worried I wouldn't want to spend time with them anymore." I shrug. I probably shouldn't have told him that. He'll think I've been thinking about marriage and babies with him.

Which I have.

Sort of.

But he doesn't need to know that, yet.

"Well, she's right about the marriage and babies part."

Whaaat?

He keeps right on talking nonchalantly, as if what he said wasn't a big deal. "But I know for certain you would never abandon those kids. I'm sure you'll always be a part of their lives in some capacity."

"You're right. I won't ever abandon them. What they fail to consider is they'll move on with a new family and leave me behind." I'm emotional thinking about losing one of my kids. I need to shake it off, and quick. "Did Ivy talk to you? She was fangirling over you something fierce when we were doing our nails and hair."

"Yeah, she did. She's got a lot of passion tucked away in that little body of hers." He huffs out a laugh. "She asked if she could shadow me for a day. I said I'd tee it up over school vacation, so it didn't interfere with her classwork."

I hug him close in gratitude. "Do you think your boss would mind?"

Oliver stalls for a second, as though he's searching for the right answer. "He won't mind. I know for sure he'd be happy to support and encourage the next generation of entrepreneurs."

"You know, she's only eleven. She can wait to shadow you at work. It doesn't need to happen anytime soon. Thank you though. Her dream is to become a CEO of a Fortune 500 company."

"Yeah, she mentioned that. I think, with her tenacity, she should be able to make her dream come true. Never know, she may come to work with me one day."

THIRTY-THREE

-kate-

WE'RE BARELY IN THE DOOR WHEN OLIVER TUGS ME AROUND TO face him. Sliding his hand under the hair at my nape, he directs my face up toward his. He whispers against my lips, "Need you, Kate." He takes my mouth in a ferocious kiss and I readily part my lips to accept his tongue, which strokes and dances with mine. Sharing the same air, in and out, the kiss makes the world around us fall away. Oliver wraps my legs around his slim hips, his hands cupping my ass, as he strides with purpose toward my bedroom.

"I need to be inside you. It was murder spending all that time with you, yet not be able to touch you." He tosses me onto my bed, following to land on top of me. I can't help but giggle at the savage need on his face, and how much he seems to have struggled throughout the afternoon and evening. "What's funny?"

"Nothing. You're acting like a caveman."

"I'll show you how I can act like a caveman the next time you let some other man put his hands on you."

I'm confused as to what he's talking about. He must see I'm not following.

"Roman." He huffs, his eyebrows nearly reaching his hairline. I still don't get what the problem is. Roman's a forty-five-year-old man, who acts more like a favorite uncle than anything else. "He hugged you a little enthusiastically when we arrived this afternoon. I don't like seeing you in another man's arms."

Whaaat? "You can't be serious."

"Deadly."

I attempt to sit up. I need to be on a more even level with him lording over me, but he keeps me pinned to the bed.

"He's like my favorite uncle. You can't possibly think anything more than that is happening. He's nearly twenty years older than me." I shake my head. "That's just ... ewww!" A shiver runs down my body at the thought of anything even remotely romantic happening with Roman. I mean, he's a sweet man and I've often wondered why he's still single because I guess for forty-five, he's good-looking. But no, just no! Actually, now I think about it, I wonder if Emma would like Roman. Now, that's something to think about.

"I can see your brain ticking over. What are you planning, Sunshine?"

"I just had a thought. Maybe I should introduce Roman to Emma. She's thirty-seven. Do you think Roman's too old for her?"

He leans forward, kissing me with a smile on his lips, shaking his head slightly. "How about you let them work out their own love life, and we'll concentrate on ours? Hmmm?" He gives my nose an Eskimo kiss, then takes my mouth in a full-on assault, leaving my mind blank of everything except him.

Slowly, both sets of clothes are removed, leaving us gloriously naked. Feeling Oliver's warm skin against mine is heaven. The fine dusting of chest hair tickling against my rigid nipples, while his hard dick rubs teasingly against my pubic bone. He turns my body on like nothing I've ever experienced. I'm already wet, my sex soft, ready to take him into my body.

Oliver leisurely lowers his hips to line his dick up with my entrance, and at an excruciatingly slow pace, enters me with short shallow thrusts, gradually increasing in depth and power. He knows how to bring my body the maximum amount of pleasure. My hands roam the expanse of his back, reveling in the feel of his strength and power. My feet press into his tight ass, urging him impossibly deeper. He takes the hint, picking up the pace. Our groans and panting breaths fill the space around us.

"I love your pussy." He breathes into my ear. Nipping my lobe, he moves lower to press open-mouthed kisses to my neck.

"I love your dick." My walls tighten, ready to explode, letting Oliver know I'm close. We both groan as I erupt, detonating his own orgasm. We fly into bliss together.

Groaning.

Grinding.

Grasping.

Kissing.

"Do you think sex between us will forever get better? Each time we come together, it's better than the time before." I sigh as Oliver keeps his lower half joined to me, sliding in and out lazily. Rising on his forearms, his hands cocoon the top of my head, while his thumbs soothingly brush my hair away from my face. He's looking deep into my eyes, as though he's attempting to see all the way to my soul.

"I don't know, but I'm willing to test the theory." He wiggles his eyebrows up and down. "Give me a minute, and I'll be ready to go again. Purely for research purposes, of course."

"Of course." I can't help but giggle at this comical side of him. He groans, giving a gentle thrust to remind me he's still inside; as if I'd ever need to be reminded. He gently slides out, getting a warm cloth to clean up the evidence of our coupling.

Snuggling into Oliver's arms after another round of breath-taking lovemaking, I feel sated, safe, and loved—even though we haven't said the words, our bodies make it abundantly clear. I've never felt this cherished or important in a man's life before. I want so much more with him. I want everything, and I'm starting to believe he wants the same with me.

THIRTY-FOUR

-kate-

TOMORROW IS THE LAST DAY OF SCHOOL BEFORE CHRISTMAS BREAK, so I plan to spend my evening wrapping Christmas gifts. That way, I can give Emma and her boys their gifts tomorrow, and Oliver isn't here to see what I got for him. My body naturally moves to the upbeat Christmas music I'm playing through my Bluetooth speakers as I cut paper to size, fold, and tape. Applying bows and name tags, I get lost in my head, thinking about my sexy times with Oliver. He certainly knows how to please a woman, in all ways.

My favorite has to be the wall sex, though. Just thinking about it makes my lady parts clench in readiness.

I had given Oliver a key because some nights he's late coming home from work. I had just stepped out of my bathroom with a towel wrapped around my hair and another around my body when he walked in.

He took one look at me and I could see his eyes darken— his intent written all over his impressive face and body. He stalked over to me, undid my towel, dropped to his knees, situated one of my legs over his shoulder, and kissed, sucked, licked, and nipped at me as though he hadn't seen me for days. I've never experienced anything like Oliver's mouth on my body before. I never knew oral could feel as sensational as it does with him. My previous boyfriends seemed to do it out of some form of obligation or something equally stupid. They certainly never got into it like Oliver does. He makes me feel like he could stay there all day. His talented mouth worked over my sensitive lips and clit while his fingers leisurely pumped in and out of my channel. I held onto his head for dear life because it was difficult to remain standing with such an onslaught of attention.

As I came down from my orgasm, Oliver dropped his pants, picked me up, pressed my back against the wall, and thrust his engorged dick inside my body. I've noticed he has this habit once he's inside me; he pauses for a bit, studying my face closely before moving. Almost as though he wants to make sure I'm genuinely on board for what's about to happen. He pounded me wildly. I was worried I was going to break through the drywall, but at the time I didn't care. It felt beyond amazing. When he's inside me, he's one hundred percent focused on my body and my pleasure. He says his pleasure and enjoyment comes from seeing me satisfied and falling into an orgasm-induced coma. *Ha!* Pretty sure I've had several of those over the past few weeks.

I don't think we actually spoke until we'd both calmed down somewhat. With a genuine smile, he'd said, "Hey." I could only respond in like, snuggling my face into his neck, as he carried me into the bathroom so we could both wash off.

I finish my task, deciding to check my email. I find a new message from Ella and Bob telling me they'd like to meet. They're going to be working on a new school in the future and would like to discuss the possibility of working with me on the project. Oh my gosh! That's a no brainer for me. I absolutely loved working with them. I learned an enormous amount, and it felt fantastic to help the community develop its education program for their elementary students. It was truly an honor, as well as being a humbling experience.

We take a lot for granted here. Resources and support for our schools are plentiful when compared to the schools Ella and Bob are establishing in remote communities. I might check in with Oliver to see if he would also be interested in helping since he was previously involved.

I respond to their email, telling them I'm definitely interested, and when I'm available to catch up for a coffee and chat. Christmas break starts tomorrow so I have some time on my hands. I'll spend time getting my program organized, as well as spending extra time with my favorite kids.

Today was crazy hectic. The kids were extremely excited for Christmas, so they were a bit wild. I didn't mind their excitement. In fact, I found their excitement fed my own. I'm about to head over to visit the kids tonight instead of tomorrow because Roman's organized a special Christmas outing for them with kids from other homes. I dress in my black skinny jeans, a pink sweater, and my brand spanking new red Converse. I won't see the kids again before Christmas. Gathering my gifts for them, I leave a light on for later and make my way over to Lloyd Avenue.

Arriving at the house, I bounce up the steps, wondering what they'll want to do tonight. Even though I could probably walk straight in, I treat this as their home, making sure I show the same respect I would when visiting anyone I know—I always knock on the door.

I knock and wait.

I'm a little surprised that nobody has answered the door, so I knock again, then try the door handle.

It's locked. I guess it's not that unusual, but it *is* unusual for nobody to be home. Roman was expecting me, even though the kids have no idea I'm visiting tonight instead of tomorrow.

Walking around the house, I attempt to look in the windows, but all the blinds and curtains are closed. Now that *is* unusual in a house full of kids with only one adult. I walk back around to the front of the house and sit on the front step wondering where they may have gone. Maybe they went to the park a couple of blocks away. I wander toward it, hoping to find my crew. Arriving at the entrance, I look around, but can't see anyone familiar to me. I guess they're not at the park. I'm confused because Roman knew I was coming this afternoon—after all, it *was* his idea. Pulling out my phone, I decide to shoot Roman a text.

Me: Hey, I'm out front
Me: Where are you guys?

I sit, waiting for a response, but nothing is forthcoming. I wonder how long I should wait around? It won't be long before it's dark. I'm not sure what to do, and as I decide to head home, my phone chimes with an alert.

Roman: Hey, busy atm
Roman: Can I call you in 20?
Me: Sure
Me: Hope everything's okay

Maybe I should wait here until I speak with him. I don't want to go all the way home, only to have to turn around and come back again. I decide to walk around the back, making myself comfortable. While I wait for his call, I'll read the book on my phone. I'm getting to a raunchy part of the book when my phone rings. I quickly press the button to accept the call. "Hey, Roman. Did you forget I was coming over today?"

"Hey, Kate. Sorry. No, I didn't forget, but something's happened which was out of my control." He sounds unlike the

Roman I know and love. "I don't know how to break the news to you."

"Are the kids alright? Nobody's hurt?"

My heart's beating hard, and my panic is rising. Getting up, I pace across the back porch, wrapping my free arm across my stomach, as if I can protect myself against anything awful he might say.

"Ah, no. The kids are okay. Nobody's hurt. It's nothing like that." He rushes to reassure me.

"Then what's happened? Why aren't you guys here?" I question because I still get the sense something's wrong.

"We were shut down. Early this afternoon, I received a call telling me to pack the kids up. I had to bring them to the main center in the city."

I can't believe what I'm hearing. "Whaaat? What do you mean … shut down? I don't understand. How can they shut down like that? How could they kick the kids out of their home this close to Christmas with no warning?"

The shock of the news is making it difficult to breathe. I don't understand what's happened and why. Who would do such a drastic and invasive thing to these kids? They've already had enough turmoil.

"I don't know all the details yet. I'm probably not supposed to be telling you anything, because you're a volunteer and not an employee. They've shut down the fifteen homes spread throughout the city and brought everyone into the central facility. I don't know any more than that. I'm sorry I forgot to let you know we wouldn't be home when you arrived. I got caught up getting the kids packed up, moved, and settled."

He's majorly apologetic when my feelings are the least of anyone's concern.

I pause in my pacing, looking into the backyard full of many wonderful memories with the kids. "Please don't apologize to me, Roman. Your focus should always be on the kids, exactly where it has been today. How are they taking it?"

He lets out a sigh. "Oh, you know what they're like. Their walls went straight back up, and they closed themselves off from the disappointment. Pete's using humor to get through, which is driving Sammy up the wall, because she wants everyone to take things seriously. Evelyn's been tearful, and Ivy's stuck close by to support her. Jack and Blake have been super quiet, keeping to themselves."

I can picture him running his hands through his messy hair as he's talking with me on the phone.

"Do you think this is permanent? Will I be able to see them?" My gifts seem petty now, but I still want to give them to the kids.

"I know nothing at this point. I'll try to keep you in the loop if I can. I'm sorry." He sounds knocked down and defeated. Tired.

"No, that's okay. I understand. You focus on the kids. Tell them I love them and I'm still around. Okay? Maybe if you find out more, you can let me know?"

"I will. Take care of yourself."

"You, too. Bye."

Roman disconnects the call, leaving me feeling dumbfounded and lost. I sit on the steps in a daze. I don't know what to think, or what to do with myself. I'm unsure how long I sit, but a chill has reached into my bones. It's completely dark, and I decide to make my way home.

Once home, I make myself a warm drink and sit on my couch, contemplating what I can do to help. I check my emails to find I have a reply from Bob and Ella. Our schedules don't align for another six weeks, so it will be some time before we can discuss their plans. I pick up my book, but my mind won't switch off and I'm unable to concentrate on the sexy times I'm attempting to read. Turning on the television, I watch my favorite comedy talk show. The host is a bundle of fun. She'll help to break me out of my gray mood.

I must doze off at some point because I wake up to my phone ringing. Before I answer, I notice it's Oliver. I quickly accept the call. "Hey."

The relief that fills me, knowing he's on the other end of the phone, is powerful. He was the first person I wanted to talk to about the kids this afternoon. It's scary how much I've come to depend on him. Especially since I swore I wouldn't depend on another man.

"Hey, Kate." I take the phone away from my ear, because it's not Oliver on the phone, even though it says it's him.

My heart races and my hands grow sweaty. "Who is this, please? Where's Oliver? Is he okay? Please tell me he's okay!" I stand to pace my living room. I don't think I can handle any more bad news today.

"Hey, calm down. It's me, Jase. Oliver's okay. He asked me to contact you, because he won't be able to make it to your place tonight."

"Oh." The disappointment I feel is palpable. "Is everything okay?"

"Sort of. Everything with Oliver is okay. He's been called in to help sort out a work-related issue and it'll probably be an all-nighter."

"Really? That boss expects an awful lot from Oliver. He gives up an enormous amount of his personal life for his job." There's a long silence on the other end of the phone, and I check if the call has been disconnected. "Jase, are you still there?"

He clears his throat. "Yeah, I'm still here. You're right, the boss does expect a lot from his employees, but he *is* fair. This is a temporary crisis and once it's sorted out, things will return to normal. How about I give you my number? That way, if you ever need anything and can't get hold of Oliver, you can call me."

"Oh, thanks, Jase. That would be great. Maybe text it through to me and I'll add you to my contacts list." I guess that's it then. "Bye, Jase. Thanks for calling me. Maybe I'll see you soon?"

"Sure thing, Kate. Take care. See you soon."

He disconnects the call and within the next few seconds, I receive a text message with his contact details. As I save it to my contacts, I feel like this information may be handy if I ever want to surprise Oliver since they work together.

I've had a lousy evening; missing out on seeing the kids, and now missing out on seeing Oliver. I stop, taking a minute to remind myself that it wasn't my home taken away from me today, and it's not me who has to work all night to sort out some type of crisis at work. Perhaps I'll have a glass of wine and read my book while soaking in the tub before going to bed. Maybe tomorrow will bring some positive news.

THIRTY-FIVE

-oliver-

"WHAT DO YOU MEAN, THE MONEY'S FUCKING GONE?" I YELL INTO the phone at Marcus, the CEO of *The Parkerville Project*. I can't believe what I'm fucking hearing.

"We received a call from the bank early this morning, informing us they were foreclosing on our properties. The only one we can use is our central facility in the city because we own that building outright. That was the initial purchase for the organization, courtesy of you. It's the only building we have left." Marcus patiently explains to me, clearly as exasperated as I am. Marcus is the only person I have contact with over at *The Parkerville Project*. I like it to be kept on the down-low that I'm a major contributor. That's why Roman didn't know who I was when we met.

"Where did the money go? It can't have fucking disappeared. I gave you a check for one million dollars last quarter."

I stand, pacing along my floor-to-ceiling windowed wall, overlooking downtown.

"We're going to have to employ a financial investigator to find out what happened. I'm sorry I don't have more information. I don't understand what happened."

"Send all of your financials over to my office. I'll take a look to see if I can track the money. I'll need access to everything associated with *The Parkerville Project* financials. I'll expect to receive them within the next thirty minutes. If I can't find the trail, then we'll get a financial investigator in to do what needs to be done."

I disconnect the call, expecting my request to be followed since I'm the major financial contributor of the organization. I buzz Jase into my office.

Jase strolls in as if I've got all fucking day. "'Sup boss?"

"Cancel everything on my calendar for the next two days, starting from now."

He looks gobsmacked. I *never* cancel anything. *Ever.* "But you have that follow-up meeting with the Vegas investor—"

I cut him off with a slash of my arm and a stern look. "That's going to have to wait. I just got off the phone with Marcus from *The Parkerville Project*. He informed me the bank has foreclosed on most of their properties because all the money has fucking disappeared."

"What the fuck?!"

"Exactly my sentiments. I've asked him to send me all of their financials. I'll work on following the trail to figure out what's happened to the money." I run my hand through my hair. I'm overwhelmed at the task ahead of me, but I won't ever show that to anyone—not even Jase.

"Sure thing. I'll get right on rescheduling everything for you. I'll order lunch in, and clear the schedules for the team leaders—they can help you work through everything." He turns around as he reaches the door. "I'll help in any way I can. Those kids need those homes to feel safe and secure."

I fucking know that. That's exactly why I'm prepared to put my business on hold.

Forty minutes later, I'm sitting at my desk, attempting to work out the best approach for tackling the problem at hand. The financials were finally delivered, and I've begun to sort them into piles. I've got a profusion of files and papers to sort through, and I think the best approach would be to start at the most recent documents and work my way backward.

I've probably been going strong for about an hour when Jase walks in with our lunch, making himself comfortable on the other side of my desk.

He surveys the mess on my desk, sideboard, and floor. "You're going to need more than two days to go through all of this, even with the help of the team leaders and me."

He passes my lunch over, unwrapping his sub while I do the same. "I'll pull an all-nighter tonight and work across the entire weekend if I need to. Can you contact Kate on my phone? Let her know something important has come up, and I won't be able to make it tonight. If I talk with her, I'll cave and go home. I need to invest the time to sort out this issue as quickly as possible for the kids."

Don't think I didn't notice I referred to Kate's place as 'home'. I've felt that way for some time now. The feeling only became stronger when she gave me a key, enabling me to come and go as I pleased.

Lunch passes quickly, and I'm back sifting through the piles of documentation on my desk and scattered throughout my office. My team leaders arrive to help sort through, and hopefully find a trail that will explain what's happened. We're working solidly, unaware of how much time has passed. When I glance at the clock, I'm shocked to see it's after nine.

I call over, "Hey, Jase, did you contact Kate?"

"Oh shit, sorry. I'll do it right now."

I feel like shit for blowing her off, but she has a powerful hold over me. If I make the smallest contact, I'll be distracted and I can't afford to lose focus at this point.

I hear Jase on the phone with Kate. He's looking at me, giving me the evil eye. He responds to whatever she said, then offers his contact number to her.

What the fuck?

That's unnecessary. It'll only be tonight, and maybe the rest of the weekend, that I'll be out of contact. No need to fill my shoes yet! He texts his information to Kate and hands my phone back.

"What the fuck, man? You still haven't told her who you really are? That poor woman thinks 'your boss expects a lot from you'. When are you going to tell her that you *are* the fucking boss?"

He's totally pissed, and with good reason. He's been on my case for the last several weeks to be honest with her. I'm not ready. I know she won't respond well, and I'm terrified I'm going to lose the best thing that's ever happened to me. I need her to be fully invested in our relationship. I need her to be as attached to me as I am to her —so she won't leave me when she finds out who I am. I've never lied to her. She knows my real name; she knows I work in corporate investments in the city; she knows I live in the city, near work; she knows I earn more money than she does; she knows the *real* me, behind the corporate persona. I remind myself she could search me online or her brother could tell her who I am before I get the chance —which would be disastrous.

"I haven't found the right time to tell her. When she finds out who I am, how much money I'm actually worth; she'll run for the hills. I can't afford to lose her, Jase. It would ruin me. More than any financial loss ever would."

I know I've shown Jase my vulnerable underbelly, and he could easily use the information against me, but all I see in his eyes is compassion and understanding. He knows Kate is as down to earth as they come and has the biggest heart and kindest nature. He knows the impact she's had on me since she came into my life.

"Look, man, I know you're worried. But the longer you take to tell her, the worse her response will be."

He pats me on the shoulder, leaving my office to organize dinner for us, while I slump down in my chair, feeling like shit.

It's been more than three fucking days since I've seen Kate, and I'm like a junkie having withdrawals. I've made no direct contact with her. I can't bring myself to speak with her because I miss her so fucking much that I ache. I was worried if I heard her voice, I'd break and go to her. I've barely slept, only an hour or two here and there on the couch in my penthouse, before showering and returning to my office. It'll all be worth it. I found the trail of missing money. My missing money, since I fund ninety percent of the organization.

For me, it's been fucking personal!

Someone's gradually siphoned the money off into offshore accounts over the past few years. The trail shows money going into several different accounts held in different names, each to a value less than $10,000; meaning an FBAR report didn't need to be supplied to the IRS. It would have taken a great deal of know-how, and time to set the system up, and to fly under the radar for as long as they have. Now we need to work out the 'who'—though I have my suspicions.

I've spoken to Marcus about bringing in a financial investigator, and he's on board. Mike, the PI I used to find Kate, gave me his recommendation. I've set up a meeting with him and Marcus for tomorrow morning—Christmas Eve. Marcus has asked to hold a meeting for all interested parties, allowing us to report what we've discovered thus far, and our next steps moving forward to right the company. I've readily agreed that people need to be kept informed, but I don't want to spook the perpetrator just yet. To allow us some additional time, the meeting will be held at the end of next week in my offices here at Stone Tower.

I'm beyond shattered, but wild horses couldn't keep me away from Kate any longer. I need to see her, smell her, touch her, and feel her body wrapped in my arms, against my body.

Shutting down everything in my office, I lock the door to keep any sensitive information safe, driving straight to Kate's place without stopping.

THIRTY-SIX

-kate-

MARGIE AND I ARE BUNDLED UP IN OUR WARMEST COATS, SITTING ON the front porch. I sit on the step and Margie sits on a chair, enjoying a cup of tea while she catches me up on the shenanigans in our street. It's Christmas Eve and I haven't seen or heard a peep from Oliver since Friday morning, when he woke me with delicate kisses along my neck and shoulder before he left for the office.

"Did you see Pete and Joe going at it yesterday afternoon?" Margie asks with a giggle. "I swear, I don't need a TV with those two down the street."

I giggle as well. "Yeah, I can't believe Joe cut the branch off Pete's tree like that. Just because the leaves fell onto his driveway this last fall." I look over at the poor, butchered tree. "As if the leaves on the rest of the tree won't fall and blow over the fence."

"Right! The leaves that fell on his driveway didn't only come from the branch growing over his side of the fence." She laughs extra hard, causing tears to escape her eyes from the force.

"I'm not sure if they would survive if one of them moved from the street. I think they keep each other going with their antics."

"True, very true." Margie looks thoughtful. "So, I haven't seen young Oliver's car in your driveway for the past couple of days. Everything going okay?"

I shrug. "I guess so. There's been a big drama at work he's had to sort out, so he's been radio silent. I've only heard through Jase, a guy who works with him, that he couldn't leave work to come to see me." I give Margie a weak smile. "I've missed him beyond what I thought was possible, Margie. The depth and strength of my feelings toward him scares the living daylights outta me—if I'm honest."

She pats my arm. "Ah, that's the sign of a strong bond, Katie-girl. Only the best stuff is experienced at an intense level which is scary. That's the stuff worth holding on to." She nods down the street. "Speak of the devil. I believe this is him roaring down our street now."

I turn my head in the same direction as Margie, and sure enough, Oliver's car is slowing down to enter my driveway. As soon as he has the car in park, the engine cuts, and he opens the door. His long strides have him directly in front of me within seconds. He picks me up bridal style, then turns to Margie.

"Hi, Margie. Sorry, but I need to steal my girl away. Hope you don't mind."

He's still looking at me with that fierceness I've come to expect from him. He has dark smudges beneath his eyes and his usual short, tidy scruff looks unruly.

Margie waves us off with a slash of her arm. "Oh, pish posh. Don't let me stop you from having your sexy times. Have fun."

She winks at us as she rises to move inside. Oliver takes me inside my house, kicks the door closed, and orders me to lock it.

"Hey," he whispers as he runs his nose up my neck to my ear, then pulls back to peer into my eyes.

"Hey." I'm at a loss for words. I've missed him terribly, but I don't want to sound like a needy child who can't let her boyfriend get on with his job.

He blows out a long breath, his shoulders dropping into a more relaxed position. "I've missed you, Sunshine."

Oh wow. Blowing out a long breath, I study his eyes full of sincerity and release the tension from my body. "I've missed you terribly, Oliver. I didn't realize how accustomed I'd become to seeing you every day."

We both move forward at the same time to meet in a gentle kiss —a meeting of the lips—with heavy sighs and palpable relief. The kiss quickly amps up in a way I never dreamed possible before him.

I've fallen in love with him—the realization hits me with the force of a ten-ton truck. I pull him in tighter to my body as he carries me to my bedroom. Sitting on the edge of my bed, he gently pulls away from the kiss. I miss him immediately, attempting to follow his lips, garnering a smile from him.

"As much as I want to be inside you right now, I owe you the biggest apology first." I try to interrupt, but he presses his finger over my lips, shaking his head. "No, I do. I wanted to call you many times, but I knew if I heard your voice or even read a message from you; I would get too distracted from the urgent work that needed to be done. People, good people, were relying on me to solve the problem as quickly as possible, and I couldn't let them down."

"Oh, Oliver. Your work ethic knows no bounds. I won't sit here and say it didn't matter, but your radio silence hurt me. I understand your work is important. It sounds like whatever happened was pretty major, but I didn't like feeling that I wasn't important enough for you to take five minutes to check in with me. It made me feel small. Perhaps I'm more invested in this relationship than you are? But then you're here, explaining why you couldn't communicate, and I feel like such a selfish ass." That all gushed out of me at once. I hadn't acknowledged to myself that I felt that way. I pull him close, pressing my forehead against his. "Maybe we could find some middle ground?"

"I'm sorry. I truly am. My intention was never to make you feel small, or that I'm not invested in this relationship. I'm an ass. I'm not making excuses, but I'm used to focusing on my work and only on my work. Our relationship is relatively new and I forget I need to consider my partner. I was too busy focusing on how *I* felt and didn't consider how *you* would feel. For a long time, I haven't had to answer to anyone. I hope you can forgive me. I promise to do better next time."

He kisses the tip of my nose.

"I can understand when something important needs to be accomplished. I would appreciate better communication next time, though. It would have only taken you a couple of minutes to make contact. I would have understood that you needed to work. I would never try to take you away from your job because I know how important it is to you." I kiss the tip of his nose. "I missed you more than I thought was possible, and I was worried about you."

His expression is incredulous. He's clearly not used to having someone worry about or show concern for him. Every time I've shown my care and concern for him, it's as if he's never experienced it before.

"I truly am sorry. Having someone who worries about me is unfamiliar territory. It won't happen again."

I nod in acknowledgment. "I'm prepared to let it go this time, but if it happens again, I won't be so forgiving."

He moves forward, capturing my lips roughly, while his hands reacquaint themselves with my body. "I could do with a shower. Come with me."

He picks me up as though I weigh nothing, carrying me toward the bathroom. Sitting me on the vanity, he turns toward the shower to start the water, winking at me over his shoulder while adjusting the temperature.

Oh yeah, shower sex. That's my second favorite, behind wall sex with him.

We both undress, stepping under the warm water together. Oliver grabs my jasmine soap to wash my body. He's always looking after me, but I take it out of his hands, soaping up his big body with care—it's my turn to look after him for a change. Being in the shower together is a bit of a tight squeeze, because of Oliver's size, but we've made it work before. It means our bodies 'accidentally' rub against each other—*what a shame!*

I want to wash him down and give him some TLC because he looks exhausted. Touching Oliver's chiseled body is such a decadent experience—I cherish the privilege every time I get to put my hands on him. It should be a criminal offense for any one man to be this utterly perfect. From his classically handsome face to his strong, broad shoulders, down his chiseled torso, to that notable V which leads to an impressive dick, by any standards, resting between two strong and powerful thighs. A sudden feeling of gratitude over- whelms me, as I recognize the intimacy of experiencing this with Oliver; that I'm the woman who gets to *see* him and *feel* him like this. As I glance up, the green that I love so much is disappearing as his pupils dilate. His breathing is shallow, his nipples pebbled, and his engorged dick is rising to prepare for action.

He takes the cloth out of my hand, dropping it to the floor. He twists his body under the water to rinse off, then he comes for me with delicious intent written all over his face and in his taut body. His body gives off an aggressive vibe, yet his touches are gentle and delicate on my breasts until my nipples peak to his liking. Bending down, he sucks one into his warm mouth, drawing a sigh from me. Even though my body is wet from the shower, the warm wetness of his mouth is sublime, as he moves between both breasts to give them equal attention. I can't help the moan escaping from deep in my body—a satisfaction which is impossible to suppress. He presses his fully erect dick against my lower abdomen, showing me what my response does to him.

"I love your tits. One day, I'm going to fuck them and paint them with my cum," he growls out, then presses my back up against the cold tile. The difference between the front and the back of my body is significant, adding to the sensations Oliver is endowing on me as he presses my boobs together, kissing them gently and rubbing his beard across both globes. All I can do is moan at the thought of him sliding his big dick between them. The guy is incredibly sexy. His dirty mouth adds a level of heat to our sex that I never anticipated I would enjoy as much as I do.

He grabs my ass cheeks in both hands, lifting me easily. As I wrap my legs around his slim hips, he lines up his dick, drawing me down in one powerful thrust. He groans while all thought escapes me. My breath pushing out of my body, my eyes closing in bliss. He fits my body perfectly, touching all the parts inside I wasn't aware of before.

As is Oliver's usual MO, he pauses, fully seated inside me. He intently studies my face—my eyes, my lips, and a general all-round check-in that I'm with him. I take his bottom lip in a small bite, followed by a gentle kiss. As usual, he takes over, devouring my mouth. We kiss tenderly, tasting, breathing each other's breaths. He begins to move inside me. He pulls his body away slightly, allowing us to watch his dick moving in and out of me in smooth, precise glides—so hot! I'm on fire; the sensations inside me seem to be growing and expanding exponentially. For a spell, I worry the feelings are too big and that the resulting explosion may tear me apart.

"Harder. Harder, please, Oliver," I moan out. I'm almost there. "Keep hitting that spot. Yeah, that one right there!"

His warm breaths coat the side of my face. The feel of his muscles shifting and flexing under my hold adds to my lust. My breasts press against his slick chest, and I swear our hearts beat a matching tattoo.

"Come for me, Sunshine. Give it to me," he whispers in my ear, nipping the lobe.

It's then that I break.

My vision goes black for a second, and my breaths stall in my chest. For resplendent moments, I'm suspended in that extraordinary place outside of reality. My channel spasming around his dick, holding him tight, as my arms hold him tight to my body.

"Oh yeah. That's it, Sunshine, give it all to me!" He breathes out between grunts, as his thrusts become erratic. "Your pussy's strangling my cock … just the way I need it."

He falls apart; his dick pulsing and jetting out his cum into my body. I don't know how he holds me up and remains standing at this point. Squeezing my pussy as tight as I can around his dick, I run my hands soothingly up and down his back in a gentle glide, calming his body through his orgasm.

Oliver buries his face in the crook of my neck, blowing out a hot breath. "Fucking you is my favorite thing to do, behind being with you in any way that you allow me in your life."

Oh, my heart, he's too much with his sweet words. "Same for me, big guy. Same for me." I press delicate kisses where his neck meets his shoulder.

We stay in each other's embrace until the water cools. He carefully slides out of me and we both groan at the immediate loss of intimate contact. Gradually, he slides me down his hard planes until my feet make contact with the floor. He doesn't let go until he's sure I've got steady legs. We quickly rinse off, then turn the water off and step out to dry off.

I'm sitting on the couch with a glass of wine, while Oliver orders Thai delivery for dinner. I feel deliciously stretched and worked over in the best possible way. Thinking about what he does to my body makes me blush.

Oliver breaks me out of my thoughts as he sits on the couch beside me. "It'll be about forty-five minutes. I ordered enough for Margie too, if you want to let her know."

I smile at his thoughtfulness. "Sure, I'll text her now."

After messaging Margie to invite her over for dinner, I put down my phone and turn my body toward him. He rests his hand on my thigh—I don't think he realizes the sensations he provokes in my body with one simple touch.

"So, tell me what I've missed in your life over the last few days."

Where do I begin?

"I've been feeling a bit numb, to be honest. I had planned to surprise the kids on Friday afternoon, but when I got there, nobody was home. When I finally got in touch with Roman, he told me the fifteen homes belonging to *The Parkerville Project* had been shut down. All the kids had to move into their central location in the city."

I don't even register I'm crying until Oliver pulls me onto his lap and gently wipes my tears with his thumbs. "Kate. What did Roman say happened?"

THIRTY-SEVEN

-oliver-

IN MY SINGULAR DETERMINATION TO SORT OUT THE ISSUE FROM MY end, I didn't even consider how the news of the closures would affect Kate. It just goes to show, I'm not used to having to consider another person in my daily life. Maybe she would be better off if I stepped out of her life? She doesn't need someone as selfish as me messing her around.

I don't think I can give her up, though—proving exactly how fucking selfish I am.

She has the biggest, most generous heart, and she would have taken what happened quite hard. I'm not surprised she's emotional about it. I wish I could tell her of my involvement in the project, but that would expose who I am, along with my financial status.

I'm not ready.

See, fucking selfish!

She sucks in a shuddering breath. "Roman couldn't tell me much. Only that the homes were closed down, and the kids had to be moved to the central location. That means they no longer have room to take in street kids or give them a meal and a safe place to sleep. The repercussions are enormous and far-reaching for all the kids involved. My heart breaks for them." She blinks up at me.

"Right on Christmas. What a crappy thing to happen at such a special time of the year."

Mmm, Roman shouldn't be telling Kate anything because she isn't an employee. I can understand his loyalty to her, though. From my understanding, she's only one of a few people who regularly volunteer their time to the program. It's almost like she is an employee.

She looks up at me with teary eyes. "Roman said he's not supposed to tell me anything because I'm not an employee, but he said he would try to keep me in the loop as much as possible. I don't know how I can help."

"I'm sure you could visit the kids," I say, brushing a loose lock of damp hair behind her ear.

"Roman suggested I give it a few days until the kids settle in. He'll let me know when he thinks they're ready. Luckily, I'm on vacation until the Monday after next."

There's a knock at Kate's front door. I open it, finding Margie holding onto her cane with a cheesy grin on her face. She gives me an exaggerated wink and steps inside.

"I have to say, I'm a little disappointed you two have finished already. I would have thought you'd have more stamina for a man your age." She giggles, patting me on the arm as she walks past me into Kate's home. This woman is hilarious, and while I don't mind her cheeky comment, I know Kate will be mortified. This should be fun.

Kate stands to embrace Margie with their usual affection. Margie pulls back, looking Kate dead in the face. "Well, that's a shame." Kate looks at her questioningly. "You can still walk. I anticipated you to be limping, at the very least."

Understanding dawns on Kate's face and that adorable blush of hers rises to take over her neck and face. I know exactly where that blush starts, and it's got me thinking all kinds of inappropriate thoughts in mixed company.

"Oh, Margie, you have no filter at all." She covers her face with her hands to stem the giggle that's trying to escape. Kate gives up, and they both fall over each other in laughter.

I can't help but join in with them. We're interrupted by another knock at the door, which is hopefully dinner. Collecting my wallet, I answer the door—exchanging a wad of cash for our delicious-smelling meal. We all move into action, preparing the table, dishing out food, and getting drinks before sitting down to eat.

We chat while we eat. The ladies update me on the latest adventures of Pete and Joe—eliciting more giggles from them, and a shake of my head from me.

"Did you tell Oliver you got an email from Bob and Ella inviting you to help them set up another school?"

Kate looks at me. "Uh, no, I hadn't got that far in catching him up on the events of the last few days."

The pride I have for her fills my whole body. She's brilliant in her chosen profession. Bob and Ella are very selective about who they invite to work with them on projects—only wanting the best of the best. Kate definitely fits the bill, especially after the exceptional work she did at the last school.

"Tell me about it. Where's the next project?" I already know, because my foundation is the largest financial contributor to the project.

"Oh, well, it's going to be a while before we can meet to talk about it. I don't know any details yet. I'm sure they'll fill me in on everything when we meet in six weeks. At this stage, they wanted to know if I was interested in working with them on their next project." She takes a sip of her drink, then turns back to me. "Do you think you'll work on building the next school for Bob and Ella?"

I wasn't planning on it, but maybe I should. "I hadn't given the idea any thought, but I don't think I'd be opposed to the idea if it means not being separated from you."

She smiles at me as though I've given her the best news ever. Her whole face lights up, and it's an arresting sight.

"Oh, that sounds wonderful. You two working together to build and set up a new school."

I nod slowly, turning my attention to Margie.

"Did Kate tell you that's how we originally met?"

Margie holds her hand over her heart, shaking her head in the negative. "No, Katie-girl never got around to telling me how the two of you met."

I tell Margie about meeting Kate for the first time. How she was constantly in my thoughts for over a year before I decided to track her down. I don't think I've ever shared that information with Kate. She looks surprised, to say the least.

"Oh, I never knew that! You were constantly in my thoughts, as well. I thought I'd built you up to be way better than you were."

"The relief I felt when I saw you at the renovation project those months ago knocked me on my ass," I tell her honestly.

We're both lost in each other until Margie clears her throat. "That sounds like a fated meeting to me. Now I'm going to go home for the evening. Thank you both for dinner, and I'll see you two later."

Kate and I both stand—she hugs Margie goodbye, and I walk her next door. Before Margie steps inside, she presses up on her toes to peck my cheek. "You are very good for her, Oliver. She looks happy and content now she's with you. Thank you."

She moves inside, locking her door, not allowing me to respond. I head back to Kate's, finding her clearing up from dinner. We work together and finish up quickly so we can go to bed. I haven't finished showing Kate how much I missed her over the past few days.

Waking up with Kate on Christmas morning is the best gift I've ever been given. Her warm, naked body pressed against mine in slumber, touching at every available point, fills me with gratitude that I found her. That she's now part of my life. Looking down at the top of her head resting on my chest, I gently smooth her wild curls away from her face—so I can admire her perfection. The dusting of freckles across her nose, which she tries to cover with makeup; her delicate auburn lashes, laying flush against her pale cheeks; and those tempting pink lips, slightly open in rest.

Her hand resting on my abdomen slowly comes to life, indicating my quiet appreciation time is coming to a close. She nuzzles in closer, then stretches out and slowly opens her eyes, exposing those guileless cobalt irises to me.

She tilts her face up to mine as a slow smile spreads across her lips. "Merry Christmas, Oliver."

"Merry Christmas, Sunshine." I lean down to kiss the tip of her nose. She rolls out of bed and sprints for the bathroom, spoiling my fun. She has a thing about brushing her teeth before she lets me kiss her in the morning. Sometimes I'm able to catch her off-guard, but most of the time she's too quick.

When she returns to my arms, she has a mischievous look on her face. "Do you realize it's only been three months since we met for the second time?" She's glancing between my eyes and my mouth. I lick my lips temptingly, striving to distract her from the conversation. I'd rather use my mouth for something other than talking. "It feels like I've known you forever. I want our first Christmas together to be super special." If only she knew that we have known each other forever—sort of.

She moves forward, initiating a kiss and boosting my Christmas gratitude into the stratosphere. Any time she makes the first move toward intimate contact, it's like I've won a prize. As often as I've taken her body, I always want more. Every time, I promise myself to let her take the lead next time, but I can't help myself. I inevitably end up taking control—this time is no different. Even though she started this time, I'll be the one to finish it.

After a shower and a light breakfast of waffles, we sit on the couch to exchange gifts. I made sure not to go overboard with gifts, as I didn't want to make Kate feel uncomfortable. She's always chastising me for spending money on her, so I held back. I bought her a pair of Jimmy Choo Gin flats, made to order in red—her favored shoe color. I figure they'll be comfortable for her to wear to work, because she doesn't seem to wear heels very often.

"Oh my gosh, these are so pretty. Thank you." She quickly takes her woolly socks off to try on her new shoes. They fit her perfectly.

She throws herself at my body as if I've given her a new yacht, instead of a measly pair of shoes. Her genuine gratitude for the simple things is extraordinarily rare in my world.

Her second gift is probably more for me than for her—a sexy La Perla cranberry balconette bra, which is going to display her tits magnificently, and matching panties. I can't wait for her to put them on, so I can peel them off … with my teeth.

As she opens the box, the stunning blush I adore rises from her chest, covering her neck to her cheeks. Oh yeah! I love that fucking blush; especially now I have first-hand knowledge of where it originates. She picks up the delicate items, looking across at me. "These are stunning, Oliver. I feel rather spoiled and decadent." She leans forward to kiss me, gently at first, and then more forcefully. "I can't wait to wear them. There's something, so … so tantalizing about wearing something this sexy underneath your clothes. Other people don't know what's there, but I do. It makes me feel fiercely feminine and powerful."

And there goes my cock. It's already a constant battle to keep it under control around my exquisite woman, but when she talks like that, I've got no chance. I shift uncomfortably on the couch, discreetly adjusting my wayward cock.

Kate moves off the couch to retrieve the gifts she bought for me, and I can't help but admire her round ass as she bends down. She's got three gifts in her hands and her face is pinched in uncertainty.

"Are those for me, Sunshine?"

She bites the side of her thumbnail. Something she does when she's unsure or nervous. "Uh yeah. I hope you like the things I chose for you. They're certainly not as decadent as the gifts you've given me."

It's been years since I've been given a gift at Christmas time. "I know I'll love anything you've chosen for me because it came from your tender heart." She blushes again, handing the first gift to me.

I unwrap the box, opening the lid to find a pair of red socks. I look up at Kate with a smile on my face, because I get the reason behind red socks. She tucks a lock of hair behind her ear. "I love having red shoes on my feet. I'm unsure when it started, but it's the only color I'll wear. I didn't think you would like to wear red shoes, and you especially can't wear them to work, but I thought, maybe you could have red socks as the next best thing. In my opinion. Of course." The explanation gushes out of her. Whenever she's nervous or anxious about something, her words come pouring out of her mouth, but she has nothing to feel anxious about here.

"I love them. Actually, I've been thinking about getting a pair of red Converse so I can match you."

Her face lights up the entire space, and she breaks into a giggle. "Oh, I'm relieved you didn't think I was stupid."

"Never, Kate. I would never think you're stupid."

She hands me the second gift to open. Inside are two pairs of red boxer briefs. I get the sense there's a bit of a theme happening here. Kate picks them up, turning them around to show me the back. Printed on one pair is, 'This is mine', and on the other pair is, 'Property of Kate'. I can't help but burst into laughter, and Kate quickly joins me.

"I'll wear these with pride. I love them."

"I'm seriously pleased. They had a no returns policy and they're too big for me to wear." She giggles again as she hands me her last gift.

Opening the box, I find a booklet of a dozen handmade love vouchers. Each one offering a variety of experiences Kate's willing to share with me—massages, a picnic in the woods following a hike, specially made favorite meals, breakfast in bed, movie night of my choice, and more. She's put a great deal of thought and care into this gift. My nose tingles, and I'm working hard to keep my emotions at bay. I whisper a simple, 'thank you', pulling her into my arms and burying my face in her neck. This gift shows me Kate's planning to keep me around in to the future. I'm overwhelmed with how full my heart is when I'm with her.

"I know it's not much. I don't have a lot of money to spend, so I tried to make it as special as I could. I hope you like your gifts, Oliver."

I look into her eyes, full of compassion. "You have no idea what your gifts have given me. Having you wake up in my arms this morning was a gift, but this … this is next level. Thank you doesn't seem enough."

I press my lips against hers, brushing back and forth, then I slide my tongue forward to participate in the kiss. It doesn't take much coaxing these days for Kate to open up to me. Our kiss is passionate, deep, and all-consuming.

Margie, Kate, and I are expected at Kate's parents' for lunch. I don't want us to be late, which means we need to stop.

I'm more nervous than I've previously felt as we arrive at Kate's family home. This time *I know* they're the family who took me in after Mom died and while Dad was in the hospital. I'm not sure how they became involved, and I don't remember them clearly. I *do* remember feeling I was welcome here, and I adored their baby girl —Kate.

I want to confess who I am. Then I can tell Kate's mom she can stop praying for me; because I am safe, I am happy, I am successful. But I haven't told Kate about my childhood yet, and she deserves to know before I share that information with the rest of her family.

With Christmas greetings out of the way, we sit down to yet another delicious meal prepared by Kate's mom and nan. The food is utterly delicious and serves to remind me it's been a long time since I last celebrated Christmas to this extent. Everyone is supremely happy to be together. The chatter around the table is only paused to take another mouthful of delicious food.

Mr. Summer asks Kate, "Did you find out any more information about what happened with *The Parkerville Project*? Any idea when the kids will go back to their regular homes?"

"Nope, nothing yet. Roman wasn't supposed to tell me anything. I doubt he's going to be able to keep me updated, even though I asked him to." She sighs, her shoulders slumping in defeat. "I feel terrible for the kids. They've had enough upheaval in their lives. They didn't need this."

Mrs. Summer finishes chewing the food in her mouth. "Yes,

those poor darlings. I wish we had enough room for them to come here. I would happily take those precious souls in."

I know she would in a heartbeat—she's deeply maternal. She's already made me feel remarkably welcome here, with minimal effort.

After our bellies are full of delicious food, we retire into the family room to exchange gifts. I'm shocked to discover they've included me in the gift exchange. I bought for Kate's family and Margie, but in no way expected to be receiving anything in return. I was very wrong. They've included me at every turn. I hope to be part of until my dying day.

Leaving Kate's place, I drive toward my sterile penthouse to get ready for my meeting with Samuel, the financial investigator Mike recommended. As I'm driving, I run through these last months with Kate. She's completely changed the way I feel and the way I think. I can't believe I ever thought 'a couple of nights' with her would be enough. I want to be a better man for her, be everything she needs me to be. Disappearing on her for days at a time is definitely unacceptable behavior, and won't ever happen again.

The realization dawns on me that Kate and I have only ever been out on a couple of dates—one of which ended in me punching her ex and her in tears. I need to rectify the situation because she deserves the world.

My meeting with Samuel takes longer than expected. I walk him through my discoveries and my suspicions of Errol, the finance officer at *The Parkerville Project*. He looks through the files and notes I've made, then explains his process for tracking the culprit. He's concerned Errol may have already attempted to cover his tracks as soon as we made the discovery.

He's reasonably confident he can trace the money to the

source, finding the proof we need to have Errol arrested, and a conviction made. We only have a slim chance of getting the money back. The theft needs to be proven, and the money also needs to still be in the accounts. Jase works diligently, making copies of the files and notes Samuel will need to work through the investigation. As he leaves, he promises to be in touch early next week.

I spend the next hour organizing a surprise weekend away, down the coast, for Kate and me. I'm assuming she won't be seeing the kids any time soon, as her usual volunteering is on hold at this point. This may help take Kate's mind off of missing them. Once I've got everything squared away, I send her a text.

Me: I've got a surprise for you

It takes a few minutes to receive a response from her and I'm impatient for her response. I can't contain my excitement for her reaction.

Sunshine: Oh yeah
Sunshine: Will I like it?
Me: Of course you will
Me: Pack a weekend bag
Sunshine: What? Why?
Me: We're going down the coast for the weekend
Me: Don't worry, I'll have you back in time for your family dinner on Sunday night

Those annoying dots bounce on my screen, then stop, then start again. This doesn't seem like a good sign. My phone rings and her stunning smile lights up the screen.

"Hey, Sunshine."

"Are you serious? A weekend on the coast?"

She must be excited because she didn't even bother to say 'hi'.

"Yeah, I am. I figured you're probably free, and I missed you terribly on the days I had to work. I also realized on the way to my place this morning, we've only ever been on a couple of dates, and that's not good enough."

I'm holding my breath, hoping for a positive response.

She sighs. "Yeah, I'm definitely free this weekend because of what's happened." She still sounds heartbroken. "I would love to spend the weekend on the coast with you. Even though it's way too cold to go into the water, we can still have a wonderful time."

The breath I was holding in anticipation of her response, releases. "Yeah?"

"Yeah," she whispers. "I think it's just what I need to take my mind off of the kids', and it will also give *you* a break from working excessive hours. An extra bonus will be having you all to myself, totally uninterrupted. When do we leave?"

"It's only an hour's drive from your place. I'll pick you up around four. Be ready."

"Oh, I will be."

She squeals as she disconnects the call. I guess she's happy about our little getaway—which was exactly what I was hoping.

I buzz Jase, explaining to him I'll be unreachable this weekend and my reason. I can hear his smirk through the phone when he responds with his typical, 'yes boss'—*smartass*.

I'm *never* unreachable. This is an extremely rare occasion. Kate's changing me in a great many ways.

I spend the rest of the day ensuring I've got everything ready for a hectic workload next week; I still need to catch up on what I've ignored these past few days while dealing with the shit show that was *The Parkerville Project*, as well as the Christmas break. Heading upstairs to my penthouse to pack myself a weekend bag, I mentally plan what I'll need to take with me—not that we'll be needing too many clothes for what I have planned. I do, however, want to take Kate on at least one or two outings. I pack the photo I found of Kate, Toby, and me sitting on her parents' couch. It's time I opened up to her. This weekend will be the perfect opportunity to do so.

The drive to Kate's is frustrating—traffic is a fucking nightmare to get out of the city center at this time of day. The city always seems to have road closures happening at all hours of the day and night, exacerbating the problem. I arrive at ten past four, aggravated at being late. She must have been watching for me because she comes out her front door, beaming while dragging her duffel down the steps. The moment is reminiscent of the first time I laid eyes on her. I quickly exit my car to help with her bag, taking it from her as I steal a gentle taste of her lips. Once her bag is situated, she locks up, saying goodbye to Margie. We're on our way out of the city, toward our weekend getaway destination. My shoulders relax as I place my hand on Kate's shapely, jean-clad thigh.

I glance over. Kate's worrying her bottom lip. She doesn't look quite as relaxed as I feel, and I get the sense something's bothering her.

"Everything okay over there?" I ask, keeping my eyes on the road.

From my periphery, I see her look over at me. "Uhm. I'm not sure how to say this, so I'll just say it." She sighs and takes a deep breath. "I was so excited when I spoke to you earlier that I agreed to this getaway without thinking about how I'm going to pay my half of all the expenses. You're always spending your money on me, and I don't want to take advantage of your generosity. I feel as though I'm unable to reciprocate fairly."

I squeeze her thigh. "Don't even give it a second thought. I invited you away, which means I expect to cover all expenses for this weekend. Please don't worry about money, I've got it covered. It' won't break the bank. Truly."

I smile at her, squeezing her thigh again, hoping to ease her concerns. I need to lighten the mood. "So, did you pack anything sexy?"

She laughs and her shoulders relax; I've achieved my goal.

"I'm not sure I even own anything sexy, to be honest. Trust you to be thinking about that stuff." She rolls her eyes.

"I'm a man and you're a beautiful woman. I'm always thinking about that 'stuff' where you're concerned. Are you saying you don't think about that 'stuff'?" I scoff. I'm offended if that's the case.

"Of course I do. I'm just not as direct about it as you are."

Well, that makes me feel marginally better. The drive down the coast continues with general small talk about the scenery and what she would like to achieve next week before she returns to work.

We finally pull up to the property I've rented for the weekend, and it's as impressive in real life as it was in the photographs I saw online. I'm surprised it was available at such short notice, but I guess not everyone wants to be on the coast during winter. Kate's eyes are wide in surprise as her jaw drops. She seems impressed with the property.

With wide, excited eyes, she turns to me. "This is where we're staying?"

I nod. "Yep. This okay? I didn't want to stay in a hotel. This felt more … private." There were other, more spectacular properties, but I didn't want to overwhelm her.

"Oh my gosh, I can't believe you even have to ask. I've seen places like this on TV or online, but never in real life."

She leans over, wrapping her arms around my neck, awkwardly pulling me down toward her for a kiss full of joy and gratitude. We eventually separate to exit my car, collect our bags, and make our way to the front door. The butler, who will look after us this weekend, already has the door open in welcome.

"Good afternoon, Mr. Stone, Ms. Summer. I'm Gerald. I'll be looking after you this weekend. Please allow me to take your bags and show you around the property."

THIRTY-EIGHT

-kate-

I CAN ONLY GAPE. *A FREAKING BUTLER!*

This is unreal, and so far removed from my life experiences to date. I glance at Oliver, checking this is real, but he's taking it all in stride as if he does this sort of thing every day. We enter the spectacular steel blue and white weatherboard home to a massive open-plan living area with high-vaulted ceilings. The flooring is light bamboo, making the space feel even larger. The few walls are pale gray, with enormous windows across the entire back of the space. I can't help but be drawn to them, admiring the spectacular view of the breathtaking, white, sandy beach below.

I turn around to find Oliver watching me, almost as if he's waiting for my approval. I walk back to him, wrapping my arms around his torso and kissing his bristly chin. "This is out-of-this-world phenomenal. I've got to be the luckiest woman around. Thank you for organizing this awesome place for us to stay this weekend."

I press up on my toes to kiss his full lips, meaning for a gentle touch, but Oliver takes over, deepening the kiss, making it almost obscene. I sense Gerald in the room and reluctantly pull away.

Oliver winks at me, wrapping his arm around my shoulder, turning us toward our butler—*our own freaking butler!*

As Gerald shows us around the property, we learn that the glass doors across the back of the house can be opened fully and hidden inside the outside walls—which would make it feel like we're outside. If the weather was warmer, I'd have those doors tucked away the whole time we were here. As we step out of the master bedroom, a hot tub is situated on an enormous covered outdoor wooden deck, which is bigger than my entire house. Oliver tells me he has plans for me and that hot tub later—my lady parts cheer in excitement—I can't wait! The master bathroom boasts the most glorious shower, which has shower heads coming from all directions. But it's the bath that catches and holds my attention. I'd say five people could fit in that tub, and I'm dying to drop into the warm water with my man. The property has a tennis court, as well as a private limestone pathway, which takes us down to our very own private beach, complete with a stone fire pit. Gerald leaves us alone after telling us dinner will be served on the outside deck at seven.

We leave our bags and put on our coats, deciding to navigate the pathway to investigate our very own private beach—*even if it is only for the weekend.* Holding hands, we make our way down the winding limestone path until we hit the white sandy beach. The sun is sitting low on the horizon, bright orange and red hues fighting to be the last vestiges of light. It won't be long before they lose their battle, and it becomes dark. The wind carries the smell of salt off the water and the air is decidedly cold. I snuggle closer to Oliver, taking advantage of his size and warmth to protect me against the chilly wind coming off the bluest water.

With his front to my back, he wraps both arms around me, kissing the top of my head. "I love the beach. I never got to spend time here growing up. When I have any spare weekends, I occasionally choose to escape to the coast."

I suck in a breath because it's the first piece of information he's shared with me about his childhood. I want to bombard him with questions, but I don't want to push him on a topic I sense is difficult for him. "I can see the appeal. It's truly special here; relaxing and peaceful. We're never going to want to leave this place," I whisper.

He tightens his hold and we both spend quiet moments looking out at the water, our toes buried in the cold, soft sand, as the sun drops below the horizon. The sunset is almost as magnificent as the man holding me, as though he's never going to let me go.

I hope he never wants to let go.

We meander up to the house, guided by the solar lights along the pathway, and wash up ready for dinner on the enclosed portion of the back deck. A toasty fire, situated to warm inside as well as the area out here, is making the space cozy.

Gerald, did I mention we have a freaking butler, brings out wine, crusty bread, and a large bowl full of seafood arrabiata—*yum.* Perfect for our current location. Over dinner and a couple of glasses of wine, we talk about what it would be like to live on the coast as a local, as opposed to being a tourist. It sounds to me as if Oliver would love to live on the coast and simplify his life.

THIRTY-NINE

-oliver-

I WANT TO OPEN UP TO KATE TONIGHT AND SHARE MY CHILDHOOD, but I'm unsure where to begin, or even if it's appropriate at this point in our relationship. I'm sitting in the hot tub, waiting for her to join me, lost in my head, when I hear the door open and close. She steps out in an olive-green bikini, and I almost swallow my tongue. Those tiny triangles on her tits barely cover her nipples, and the triangle at the apex of her thighs is not much bigger. Her silky fiery-colored hair is twisted up in some type of knot on top of her head, leaving her smooth neck and creamy shoulders exposed.

She walks toward me slowly. "I wasn't going to pack my bikini, because I figured it's too cold for swimming, but I'm glad I did."

Fuck!

She must wear that thing to the beach—*in public!*

Every asshole would be able to see her gorgeous body. "Turn around," I growl like a fucking Neanderthal. I'm going to have to find every asshole who's ever seen her in this bikini and cut their goddamn eyes out.

She stops up short. "Huh. Why?"

"Because I need to see everything every other asshole at the beach can see when you wear those tiny scraps of fabric that barely cover the essentials."

She laughs at me—*fucking laughs!* I don't see the fucking humor —at all.

"I said, turn around." I grit my teeth, my tone brooking no argument. "Now turn around, Kate. I need to see your lush ass."

She rolls her eyes at me but turns around. And yeah, it's as bad as I figured it would be. Those delectable ass cheeks of hers are almost on full display. I take deep, purposeful breaths to get myself under control.

"Get in here, Kate, before I smack that luscious ass for being on display."

She turns around, stepping into the tub while smiling and rolling her eyes at me. "You're a bit of a caveman sometimes. You know that—right?" She huffs out a laugh. "I'm only getting in the tub because I want to, and *not* because you told me."

"Only for you, Kate. You bring it out in me. From the very first moment I laid eyes on you, as you dragged that duffel behind you toward the school." I pull her in close, kissing her nose. "I've never felt this protective of anyone before. This is all new to me."

I feel the fight leave her, and her body softens into mine. I position her on my lap, her legs straddling mine. Grabbing her almost naked ass, I drag her into my body, taking her bottom lip in a gentle bite which quickly evolves into an unrestrained ravenous fucking of our mouths. She grinds her hot pussy against my thick cock, and I squeeze her ass, drawing her impossibly closer to my body. If I could drag her inside of me, I fucking would.

Guiding her hips back and forth, she rocks her soft pussy against my engorged cock, building the rhythm and intensifying the sensations. I pull my mouth away from hers to nudge her bikini top aside with my nose, freeing the globes and allowing me to suck on her luscious tits. Her sighs and moans spur me on, guiding her hips faster, sucking harder on her tits until she shudders in my arms on a long moan. She collapses forward, slumping into my body, tucking her face into my neck. She kisses and licks my pulse point gently, and I release a deep sigh of pure male satisfaction. I slowly glide my hands up and down her back until she collects herself. Raising her head, she looks between both my eyes and mouth.

"That was ..." She sighs. "I don't know. I'm lost for words. It keeps getting better and better between us."

I know exactly what she means. I'm still hard as a rock. I nuzzle into her neck, licking up toward her ear so I can nip the lobe. I move back to her jaw and kiss my way up to her mouth. I take her lips in a slow, luxurious exploration of her mouth. We kiss for what feels like hours, if not days. I could kiss her for eternity, and it still wouldn't be enough.

I reluctantly release her as she slowly pulls away. She shows me her fingers which look like prunes. "I think it's time to get out."

I nod, assisting her out of the hot tub, following close behind. Grabbing towels from the cupboard near the hot tub, we dry the excess water off and step inside to shower off the chemicals. We spend most of the night loving each other's bodies in between brief bouts of sleep.

FORTY

-kate-

I'M LAYING ON MY TUMMY WHEN I WAKE TO OLIVER'S FINGERS slipping inside my body; my body reacts immediately, my hips bucking with his rhythm. He slides my leg upwards to open me to him, then positions himself over my back and slowly glides his dick through my folds and into my pussy. We both groan at the sensation and meet in a slow, languid kiss. My body heats; tingles beginning to spread through my limbs.

"Morning, Sunshine." His kisses linger on my neck. "Hope you don't mind me starting without you."

"Why would I mind when I have this to wake up to?" I push my hips back, meeting his leisurely thrusts. "Be my guest to wake me up like this any time."

He slowly rocks into my body, maintaining solid eye contact. "I love being inside you. It's my favorite place to be. You feel too fucking good squeezing around my cock. We were made to fit together like this."

His thrusts increase in speed and power, as his hand slides under my body to tease my aching clit. All I can do is moan, begging him not to stop; I'm incapable of anything else when he's inside me. It doesn't take long and I'm exploding, coming on a loud moan, which

I couldn't hold inside if I tried. Oliver's dick pulses and he follows with his own orgasm. Sharing this level of intimacy with him is completely intoxicating.

What a way to start the day.

"Yeah, I agree. What a way to start the day."

Oops, I must have said that out loud. Without leaving my body, he rolls us to the side, holding me to him as we catch our breath.

"How did you sleep?" he whispers, carefully sliding out of my body.

"Well, there wasn't much sleep to be had, because someone kept waking me up throughout the night." Not that I'm complaining, but I'm not sure my legs are going to function today.

"Oh yeah? I don't remember hearing any complaints. A lot of moaning, and 'harder', and 'don't stop' though." He's got a huge smile on his face, while his mossy-colored eyes twinkle with mischief.

Oh my gosh, there goes my blush. I hate having such a fair complexion.

"And there's that stunning blush I adore."

"Oh, stop it! You're not being fair."

"Pretty sure I was being fair last night. I'm reasonably certain you got two orgasms to my one every time." He's laughing as if he's told the greatest joke ever, as he jumps out of bed to avoid my playful swing.

We spend most of the day relaxing around the house, playing tennis, walking along the beach, and lazing on the back deck while being spoiled with a delicious breakfast, lunch, and snacks in between. Oliver's organized a sunset cruise with dinner on a yacht tonight, which sounds divine. I can't believe I'm having this experience with him. I keep having to pinch myself to confirm this is all real.

Walking toward the pier, I spot a magnificent yacht with an enormous mast docked at the end. As we stroll along the pier, with my hand securely in Oliver's, I realize we're heading for the yacht I saw from the parking lot.

Wow, this can't be my life right now—it feels like a dream.

I glance up at Oliver to find he's watching me, perhaps waiting for my reaction. My eyes must be as wide as saucers. "Is this the yacht for our sunset cruise?" He nods. "It's amazing. You're spoiling me beyond my wildest dreams."

I throw my arms around his neck to lay a smacking kiss on his lips. It was meant to be a quick peck, but Oliver takes over. He grabs my butt and pulls me tight to his body, making the kiss totally indecent for public consumption. Eventually, he pulls away from me, leaving me breathless and dizzy.

He looks into my eyes. "You deserve the best of everything, Sunshine. I'm going to give it all to you," he whispers.

"Oh Oliver, all I need is you. Nothing else. Just you."

His steps stutter a moment as he gives me a slow nod. Dragging me to the end of the pier, we board the yacht on steroids. After a tour of the decadent water vessel, which leaves me speechless, the crew set about departing the pier and cruising out to sea.

We wander up on deck, wrapped in our warmest clothes, to appreciate the magnificent view. Even though the sun is shining, the wind is cold on my face. The crew meets our every need, barely allowing our glasses to empty.

As afternoon turns into evening, Oliver and I move inside to get out of the cold and partake in a divine seafood feast. With full bellies and glasses of wine, Oliver begins to share stories about his childhood. My relief is palpable, as he hasn't told me much about himself before this and I was worried he never would. However, my relief is short-lived as he recounts the night that changed his life forever. I rise out of my chair to settle beside him in his, wrapping my arms around him, offering the only comfort I can give him.

He's lost to his memories. The vacant look in his eyes tells me he's reliving the night the lost little boy learned his mom was never coming home to him—would never hold him, or kiss away his bumps and bruises. The little boy who just wanted his mom to hold him and tell him everything would be okay. Even though his dad survived the crash, he also lost him that night. Tears track down my cheeks. I don't want to wipe them away and possibly cue Oliver into my heartache for him, because I sense that's the last thing he wants from me.

I feel closer to him at this moment than any other moment we've shared over the past few months. He's finally let me in. Allowed me to see who he really is, and what shaped him to be the man he is today. He tells me about how *The Parkerville Project* gave him a place to stay before being placed with his first foster family, and in between subsequent families, I understand why he was volunteering at the renovation project where we reconnected. He wants to give back to the organization, which helped him when there was nobody else.

My heart breaks for this man, who missed out on so much love during his formative childhood and teenage years. No wonder he closed himself off, concentrating on his work, to the exclusion of people.

He glances at me and then back at his hands. "There's one more thing." He pulls out an old photograph, studying it silently for a few moments. "I'm the boy who stayed with you. I'm Oliver from the photo on your mantel." He passes the photograph to me and I draw in a sharp breath as my eyes land on the familiar couch with a young Oliver holding me while Toby sits next to us. The photo must have been one of several shot that day, because everything's the same. The look on Oliver's face, as he looks down at me as a baby, reminds me of how he looks at me now.

I glance up at him. *He* was the boy who stayed with us for two weeks. *He* was the boy who apparently doted on me and only smiled when he was with me. It somewhat explains our immediate connection. It's as though we were always destined to be together.

"I can't believe it. Mom and Dad are going to be so surprised."

"Do you think so?"

I nod. "Absolutely." My mind races with the possibilities of 'what if?'.

What if he had always lived with us?

What if my parents had adopted him?

What if he'd never come to live with us?

What if we'd never met again?

My thoughts whirl as we sit quietly in our cocoon, watching the dark waves behind the yacht as we sail toward the pier to disembark.

In bed, our bodies come together. Our mouths, hands, and limbs entwined in a way that somehow feels deeper and more connected than we've been before. A level of trust has settled between us, giving me a sense of comfort and a feeling of home. Lord help me, but I love this man—this complicated, overwhelming, intense, magnificent man. It's in this moment I realize that I've become comfortable with him. No longer fearing that he'll leave me for someone prettier or more interesting.

Oliver surprises me by organizing a visit to the artisan markets which are set up along the pier we visited yesterday. It's got a different vibe today, with an eclectic array of items being made for sale in front of us. A young woman, in her late teens, is making a pair of stunning rose gold earrings, with delicate rose quartz heart inlays. I notice she has a matching necklace, which she must have finished before beginning the earrings. I'm tempted to purchase the set, but it's not in the budget for me. I'm careful not to show too much interest because I don't want Oliver to spend any more money on me this weekend. It's ridiculous how much he must have paid for the accommodation and the yacht yesterday, not to mention having a butler at our beck and call.

We keep moving along, observing an older lady making the most intricate lace dress overlay I've ever seen, and a man blowing glass to create a unique set of wine goblets. Loads of people with enormous talent.

I drag Oliver toward a woman about my age, making homemade ice cream. We end up in an argument because I want to pay. I eventually win, and we enjoy the tasty treat as we continue exploring the various stalls. We spend hours wandering through the maze of stalls and displays, stopping to chat with the crafters about their products and praising their talents.

I excuse myself to the restroom. When I return, I find Oliver speaking with the jeweler who was making the earrings I was admiring. I see him slip her something with a nod and a smile. He says something to her, then makes his way toward me. She waves to me with a grin and then strolls off toward her stall.

"Are you ready to leave? We need to get on the road if we're going to get you home in time for dinner with your family."

"Yeah, sure. I didn't realize how late it was." I stop to face him directly. "I had the best weekend with you. Thank you for spoiling me." I pause, looking into his glittering green eyes. "And thank you for sharing your story with me. I know it wouldn't have been easy, but I appreciate you trusting me." He seems lighter today, not as bogged down.

I press up on my tiptoes, kissing his lips gently with gratitude. He kisses my forehead, giving me a stiff nod. The tick in his jaw reminds me it's a difficult topic for him. Placing his hand at the small of my back, he guides me to the entrance of the markets.

We make our way back to the house to pack our belongings. It doesn't take long and we're on the road, heading back to the city. As we get closer, I can't bear to let him go. Without thinking of the repercussions, I blurt, "Do you want to come to dinner with my family tonight? We could tell Mom and Dad who you are. I know Mom will be relieved to learn you're okay after all these years."

Even though I surprised myself with the invitation, I don't want to rescind it. I want him there with me. It's not like he hasn't joined our family for dinner before, but now I want him to come to *every* family dinner.

He glances across to me, eyes crinkled at the corners, lips spread wide. "I'd love to. How do you think your parents will take the news?"

"I think they'll be over the moon. You know you're always welcome. Mom always makes enough food for an army—it won't be any trouble."

Mom's always made it a point to have more than enough food, just in case we want to invite any friends over. It's a sort of open-house policy where our friends are concerned. "I'll message her to let her know Oliver's coming to dinner."

Me: Hi Mom
Me: Is it okay if Oliver comes over for dinner?
Mom: Of course it's okay
Mom: Oliver's always welcome here
Mom: Especially now he's your b-o-y-f-r-i-e-n-d
Me: Mom!! *eye roll emoji*

I sigh, rolling my eyes. Oliver notices, looking at me quizzically.
"I think Mom's excited you're my boyfriend."
He chuckles light-heartedly and lays his hand on my thigh.

Dinner is a quiet affair; Mom, Dad, Oliver, and me. Which works perfectly for the news Oliver has to share. I can tell he's nervous, so I'm doing everything I can think of to calm his nerves. I stay close, offering him small smiles and gentle touches. I hope he knows I'm here for him.

As we eat dinner, I take the first step for him. "Mom. Dad. Oliver has something he would like to tell you both."

He looks across at me, full of anxiety. I nod, letting him know it's okay, while smoothing my hand up and down his back, attempting to soothe him.

Clearing his throat, he begins his story.

By the time he's shown his photograph to my parents and told them his story, we're all in tears. Mom hops up from her chair, pulling Oliver up into the tightest hug I think I've ever seen. Even Dad joins in.

"I'm not sure how I came to live with you or why I left. I'm hoping you can fill in the blanks for me."

Dad clears his throat, clearly emotional. "Uh, well, my friend was working as a counselor for the Department of Children's Services when your case came across his desk. They only needed something short term for you until your father was released from the hospital. He asked me if Emily and I would be willing to look after you until your father was well enough to be released."

Mom takes over. "We fell in love with you immediately. You were such a sad, lost little boy. You had lost more than anyone ever should. Kate seemed to have a special place in your heart—the way you constantly doted on her. It was truly special to watch your sadness vanish when you were with her."

"After I left here, I was taken to a house which was part of *The Parkerville Project*. My father was arrested and eventually sent to prison for drunk driving, causing death. I never lived with him again." Oliver shares.

My mom gasps, holding her hands to her throat. "Oh no! Why didn't they bring you back here? I don't understand." She looks across to Dad. "We would have kept you as part of our family. We would have loved you and given you a solid family."

I think Oliver needed to hear that. His posture relaxes significantly as his face smooths out. Somehow finding peace knowing that he *was* wanted.

FORTY-ONE

-oliver-

THIS WEEK IS GOING TO BE A FUCKING NIGHTMARE. I NEED TO CATCH up on what I missed last week, in addition to staying on top of the situation for *The Parkerville Project*. My *CornerStone Foundation* can't even step in to help financially for the next two quarters, as we have already designated those funds for the *Schools for Everyone* project. I wish I had enough money available to help both organizations simultaneously, but I still have a company to run with employees to pay. I call Jase into my office to run through my schedule and plan for *The Parkerville Project* meeting on Friday for any interested parties.

After we've finished going over everything work-related, Jase lingers with a smirk on his face. "So, how was the weekend away?"

I lean back in my chair. "It was the best weekend I've had in living memory."

Jase's eyes widen as his smirk becomes a full-blown smile. "That's great news, Oliver. I'm genuinely happy for you, man. I don't suppose she has a sister?"

I laugh, typical Jase. "Uh, that would be no. Only Toby. Hey, did you recognize him—Toby Summer?"

"Yeah. He's been singing up a storm for several years now. I did my best not to go all fangirl over him because I'm sure he gets tired of it."

"Huh. It was just me then. I didn't make the connection until I was explicitly told at Thanksgiving dinner with Kate's family. I feel like a dick now."

"Nothing new there, you are a dick." He laughs as he rises from the chair to leave.

"Fuck off, asshole. Get to work or I'll dock your pay!" I laugh, turning back to my computer, but not before I notice him giving me the bird over his shoulder. I'm lighter today. My weekend with Kate was exactly what I needed. Sharing my story with her and her parents lifted a burden off my shoulders I hadn't realized I was carrying. Knowing they didn't give me up, that they would have kept me settled a part of my soul that's always felt fractured. Yes. The weekend was the best I've had in living memory.

I get stuck into catching up on emails, phone calls, and reports needing to be finalized for our current clients. Even though I've got a lot on my plate at the moment, thoughts of Kate constantly invade my mind. Of wrapping her up in my arms, and the way our bodies fit perfectly together.

Over the next few days, I work with dogged determination to catch up and get on top of everything that needs to be done. By midweek, I'm thinking I need to chase up Samuel. I need to know how he's progressing with the investigation. It would be much better if we had more information for the meeting we have planned on Friday.

I buzz Jase. "Can you get hold of Samuel for me? I need an update."

As I'm on the line, I hear Jase's other line buzz, so he disconnects our call. When he buzzes me, he announces Samuel's on line one for me. Well, that's good timing. I press the line and answer. "Hello Samuel, what do you have for me?"

"Well, I traced the money and offshore accounts. Your suspicions were correct. It was Errol. I've contacted the FBI, the SEC,

CFTC, and other necessary authorities. They'll be moving in to arrest him with an appropriate search warrant this afternoon. They want to ensure the case is as watertight as possible to reduce any chance of him escaping prison time. They're also working to increase the chances of *The Parkerville Project* getting as much of their money back as they possibly can."

Well, that's a relief. "Thanks. That's good news for us."

"No problem. It was a straightforward process for me. You had already done most of the work to find the money. I'll continue working with the authorities until they no longer need my input."

"Sure. Let me know if there's anything further I can do to help the process along."

"I'm sure the FBI and other agencies will need to speak with you and Marcus at some stage."

"Of course. I wouldn't expect anything different. Thank you for everything, Samuel. I'll speak to you soon."

"No problem. Bye for now."

Disconnecting the call, I wipe my hands down my face. When I look up, Jase is standing in the doorway, waiting to hear the latest update.

"They got him. It *was* Errol. The FBI is arresting him this afternoon."

The relief is overwhelming, and suddenly, my body sags with exhaustion. I didn't realize the toll this issue was taking on me. My shoulders release and some of the built-up tension leaves my body.

"That's great news. Do you want me to get Marcus on the line for you? You can give him an update."

"Yeah, thanks, Jase." He nods, stepping out to organize the call.

I spend the next fifteen minutes on the phone with Marcus relaying the information I received and finalizing plans for the Friday meeting. I'm pleased that we have more information to give to the interested parties. I speak to the bank, which holds the mortgages to the properties, informing them of the situation. Unfortunately, the situation from their end remains unchanged. We have ninety days to come up with the remainder of the mortgage, or we lose all the properties under *The Parkerville Project* umbrella.

FORTY-TWO

-kate-

OVER THIS PAST WEEK, I'VE CAUGHT UP ON MY CHORES AROUND MY little house, worked in the garden, prepared my program for the next term, and prepped my activities for the first two weeks back. Today I'm going to treat myself to brunch out with my colleague and friend, Emma. She's ten years older than me and has two sons who are at school, one of whom is in my class. She left the corporate world when she gave birth to her oldest boy, Lachlan, to be a stay-at-home mom. Before her youngest son, Austin, was born, she decided to become a teacher. She wanted to be available for her kids before and after school and during school vacation. Her husband left her because he felt she wasn't the same person he'd married, and decided the two boys—particularly Lachlan—were too much trouble. He wanted a corporate wife and the life that goes along with that—*asshole!* The boys are with Emma's parents today, giving Emma some time for herself.

I'm sitting in a booth near the window, inside our favorite catch-up spot, when she enters. She has the biggest grin and looks pleasantly relaxed. We hug in greeting and then get to the important business of ordering our coffee and cake. We catch each other up on our Christmas vacation shenanigans. When I tell her about what happened to the kids I volunteer with, she's visibly upset, offering to help in any way she can. I go on to tell her about my weekend away with Oliver, and she's genuinely happy for me that things are going along smoothly.

"So, have you done the obligatory social media search on him yet?"

She's big into social media. Me, not so much. I've always been a pretty private person—the appeal isn't there for me. I've learned from Toby that social media isn't all it's cracked up to be.

"Uh, no. You know I'm not into all that stuff." I wave her suggestion off.

"Geez girl, I think you're the only twenty-something I know that isn't all over social media. I can look him up if you like?" She gets out her phone, ready to search like the skilled social media stalker she is.

I laugh and wave her off. "No, it's okay. I'd prefer to learn all about him from him, rather than a third party. Thanks for the offer, though."

She shrugs carelessly, tapping her phone. "That's okay. If you change your mind, you know where to come." She finishes her sentence with a saucy wink.

We say our goodbyes because Emma needs to run a few errands before picking up her boys. I meander to the park across the street to take a stroll on this cold, but sunny afternoon. I visit the market to purchase the ingredients to make Nan's famous chili because Oliver said he's attempting to make it to my place in time for dinner tonight. He's been working late every day, catching up on the work he missed because of Christmas and the big drama that happened. After the market, I drive home to prepare dinner. I also need to work out if I have anything sexy enough to wear as a special treat to seduce my sexy boyfriend.

After spending twenty minutes rifling through my cupboard and drawers, I come up with my cute herringbone skater skirt, and a gray crossover top, leaving my midriff bare. I wear my red Converse that Oliver bought for me, and dry my hair in loose waves down my back. The chili is almost ready when I hear Oliver come through the front door, dropping his keys on the table where I usually leave mine. He spends most of his time here. It's almost like we're living together. His footsteps come closer and I prepare myself for seeing him in his suit—*so hot!*

He stops in my bedroom doorway, rolling up his shirt-sleeves; he must have already relieved himself of his jacket and tie in the living room.

Mmhm, those forearms.

His eyes trace up and down slowly, from the top of my head to the tips of my toes, raising his eyebrows and smirking. I'm checking him out too, pausing on the zipper of his pants, which appears to be growing before my very eyes—*oh my.*

Yes, please.

Licking my lips, I continue trailing my way up his torso until I get to his face. His smirk is gone, replaced with a hungry look that makes my panties wet and thighs clench. He leaves the room, confusing me with his sudden departure. After about thirty seconds, he returns, making a beeline straight for me. Crowding my space, he presses his body tight against mine. One hand lands on my hip while the other goes to the back of my head, underneath my hair, holding me in place.

"Hey," he whispers against my mouth.

"Hey."

His mouth crashes down on mine, his tongue parting my lips to make its way inside. His kisses make me dizzy and incoherent. All I can do is hold on for his delicious assault. Warmth spreads throughout my body, my sex softening in preparation. Wrapping my arms around his neck, I pull him in as close as possible. He slides the hand at my hip down to the back of my thigh, which he smoothly lifts, wrapping my leg around his hip. This close, I can't miss the unmistakable erection filling his trousers. His other hand smooths down my back to my butt, raising my other leg, lifting me completely off the floor, and locking me in position at his waist. I love this show of pure masculine strength. It's such a freaking turn on.

He takes the few steps required to get to my bed, sitting on the edge with me wrapped around him. He slows the kiss, moving to lick and kiss along my jawline, up to my ear. "You look sexier than sexy in this getup, which means you can never wear it in public," he whispers.

I pull back, searching his face. I can't tell if he's joking, or if he's serious. His face looks serious, which suggests he means what he's saying.

"Tell me you're joking." I pause, waiting for him to confirm that he is, indeed, joking, but he appears to be standing firm. "You can't be serious. You can't possibly think I'll be okay with you telling me what I can and cannot wear when I go out in public. I thought you were messing around with the bikini comments, but I'm starting to think you weren't joking at all."

He shrugs his shoulder, looking me dead in the eye. "I'm deadly serious. You're mine. That means nobody gets to see how sexy you are, except for me."

Uh, I don't think so big guy.

I push away from him, or at least I try to push away from him, but he has a vise grip on me which isn't allowing any leeway.

"I'm not the kind of girl guys look at and think, 'hey, she's sexy'. I'm also not the kind of girl who goes around flaunting her body. I never pair these items together, but I thought I would *attempt* to look sexy for you tonight. I wasn't sure I could pull it off until you looked at me and went all caveman." His clenched jaw is crazy tight as he huffs out a breath, but I place my fingers over his lips to stop him from speaking. "Oliver, you have nothing to worry about. When I'm out in public, I'm quite a conservative dresser."

He's still trying to interrupt me, so I press my fingers harder against his lips, shaking my head. "But, it *is* my choice what I wear. I won't have you, or anyone else, tell me what I can and can't wear. I make my own choices. If I want to walk down the street in a negligee and hooker heels, then that's what I'll damn well do, and you won't be able to stop me. Understood?"

I remove my fingers, allowing him to speak.

He shakes his head. "Sunshine. You have no idea how strikingly gorgeous you are."

Now it's my turn to shake my head. "You make me feel beautiful, but I was never beautiful enough to keep a boyfriend before. I'm still waiting for you to wake up and notice I'm not all that." Even though I'm feeling more confident in myself and haven't felt the worry I originally did since dating Oliver, the thought of him leaving me for someone more attractive sneaks up on me now and then. Not that he gives me any reason to feel insecure. Quite the opposite. He makes me feel completely secure and adored. I look down at our laps because I can't bring myself to see the pity in his eyes.

Using his finger, he raises my chin. "That's on them, Kate. If they were too stupid to see what was in front of them, then they weren't the right person for you. And, quite frankly, I'm ecstatic they didn't, or I wouldn't be here with you now." He kisses the tip of my nose. "I'll attempt to tone down my caveman tendencies, but I can't make promises. I want to keep you all to myself. I'm not good at sharing."

I nod. "I'm guessing that's as good as I'm going to get from you." I give him a small smile. "It's not like you're ever going to have to share. I'm not *that* girl. I won't ever stray. Just keep it in check, okay?"

He nods at me, kissing my forehead.

"C'mon, let's have dinner before it burns. I cooked Nan's chili."

Kissing the tip of my nose, he releases me to stand on my own feet. Grasping his hand, I drag him through to my kitchen, where I see the burner has already been turned off.

"I turned it off because I thought we'd be busy for a while." He shrugs, giving me a boyish smile. "I didn't want all of your hard work to go to waste."

Probably a good idea too, because we were seriously distracted there for a bit. I serve up two bowls and we move to my small dining table to eat and chat about our day. Oliver tells me he's getting on

top of his work. He's also happy with the preparations for an important meeting tomorrow morning.

After dinner, we clean up and move to the couch, each with a
glass of wine to wind down from the day. We turn in for the night,
picking up from where we left off before dinner.

Even before I open my eyes, I immediately know I'm on my own. I
sense he's already left to start his day. I roll over to my bedside cabi-
net, grabbing my phone to check the time. It's after eight, which
surprises me. I rarely sleep this late, but we were up half the night,
loving each other's bodies.

I have a missed call from Roman. That must have been what
woke me up. Maybe I can see the kids. I quickly press the icon to
return his call.

"Hi, Kate, thanks for calling me back." Roman sounds frazzled.

"No problem. Have there been any fresh developments? Can I
see the kids?"

"Sort of. Look, I was supposed to go into a meeting today to
get an update on what's happening, but I can't go. Evelyn's sick
and I don't feel right leaving her when she's feeling unwell." He
huffs out a sigh, and I visualize him running his hand through his
messy hair.

"I can come and look after her. That way you can go to the
meeting. I don't mind." I climb out of bed so I can get ready to go.

"Nah, you're back at school on Monday. I don't want you to get
ill. Can you go to the meeting on my behalf and then let me know
what's going on?"

"Uh sure. Will it be okay for me to go, since I'm not an
employee?"

"I'm pretty sure it'll be okay. It's a meeting for anyone who's
interested. Not just employees of *The Parkerville Project*. Would you
mind?"

"Not at all. I'll go, and then I'll call you to give you the
rundown. What time does it start?"

"Cool. Thanks, Kate. It starts at ten. I'll text you the address. I can't tell you how much I appreciate this."

"No worries. I better get moving. Tell Evelyn to get better soon. Talk later."

"Bye."

I end the call and immediately step into the bathroom to get ready. After my shower, I dress and check my phone for a text from Roman.

Roman: Thanks again Kate
Roman: The meeting is on the 38th floor of Stone Tower, 1151 Mayfield Ave in the city center
Me: No worries. Chat later

I'd better get moving, or I'll never make it in time. I grab my purse and keys and make my way into the city. While I'm on the bus, I figure I could meet Oliver for lunch, so I send him a message.

Me: Hey boyfriend, I'm coming into the city at the last minute. Want to meet for lunch?

He said he was going to be busy this morning. Hopefully, he'll see my message before lunchtime and respond. I step off the bus and make my way toward Mayfield Avenue. I don't come into the city often, so I use the map app on my phone. I'm surprised it works on my older model phone.

The building it directs me toward is completely different from all the other tall buildings around it. Slim gray bricks of different sizes and shades are stacked for the first three floors, and as I raise my head to look up at the structure, the bricks give way to stone, cut in slim lengths to form a chevron pattern for the rest of the tower. Above the archway for the main doors, is large stainless steel lettering spelling out STONE TOWER. The building is like nothing I've seen before and as much as I try, I can't see all the way to the top. I must remember to tell Oliver there's a building in the city with his name on it. That should give him quite the ego boost I expect, though he probably already knows about it since he works in the city.

I step into the lobby, which continues with the gray stone theme on the floors enhanced by stainless steel counters, behind which sits a very attractive woman. I step toward the counter to check the meeting is on the 38th floor.

The woman gives me a friendly smile. "Welcome to Stone Tower. Can I help you?"

"Hopefully. I'm here for a meeting about *The Parkerville Project*. I believe it's on the 38th floor, but I wanted to check." I tuck my hair behind my ear.

"Oh lucky you checked, it's actually on the 48th floor. Conference room five. You can take the elevator to the left. It will take you all the way up."

"Thanks. Have a great day." I smile, waving as I walk away.

"You, too."

I press the up button. Luckily, I checked. Maybe it was moved, or maybe Roman accidentally pressed the wrong number when he messaged me. I step into the elevator when it arrives and press the button for the 48th floor. The elevator is decadent, all mirrors and stainless steel, with a gray stone brick floor which matches the façade of the building. I arrive at the correct floor quickly and exit to find another desk.

The older lady behind the desk raises her head and smiles at me. "Can I help you?"

"I'm here for *The Parkerville Project* meeting in conference room five. I think I'm slightly early, but I didn't want to be late."

"Oh, of course. I always think it's better to be early than late. Please complete this sign-in sheet, and I'll show you through."

I write my details on the sheet, giving my name, contact email, and phone number. I see I'm the fifth person on the list. The woman then comes out from behind her desk to show me to the correct room.

"There's tea and coffee over on the side table. Help yourself to any of the pastries."

I make my way over to a chair in the back to drop off my purse.

Making myself a cup of coffee, I select a pastry, since I didn't eat breakfast in my rush to get here. The other attendees are milling about and chatting. I don't know anyone, so I keep to myself. I get comfortable in my chair tucked in the back corner and watch as more and more people arrive. The space becomes crowded, making it so I can no longer see the front of the room. That's okay, as long as I can hear what's being said.

Right at ten o'clock, a man clears his throat to gain everyone's attention. I set my phone to record the meeting, in case I miss anything important and Roman wants to hear what they said. I notice a message on my phone screen.

Big O: Hey Sunshine, I'd love to catch up for lunch
Big O: Where do you want to meet?

I'm unable to respond as the man introduces himself. "Good morning everyone, my name is Marcus Trainor, and I'm the CEO of *The Parkerville Project*. As you are aware, we are currently having some financial difficulties and decided to call this meeting to inform all interested parties about what's happening. First, I would like to thank Mr. Stone for allowing us the use of his building for this meeting. I would also like to take this opportunity to thank him for the major contribution his charitable foundation, *The CornerStone Foundation*," I've heard that name before, "has made to our project over the past many years. Without its ongoing support, *The Parkerville Project* would have closed its doors long ago. It was also Mr. Stone, who stepped in when the trouble first hit. He worked tirelessly to identify what had happened to the money, which was supposed to be paying our mortgages and wages for our paid staff." He pauses as a chair scrapes. "Without further ado, I would like to introduce Mr. Stone."

Everyone claps politely, then Mr. Stone clears his throat and speaks. "Thanks, Marcus, for your kind introduction." I know that voice; the deep, rich timbre, but in a different context. He continues. "It has been my pleasure to help *The Parkerville Project* over these past years." I suck in a breath, because Mr. Stone is *MY* Oliver. I can't hear anything else over the rush of blood to my ears. My breaths stall in my chest and I'm getting dizzy. All the noise and air has been sucked out of my space—I feel like I'm in a vacuum. Closing my eyes, my body shakes as a tremor moves through it. I can't believe I didn't put two and two together:

Stone Tower,

The CornerStone Foundation,

Mr. *Stone,*

Oliver *Stone—my boyfriend.*

I need to get out of here, but I don't want to make a scene, and I certainly don't want Oliver to know I'm here. I wait for my body to calm—taking deep, measured breaths—then I rise slowly from my seat and walking quietly toward the door. Luckily, I'm on the shorter side and the room is packed—he probably won't see me leave.

As I pass through the door frame, I glance up to find Jase's stunned face. He attempts to reach for me, but I move quickly past him, shaking my head. Making a beeline for the elevator, I struggle to keep my tears at bay. Thankfully, the car arrives quickly and I step inside, pressing the button to close the heavy doors. As the doors close, Jase is watching me with concern.

Maybe I should have taken Emma up on her offer to check on Oliver's social media. I'm such a fool.

What in the hell is he doing with someone like *me?*

He could have any woman on the planet.

I catch the bus home, put myself to bed, and sob my heart out until I fall into an exhausted sleep.

FORTY-THREE

-oliver-

THE MEETING COMES TO A CLOSE, AND AFTER A LONG DISCUSSION with Marcus, I make my way to my office. I'm about to sit down to check my phone to see if Kate's suggested a place to meet for lunch when Jase interrupts me by throwing a sheet of paper on my desk. He looks thunderous—anger is rolling off him in waves. I don't think I've ever seen him like this before.

"What's this? And what's up your ass?" I pick up the sheet of paper. It's the sign-in sheet for the meeting.

"Take a look at the names on the attendee list for the meeting. Then you tell me what's up my ass."

I scan the document and all the blood leaves my face. I look up to Jase, then back down at the page, hoping against all hope that I read the name in the fifth space incorrectly.

"Tell me it's not true. Kate was in that meeting?"

"Yep. But she left early, close to tears. I tried to stop her, but she brushed me off." He shakes his head, pacing in front of my desk with his hands on his hips. "You hadn't told her, had you? I told you to tell her, man. You fucked up. You fucked up big time."

I get up, tipping my chair over in the process, collecting my phone and keys, then stalk out of my office without a word.

I have to get to Kate.

I need to explain.

I have to fix this.

I can't lose her.

She's the best thing that's ever happened to me.

With city traffic, it seems to take forever before I'm banging on Kate's door. I figure she wouldn't appreciate me letting myself in at this point. There's no response, so I bang harder, calling her name. Still no response. I decide to risk it and let myself in. I move through her silent home, walking from room to room, hoping she's here. I finally get to her bedroom and my heart shatters.

Pieces falling at my feet.

Leaving a bloody mess on her floor.

I did this to her.

She's curled up in the smallest ball in the middle of her bed, hiding under her blankets, and hugging the pillow I use. I take my shoes, jacket, and tie off, then climb in behind her slight form. Wrapping my arms around her, I endeavor to work out a way to make this better, but my mind isn't cooperating.

After several minutes, Kate begins to stir and I feel the moment she realizes she's not alone. I swallow hard and kiss the back of her head.

"Please let me explain," I whisper.

She shakes her head, attempting to extricate herself from my hold. "Please leave. I don't want you here. I don't even know you."

I tighten my hold. "You *do* know me, Kate. You know me better than anyone. I'm not leaving until you let me explain."

She starts to struggle against my hold, so I loosen my grip because I don't want her to hurt herself. She stands from the bed, brushing her tangled hair from her face. Her eyes, red and puffy, cause a fracture in my heart—I did this to her. I watch her steel herself, standing ramrod straight, looking me straight in the eye as I sit up.

"I said I want you to leave. I don't want you in my home. Please give me back my key and leave now, or I *will* call the police."

I can't believe she won't hear me out. "Please, Kate. It'll be okay. Let me explain."

"No!" she shouts, her face red with anger. Her small hands fisted at her sides. "Get out! I don't want you here. You're a stranger. I can't believe I let you into my life, my home, my family, and in my bed when I barely know you at all." She takes a deep breath. When I don't make a move, she screams, "Get out!" Her body shaking in rage. I stand because I don't want to make things worse. Grabbing my jacket, tie, and shoes, I remove her key from my chain, placing it on her table, then step toward the front door.

"I'm leaving. For now. I'll give you space, but I'm not letting you go, Kate. I told you, you won't be able to get rid of me even if *you* want to end this relationship, and I meant it."

I leave and close the door quietly behind me, ensuring it's locked.

Knocking on Margie's door, I ask her to watch over Kate for me, giving her my business card in case she needs anything. Climbing into my car, I drive back to my empty penthouse, feeling like the biggest piece of shit on the face of the earth.

I'm empty. My heart left in pieces on Kate's bedroom floor.

Pulling out a bottle of scotch and a glass, I pour myself a drink. After swallowing it down, feeling it burn, I decide to forfeit the glass, making myself comfortable on my couch with my new friend.

FORTY-FOUR

-kate-

I'M TRYING TO CALM MY BREATHING WHEN THERE'S A KNOCK AT MY front door. My temper rises again. Why can't he just leave? Leave me alone! "Go away!" I shout through the door.

"I'm not going anywhere, young lady. Now open this door, or I'll get my key and let myself in."

I quickly move to open the door in relief that it's not Oliver. There's also a minuscule amount of disappointment that he gave up so easily. I remind myself he was doing what I asked him to do.

Margie looks at me closely. "You look awful, Katie-girl. What happened?" She moves into me, wrapping her arms around my body in a fierce hug, hitting the back of my legs with her walking stick. The small amount of composure I had collected breaks apart and the tears start all over again. I'd have thought I would be too dehydrated to cry any more, but apparently, I have an endless supply of tears.

"Oh, Margie, I'm such an idiot. If there was a prize for the biggest idiot, I would take it out."

Margie guides me to my couch, then makes her way to my kitchen, making me a cup of tea. Tea fixes everything, according to

Margie. She's walking short distances without her cane already. She's truly astounding.

"You're not an idiot. Not at all. Now tell me, what has you in such a state, and poor Oliver looking like his puppy just died?" She pats my thigh, handing me my cup of tea.

"You saw Oliver?"

"He knocked on my door, asking me to keep an eye on you. He looked ... broken. Much the same as you do." She sighs. "You young people don't know a good thing when you've got it." She looks wistful, as though she's remembering her own good thing. "Tell me what happened, Katie-girl." Her voice is soft, coaxing.

Closing my eyes, I take a deep breath. "He's Oliver Stone. *The* Oliver Stone. He owns a freaking building in the city and has his own charitable foundation." I look at her puzzled face. "I had no idea who he was. I feel like such an idiot."

Margie still looks puzzled. "So? Who cares if he has a building and a charitable foundation? Why does it matter?"

"He lied to me. He told me he worked in corporate invest-ments." I huff. How can she not understand what this means?

"He *does* work in corporate investments. It says so right here on his business card."

She pulls a card out of her bra, handing it to me. Clear, bold text slaps me in the face:

I flip the card over to find his contact number and email. "Why do you have his business card?"

"He gave it to me in case I needed anything. Such a sweet boy." She takes the card from me, slipping it back into her bra as though it's a prized possession. "Now tell me why him owning a building and having a charitable foundation is such a problem?"

I turn my body to face Margie, thinking about how to explain it to her. "Maybe he didn't lie, as such, but he also wasn't completely honest with me. I already felt at a disadvantage in our relationship because of the way he looks as compared to the way I look." Margie tries to butt in, but I hold up my hand to stop her. "I had become comfortable with the idea that he was in this relationship for the long haul. That he wouldn't dump me in favor of someone prettier or more interesting. He ... he made me feel beautiful. I was starting to relax into our relationship. But now this." I slap my thighs. "He's obviously beyond wealthy, and that takes him way out of my league. I'm a kindergarten teacher struggling to pay off my mortgage and driving Nan's car. I buy the cheapest clothes I can find and get my hair cut once every six months to save money." I take a breath. "I wouldn't have any clue how to live in Oliver's world. Let alone keep a man like him interested in me long term." I wipe frantically at the tears streaming down my cheeks as Margie moves in to hold my body to hers in comfort.

This discovery has cut to the core of my past hurts. One of my previous boyfriends at college thought it was okay to be dating multiple women because he had money. He couldn't understand why I was upset about his philandering ways when I discovered his infidelity. He informed me that all wealthy men have a wife at home, and lovers on the side—it was almost expected of a man with a solid bank balance.

"My dear, dear girl. I've got a feeling that might be exactly the reason that boy withheld the information from you." She pulls back, looking at my face, wiping my tears away. "I also think that maybe, just maybe, he wanted to live in *your* world, not the other way around."

"He must have been having a good laugh at my expense. I was always telling him he's too frivolous with his spending, buying me coffee and pastry every day, as well as lunch. That weekend away seemed extravagant. While I was blown away by it all, Oliver looked so comfortable with the luxury and decadence of having a butler and a yacht with a full staff." I sniff, getting up to find my tissues to blow my nose and clean up my face.

"I doubt he was laughing. He probably thought it was refreshing. Can you imagine his life? I'm betting everyone around him wants something from him. But you only wanted him. Maybe that was what he was looking for? Don't be so hard on the boy. At least give him a chance to explain."

I nod, but I need some time to organize my thoughts and emotions. "I think I need some time to digest this new information."

"Fair enough. But don't take too long." She stands up. "I need to get back home. My show's about to start." I stand too. I hug Margie and walk her to the door. I watch her until she goes inside and I hear the locks engage, then I step inside to lock myself in for the night.

I check my phone, noticing I have a couple of missed calls from Roman. Shit, I completely forgot the reason I was in that meeting in the first place. I'll call him tomorrow. There are also several texts from Oliver.

Big O: I'm sorry Kate
Big O: I can explain everything
Big O: Please don't shut me out

I notice he didn't call me Sunshine. I can't blame him, since I was screaming at him to leave me alone the last time I saw him. Certainly not my finest moment. Turning my phone off, I decide to have a steaming hot shower, followed by a hot chocolate. Then I put myself to bed for the night.

Sleep is difficult to find—my bed feels terribly empty; blistering cold and lonely without Oliver here.

I must have fallen into a fitful sleep because I wake to banging on my door.

Looking out of my window, I find Oliver's car parked in my

driveway. I'm not ready to see him. I need some time, some space. I stomp to my front door and without opening it:

I tell him to go away.

To leave me alone.

To give me some space.

I hear a muffled, "I'm sorry, Kate." And a thud through the door, which triggers another stream of tears. He sounds achingly sad and defeated. I turn my back to the door, sliding down the wood until my butt hits the floor, waiting to hear his footsteps take him away. It takes what seems a million minutes until I hear him walk away and his car engine roar to life. I cover my face with my hands, letting the tears flow, expressing my heartbreak in the only way I can. Eventually, I pull myself together, deciding to go about my day as usual.

It's better this way.

Better that I leave him before he leaves me.

Not that it hurts any less.

As I'm going through the motions of my regular Saturday chores, my laptop is taunting me. It would be easy to type his name into the search bar—I do well to resist the temptation through most of the day.

I return Roman's call from yesterday, apologizing profusely for letting him down. I told him I became unwell in the meeting and had to leave. He was completely understanding, telling me there are a heap of illnesses circulating at the moment. He got the information from one of his colleagues who attended the meeting. Apparently, Oliver's the person who worked out what happened to the money. He's the one ensuring that a conviction is brought down on the perpetrator. I'm proud of him. He's been working hard to sort out the problem.

That must have been the work issue that caused him to disappear on me right before Christmas. Why didn't he tell me then? He could have easily explained that he was working to sort out the problem of the closures of *The Parkerville* properties.

After a dinner comprising toast, because my stomach is unsettled, I sit on my couch, attempting to read my latest book. I can't concentrate on the words on the page with all the confusion in my head. Looking across at my laptop, which has been taunting me all day, I chew on my thumbnail, debating whether to take a quick peek.

The laptop wins. I put my book down and pick it up, turn it on, and open my favored search engine. I type 'Oliver Stone' into the search bar and hit the return button. Instantly, the results load and at the top, it says: 'About 142,000,000 results (0.45 seconds)'. *Crap!*

The initial results are for Oliver Stone, the American film director, but as I scroll further down the page, there are some pages for my Oliver. I click to images and the screen fills with hundreds of images of him. Mostly in suits entering or exiting special events. He looks different, more stoic, less free. Scrolling through, there are several with extremely attractive women, lots and lots of different women. Each one is extremely pretty—model-worthy. There's quite a few of him with a petite blonde woman. I wonder if that's Sonia —if it is, she looks eerily similar to Crystal. The two of them look spectacular together. I feel like I'm going to be sick—my meager dinner fighting its way to the surface. Taking deep breaths, I manage to keep it at bay. Shifting back to the 'all' tab, I notice the first link is his company website. I click through to find information about Oliver Stone, the CEO of one of the most successful corporate investment companies in the US. The information is very bland and generic, telling prospective clients about his educational background, achievements, and career highlights and goals. Nothing personal to find here. I click out and check a few gossip sites, each one speculating about his relationship status with the latest woman on his arm. I come across an article from forbes.com, listing the richest men in America—Oliver is second on the list, and first for men under thirty-five. He's touted as a genius in his field, the likes America has never seen.

My head is spinning with the information and I close out of the search, shutting down the machine as if it's burned me. I don't know what to think. Yes, I knew he had more money than me. It was obvious in the car he drives, the suits he wears, even his casual jeans are an expensive brand. But never in my wildest dreams did I think he was a billionaire! He certainly never gave off that vibe with me.

A freaking billionaire, for goodness' sake!

What in the hell is he doing with me? I don't understand. I look around at my humble house and I wonder what he thought of it.

I repeat my routine from last night—hot shower, hot chocolate, and then bed. Once again, sleep is an evasive creature. I feel like I've been put through the wringer when I once again wake up to banging on my front door. Looking out my window, I see his car in my driveway again—I don't even have the energy to respond today. I sit in silence, hoping he'll go away. I feel even worse. Today is his birthday, and I know he has nobody to make a fuss over him. But my heart is cracked like glass—it won't take much to shatter it completely.

I can't do it.

I can't let him in

My phone alerts me to a new text.

Big O: Please let me explain

Big O: Let me in. We need to talk

Big O: It wasn't my intention to hurt you Kate

I decide to stay with my parents for a few days, just in case this becomes a daily occurrence I'm not prepared to deal with. I start back at work tomorrow, and I need to be at my best for my students. I pack what I need, letting Margie know I'll be gone for a few days and she can call me if she needs anything.

Arriving at my childhood home, a sense of calm and ease which comes with familiarity washes over me. My brother's car is parked in the driveway, which also lifts my spirits. We share a special bond, not sure if it's because we're twins, or because we have always been close. He's not only my brother, but he's also my best friend. I move to grab my duffle out of my trunk, preparing myself for the bombardment of questions I'm bound to encounter when I announce I'm staying for a few days.

Toby must have been at the front window, because he comes out to help me with my bag before I've even closed the trunk.

"Hey, Squirt. You moving in?"

"Uh, yeah, just for a few days." I give him a side hug, hoping he won't notice my still puffy eyes.

He studies me closely. "What's up? You've been crying and now you're moving in with Mom and Dad. Something's wrong."

I wave him off. I should have known he'd notice. "It's nothing. Don't worry about me. How come you're here?"

He lets it go, knowing that I'll talk to him when I'm ready. "I'm going to be busy in the recording studio starting next week, so I wanted to spend as much time with Mom and Dad as I could. You know what my life gets like when I get in the zone." He laughs lightly. "The entire world ceases to exist, except for my music." I nod because I'm well aware he gets one hundred percent absorbed into his creative process when he's working on an album.

We step inside and Mom and Dad are waiting at the entrance with concerned expressions. Mom moves in for a hug. "Wow, aren't we extra lucky today? Both of our children decided to spend the day with us."

Dad pipes in, "It looks like Kate plans to spend more than just a day with us, Love."

"Hey, guys. Do you mind if I stay for a few days? I need a break from my place for a bit. If that's okay?"

Mom waves me off. "Of course, Katie-girl. This will always be your home. You know we love having you with us. I'll put some fresh bedding on for you."

She wanders off to change the bedding, while Toby takes my duffle through to my childhood bedroom. I'm not sure where Shane is. He's usually Toby's shadow, not that he needs his bodyguard when he's home with us.

Dad puts his arm around my shoulder, guiding me into the kitchen. "C'mon, I was just making a cup of coffee. You want one?"

"Thanks, Dad. I'd love one."

He winks at me, getting to work, making my coffee the way I like it. When he's done, he nods his head toward the closed-in back porch and we make our way outside. We're getting settled when Mom and Toby make their way out to join us.

"So, Squirt, what's up? Maybe we can help?"

"Toby, Love, leave her be. She'll talk when she's ready." Mom smiles gently at me, setting off the waterworks all over again. I can't believe I have any water left in my body at the rate I've been crying.

"I feel like an idiot. A complete and utter idiot," I mutter.

Mom moves closer, stroking her hand gently up and down my back in comfort. "Now I doubt that's true. Why don't you tell us what happened? Then we can decide for ourselves."

I look up into the faces of the people I trust most in this world. They've always been upfront and honest with me. Like the time I wanted to sing as part of a duet with Toby, but I sounded like a dying cat. Mom gently told me I couldn't hold a tune, but maybe I could be his manager since my strength was being organized. I know they'll be totally honest with me.

"I found out that Oliver isn't who I thought he was. I feel like such a fool. I can't believe I didn't see the clues."

Toby sits forward in his chair, clearly on the defense. "What do you mean 'he isn't who you thought he was'? Did he cheat on you? Is he married or something? I'm pretty sure he was single. I'll kill him."

"Calm down, Son. There'll be no talk of killing anyone," Dad says in a firm tone.

"No, nothing like that. He's *Oliver Stone*." I look at them with wide eyes, like 'duh'. "*The* Oliver Stone. *The billionaire*, Oliver Stone," I say with an exasperated huff.

Mom, Dad, and Toby all look at each other in confusion. Don't they get what this means? What is *wrong* with these people?

"Uh, I hate to break it to you, Sis. But I already knew who he was. I assumed you knew." He shrugs, looking amused at my lack of knowledge.

"How did you know? And how would *I* know? I don't keep up

with the business world and I'm not on social media. I had no idea. I felt blindsided. I mean, I figured he earned a lot of money judging by his car and clothes and stuff, but I had no freaking clue he was a billionaire!" I throw my hands up in frustration. I look at Mom and Dad. "Did you guys know?"

They both shake their head in the negative. "We're still getting over the surprise that he's the Oliver we cared for when you two were babies. What does it matter?" Mom asks gently while Dad says, "He seemed pretty normal to me." He shrugs. "How does Oliver, being a billionaire, change anything?"

All three of them are looking at me, anticipating my answer. I can't believe I have to spell this out to them. "It changes every-freak-ing-thing."

Dad rubs his chin in contemplation. "Am I missing something here? I don't understand why the size of his bank account changes anything. That boy is so far gone for you, it's not funny." He looks at me, waiting for my answer. "Toby's loaded, but you still love him."

How is that even the same thing? Toby's my brother. Of course, I'm going to love him.

"Well, for starters, he wasn't honest with me. What else don't I know about him? Second, I don't know how to be the girlfriend of a billionaire, and third, and probably most importantly, what's he doing with a girl like me? When he can have anyone he freaking wants. He'll probably have a bevy of women at his beck and call, just like Keith did. Remember Keith? The one who thought, because he had tons of money, it was okay to date several women at once." I take a deep breath because all of that came out in such a rush.

Mom tsks me, while Toby responds, "It seems to me you were doing an okay job at being the girlfriend of a billionaire because he was hoping to keep coming to our family dinners for as long as you'd let him." He looks at me pointedly.

Damn him for making sense like that.

Then Mom butts in. "Kate, in any new relationship, there are going to be things about the other person that you don't know. You learn about them along the way. That's a natural development. You can't expect to know everything about a person in such a short time. I can guarantee you haven't told him everything about you."

True, but hiding that you're a billionaire is pretty major. It's not like learning he doesn't hang his towel up after his shower—*right?*

"I didn't think we brought you up to be judgmental of other people. He shouldn't be punished for mistakes made by other men you've previously dated." She gives me a disapproving look, making me feel small.

Dad huffs, looking at me sharply. "I need you to explain the 'third' comment. Something about 'a girl like me'?"

What is it with these people? They don't see the disparities between the two of us. I know they're my parents and all, and they're supposed to only see the good parts, but let's be realistic here.

I straighten up. I need them to hear what I say. Understand what I say. "I already felt like I wasn't pretty enough to be with Oliver."

Dad attempts to interrupt, but I hold up my hand in the universal sign of stop. Mom's looking at me with sympathy because we've already had this discussion.

"Please, let me get it all out before you tell me you think I'm wrong." I fiddle with the bottom of my t-shirt. "He is *incredibly* good looking and I've had an awful time keeping the interest of past boyfriends."

"That's because they were crap boyfriends. That had nothing to do with you. Just, maybe, poor choices on your part," Toby interrupts on a growl.

I give him a small smile. "Either way, they've all strayed for someone prettier or more interesting. Or because they felt they were entitled to date more than one woman at a time. It took Oliver a while to convince me to give him a chance because I don't trust he'll stick around. He's breathtakingly handsome, kind, and generous to a fault—he certainly *could* have the cream of the crop. The images I've seen of him online, with a bevy of attractive women, support this." I take in a shuddering breath. "As you know, he persisted, and I gave in. He was very convincing and, to be honest, I was actually beginning to feel beautiful. I was growing more confident and less worried he would cheat on me. That took a lot of faith on my part." I stand up and move to the railing, leaning my back against the post. "But this adds an extra layer for me. Not only is he *that* good looking, but he's also loaded as well. How appealing is that to most women out there? I can't risk my heart. I'm already in deep with him. I don't think I would survive."

Toby stands, wrapping his arms around me in a tight hold, allowing me to cry into his shirt. "Hey. You know, I saw him out to dinner with another woman. I could plainly see she was flirting with him—like a full-on assault. I heard him shut her down. Point blank. I honestly don't think you need to worry about him cheating on you, or being interested in anyone else." He squeezes me tighter, kissing the top of my head. "When I confronted him about it, he was genuinely upset that I would think him capable of cheating on you. My gut tells me he's a good guy."

Mom passes me the tissues to blow my runny nose. I must look a complete wreck. "Maybe the attraction to you is that you're *not* after him for anything other than the man he is? Perhaps he could see your genuine interest in him as a person, rather than what you could take from him. Maybe, just maybe, you give him something else he's been searching for—something all the money in the world can't buy," she says, giving me a soft smile.

Dad pats the chair next to him, directing me to sit down. "I recognized in him the same determination I had to win your mother over. He made his interest in you, and a future with you, very clear to all of us. He's an intelligent man. You have to give him credit that he knows what he wants out of life. I think you need to give him a chance to explain."

Everyone seems to be on Oliver's side. "But he kept something huge from me. Don't you understand? I feel like I don't really know him."

"Just give him a chance. Okay?" Mom nods at me. "He must have had his reasons. Now I need to get lunch started. You three relax."

"I need some time to get my head around it."

She squeezes my shoulder as she passes, reassuring me she understands. Gradually, Dad moves inside to watch TV, and Toby goes to work on some song that won't leave him alone. Thank goodness I'm back at work tomorrow. The kids will keep my mind busy and away from all things Oliver. I head upstairs to my bedroom to unpack for the few days I'll be here, choosing an outfit to wear tomorrow. My phone alerts me to a text.

Big O: I miss you x

The tears roll from my eyes, slowly down my cheeks, dripping onto my phone screen. I miss him too, but I'm not sure I can trust him, trust his intentions. I'm exhausted and completely wrung out.

FORTY-FIVE

-oliver-

I'm in the office at the ass crack of dawn. Not even a workout can extinguish the anger I have trapped inside my body. I *know* I've only got myself to fucking blame, but the need to fucking punch something is strong. I spent most of the weekend here working; attempting to take my mind off Kate, but it's not fucking possible. She takes up all the real estate.

Hours pass as I work on our major accounts. Employees begin to trickle into the office; lights going on, computers booting up, and a steady stream of idle chatter breaks my silence.

The fucking noise is annoying as fuck.

I glance up from what I'm doing to find Jase leaning against my doorframe. "I don't pay you to stand in my fucking doorway, staring at me. Get to fucking work," I grumble at him.

He steps forward, closing the door behind him. "You look like you've gone ten rounds with Tyson. Are you okay?" He makes himself fucking comfortable in the chair opposite my desk, resting his foot on his opposite knee, slouching back like he's got all fucking day to fucking sit and fucking chat.

"No. I'm not fucking okay and I don't want to fucking talk about it. I just want to get on with my fucking work. Can you get me the files for the Rhinecourt account? I've had an idea I want to follow up."

He rises from his chair, giving me a nod. "Sure. I'm here if you want to talk, though. I know I'm *only* your assistant, but I also consider us friends."

Well, he knows how to make me feel like a fucking piece of shit.

He taps my desk, stepping out to get the file I requested. He quickly returns, placing it on my desk without speaking.Closing the door with a snick behind him, he silently leaves my office. I get to work on the account, discovering my idea will work; making Ms. Rhinecourt an additional thirty million dollars within two years.

My phone buzzes from Jase's line. "Yeah?"

"I've got Gloria from *Coffee and Cookies* on line one for you."

"Can't you fucking deal with her?"

"I tried. She specifically wants to speak with you. Sorry, boss." He sounds somewhat apologetic.

"Fine, put her through."

I press the correct button to accept the call. "Hello, Oliver Stone speaking."

"Oh, hi, Mr. Stone. My name is Gloria—"

"I know who this is, my assistant informed me. How can I help you?" I know I'm being a fucking dick, but I'm not in the fucking mood.

"Oh, of course. Um, I've been delivering coffee and pastries to Kate, as per your request."

That perks me up.

"I wanted to let you know she canceled the ongoing order today. She also said that no matter what you said, she would no longer accept the gift of coffee and pastries daily."

Fuuuck! I'm losing her.

"Thank you for taking the time to let me know personally, Gloria. Please send through the final invoice and we'll be sure to get that squared away for you."

"Sure. No problem. If it's any consolation, she looked devastated."

"Thanks. But it's no consolation to me to know she's sad. Good-bye, Gloria."

I disconnect the call and throw my pen across the room. I wish it was something more satisfying, to be honest. It doesn't give me any satisfaction to know Kate's devastated.

I'm the fucking asshole who's made her feel that way.

I only ever wanted to make her happy.

Protected.

Loved.

Secure.

I've failed on every level.

Honestly, if I think about it, what do I know about relationships? The last healthy relationship I witnessed was my parents' relationship when I was seven. I only ever viewed that relationship through the eyes of a child. Clearly, I don't know what I'm doing. She's probably better off without me in her life. She deserves to have the best —the best husband, a family. I don't know the first thing about any of that. Thinking about leaving Kate leaves me feeling cold. I can't fucking do it. I'm going to fucking fight for her if it's the last thing I fucking do. Selfish, I know. But too fucking bad. I pace my office, stopping to look out over the city, when there's a knock on my door.

What the fuck now?

"Come in," I call out.

Jase opens the door and steps inside, closing the door behind him. "What was that about? Gloria was pretty cagey and wouldn't tell me anything. Demanded to speak only to you."

I tuck my hands in my pockets as my shoulders slump. "Kate canceled the ongoing coffee and pastry order. She said she would no longer accept the gift from me. She asked her to stop bringing the delivery, no matter what I said." I huff out a breath, running my hands through my hair. Jase's face is full of concern and sympathy. "I know you're dying to tell me 'I told you so', but I don't fucking need it right now."

"I wasn't going to say that. I would never kick you while you're down. There's no fun in that." He shrugs. "What are you going to do?"

"I don't fucking know. She won't talk to me. Won't even answer her front door. Hasn't returned any of my messages. I think I've lost her. The one woman I want and she doesn't want me." I slump down in my chair, releasing a deep sigh.

"Well, you're not going to give up, are you? That's not the Oliver Stone I know."

I rub my hands down my face, noticing that my normally short beard is getting out of control. "Of course not. I'm trying to fucking give her some space and time to come to terms with what she's learned about me." I glance over at Jase. "It might kill me to give that to her, but I fucking will. I owe her that fucking much. Then I have to come up with a plan to win her back."

"Well, if there's anyone with enough determination to break through the fortress she's building against you, it would be you." He leaves my office, closing my door with a sharp click.

I'm close to calling it a day, because I can't concentrate for shit and my new friend, *Lagavulin*, is calling my name, when a new email catches my eye.

Re: Update on Banking Situation

From: Marcus Trainor

To: Oliver Stone

Hello Oliver

I've just received word from Mutual Banking Trust that our ninety-day deadline to pay the remainder of the mortgage started from when the first payment was missed, which was two months ago. This means we have thirty days to raise the funds to save the properties.

I've been looking at the number of kids we have on the books and I think we can realistically reduce the number of properties by two. This solution will mean we have no room to take on any additional kids, or we will have to house them in our central location, which isn't ideal. The beauty of the homes is that it gives the kids a sense of belonging somewhere. It's like a home with a parent and siblings.

We've got seventy-six kids on the books at the moment. We can move a couple of kids around to fill thirteen properties to capacity, offloading two homes.

These changes will reduce the mortgage slightly.

Please let me know if you have any further suggestions or any other way you think we can solve our problem.

Kindest regards

Marcus

CEO

The Parkerville Project

I read the email twice, my jaw clenching. This is a fucking disaster. What kind of sick fuck steals from homeless kids? I can't wrap my mind around it. My head thumps a steady beat as a result of the email.

My line buzzes again. "Hey, I'm sorry, but I've got Glen from *Lenny's Luscious Lunches* on line one. He will only speak with you."

Fuck, here goes. I bet she's canceled the lunch orders now.

"Put him through." I pick up the correct line. "Hello, this is Oliver Stone."

"Hi, Mr. Stone. My name's Glen from *Lenny's Luscious Lunches*. We had a standing order to deliver a range of lunches to a Kate Summer, over at Northwood Elementary at your request."

"Yes, I'm aware. How can I help you?" I don't know why I asked that question when my gut is telling me exactly why he's calling.

"Well, when our delivery guy took lunch to her today, she canceled the ongoing order. She said we were to stop delivering lunch to her, no matter what you said." He sounds unsure of himself. "Uh, I wanted to check with you that she had the authority to decide?"

I clear my throat. "Of course she does. If she no longer wants lunch, then that's most definitely her prerogative. Please send through the final invoice to finalize the account. Thank you."

"No worries. Bye."

I disconnect the call before I crush the phone in my hand. She's certainly sending me a clear fucking message—she no longer wants to have anything to do with me. I want to talk with her, but there's no point while she's in class. She never accepts any calls. I'll stop by her place later this evening when I know she'll be home.

Stepping out of my office, I catch Jase returning to his desk with a coffee. He spots me. "Did you want one?" He gestures to his cup. "I can make you one."

"Nah. I'm okay. You got a minute?" I nod my head toward my office. "Bring your tablet and coffee."

He collects what he needs, following me into my office. We both sit, and I turn my screen around to show him the email from Marcus.

"Fuck, thirty days?" He looks at me in disbelief. "What can we do to get that kind of money together in thirty days?"

"That's what I'm hoping we can brainstorm. I don't want them to lose a single fucking property. It's too damn important. Even if I have to put work on hold again, I'm going to sort this shit out." I run my hands through my hair, looking at Jase. "Any ideas? We need to raise $10,000,000 to buy the mortgages outright, staff wages, running costs, and everyday costs associated with raising kids quickly."

Even though I have an abundance of money on paper, most of it's tied up in assets and portfolios. The money I have on hand won't cover the mortgage. I can give some to the cause, but not enough. "I can personally put in two million, leaving us eight to find."

He shakes his head. "You've already lost enough money because of this disaster. How can you be happy to contribute even more?"

"This is important to those kids. They need a stable environment. It means a lot to me too because of my history, but mostly, it means the world to Kate. She's been devastated by what happened. I need to sort this out as quickly as fucking possible for the kids, for me, and especially for Kate."

Jase sits, rubbing his stubbled chin, thinking but remains quiet.

"Remember that gala dinner I went to last year? They organized it to raise awareness and money for the city's homeless women's shelter."

Jase nods. "Yeah, vaguely. Tickets cost a bomb, if I remember correctly."

"Exactly. It was $5,000 per ticket. They also held an auction. They raised close to $6,000,000. Maybe we could do something like that?"

A sense of hope blooms that perhaps we could pull this off. The tickets will have to be more expensive and we would have to sell a lot of them, but I think it might be possible.

"That will be difficult to pull off in the time frame we have to work with." He doesn't look convinced.

"Well, we fucking have to. I'm going to take the lead on this project. Let's work out which accounts I can pass off to the team. I'll keep the most important ones, enabling me to focus on organizing this event."

Jase looks at me as if I've lost my mind. Maybe I fucking have. I usually begrudge taking time away from my 'real' work, and yet here I am doing it for the second time in less than a month. We spend the next few hours going over our accounts. I offload most of my accounts to my team, leaving me with half a dozen to manage. Once the gala's over, I'll pick them back up. Jase and I also make a basic list of where to begin and what will need to be done—I need to hurry.

To get the ball rolling, I spend the afternoon contacting the necessary people and organizations I need to contact. I shoot off an email to Marcus, informing him I'm working on something which may help. I send off emails to a couple of large, reputable hotels, explaining my purpose and asking if they'd be prepared to host such an event at a heavily discounted cost, allowing us to give as much money to the cause. I write emails to galleries, travel agents, designers, and importers to request donations that can be used in the auction. I've requested items with a minimum value of $10,000. This way, bidding can start at a reasonable figure—giving us the best return. I've also asked them to put me in touch with anyone else they think might like to help. I can't do any more than that for today, so I call it a night and drive to Kate's.

I don't see Kate's car in the driveway when I arrive, but I get out to knock on her front door, anyway. No answer. I try calling her but my call is sent straight to voicemail, which is no surprise. I try knocking again, louder, knowing she won't answer, but I don't want to give up. I decide to sit on her front step, waiting for her to come home. After what seems like hours, but is probably less than fifteen minutes, I hear Margie's locks disengage and her door open.

She steps out with her walking stick. "What are you doing sitting on Kate's step?"

Taking a deep breath, I stand. "Hi, Margie. I'm waiting for Kate to come home. Any idea when that'll be?"

Margie studies me closely. "You look like shit, young man. Come in. I'll make you a cup of tea."

I follow her inside a space that's a mirror image of Kate's. Margie sets about making tea in her small kitchen, while I sit at her two-person dining table. She places a pot of tea on the table, along with two china teacups and matching saucers. We've done this several times before, when she first came home from the hospital.

"Kate's gone to stay with her parents for a few days. She seemed rather upset, saying she needed some family time." She studies me closely, as if she'll find answers why Kate was upset. "Want to tell me what happened?"

Maybe Margie can help me out if I tell her what I did. "She found out something about me she wasn't expecting, and I guess she didn't like it."

Margie pats my hand. "What did she find out, Oliver? What were you hiding from her?"

"I was eventually going to tell her, but I knew she would balk at being in a relationship with me if she knew. I needed her to be fully invested in our relationship. Before I told her, I needed her to be in love with me. It was the only way I could think to keep her." I sigh, gazing into my tea. I realize I can't keep someone who was never mine to begin with.

"You're talking in circles, young man. Why would you think Kate wouldn't want to be with you?" She looks at me sternly, as if I'm not giving Kate full credit for the type of person she is.

"I'm a billionaire, Margie. There's no other way to say it. Kate was already gun shy to date me because she had some ridiculous notion that she's not beautiful or interesting enough." I snort in disgust. "Which is utter bullshit!"

"Mhm. I agree with you there." She nods in agreement.

"When we first met, she looked at me with interest. Like a woman does when she likes what she sees. It was purely based on physical attraction. Do you know how many times a woman looks at me in that way?" I look at Margie and she shakes her head in the negative. "Never. Exactly never." I breathe out. "It was refreshing to be ogled for my body, and not my bank balance." Margie snorts out a laugh. "At university, women could see my earning potential based on my academic program. Once I started my company and making money, I still attracted women who were after my bank balance, not me."

Margie nods along. "I don't think many men would consider that to be a burden."

She's probably right, and for me, it wasn't a burden until Kate came along, showing a different kind of interest—one I liked.

"You're probably right, Margie. But it was something new for me. I'll never forget how she made me feel like a man, instead of a meal ticket. There was something truly special about her—I immediately felt drawn to her. I couldn't fight it. I tried to find her because I couldn't stop thinking about her. As I told you, I even hired a private investigator and then I bumped into her. To me, it was a sign we were meant to be something to each other." I shrug. "I sound like a fucking pussy."

Margie pats my arm. "I get it. I really do. Kate is truly special. She has the power to draw people into her orbit; she doesn't realize her potency, because she's especially sweet." She takes a sip of her tea, then glances up at me. "But you've hurt her, Oliver. She feels betrayed ... lied to." Margie squeezes my arm to stop me as I try to interrupt. "I know you didn't tell her any untruths, young man, but you also weren't completely honest with her. I can understand why, because I know you had a difficult time convincing her to spend time with you. But when you had the chance, you should have told her. I think it made things much worse with the way she discovered your secret."

I nod because I fully agree; it would have been much better if Kate had learned who I was directly from me, instead of the way she did.

"What can I do? She's completely shut me out. She kicked me out, won't speak with me, won't even return my texts. My calls go directly to voicemail, and now I find she's left her own home to avoid me."

I can't believe the lengths she's fucking gone to.

"You've got to give the girl some time. She needs to come to terms with the reality of who you are and what that means. Give her some space. It's what she needs right now. Maybe if she misses you a little, you'll have a better chance of winning her back." She squeezes my arm and looks at me with such compassion.

"Thanks. I guess I'll go home and let you get on with your evening." She stands up with me, giving me a hug I desperately needed. It's ironic. I'd gone years without that type of affection, never giving it a second thought. Until now. Now, I miss that simple gesture of intimacy so very much. I'm terrified I'll never have it again.

Once again, I head home to my empty penthouse—*alone*.

I'm responding to an email from the *Four Seasons* when there's a knock on my office door. Annoyed at the interruption, I call out, "Come in."

I remain focused on the email, which is offering me a great deal for the privilege of hosting the gala. They've even offered us the use of their PR people as well as their event manager. A throat clears. Looking up from my computer, I find Jase standing next to a very pissed off Toby, with Shane hovering near the door. I sit back in my chair, gesturing for both of them to take a seat.

Toby doesn't waste any time. "You've hurt my sister. I told you to watch your fucking back if you stepped out of line with her. You wanna explain what happened before I pummel you into the ground?"

I explain everything to him, in detail. How much his sister means to me, what I hoped for in the future, how she found out about who I am, and why I kept my secret. As I work through my explanation, his anger dissipates as his shoulders relax and the tension leaves his face.

"If she would give me a chance to explain, we could put this behind us and move forward together. I don't want anyone else but her. She's it for me." I shrug. "I want her in my life, but I'm prepared to give her some time. Then I'm going after her, and nothing is going to stand in my way."

Toby nods approvingly. "Sounds fair to me. If I can help, let me know. I want my sister to be happy. She was happy with you, and I could see her confidence steadily growing."

Jase pipes in. "Did you get the email you were expecting from the *Four Seasons* about the gala that you're organizing?"

"Yeah, I was just reading it. Their offer is incredibly generous."

"What's going on?" Toby asks.

Jase explains what I'm attempting to achieve for *The Parkerville Project*. "Oliver's putting his business on hold to work on this gala because this is immensely important to the kids and Kate."

Toby looks thoughtful, rubbing the stubble on his chin. "Have you got the entertainment organized yet?"

Jase and I look at each other. "Shit, didn't think of that."

"I could do it. Not to be boastful or anything, but I *am* a four-time Grammy winner. I can pull a pretty decent crowd. I would also be happy to auction off some of my time, or something along those lines." He shrugs carelessly, as though he hasn't just made my day.

Shane steps further into my office, away from the door. "You'll need to check your calendar, Toby. Things are getting busy for you."

Toby waves him off. "We'll work around it. No problem."

Not only is he prepared to help me win Kate back, but he's also prepared to help with the gala.

I get up from behind my desk, stepping around to shake his

hand. "Thanks, man. That would help us out, and it means the world to me you've even offered."

"No problem. What date is the event? I'll let my manager know, so she can get in touch with you. We can even use my PR people to help spread the word."

I give him the details and he leaves my office, looking much calmer than when he arrived. I also feel a marked improvement in my mood, knowing I have his approval and support when it comes to Kate.

FORTY-SIX

-kate-

THE PAST WEEK AT WORK FELT LIKE A CHORE, MAKING ME EVEN more miserable because I've always loved my job. I've always found solace and joy in it. It's taking all of my energy to put one foot in front of the other at this point—it's like I'm walking through molasses—I don't even want to get out of bed in the morning. One day runs into the next and I'm not sure what day it is, or how much time has passed.

The world is drab and gray without Oliver.

I'm lifeless and disinterested in life, work, eating, reading, the kids—everything. This is my choice and I have to keep reminding myself. I could have let him explain, but I wanted to protect myself —it's better this way.

I'm able to fake it for my students, but Emma sees right through my façade. She's been begging me to open up to her, but I'm worried she'll throw it back at me, that I should have searched him online when I had the chance. I trudge through the week, with a promise to Emma that we'll meet for our regular coffee and cake catch up next weekend. She's even invited Margie along because she knows I won't deny Margie an outing to her favorite coffee shop.

Oliver hasn't contacted me for a few days I guess he's given up, so I decide it's safe to move back to my place. I felt awful leaving Margie on her own and it's time to get back to my routine. Mom and Dad are worried I'll have too much time alone and spend my time wallowing.

It hits me hard when I open my door, seeing evidence of Oliver in my space. Socks he left behind, his toothbrush and shaver on the bathroom counter, a couple of t-shirts and workout shorts in my bedroom. The hardest of all is his scent on my bedding and the towel he used—the intoxicating scent that encompasses Oliver. The scent I associated with warmth, caring, home … *love*. I decide to strip my bed, remaking it with fresh linens, blankets, and a quilt. I change the towels and put everything into the machine. I find a box, and moving from room to room, I collect and pack Oliver's things. I'll let him know he can come and collect them from my front porch. I save one shirt, tucking it under my pillow. Losing him completely is something I can't bear.

Maybe I'm a masochist?

Sleep is hard to come by, and I end up burying my nose in his shirt, using his scent to help me fall into a fitful sleep.

Saturday afternoon comes around and it's time to collect Margie and meet Emma for coffee. I'm not looking forward to this, because I know they're going to meddle. Margie and I arrive at the coffee shop to find Emma already seated at our favorite table by the window. We all greet each other with hugs and move onto the important business of ordering our coffees, along with a selection of delicious cakes and slices we can all share. The conversation starts out light as Margie and Emma catch up, allowing me to zone out. My friends eat; however, I can't bring myself to take even a small bite. I usually love my coffee, but even that's lost its appeal.

Margie clears her throat, placing her fork on her plate. "How are you doing, sweet girl?"

"I'm okay." I look anywhere but at Margie because she'll see right through my lie if she sees my face.

"No, you're not. You've been struggling all week, and I want to know why?" Emma huffs out, giving me a sympathetic look crossed with a motherly scowl. *Geez.*

"Did she tell you what happened, Emma?" Margie asks.

Here we go.

"No, she won't share. Which means I can't help her." Emma seems hurt, making me feel like the lowest of the low.

Margie goes ahead, sharing my heartbreak with Emma.

In detail.

As though I'm not even sitting at the same table as the two of them.

Nothing's left out.

Emma looks at me with a 'what-the-fuck?' look, and I shrink down.

"What the hell is wrong with you? Anyone would kill to be in your shoes," Emma whisper yells at me in exasperation.

"Exactly! He could have anyone. It's just a matter of time before he cheats or he'll leave me for someone much more suited to his billionaire lifestyle." I huff. "I'm already in too deep. When that happens, I won't survive. I need to get out before I'm in any deeper."

Emma calms slightly, her expression full of compassion. "I hate to break it to you, girl, but you're already in as deep as you can possibly be."

Something over my shoulder catches Margie and Emma's attention. Margie's smiling and Emma sits up straighter, smoothing out her hair. I turn around and am shocked stupid to see Oliver striding toward our table with purpose—his intent written all over his impressive face. He looks stunning; as usual.

How on earth did he know I was here? I don't remember ever telling him about this place. It's not as though the café is in a prominent position, and he saw me in the window as he walked by. I turn back toward Margie and Emma, noticing Margie give a not-so-subtle wink to Oliver. *She wouldn't have. Would she?*

"Hello, ladies." He nods, with a half-smile, toward Margie and Emma, and then his mesmerizing green eyes zero in on me. "Kate."

Margie stands, giving him a hug, then introduces him to Emma. "Emma, this is Oliver, Kate's beau."

Oh my gosh, he's not my beau anymore. Did she listen to a word I said?

Oliver holds out his hand to greet Emma. "It's great to meet you, Emma. Kate's told me a lot about you."

Emma blushes, placing her hand over her heart. "Nice to meet you as well. I hope she's only told you the good things about me. I wouldn't want you to get the wrong impression." She giggles like a schoolgirl and I roll my eyes. *Oh, Emma.*

"Most definitely only good things. Kate has a lot of respect for you." He turns to me. "Kate, do you have a few minutes to talk?"

I can't talk to him here in front of my friends. I know that I'll become a mess and break down and I certainly don't want to do that in a public place.

"I can't right now. I'm catching up with my friends." I turn my back to him.

Margie and Emma both do a double-take. I'm being a total bitch, which is out of character for me.

He steps to the side, placing him in my periphery. "I've given you time. I've been extraordinarily patient. It's time you allow me to explain." He's speaking calmly, but his body is as tense as a rubber band ready to snap.

I stand up, turning to face him. "I need more time. I can't put a time frame on coming to terms with the reality of not knowing the man I was sleeping with." I whisper-yell at him. Several people are now watching our exchange, making my annoying blush rise.

Running his hand through his hair in frustration, he mutters something unintelligible under his breath. He bends forward, situates me over his shoulder fireman style, wraps his arm around my legs, and stands up to exit the coffee shop. At first, I'm downright shocked I don't react, then I animate and begin to struggle in his hold. When I glance up through my unruly hair, Margie's smiling and Emma's clapping her hands and bouncing on her toes like the kindergarten children I work with every day. He keeps moving, ignoring my attempts to wriggle free. Nobody seems to think anything of a man walking down the street, with a struggling woman slung over his shoulder.

What is wrong with people? He could be a serial killer for all they know!

He stops at his car, releasing the locks. He climbs into the passenger seat, positioning me so I'm straddling his lap.

I've missed this. This intimate contact with him.

One strong arm bands around my lower back, holding me tight to his hard body, while his other hand cups the back of my head. I've nowhere to go, and it's impossible to avoid his eyes in this position. He's studying my face intently. I wonder if he can see my pain and hurt from his betrayal.

The lack of sleep, the lack of life.

He still looks as handsome as ever, even with dark circles under his eyes, an untrimmed beard, and messy hair. I can't help but notice the firmness of his chest under my hands and his muscular thighs beneath my butt. It's not fair. Being this close to him devolves my ability to think rationally. This is a dangerous situation for me to be in with him.

"I need to explain, Kate. You're being unfair, and I won't let you throw away what we have. It's too special to give up." He reverently tucks a lock of hair behind my ear, glancing between my eyes and my mouth. "Give me ten minutes. If you don't like what I have to say, I'll walk away. It'll kill me to do it, but I'll honor your wishes."

I nod. "Okay." I'm surprised at the steadiness in my voice.

His chest rises and falls under my hands as he takes a deep breath, closing his eyes for a moment. "Remember when we met?"

I nod.

"I thought you were beyond gorgeous from the instant I laid eyes on you. You were all sweetness, sunshine, enthusiasm, and bright smiles. You hugged Jase and me like we were old friends." He huffs out a laugh. "When I noticed you checking me out as though I was a piece of meat, it made my day."

My body heats as my blush rises from my chest. I was hoping he hadn't noticed that.

He gently strokes my cheek with his thumb as he whispers, "I love your blush."

Oliver holds firm as I attempt to break eye contact by tilting my head down. "You're the only woman I've ever met who looked at me like a man, rather than a walking line of credit."

He looks awfully sincere and I'm shocked. I assumed he had women all over him all the time, solely based on how he looks. I berate myself because I never took the time to think about our relationship from his side. Some of the fight leaves my body.

"When I came home, I couldn't spend time with another woman without comparing her to you, and how you made me feel in the short time I spent in your company. The connection I felt with you was nothing I'd ever experienced before—it was immediate. To be honest, the unfamiliar feeling knocked me on my ass. I think our childhood connection explains that somewhat."

Well, that's a bit of a surprise.

"I tried to get you out of my head, tried to convince myself I had built you up in my mind to be better than you were, but I couldn't shake thoughts and images of you out of my head. I even hired a private investigator to track you down."

Oliver's told me this before and it's no less creepy this time around. "You realize how creepy that sounds? Right?"

He nods. "I know. Jase told me I was acting like a crazy stalker."

I can't help the chuckle that escapes.

"When I laid eyes on you at the renovation project, I couldn't believe my luck. I thought the universe was finally working in my favor. I knew I had to have you in my life, but you were incredibly wary of me. You were caught up on the idea that you weren't beautiful or that you wouldn't be able to hold my attention. Which is utter bullshit!" He sighs. "I knew I had to tread carefully with you." He looks out of the window, then back to me. "I felt as though you were never as invested in our relationship as I was. As though you had one foot out, ready to run in the opposite direction." He whispers, his face pained. I attempt to interrupt, but he continues. I've clearly hurt him. The fortress I've kept around me, the one he's been working to break through, has ultimately damaged the man I know I've fallen in love with. "I was prepared to move this relationship along at your pace, as long as you would let me be a part of your life. I thought once I felt you were fully invested like I was, I would tell you about my money."

At this moment, I feel seriously small. I made him feel as though I was never fully invested in us. I've unintentionally hurt him, and that hurts me.

"I never intended to keep it from you, but I didn't want to give you another reason to keep me at arm's length. I sensed my money would be an issue for you." He takes a deep breath. "Kate, I am truly sorry you found out the way you did—it was never my intention. I never wanted to hurt you. I've only ever wanted to make you happy." He looks deeply into my eyes, his voice gravelly. "Please accept my apology."

Looking into his eyes, all I see is sincerity, heartbreak, and truth. I nod as tears fill my eyes, spilling over to track down my cheeks. "Oh, Oliver. I accept your apology, as long as you'll accept mine. I didn't realize how much I was hurting you by holding back to protect myself."

His shoulders visibly relax, tension leaving his body.

"I'm scared, Oliver." He holds my head steady as I try to look down at my lap. "I *am* more invested in this relationship than you realize. I'm in deep, Oliver, and I know I won't survive *when* you tire of me." I swallow hard. Now's the time to explain my fears. "I, uh, dated a guy in college who had money. Old family money, but lots of it. I found out he was dating several women at the same time. When I confronted him about it, he blew me off. Said it was expected for guys with money to have a wife as well as lovers on the side. He didn't see the big deal."

Oliver brushes his warm lips over my mouth with a gentle touch. "Well, that guy was a dick. It's not an expectation for wealthy men to be with several women at the same time." He kisses the tip of my nose. "I want you, Kate, *only* you. You're everything I didn't know existed in this world." He kisses me gently again, keeping it chaste. "I don't think you realize what *you* give to me. When I'm with you, I feel a sense of peace I haven't felt since I was a boy and Mom was still alive. I feel at home with you, as though I can finally take a breath. That feeling is beyond anything my wealth can buy me. You give me *so* much." He kisses the tip of my nose as punctuation.

I take a deep breath and look at him, really study him. He's profoundly vulnerable at the moment. "I'm sorry my past relationships have had such a negative impact on us. I feel awful because I did promise I would work on my issues, but I can see I never did. I only pushed them aside." I run my hands through his hair, massaging his scalp, bringing them to rest at the base of his neck, allowing me to play with the strands resting on his collar. "I don't know how to be the girlfriend of a hot billionaire." My voice is small, unsure.

He laughs and the final tension he was holding leaves his body.

"That's the whole point. I didn't want you to be the girlfriend of a *hot* billionaire. Underneath all of that, I'm just a man who wanted you to be *my* girlfriend." He rubs my cheek with his thumb, smiling at me. "Think you can do that?"

I'm still unsure. "I promise to try. But I don't know the first thing about your world; living in your world. Is that why I've never been to your apartment? Because you already know I won't know what to do? Or how to act?"

Shaking his head in the negative, he tells me, "No, Kate. Not at all. I don't care about all of that. It's not important to me. I want to be in *your* world, where the sun shines and there's joy and love; *that's* why I never took you into mine." He looks out the window again, as though he can't look at me. "It also would have given away how much money I had. I live in the penthouse of Stone Tower." He huffs, running his hand through his hair; I can see that's why his hair is such a mess. "Before you came into my life, I only left my building for business meetings or socially expected appearances at fundraising events. I was pretty reclusive. The life I led was sad and hollow. Before I met you, I didn't realize it. The business of making money was my sole focus. I'd been hurt as a child and as an adult, so

I locked myself away. I don't have friends and you know I only have my father."

My heart breaks for this wonderfully complicated man. He's had such a sad and lonely life, surrounded by people who don't see him as a person—only as a means to an end.

"What about Jase? I thought he was your colleague and friend. Who is he to you?"

He looks sheepish. "He's my assistant. I employed him over six years ago now. Over the years, we've grown close. He's almost like a brother to me." He shrugs. "If it's any consolation, he's pissed at me for not telling you sooner." He kisses the tip of my nose. "It's because he was working to improve people's perception of me, that we were working on the school, and then again on the renovation where we met for the second time."

"Well, I'm happy to know you've had at least one person in your corner." I huff out. "All those times I was telling you that your boss expects too much of you. You *are* the freaking boss!" I sigh. "You must have been having a good laugh at me."

"Never, Kate. Never. It made me feel like absolute shit that I was keeping something monumental from you."

I lean in to kiss him, gently pressing my lips against his mouth. At the feel of his lips against mine, I release a heavy sigh of relief. I thought for sure I would never touch him in this way again. His lips move against my mouth, licking his tongue over my bottom lip, encouraging me to open. We get swept up in long, drugging kisses; our breaths choppy.

He pulls away and his eyes flit between mine. He still seems worried. "I need to confess a couple more things to you before we move forward." He looks down and then back up at my face. "Full disclosure. No more secrets."

Oh, gawd. This doesn't sound good. I brace myself for whatever he's about to tell me and nod, encouraging him to go on.

"There's no easy way to confess. It's probably best if I just say it. When your car broke down, I asked Max to replace everything mechanical. Your car is pretty much brand new, apart from the body and interior." My mouth drops open. I'm completely shocked.

I don't know what to say. "I wanted to buy you a new car, but I found out you were attached to it because it was your nan's car, so I worked around it." He brushes his nose along mine. "Please don't be mad. It kept letting you down and I was worried you'd be left in a dangerous situation."

I'm stunned. "Oh, Oliver. You sweet, generous man. Thank you for taking such good care of me, even when I didn't know you were doing it." I smile gently. "Nan's car does mean a great deal to me. I can't explain how much it means to me that you were respectful of my sentimental attachment to it."

"There's one more thing." Ugh. This is crazy. "I paid for Margie's physical therapy and in-home nurse recovery program. She didn't have private insurance to cover the additional costs associated with her surgery. She would have ended up with an enormous bill which she shouldn't have had to deal with."

Oh. My. Gawd!

This man.

How can I be upset with his kind generosity toward someone he's only recently met? I think he takes my shocked silence as displeasure.

"Please don't be mad, or use this as an excuse to walk away. I only meant to help—"

I cut him off, pressing my lips to his in a kiss full of gratitude and appreciation for his kindness. I lick my tongue across the seam of his lips, encouraging him to open to me. He presses in closer, sealing our mouths, uniting us as deeply as possible with our clothes on. His hand tightens in my hair, maneuvering my head to take the kiss deeper when there's a knock on the window.

I startle away from Oliver, and we both look out of the tinted glass; finding Margie's face pressed up against it, attempting to peer inside. Oliver and I burst into laughter at the sight as he unlocks the door, alerting Margie to move away. Once she's out of the way, Oliver opens the door, helping me out and following close behind. He tucks me into his body, allowing me to wrap my arms around his torso.

Margie looks between the two of us, and she must be happy with what she sees. "Oh, thank goodness. You've made up."

She steps into us, wrapping her arms around us both in a tight hug. She's strong for a woman her age. I glance across, finding Emma holding my bag with a genuine smile as she gives me a thumbs up with a wink.

I look toward Margie but ask Oliver. "How did you know where to find me, anyway?"

Margie smiles brighter, while Oliver clears his throat, putting his hands in his pockets. "I texted him." She responds proudly. "You were being a stubborn brat, and I wasn't having it anymore."

Oliver attempts to hold in a laugh while Emma lets loose a loud chuckle. I can always rely on Margie to be straight with me.

I step forward, embracing her in another hug, full of gratitude. "Thank you, Margie. I love you big time, lady."

"I love you too, Katie-girl. Now go and have some hot make up sex."

She winks at Oliver while patting me on the arm. Emma chokes on nothing and Oliver bursts out laughing. My annoying blush takes over my whole body as if I'm on fire. I should be used to her lack of filter, but she still catches me off-guard sometimes.

"Emma's going to drop me home." She reaches back to Emma, who's still holding my purse. "Here's your purse. Off you go now."

FORTY-SEVEN

-oliver-

OXYGEN FINALLY FILLS MY LUNGS. I FEEL AS THOUGH I HAVEN'T taken a proper breath in the last two weeks. There's sunshine in my world again, color and purpose. The relief of having her with me again is monumental, and something I certainly don't intend to take for granted. I can't believe the assholes she dated in the past. They certainly have a lot to answer for, and I wish I could go back and punch Brandon in the face again.

"How about I take you to my place? I can show you where I live and work."

She looks up at me with a tremulous but grateful smile on her face. "I would really love that."

I take her hand, opening the passenger door, allowing her to situate herself inside. "We'll come back to get your car later. Okay?"

"Of course." She nods, putting on her seatbelt, beating me to it.

Closing the door, I make my way around the front to the driver's side. Getting in, I admire Kate. "You look perfect sitting there." I didn't think I'd ever have her in my car again.

"I think I would look even better if I were sitting there." She winks, gesturing to my seat.

Laughing, I let her know that's not happening anytime soon. I'm very protective of my baby. We make our way toward my building in relative silence, our hands entwined on the console between the two seats, enjoying having the other close.

"About Margie." Kate turns toward me. "I don't want her to know I paid her medical bills."

"Why not?"

"She received the best possible care. That was my goal. That's enough for me. I don't need her gratitude or feeling as though she's indebted to me for any reason."

She contemplates what I'm saying, nodding in acknowledgment. "She won't find out from me. Your secret's safe." She squeezes my thigh. "Just so you know, I think what you did for her is highly admirable and extremely generous."

As we get close to Stone Tower, she leans forward, studying the building through the windscreen.

"You know, I was quite taken with this building when I first saw it. I thought about how it was coincidental there was a building with your name on it." She shakes her head. "I can't believe I didn't put the pieces together then."

Squeezing her hand, we make our way into the parking garage to park in my allocated bay. Exiting the car, I take her hand, guiding her to the elevator. I place my hand on the security panel to call for the elevator.

Her eyes widen as she laughs. "This is very James Bond. Very schmancy!" She nudges my arm with her shoulder.

Smiling, I wink at her. Once the doors open, I drag her inside, pinning her to the wall with my body. "My handprint is my security. This elevator only stops at my penthouse when I press my hand to the panel. Otherwise, it's a regular elevator, requiring the user to select a floor." I gesture to the panel. "You'll notice my floor isn't available for selection."

She looks across. "The top floor is forty-nine. How many floors does your building have?"

"Fifty. I have the top floor, and the roof is also only accessible from the penthouse. There's an indoor pool and entertaining area up there. I'll show you later. The view across the city is spectacular."

Being back in her orbit settles me. Feeling her body against mine, having her smiles, her laughter, her eyes on me—soothes my soul. Moving in closer, I run my nose from her ear down her neck, gently biting her collar bone. She shivers from my attention, fisting my shirt in her hands, drawing me closer. The elevator comes to a stop and the doors open to my foyer, interrupting us. I normally appreciate the speed of the elevator, but I'm cursing it this time.

FORTY-EIGHT

-kate-

OLIVER STEPS BACK FROM ME AND HIS HOME COMES INTO VIEW. I gasp. My eyes don't know what to take in first. The first thing I notice is all the glass and the cold, sterile atmosphere of the place. It's akin to being in a fishbowl—a very decadent fishbowl. I make a beeline for the windows and am immediately overwhelmed by the view. It's magnificent.

"I bet this looks sensational at night."

Moving from window to window, I take it all in. Turning back around to face the room, my heart sinks for Oliver. It's devastatingly cold and sterile. Don't get me wrong, it's elegantly furnished and decorated, but there are no signs a person lives here—no photographs, no tossed shoes, no personality, no warmth. It drives home what Oliver was telling me in the car. My heartbreak must be written all over my face, because his expression is one of concern. Stepping toward me, he takes me in his arms.

"What's wrong?" He leans back, looking between my eyes, studying my face, while skimming his hands soothingly along my spine.

"Nothing's wrong. I'm sad looking at your space—it seems cold and lonely. I guess I didn't fully comprehend how lonely your life was for you until I saw your home."

He kisses my nose. "*I* didn't realize it until you came along. This has only ever been a place to eat, sleep, work out, and shower. Your place feels like a home to me." Taking my hand, he kisses it reverently, then steps back. "Let me show you around. Then I'm going to pack a few day's worth of clothes and we're going back to your place."

He shows me from room to room, which all looks pretty much the same. The whole place is decorated in various shades of gray, from the dark-stained, almost black, timber floors to the light-gray, almost white, painted walls. The rooftop is the most divine feature, besides the view from every room in his penthouse. The Olympic-sized pool with a built-in spa at one end is to die for. Talk about how the other half lives. I don't think my eyes could grow any wider if I tried.

Oliver takes me downstairs to his offices, some of which I've already seen, which occupy the next two floors below his penthouse. The gray stone floors, steel, and glass give a modern feel to the space. Oliver's office comprises of a suite of rooms—one being his actual office, a large meeting room, a fully contained kitchenette, and a well-appointed private bathroom. Windows line all the external walls, affording an outstanding view, which I bet he rarely takes time to enjoy.

"Do you really use all this space?" I find it unbelievable that one person needs this much space at work. It's like a mini apartment.

"Well, yeah. Mostly." He looks around like he's seeing it for the first time. "I guess it must seem decadent. I put in long hours and a lot of it is about convenience. This way, I don't have to run upstairs."

We head back up to his penthouse after he uses his handprint at the elevator, which blows my middle-class mind. He seems in a hurry to pack up and get out of here.

"What's the rush?" I ask. *Maybe he doesn't like having me in his space?*

Without looking up from what he's doing, he responds, almost absentmindedly. "Hmm?"

"You seem as though you're in a rush to get me out of your space."

He puts down the t-shirt he was holding and steps into my space. Cupping my face in his large hands, he tilts my head back gently to peer directly into my eyes. "Since I started spending time at your place, I don't enjoy being here. It feels cold and lonely. These past two weeks have been hell. I spent as much time as possible in my office to avoid the loneliness I feel when I'm up here. I only came up here to shower and change. I got little sleep, because my body refused to settle without you near." He kisses my forehead and the tip of my nose as my heart smashes into tiny pieces all over the floor.

I swallow down my guilt. "I'm sorry, Oliver."

I've been such a bratty bitch. If only I'd given him the chance to explain the day I found out. I was distraught and went straight into self-preservation mode. I wasn't thinking rationally.

I hurt him … deeply.

I don't deserve this man. But I'm not letting him go again.

"I'm honestly sorry I acted horribly toward you."

He shakes his head in the negative, giving me a gentle smile. "You have nothing to be sorry for." Well, that's an absolute lie. He kisses my forehead and the tip of my nose as if to reassure himself I'm here. Since the café, he's had his hands or some other part of his body in constant contact with mine. "Promise me you won't ever leave me again," he whispers. His vulnerability is palpable.

Pressing up onto my toes, I kiss his bristly chin, ensuring I have his eyes when I throw his words back at him. Unequivocally telling him, "I promise you won't be able to get rid of me, even if you try." I only hope I can keep my fears at bay to keep my promise. He takes my mouth in a possessive kiss, which has my body heating instantly and toes curling. I lose all sense of time as the kiss progresses to something deeper, something that expresses the loss we both felt over the past two weeks. It's full of relief for our reunion and the promises we've made to stay together.

Oliver finishes packing, and we make our way down to his car. I can't wait to get Oliver back to my place. I'm going to give him some tender loving care in an attempt to make up for my unforgivable brattiness these last weeks.

FORTY-NINE

-oliver-

THE TENSION I'VE BEEN CARRYING ACROSS MY SHOULDERS THESE past weeks dissolves as soon as I step foot inside Kate's home. My breathing deepens and that sense of peace and calm only she provides washes over me. I spy a box packed with my clothes near the front door. I look at Kate and she blushes.

"I collected all of your things with a plan to give them back to you." She looks down at her feet.

Stepping into her space, I use the tips of my fingers to tilt her face up to mine. "I guess that's to be expected. Let's unpack all this later. I've got some reacquainting to do."

I take her mouth in a rough kiss, expressing all of my frustration over the events of the previous weeks. I work hard to restrain myself, gentling the kiss and slowing down to savor our reunion. My body's alight with anticipation for having Kate's tight pussy choking my cock. Without breaking our kiss, I lift Kate beneath her ass, encouraging her to wrap her legs around me; noticing she's lost weight. Her arms automatically wrap around my neck as I kiss her all the way to her bedroom—I need a bed for this. I want to take my time with her. I need to show her how much I missed her and how much she means to me. Later, I can take her hard and fast against the wall. One of my favorite things to do.

As eager as I am to get to the main event, I need to slow down, take my time—I've got two weeks to make up for. I lay her gently on the bed, still tasting her mouth, absorbing her breaths, stroking her tongue. Our hands roam, reacquainting ourselves with each other's bodies. I remove the fabric between us—desperately needing to feel her skin against mine. As more of her silky skin is exposed, I trail my hands and lips over her body—tasting, touching, licking, and nipping, paying her luscious tits special attention.

Her breaths quicken as her body trembles in response to me. "You've got too many clothes on." She begins eagerly pushing and pulling at my clothes. "Get them off. Please. I need to have your skin against mine."

I kiss the tip of her nose and push myself up from her bed to remove the offending items as quickly as possible. "Anything for you, Sunshine."

I can't tear my eyes away from her. She's fucking stunning. The puffiness of her lips from my kisses fills me with male satisfaction. I mentally congratulate myself for marking her spectacular tits with a beard rash caused by my eager attention. Removing my shirt, I discard it quickly while she watches with half-lidded eyes. Sitting up, she shuffles to the edge of the bed, coming close enough to reach me. Kate immediately releases my belt buckle, quickly followed by the button and zipper in one swift motion, then she wriggles my jeans from my hips so they fall to the floor. I toe off my shoes, then slip my jeans and socks off. As I stand up, I remove my boxer briefs and kick them away. My heart is beating desperately fast. I'm worried it's going to explode right out of my chest. Kate moves forward quickly, licking straight up my cock, from my balls to my tip, then she takes the length in her mouth and moans. The vibrations shoot through my cock to my balls and I can't stop the groan that escapes in pleasure—my head dropping back on my shoulders in ecstasy. Her hot, wet mouth surrounding my shaft is unreal. It takes all of my willpower to fight the urge to grab her head and fuck her mouth into oblivion. It's such a turn on to know she's as desperate for me as I am for her.

I attempt to pull away, but Kate grabs my ass, holding me close. Who am I to argue with the lady? She sucks and licks my cock like it's her favorite treat and she's been deprived for too long. The vibrations caused by her little moans send my cock into hyper-drive. It feels so fucking good to have her mouth on me, taking me into its warmth, but I need to be inside her tight pussy when I come—which will happen too soon if I don't stop her.

"Kate, your mouth's sensational, but I need to be inside your hot pussy when I come." I groan as she pulls away.

I push her onto her back, dropping to my knees and spreading her legs further apart with my shoulders. Studying her glistening pussy, I use my fingers to spread her lips. "You're already incredibly wet." I slide a finger inside slowly. We both groan at the sensation. "Your pussy's gripping my finger extra tight to welcome me home."

I slide out and back in slowly, then lean forward to swipe my tongue up her slit to her clit, nipping gently with my teeth. Kate's body jolts off the bed and I place my hand on her trembling tummy, to keep her still until I've tasted my fill. A long moan emanates from her and she attempts to thrust her hips in time with the pumping of my finger. As I slide out, I replace one finger with two, causing Kate to whimper. I scan her curvy body, finding her massaging those firm tits, her head thrown back in ecstasy. Her pussy convulses around my fingers as she falls apart. Her body trembles and her legs tighten around my head. I gentle my fingers and my kisses, then slowly move up her body, laving her trembling flesh with kisses until I get to her breasts, which I suck into my mouth.

"Oh my God," she whispers reverently. "I can't believe how good you are at that." She giggles, and it's the very best of sounds. I want to hear it every single day.

"What's so funny?" Smiling, I look up at her flushed face. Feeling fucking fantastic that I can make her happy.

"Nothing. I'm just happy." She sighs. "I missed you more than I ever thought would be possible."

"You missed my tongue and fingers," I state as a joke. I know exactly what she means—I missed her desperately.

"Well, I missed those too, but I missed *you* beyond belief. The time apart made me realize how important you are to me, and how much I love spending time with you."

She moves in to kiss me, but it's impossible to be passive. I swipe my tongue over the seam of her lips, encouraging her to open up to me. Our tongues move in a familiar dance. It's seriously hot that she can taste herself on me. I bite her bottom lip, then lick away the sting. Shuffling her up the bed, I position myself between her thighs, swiping the crown of my throbbing cock through her slick, swollen folds. Locking eyes with Kate, I slowly slide my cock into her tight heat. I hold there, maintaining eye contact to check she's still with me. Her pussy feels heavenly, strangling my thick shaft. Right here is where I belong. I vow right now we'll never spend time apart again.

She attempts to tilt her hips, encouraging me to move. "Please move. I need you to move," she pants.

I teasingly slide almost all the way out of her channel and then back in, slowly. "Anything for you, Sunshine. Watch my cock sliding in and out of your tight pussy. Watch us joining, the way we're meant to."

She looks down between our bodies, groaning. "Feels so good." Her feet come up, pressing into my ass, as she tilts her hips upward. "Harder. Please!"

I slide out, careful not to leave her body, and then slam back in. I repeat the process over and over—a gentle slide out, a hard slam in. A sheen of perspiration forms over both of our bodies, making our hot skin slick. The scent of sex fills the air, a heady scent that turns me on further, making my cock lethally hard. Her pants and my grunts adding to the sound of skin slapping against skin. Her internal walls begin to contract, strangling my cock. I hold on to my rhythm as long as I can until I feel her quake and break apart beneath me, giving me permission to let go. My thrusts become frantic, leading to my own explosive release. Tingles shoot down my spine as my balls tighten up; blackness forms around the edge of my vision as I come, and come, and come some more. I throw my head back on a long groan. My entire body shudders with my orgasm that doesn't seem to have an end.

I collapse to the side of Kate, rolling her with me, keeping my cock inside the haven of her body. We're both working hard to catch our breath. I gently swipe the hair stuck to Kate's face away, checking she's okay. She graces me with a shy smile and nuzzles into my neck.

I kiss the top of her head. "I'm gonna want to repeat that. Several times." She giggles and I groan as her walls squeeze my half-spent cock. This is the only place I want to be for the rest of my days.

I tenderly carry Kate into the shower and can't resist the pull to take her again. Holding her against the tiled wall in my arms, I pound relentlessly into her body until she cries out her release and I swiftly follow with my own. I'm never going to get enough of this kind-hearted, sexy woman.

After we've dried off, Kate puts together a plate of cheese, crackers, and fruit for a picnic on her bed. As I'm moving the pillows to make us more comfortable, I discover one of my t-shirts hidden under her pillow. Holding it up, I raise an eyebrow to Kate in question, eliciting a shy smile and her breathtaking blush.

She casually shrugs her bare shoulder. "I couldn't bear to give up everything. I was going to keep that one, hoping you wouldn't notice." She looks away from me, embarrassed.

I carefully draw her face back to mine, kissing the tip of her delicate nose. "You can keep them all."

As we eat, I mention the gala I'm organizing, and how Toby offered to be the entertainment. When I explain we only have two weeks to get the funds to save the kids' homes, she immediately offers to help in any way she can. We work on making a plan for her to stop by my office on Monday after she finishes work to look through what we've done so far. Tickets went on sale last Monday, making fine-tuning the event a priority.

I also tell Kate about my visit with my father and his counselor. I think we cleared the air during our two-hour meeting. He carries a great deal of guilt for the accident which killed Mom, but his biggest burden is not being the father I needed growing up—that he checked out, leaving me to grow up on my own. It was probably the most honest and open discussion we've had, and I'm hopeful we'll be able to forge some kind of relationship moving forward. Kate's ecstatic for me, which I knew she would be. I now have a standing appointment every second week with him and Dr. Wyatt at *Square One*.

We spend the rest of the weekend in bed, reacquainting ourselves with each other's bodies and showing the love and affection we have for the other, without saying the words. I have this desperate need to constantly have some part of my body touching hers—as if the constant touch reassures me she's still with me. Kate's easy with her affections, and I feel the fractured part of my soul settle for the first time in a very long while.

FIFTY

-kate-

OVER THE LAST TWO WEEKS, OLIVER AND I WORKED SEAMLESSLY together, preparing for the best gala event possible. He and Jase had already done the bulk of the work before I stepped in to help. Mom, Dad, Toby, and even Margie have helped wherever possible, and I know we've given the event the very best chance of success. The response from the rich and famous has been mind-blowing. Tickets sold out within forty-eight hours and offers came in from far and wide for the use of vacation homes, personal jets, and dates to be auctioned for the cause.

Tonight's the big night, and it seems I have a flock of hummingbirds taking flight in my stomach. Oliver insisted on taking Mom, Margie, and me shopping for our dresses and shoes for this event; which I reluctantly agreed to after we had a massive argument. I laid down some serious boundaries regarding his use of money where I'm concerned.

I don't want it.

I'm not interested in it.

I don't want his money to change who I am as a person—who we are as a couple. I know he has money, lots of it. I know there will be certain aspects of life with Oliver I will have to accept, but I don't want him to ever think I'm with him because of his money or for what he can give me.

He wasn't happy, but he eventually acquiesced to my 'unreasonable' request—*his words*. If it were up to him, I would have had a full day of pampering, with someone doing my hair and makeup. I wouldn't have felt like me.

I shower, washing my hair, shaving, and scrubbing my body with extra care, ensuring its smooth and silky. I've never been to an event like this and as excited as I am, I'm also nervous I'll struggle to meet society's expectations of what a billionaire's girlfriend should look and dress like. I only hope I don't embarrass him.

I blow my hair, styling it into smooth waves down my back, and apply my makeup, with a focus on my sapphire eyes, balancing it out with a pale matte lip color. I blew my budget to purchase some sexy red lingerie to wear beneath my dress to help me feel empowered.

I slip my feet into my red satin sandals, which have a single strap across my toes, painted in the same color. I get to work wrapping and tying the lustrous laces around my ankles and lower calves. Standing up, I'm a little wobbly because I'm not used to wearing such high heels. I have been practicing for the last few days, but the wobble is real. Ballet flats are my go-to for work and my Converse for the weekend, so I feel a little odd.

I carefully slide into the elegant, full-length black V-neck, off-the-shoulder satin dress. The fitted bodice shows off the top of my boobs sensationally—*Oliver may well swallow his tongue*. Hidden within the gathers of the full skirt is a long split, which goes all the way to the top of my thigh. The dress is actually very demure until I step forward, exposing the full-length split—making me feel sexy. The best thing about this dress is the hidden pockets, meaning I won't need to take a purse—*yay for me*.

I spritz some of my favorite perfume on my pulse points, finishing with the diamond stud earrings my parents gave me for my twenty-first birthday. I'm putting my essentials in my pockets when there's a knock on my front door.

I hurry to the door as quickly as I can in my heels, opening it swiftly to find Oliver, looking absolutely edible in a dark green tux which appears almost black. Fitted to perfection across his broad shoulders and tapering in at his slim waist, showing off his masculine physique. My eyes rake down his body and up again in heated appraisal. When I finally make my way up to his face, I see the same appreciation in his eyes, making my heart skip a beat and my skin to warm.

He steps into me, one hand tightening around my waist, one to the back of my head under the fall of my hair. He pauses then kisses my forehead. "You look otherworldly." He sucks in a breath. "You've stolen all the air from my lungs." His warm hands come up to cup either side of my face as he whispers, "Can I kiss you?"

I can only nod. The reverence in which he spoke has stolen my voice and my heart. I can't help but wonder how many times I can fall in love with him. He moves in slowly, and my eyes close of their own volition to prepare for the potency that is Oliver. At first, his kiss is gentle, almost sweet before deepening, becoming more demanding. I'm unsure how long we kiss, but we're interrupted by a throat clearing behind Oliver. He presses his forehead to mine, winking at me with a soft smile and a chuckle.

"C'mon you two, we haven't got all night." Margie huffs. "I imagine it would be poor form for the hosts to arrive late to their own event." We all snicker at that comment, making our way toward the waiting limo after locking up.

Once we're settled and on our way, Margie studies the two of us for several beats. "I must say, you two make a handsome couple. You'll make beautiful babies."

I almost choke at her blasé statement, but Oliver takes it in stride. "If our daughters are as kind-hearted and as beautiful inside and out as Kate, I'll be the luckiest man in the world."

My heart melts and I feel completely secure with Oliver right now. I lean across to whisper in his ear, "I'm hoping we have little boys who have a generous spirit and look just like their daddy." Then I kiss his neck, just below his ear. "I didn't get a chance to tell you how edible you look in your tux, Mr. Stone." He kisses my exposed shoulder, making my body heat.

I have to keep reminding myself we have Margie in the car, and our PDA needs to be kept suitable for public observation.

Margie turns to us with a small smile. "I'm extremely proud of you two. I know tonight's going to be a tremendous success and I want to thank you for including an old lady." Margie's eyes look glassy as she nods her head once, turning away to stare out of the window. The outfit Oliver bought Margie for this evening is lovely; a muted mossy green, with lace sleeves and overlay. Its fitted bodice with a scoop neck gives way to a straight skirt, stopping at her ankles. She looks great, all dolled up. I feel my own eyes burn with tears, which I barely manage to keep at bay.

We arrive at the *Four Seasons*, which has been awesome throughout the entire process of putting together such a large-scale event with very short notice. They only requested a heavily discounted payment for the food and beverages for the evening. The hotel kindly donated everything else, including the room hire, table settings, staffing, the emcee, PR, the valet parking, the auctioneer, and the event organizer.

The driver opens our door, allowing Oliver to exit the car first. He assists Margie out of the car and then helps me manage my exit, holding out both arms to escort us down the red carpet, past the paparazzi. Flashes explode as journalists thrust microphones into our faces, posing questions about who Margie and I are, as well as the designer of my dress and shoes. I can't believe anyone would be interested in who made my dress and shoes. I'm extremely nervous. I can't even remember off the top of my head. My choice of outfit had nothing to do with the cost or the designer, only that I liked it and I hoped Oliver would think I was beautiful wearing it.

Margie goes ahead, leaving the photographers to get shots of Oliver and me together. All the while he whispers 'how sexy I am' and 'how he can't wait to take my dress off later tonight', helping to calm my nerves in this unfamiliar situation. He has a confident air, which reminds me of all the photographs I've seen of him with different women, walking red carpets into events like this one. It's a bitter pill to swallow, but I manage. He's got a history that happened before I came along—it can't be erased because it makes me jealous or uncomfortable. He does nothing but dote on me, build me up, and show me how much I mean to him. We haven't said those three words yet, but we *show* each other all the time.

Oliver slows to a stop in front of one particular journalist who garners his attention. "Mr. Stone, who is your date this evening?"

He steps closer to my body, pulling me in with an arm banded tightly around my waist, looking down at me with smoldering eyes. "This stunning woman is Ms. Kate Summer." I smile and nod in acknowledgment toward the journalist.

"You're not usually the type of woman we see accompanying Mr. Stone to these events. How do you know each other?"

Did he really say that to me? What a jerk!

Pressing my shoulders back, I raise my chin. "You mean a *real* person—right? Instead of the fake women, who only want to be seen with him to raise their profile? Is that what you meant?" I'm proud of the strength in my voice because his comment dug at the very core of my past hurts. I showed some spine and stood up for myself, without being rude. *Go me!*

Oliver steps in, whispering in a deadly tone, "You can fuck off. How fucking dare you be disrespectful to my date? I will fucking dismantle your pitiful excuse for a life, piece by piece." If you were looking on, you would have no clue as to the anger emanating from Oliver. Externally, he looks as calm as a lake, but I can feel the tension rippling off of him. The reporter looks panic-stricken by Oliver's response to his inappropriate question. I tug his arm, encouraging him to move along, allowing us to get on with our night. I'm not about to let some jerk ruin our evening.

"Are you okay?" He whispers in my ear. His warm breath on my neck.

I smile at him. "Yeah, I am. Thank you for standing up for me."

"You stood up for yourself, but I couldn't let it go. I wanted to show that asshole that we're a team." And that's exactly what we are. I kiss the underside of his jaw in appreciation.

As we step inside the ballroom, my jaw drops at the spectacular sight. Everything is beyond stunning. From the table settings to the balloons and flowers, kindly donated by *Blooms and Balloons*, to the decorations donated by *Event Hire*. The large photographs show-casing the kids experiencing the day-to-day life in the homes provided by *The Parkerville Project* are a masterful addition. Each photograph is accompanied by the story of how the child came to live in one of the homes. We thought the photographs and stories would help loosen people's purse strings when it came time for the auction planned later this evening. People are already studying them, so I think they'll work a treat.

Some of the older kids will be in attendance for part of the evening, sitting at the tables with the attendees. It will be such a unique experience for them. We also have an electronic tally, showing the amount of money already raised and the amount we still need. Currently, the tally sits at $5,000,000, which includes Oliver's donation of $2,000,000 and the sale of tonight's tickets, minus the food and beverage expenses. We need to double the amount with the auction. After perusing the donated items, I feel our goal is easily achievable. The money we need will cover purchasing the mortgages outright, utilities, staff wages, health care and psych services for the kids, school supplies and after school tutoring and activities to keep them on track, as well as food and clothing for the next several months; until the missing money is recovered—*hopefully*.

Marcus approaches us with an enormous smile and a striking woman on his arm. He takes Oliver's hand between both of his, shaking vigorously in appreciation. He then takes my hands, repeating the process, almost jarring my arm out of my socket.

"I can't thank the two of you enough for all you have done to help us help the kids." His happiness is infectious and we smile broadly in return.

"It's been our pleasure to put this event together. Let's hope we reach our target of $10,000,000 tonight."

Marcus nods, then draws our attention to the woman beside him. "Please allow me to introduce my lovely wife, Celia." She smiles, nodding in acknowledgment, shaking each of our hands with a gentle calmness; quite the juxtaposition to her husband. We make small talk for a while until the manager of the hotel approaches us to confirm some minor details for the evening; ensuring we're happy with everything thus far.

The room is filling quickly and I'm embarrassingly star-struck with the number of celebrities in attendance. Even though Toby's famous, I'm very much removed from that part of his life. I've been to his concerts, but I've never met any of his famous friends. He likes to keep our family separate from his stardom and the things that go along with it. Oliver retrieves a couple of drinks for us when we spy Mom and Dad. Oliver purchased a table so Jase, Margie, Mom, and Dad could attend the event. At $8,000 a ticket, it wasn't in the budget for them. We cross the room to welcome them, hugging in our usual exuberant greeting. Mom gushes over how I look in my dress, while Dad and Oliver catch up. Right at seven, the emcee announces the entrée will be served, inviting everyone to take their seats.

A hush settles over the room as guests are served and begin eating—a tasting plate of seared scallops in a herb butter sauce, small medallions of steak, dauphin potatoes, and seasonal greens. The food is beyond divine. Marcus approaches the podium to thank everyone for attending, encouraging them to open their hearts and wallets later in the evening during the auction. He introduces Oliver, inviting him up to the stage.

Oliver strides up to the podium with sure steps and a confidence that can't be faked. Everyone in the room applauds, and he waits patiently for them to settle.

"Thank you, Marcus, for your kind introduction. Thank you, everyone, for paying the ridiculous amount of money to attend this evening." Everyone snickers and I notice they're nodding in agreement with one another. "*The Parkerville Project* means the world to me because I was once a kid who lived in one of the homes they provide." Audible gasps sound throughout the room, and I, myself am shocked he's shared such a personal part of his history with the people here. It's not something he likes to speak about and it took him a long time to share it with me. "I ended up with nobody to care for me when I was seven. The why and how aren't important for this story, but where I ended up is. The people at *The Parkerville*

Project took me in and cared for me. They kept me safe and nourished, and gave me a home." He looks at me. "More recently, they unknowingly facilitated a serendipitous second-chance meeting with my elegant girlfriend, Kate." Everyone is looking in my direction, attempting to work out who he's talking about. "Normally, I would throw wads of money at a problem, rather than giving my time. I always considered my time better spent making more money." People around the room nod in agreement. "But Kate and Jase, my longtime assistant, have shown me the importance of also giving my time. The value of rolling up my sleeves and giving my skills to help others is something they've taught me. I can't thank you both enough for the valuable lessons." He nods in our direction and I can't help the thrill that runs through my body at his words. "Of course, money is always a big help, and that's exactly why you're all here tonight. Please give generously for the kids, so they can return to their homes as soon as possible. Thank you. Please enjoy your evening."

Oliver returns to our table amid pats on the back and plenty of handshaking. Everyone stops him for one reason or another. Men and women alike attempt to get a piece of him. The women are blatant and outright slimy in their intentions—it reinforces what he's told me and why he values our relationship so much. He and Jase share a manly handshake slash back slap, slash hug thing men do. As he sits next to me, he takes my hand, kissing it tenderly, then kisses my exposed shoulder. "Thank you, Kate." His quiet words hold a deeper meaning, filling my heart with gratitude for him. I turn, kissing the top of his head.

Dinner arrives, and we all settle down to eat our meal, chatting excitedly about the various celebrities in our midst. Margie, Mom, and I excuse ourselves from the table to visit the ladies' room and freshen up. As we exit the ladies, I can hear Toby on stage, playing to the audience. Some people have moved to the dance floor to dance, while others stand in small groups talking, and others make their way along the auction table, looking at what will be on offer within the hour.

I find Oliver in the crowd and come to a screeching halt. A stunning woman with a petite frame and white-blonde hair is practically glued to Oliver's side. Her large breasts press against his body, while her hand glides down his jacket, feeling his pecs. I can't believe what I'm seeing, and I lose the ability to breathe for a moment—I think this is Sonia. The surprising thing for me is in this moment I realize I trust Oliver completely. I have no thoughts in my head that he may be more interested in her than in me. He's given me zero reasons to feel insecure in this situation, and I'm not going to let my past experiences rule my behavior.

Mom and Margie notice my inaction and step closer to me, following my line of sight. We all stop to watch them for a minute. The tension radiating off of Oliver is obvious, his shoulders drawn as tight as a bow, his head pulled back as far away from the woman as possible. He's politely working to extricate himself from her hold without causing a scene. I step forward without thought, my need to step between them and get that woman away from my boyfriend at the core of my actions. I come around behind them, approaching from the other side. Oliver looks relieved when he spots me.

I thrust my hand out toward the woman. "Hi, I'm Kate, Oliver's girlfriend." She looks at my hand as if it's covered in crap. "And you are?" I prod. She makes no move to separate from my boyfriend. However, Oliver steps up his game, stepping away from her and closer to me. He wraps his arm around my waist and pulls me into his body, finishing with a kiss to the top of my head. The tension in his body subsides.

She looks at Oliver in disbelief. "I'm Sonia. We were engaged not all that long ago. I can't believe he hasn't told you about me." She brushes her long locks over her shoulder. "I'm his one great love." She smiles a fake, saccharine smile at him. "I was telling Oliver that I would love to catch up with him sometime soon." She smirks at me, attempting a coy shrug. "For old times' sake. You know how it is?"

I was right. This *is* the ex that's been stalking him in an attempt to get him back.

"And I was just telling Sonia, I wouldn't catch up with her if she was the last woman on earth." He kisses the top of my head again and looks at Sonia. "Thank you for supporting *The Parkerville Project*. Enjoy your good evening." He sounds as if he's speaking to a stranger, and I can't help the million and one questions that fly through my mind.

Oliver guides me to the dance floor, taking me in his arms, holding me tight against his body. Tipping my chin up, his eyes capture and hold mine. "You're the only woman in this room I see … I want. Don't let that vapid woman cause you to question how important you are to me." He takes my mouth in a possessive kiss that isn't suitable for public viewing, but I relish in the feel of his mouth on mine.

"You want to hear something great?" He nods for me to continue. "I trust you completely. You've given me no reason to question how you feel about me. I feel completely confident in our relationship." I kiss his chin. "I feel sad for her, though. Her desperation was coming off her in waves." We dance for several songs until the emcee interrupts us, announcing it's time for the auction to begin. Grabbing a couple of drinks, we return to our table as the proceedings begin.

As the auction gets underway, I excuse myself under the guise of checking in with Toby, but I want to find Sonia. Eventually, I see her coming out of the ladies' bathroom and make a beeline for her. We need to have a chat.

"Uh, Sonia." I'm proud of the strength in my voice, even though I'm extremely nervous about confronting this woman.

She turns around, looking me up and down with obvious distaste. "Yeah. What do *you* want?"

"I wanted to have a quick word with you. If you don't mind?" I'm not sure what I can say to her to get the message across that Oliver is with me. That she doesn't have any chance of reconciliation. I gesture to a couple of club chairs situated out of the way. "Mind if we sit for a moment? I'm not used to wearing heels and my feet are killing me."

We move forward, both sitting at the same time. "I guess you're wondering what I want to talk about."

"I'm guessing it has to do with Oliver."

I nod. "Yeah, it does. I wanted to explain some things to you. I want to make it clear you're wasting your time. When you dumped him for a richer man, you hurt him deeply. For a long time, he closed himself off. He no longer trusted women because of what you did."

She smiles a feline smile. She seems proud of her achievement. "Oh, I realized when I last saw him how much my actions had hurt him. He obviously still loves me, if he's *still* feeling hurt after all these years."

This woman is delusional. I'm uncertain if anything I have to say will get through to her. But I try anyway. I explain how Oliver and I met. I tell her all about his efforts to find me again, and then to convince me to date him. I tell her about our recent breakup and the deep connection we share. I explain I want him for the man he is, not for the size of his bank account. I tell her the reasons Oliver wants to have me by his side. The things I give to him that money can't buy. I can't tell her how much I love him, because I haven't told Oliver yet. The details I've shared are extremely personal, but I'm hoping she finally gets the idea; there isn't any room for her. I didn't want to be unkind to her. For one, it's not in my nature and second, she needs kindness, not hate or anger. I've probably shared too many intimate details, but I wanted to get through to her. I want her to leave my boyfriend alone.

-oliver-

I DIDN'T ANTICIPATE RUNNING INTO MY EX HERE, SO SHE CAUGHT ME by surprise. Her calls, emails, and texts have ramped up over the past few weeks since her visit to my office, but it seems she's upping her game. I must remember to get Mike to investigate her. Something's changed and I want a heads up before she becomes more of a problem. I look over at Kate and take a moment to appreciate how stunning she looks tonight. She worries she doesn't fit into my world, but how she has presented herself tonight is proof she needn't worry about such things.

Kate is gorgeous in her cut-off shorts, when she first wakes up in the morning, covered in glue, paint, and glitter after a day at work, or anything else she wears. I've never seen her like this before. When she opened her door, I almost swallowed my tongue. Seeing her standing next to Sonia reinforced for me that Kate is the person for me now, and into my future. We've made a great team these past weeks, working together with Jase to organize this event. It's confirmed my original feeling—I want to marry her and make her round with my babies. She has such a genuine heart and soul, and I will be eternally grateful that she allows me in her orbit. I'll never take her precious gift for granted.

The auction is in full swing, the electronic tally showing $8,725,260. Kate is almost bouncing in her seat, excitedly watching the tally moving closer to our goal. A handful of attendees battle it out for an original artwork by a famous Japanese contemporary artist, who spends his time between Tokyo and New York. The piece eventually goes under the hammer for $1.8 million. Kate and her family are in utter shock, as the winning bid takes us over our goal for the evening. Amid cheers and whistles from everyone in the room, balloons release from the nets attached to the ceiling in celebration. Kate turns her excited face to me and grabs my face, slamming her mouth onto mine, kissing me through her smile and mine.

"We did it!"

I laugh. "We did."

The auction is momentarily paused for dessert to be served, buffet style, and Toby returns to the stage, continuing his performance with Shane's ever-watchful eyes on the crowd forming on the dance floor. Tickets for his next album tour, including a backstage pass, are up for auction tonight. He's been more than generous with his time to help us. We assemble plates of the guys' favorite desserts for them to enjoy once this set is finished. We leave our desserts for later, joining the growing crowd on the dance floor. I feel a tap on my shoulder. Turning, I find Kate's dad gesturing to swap dance partners. I reluctantly give up my favorite dance partner to share a dance with Kate's mom.

"You are stunning tonight, Mrs. Summer." She smiles shyly.

"Why thank you, Oliver." She looks around my body to check where her husband and daughter are. "I wanted to have a quick word with you, if that's okay?"

I nod. "Of course. Anytime." I brace myself. I'm unsure if this is going to bode well for me.

She releases a heavy breath, giving me a motherly smile. "I wanted to tell you how happy I am that you found your way back to our family. Despite the many difficulties you faced growing up, I'm extremely proud of the man you have become. I know I'm not your mother, but I wanted you to know I think your mom would have been very proud of the man you've become." Her words have unfamiliar emotions clogging my throat. "I also wanted to thank you. Kate's confidence has grown so very much since the two of you have been together." I'm shocked she's attributing Kate's increased confidence to me. "You're fabulous for her, Oliver, and I'm truly happy you're in her life—our lives. I know it took a lot for you to convince our girl to give you a chance, and I'm very thankful you persisted." Her approval means everything I didn't realize I needed. It's been twenty-five years since I've had a mother's approval and affection, which I'm only now realizing I've missed terribly. She must sense my turmoil, because she rubs my arm tenderly and kisses my cheek.

We swap dance partners again and I pull Kate in close, kissing her neck and exposed shoulder, then send her out in a spin and pull her back into my hard body—both of us laughing. My heart and soul feel lighter than I can ever remember, and I have Kate and her family to thank for that.

Toby performs his last song for the evening, and the emcee announces the auction will continue shortly, encouraging everyone to return to their table. One hour later, and the last item is up for bid—tickets and backstage passes for a concert celebrating Toby's next album, which hasn't been laid down yet. It goes for $225,000, taking our final tally for the evening to $13,827,380. Everyone in attendance cheers and celebrates the enormous success of the evening—popping champagne, making toasts, and reveling in our success. Kate's eyes are full of tears as Marcus approaches us. Throwing all formality out of the window, he pulls me up for an enormous bear hug, and some healthy back-slapping. Then he draws Kate in for a tight hug of appreciation.

"I don't know how we can ever thank you enough for everything you've done. I am without words to express my gratitude to you both." He looks close to tears as Celia steps closer to offer her husband support.

The evening finally wraps up and we say our goodbyes to everyone. Margie is spending the night at the Summer's home and since we're in the city, I'm taking Kate back to my place. I can't wait to get her out of that exquisite dress so I can worship her delectable body.

As soon as we enter my apartment, Kate's on me. Slipping my jacket off my shoulders and tossing it over the nearest chair. Next, she moves to my bow tie and I gently grasp her wrists, stilling her. She looks up at me in confusion, but stills when she sees the seriousness of my expression. I place her hands on my pecs, allowing me to cup her face gently in the palms of my hands, keeping it tilted up toward my own.

"I have something important I need to tell you before I spend the rest of the night worshipping your delicious body." I kiss the tip of her nose. "I love you, Kate." Her eyes widen and shimmer. "The very first moment I laid eyes on you, I felt inexplicably drawn to you. I had never felt that magnetic pull toward another human being in my life, and it caught me by surprise. When we met the second time, I knew I couldn't let you slip away. Over these past months, getting to know you—your beautiful heart, your gentle nature, your genuine soul—it only confirmed and solidified my initial feelings toward you." I kiss her cheeks. "I want to be clear. I have *never* felt this way about another woman. You're *everything* to me, and I don't foresee a time in my life when I won't want to have you in it; standing by my side, sharing my world." I take her lips in a gentle exploration and she immediately opens for me, sinking into a kiss that expresses everything we both feel.

She gently pulls back, giving me a shy smile. "I love you too, Oliver. So much. I've been overwhelmed with how big my feelings are for you. It's wonderful to finally say the words." She moves forward to continue our kiss, both of us smiling into it. We deepen it to a soul-searing level and as usual, everything falls away, and it's as if we're in a void, where we are the only people in existence.

Without breaking the kiss, her hands move to undo and remove my bow tie, while my hands move toward her zipper. As I slide it down slowly, she unbuttons my dress shirt. "You looked fabulously hot in your tux tonight. My panties have been drenched since the moment I opened my door."

I groan, moving in to take her lips in a rough kiss, biting her bottom lip, then her top lip. I swipe my tongue across and suck each soft pillow into my mouth. My need grows exponentially with hers. I slide my hands over her smooth shoulders to shuck the straps at the top of her arms. The dress slips down her body, gradually revealing a delicate red lace strapless bra, which has her perfect tits on display like the delicacy they are. Sliding the dress down lower, she has matching panties—a tiny triangle covering heaven, with ties at her hips for easy removal. My cock jumps in excitement as a drop of precum moistens the tip. Holding out my hand for Kate, she steps out of the inky pool and I suck in a sharp breath as she stands before me in her sexy as fuck underwear and satin lace-up sandals. My eyes peruse her curves from the tips of her red-painted toes, up her body, to the top of her alluring head. She is a spectacular sight, creamy skin wrapped in red, with her crimson hair falling like silk down her back. My hands move without restraint, roughly grasping the back of her neck to draw her to my mouth. I kiss up her neck to her ear, tugging on her earlobe with my teeth.

"You are the most breathtakingly sexy woman I have ever laid eyes on." She moans, pressing her body closer to mine. She slides my shirt from my arms with great difficulty, finally realizing the sleeves are trapped by my cufflinks.

We both chuckle, working to remove them, then tossing my shirt out of the way. Next, we both work to undo my belt, button, and zipper. While I toe off my shoes, she slides my underwear and trousers down my legs and discards them somewhere close by. I bend down to remove my socks and step Kate backward until I press her back against the cool glass of the window overlooking the city skyline. She gasps at the chill as I press my warm body against her front, trapping her. I take advantage of her gasp, thrusting my tongue into her mouth as I slide my hands to her hips, releasing the ties on her panties.

It's like being together for the first time all over again. Her warm skin touching mine, her breaths fanning my face—*home*. One hand skims up to massage her breast through her bra, while my other hand slides from her hip to her pussy, which is drenched.

I groan.

She moans breathily.

My cock jolts.

Dropping to my knees, I position one silky leg over my shoulder and tease her clit with the tip of my nose, then I swipe her swollen lips with my tongue. Her hips snap forward as her hands go to my hair, gripping it tightly as she moans her approval. I'll never get enough of hearing her sexy sounds and tasting her sweet pussy—it's like crack. I work her over with my mouth and when I know she's getting close; I slide two fingers inside her tight channel, causing her to break apart spectacularly. Her whole body shudders with her release, and her tits heave with her effort to take in a breath. As she comes down from her high, her head drops forward, a slow smile forming on her lips. She looks sated, but I'm not finished with her yet.

Releasing her leg, I move up her body, kissing, biting, licking as I go. I slide one hand in between the glass and her back to release her bra and catch one of her tits in my hand. Using both hands, I squeeze them together, giving them the attention they deserve. I take each one into my mouth, sucking hard on the peaks.

"I love your tits. These pretty peach-colored nipples tighten up nicely, ready for my mouth to suck and bite." She grips the back of my head, pressing me into the soft globes.

"I love how you suck them. Please never stop." Her voice is desperate.

"I won't. I'll never stop sucking your gorgeous tits." Skimming my hands down her body to her ass, I pick her up, encouraging her to wrap her ivory legs around my hips. My cock's close to exploding as it gets closer to the haven that is Kate's pussy. I slide Kate's drenched folds along my shaft, then line myself up and slide in slowly.

Painfully slowly.

I feel every glorious inch of her tight walls welcoming my cock home. Bottoming out, balls deep in this sexy woman, I study her face carefully, ensuring she's with me every step of the way. What I see in her eyes fills me with a sense of contentment and satisfaction I've only ever experienced with her.

Kissing along her jaw, I take her mouth in a luxuriously slow dance of tongues, exchanging breaths. I begin a slow seduction of my hips, sliding my cock in and out of her tight pussy with measured strokes. The sensations make my cock weep in wonder at the bliss I've found. Kate moves her hips in time with my thrusts, which gradually increase in tempo and power, driving us both higher into the stratosphere in our desire to come. Her walls spasm around my shaft as she comes on a long moan and I can no longer hold back my release. My balls draw up and I explode, whispering Kate's name reverently; my body's release leaving me breathless, my legs shaky. I carefully carry Kate to the dining table, laying her down gently, folding myself over her, because I'm not ready to leave her body.

She giggles, which feels awesome around my cock. I lift my head to check what's so funny. She brushes her hair out of her face, looking up at me with sparkling eyes. "I hope no one saw my ass pressed up against your window." She bites her bottom lip. "That could be embarrassing."

I lean in, kissing her nose, then her forehead. "We're pretty high up and the lights are still off inside. That would make it difficult to see anything. I wouldn't put you at risk like that, because I don't want anyone else to see what's mine."

She looks satisfied with my answer, nodding her head. "That was the hottest sex I've ever had, and we've had some pretty hot sex."

I can only nod in agreement. The chemistry between us is off the charts on fire, and knowing Kate inside and out makes our connection even stronger. I didn't know sex could be this spectacular.

"Every time we have sex, our connection grows stronger, and it feels more intense. I was close to blacking out then. You might kill me by orgasm." I kiss her nose as she giggles, pushing my still semi-hard cock out of her body. Lifting her in my arms, I carry her into my bathroom to we can clean up so I can defile her all over again.

My phone lights up with a call. Mike's name is on the display. "Hey Mike, what have you got for me on Sonia?"

"Hi, Mr. Stone. Well. Sonia's in a bit of a mess. She's been kicked out of her home, had her car repossessed, and all of her credit cards are maxed out."

"Huh. I knew something had happened for her to be coming after me. What about her husband?"

"He discovered she was cheating on him. That's why he's kicked her out and cut her off. As you would know, she's never held down a job—she has no income and no way to get one. I've been following her to upscale bars, where she's working hard to hook a new sugar daddy."

"How long ago did this happen?"

"From what I can gather, about four months ago now."

"How did she manage to get a ticket to the gala?"

"As far as I can tell, the man she'd been seeing attended the event, and she was his date. They're no longer together. She's having a hard time locking any one man down."

"I see. Keep a general check on her and let me know if anything changes."

"Sure thing, Mr. Stone. Bye."

I disconnect the call, sitting back in my chair, looking out of my expansive wall of windows across the city skyline. It all makes sense now. That's about the time the messages, phone calls, and emails started. I'll keep ignoring her; she'll get the message eventually and hopefully move on.

I get back to work, familiarizing myself with the new data and analysis reports which have been put together by my finance department. We're looking good for this quarter, even though my focus has been elsewhere for the past month or so. The projections for the running expenses of the company over the next twelve months are also looking good. The coming year is looking to be our best year yet, which also bodes well for my charitable foundation.

It takes two weeks for *The Parkerville Project* finances to be sorted with the bank and the foreclosure status to be dismissed. The money raised has paid off the mortgages and given the organization enough in reserve to cover the general expenses associated with the running of the properties, as well as staff wages, until we get the stolen money back. Everyone can finally take a breath.

Kate plans to spend her weekend helping the kids move back into their home and get settled into their usual routine.

Checking my emails, I notice a new email from Marcus. I click on the notification to see if there are any updates.

Re: Update on the embezzlement proceedings
From: Marcus Trainor
To: Oliver Stone
Hello Oliver
We have a court date! Our lawyer will be in touch with you within the next few days, to discuss the procedure from here and probable dates you will be required in court.
She says things look promising for a conviction and the return of funds still sitting in the offshore accounts. As you are aware, some of the money is gone, but most of it is still sitting there. The accounts were frozen immediately, preventing any further theft.
After the court convicts Errol, we're probably looking at six months before the stolen funds are returned to us. Thanks to you and your team, we have enough money to tide *The Parkerville Project* over until then.
Kindest regards
Marcus
CEO
The Parkerville Project

Well, that *is* good news! Things are looking up. I have the woman of my dreams, *The Parkerville Project* is in good shape, and my business is successful beyond my dreams. Life is good.

I make my regular call to check in on my father. They seem to think he'll be ready to move into a halfway house within the next six weeks. It's the next logical step in preparing him for living in society as a functional citizen. He'll still get the support he needs while stepping out into the real world. They'll help him secure work and settle into a routine aimed at building his independence. Their success rates are high, so I'm feeling positive and hopeful for a more productive future for my father. I only hope this step allows us to build on what we've started over the last few weeks during the visits with his counselor. I miss the involved and loving father I had when I was a boy. Not that I would ever expect us to return to that.

My mobile buzzes with an unfamiliar local number. I wouldn't normally answer a number I don't recognize, but it may be the lawyer.

"Hello. This is Oliver Stone."

There's silence for a few beats. Checking the display, I ensure the call is still connected.

"Hello."

I'm about to disconnect the call when I hear *her* voice.

"Oliver." It's a whisper. "I need your help."

"I'm not interested, Sonia. I've made my position crystal clear. Leave me the fuck alone."

I'm about to disconnect when she sobs, "I'm sorry, Oliver. I don't have anyone else to call, and I'm scared. I don't know what to do or who I can turn to."

Fuck! I can't turn my back on her when she sounds desolate. Desperate. I know she must be in a bad place after the information Mike gave me. "Where are you?"

She gives me her location. I tell Jase where I'm going and why before leaving immediately. I plug the address into my GPS as I'm pulling out of the parking garage. On my way, I can't help but wonder what's happened to Sonia. Why am I the only person she has left to call? We've been over for a long time, and until recently I hadn't heard from or seen her.

Arriving at my destination, I find a parking space as close as possible to the address. It's a small café in a bohemian part of town. An eclectic array of people, bundled for warmth, are sitting outside enjoying the sunshine on mismatched wrought-iron chairs. I exit my car, engaging the locks. A flash of white-blonde hair leaps at me, wrapping me in an embrace as I step around my car. I take a moment to gather my wits and press against her shoulders, pushing her back. She doesn't appear distressed or even mildly upset—I feel as though I've been had.

"Sonia." I push her back further, stepping away from her body. "What the fuck are you playing at? You sounded distressed on the phone, so I came to help, but you seem more than fucking fine now."

She acts coy, which I know for a fact she's not. Placing her hand on her chest, in an attempt to draw attention to her mostly exposed breasts, she says, "Oh, Oliver. It was the only way I knew to get you to come." She grasps my hand. "Come. Sit down, share a coffee with me."

I pull my hand free. "I don't have time to share a fucking coffee with you. You sounded distressed, and I came here to help. I thought you were in trouble. I've got a busy schedule and I don't have time for this shit." I snap at her. She's delusional if she thinks I have any inclination to spend any time with her.

She puts on a pout that possibly works for a ten-year-old, not a fully grown woman. "Come on, Oliver. Surely you can spend an hour with me. I need to talk with you, and you've been ignoring all of my attempts to contact you. I had to do something drastic."

I drop my head, huffing out a breath in frustration. "Do you even have a problem?"

She shrugs one shoulder. "Other than wanting you back and you not giving me the time of day?" She steps forward again, attempting to reach for my forearm, but I step back quickly.

"Then I'm outta here. I've made it as plain as I fucking can. I'm not interested in anything to do with you. We ..." I wave between the two of us. "Are not getting back together. I have moved on so far from you and our pseudo-relationship, we may as well be in different galaxies." I glare at her pointedly. "Do not contact me via email, phone, or in person. I. Am. Not. Fucking interested. I don't want to revisit what we had, because I've learned that what we had was less than nothing."

I'm a few steps away from her when she calls out to me, "What we had was special! You may not remember, but I do."

I stop my retreat, spinning around to face her. I take two steps forward until I'm in her space. My posture is intimidating and my tone says, don't fuck with me. "Oh, I remember everything, Sonia. What you meant to say was my credit card and my cock were special. There was nothing outside of that between us. I was a dumb fuck back then. I'm wiser now, and there's no way you can convince me to revisit what we had."

"You know I had a chat with your 'girlfriend' the other night at the gala?"

She says 'girlfriend' as though it's a dirty word. The dumb-founded expression on my face informs her of my ignorance.

"Yeah, she's all sweet and apple pie. Blah blah this and blah blah that. She thinks she's got you locked down, but there's no locking down Oliver Stone." She rests her hand on my pec, looking up at me through obscenely long eyelashes. "You and I were great together in bed. You were always happy to have me on your arm for events. You loved having me spend your money to look my best, and we look good together." This woman is delusional. "Not like that frumpy ginger you're wasting your time on. Oliver, she's not right for you. She doesn't know how to be the wife of a billionaire CEO. She doesn't know how to play the game. I can do all of that for you."

I grasp her hand, pushing it away. "Don't fucking speak about Kate. Don't even fucking think about her. She's a thousand times more woman than you'll ever be. The fact she doesn't know how to 'play the game' is what makes her perfect for me, in every way. She's my future, and I won't let you, or anyone else, get in my way. Now leave me the fuck alone."

Her shoulders slump as her head drops. Looking at the ground, she heaves out a long sigh. Tears fall from her eyes—she looks defeated. Maybe she's finally got the message? "You love her," she whispers.

Tucking my hands in my pockets and rocking back on my heels, I look directly at her. "Yes. I do. She's the best thing that's *ever* happened to me, and I will not allow anything or anyone to take her away from me. Not now, not ever."

"I can tell by the way you defend her. She told me how hard you worked for her and how you wouldn't let her go when she was being difficult." She sighs, looking away, then back to me. "You never fought for me when I walked away."

My eyebrows press down. I can't figure out if she's being genuine or if there's further subterfuge going on. "No, I didn't fight for you. You made your fucking choice, and it wasn't me. I was hurt and angry at the time, but I never considered fighting to get you back. Now, when I think about it, I'm relieved you walked away. Kate's shown me how powerful a loving relationship can be." She nods and I soften my tone. "Go find that, Sonia. Leave all the other bullshit behind and go find it. Don't worry about the money, find the real thing. It's worth more than any money you think you need."

I leave her on the sidewalk and drive away, feeling out of sorts. I take a long drive, attempting to center myself, then make my way back to the office. I think I got through to her this time. When I arrive, I call Jase in, telling him everything that's been going on with Sonia over the past few months. His surprise and shock would be almost comical if I weren't feeling as off center as I am. His suggestion to inform the police mirrors Kate's, but I don't think it's necessary at this point.

I need to get through the day, then I can see my Sunshine. I'm taking her out for a casual dinner to celebrate Valentine's Day. Nothing fancy. We spend too much time hidden away from the world, and I want to show everyone she's mine. It's something Kate's avoided since the beginning when we ran into her ex at the pier. She also didn't feel comfortable with the attention she drew at the gala, and the speculation about who she was to me. She's gun shy, which I can understand. But she needs to realize that all the other shit isn't important. What we have together is all that matters.

After spending the afternoon going over reports for our newest client and gathering the data to build a solid portfolio, I finally arrive at Kate's. I'll meet with him in person next Friday to discuss the options available.

Kate's car isn't in the driveway, so I'm not sure if she's home. She's in the living room when I enter. I expected to find her dressed, ready for our dinner date, but she's sitting on her microscopic couch in leggings and a slouchy sweatshirt, looking at something. I step toward the couch, bending down to kiss her.

I study her face; her blotchy skin and red eyes tell me she's been crying. "Hey. What's going on?"

She shows me what she's looking at and my heart sinks to my feet. Photographs, which had to be taken today. They appear very intimate *and* very damning.

Me looking down into Sonia's face; her looking up at me adoringly.

Sonia with her arms around me, her hand on my chest, looking up into my eyes.

Each one makes me feel sick to my stomach. Each one explains the tears—once again, caused by me. The images captured don't show the true events of the brief meeting I had with Sonia today. But to someone who wasn't there, they look intimate—as if we're lovers.

"Where did you get those photos?"

I'm fucking fuming. I move around the couch, ready to explain the images aren't what they seem, but Kate stands quickly, wrapping her arms around her body as if she needs to protect herself from a physical blow.

She whispers, "How long have you been seeing your ex?"

I reach for her, but she steps away, much like I did today when Sonia attempted to reach for me. My heartbeat explodes into a rapid staccato—panic overwhelming me. "I'm not with her. I haven't been with her for several years. You know this, Kate. These pictures don't show what truly happened today." I step forward in a weak attempt to step back into Kate's orbit. I'm cold and empty on the outer regions, and I don't fucking like it—not one single bit.

"Will you let me explain?" I ask. Not that I'll take 'no' for a fucking answer this time. I need to keep calm. She nods, but doesn't look at me. "Can we sit while I tell you what *actually* happened?"

She nods again, stepping back toward the couch, sitting as close as possible to one end. I sit in the middle of the couch—because I'm an asshole like that. I don't want to give her an inch of space.

"She called me today from a number I didn't recognize. I've blocked her calls, texts, and emails. I already told you this. I answered the call because I thought it may have been the lawyer helping us with the embezzlement issue." I run my hand through my hair, resting it at the back of my neck. "Anyway, it was Sonia. She was sobbing and sounded as though she was in trouble; she asked me to help her. She said she had nobody else to call. I should have known better, but my conscience got the better of me and I offered to meet to help her." I drop my hand into my lap, huffing out a breath. "When I arrived, I had barely made it onto the side-walk when she pounced on me before I could register what the fuck was happening." I hold up the first photo. "I pushed her away immediately and was suspicious because she looked fine; absolutely zero signs of distress. She wants me back; correction, she wants my money back. She wasn't in trouble, she didn't need my help, and she wasn't upset." I get up to pace. I've got too much adrenaline pumping through my body to sit still. "Clearly, she wanted to cause trouble between us. I had no idea someone was taking photographs. I stupidly thought she genuinely needed help; that she was in trou-ble." I stop moving to look at Kate. "I'm sorry. There's less than nothing going on between me and her. I'm not interested in her in any way, shape, or form. *You* are my entire world. Why would I throw away what we have for something which was less than nothing?"

She stands and cups my face in her small hands. "I'm sorry,

Oliver. I should have known better, but those photographs hit every single one of my insecurities. Sometimes, my demons overtake rational thought. I'm honestly sorry I doubted you, for even a second." She kisses my lips gently, then pulls back to study my face intently. "Can you ever forgive me?"

"There's nothing to forgive, Sunshine." I grasp her ponytail, tugging her head back—taking her mouth in a kiss full of apology and promise. Without this woman, I can't breathe properly. I'm not sure what it's going to take for her to finally realize the depth of my feelings for her, and that nothing, absolutely fucking nothing, is going to take me away from her.

"Maybe you should go to the police about her stalking you. She seems pretty determined and desperate. You don't know what she might be capable of." She wraps her arms around my waist, looking up at me. "I'm worried for you."

I pull her body as close as possible to my own and kiss her forehead. "I'll be okay. I made it clear today that I want nothing to do with her. I think I finally got through to her. She should leave me alone now." *I hope.* Maybe I wasted my time. "Where did you get those photos?"

"They were in an envelope sitting on my porch." She shows me an envelope with her name scrawled across the front in a feminine script. *Fuck!* That means she came here *after* our meeting. Maybe I *do* need to get the police involved.

"Where's your car?"

"When I came out of work this afternoon, all of my tires were flat. I called Max, and he came to pick it up. It's a bit weird for all of my tires to be flat at the same time." She shrugs her delicate shoulder. "He said I should have my car back by tomorrow morning. He's going to fix it overnight, so I'm not without it." She steps into me, squeezing my torso. "How about I make you something for dinner? Then we can get some ice cream since I ruined our dinner plans. My treat." She steps toward the kitchen to put something together for me, when I grasp her wrist, stopping her.

"You didn't ruin our dinner plans. Sonia did. Put the blame

where it belongs. You don't need to make me anything. I had a late lunch meeting. Just let me get changed and we can go."

"Okay. I should change as well. I don't want to embarrass you again." She steps past me and into the bedroom.

"When did you ever embarrass me?"

She rolls her beguiling denim eyes as if I should know. "Both of the times we've been seen together in public."

I can almost hear the 'duh' at the end of the sentence. I follow her into her bedroom, and as she opens her closet door, I slam it closed with the palm of my hand. She startles—I don't think she realized how close I was.

"You look perfect just the way you are, and before we go any further, I want to make something perfectly clear to you. So listen up and listen good. Not once have I ever been embarrassed to be seen with you. I always feel honored you give me the time of day." I lift her chin with my knuckle, ensuring she has to look at me. "You are stunning to me—whether you're naked, dressed for work, lounging at home, or dressed for the gala." I cup her cheeks, perusing her face. "You are so fucking beautiful, Kate. I wish you could see what I see."

A tear slips down her cheek and my heart drops—I didn't intend to upset her. I would rather cut off my right arm than see her cry. I kiss it away. "Don't cry, Sunshine. I never want to see your tears."

"It's not a sad tear, Oliver. It's a tear of acceptance. I think I finally get what you've been telling me from the start." She presses up onto her toes, gently pressing her lips to mine. "Thank you." Two simple words, but they're deeply heartfelt, easing my anxiety.

"Good. Now let's get moving. I want some ice cream." I slap her delicious ass as I pass her to change into sweats and a t-shirt.

She looks at what I'm wearing and smirks. "You realize wearing gray sweats will get you a whoooole lot of attention? Right!"

I look down at my pants and back up at her in confusion. "Why? What's wrong with them?"

"Uh, nothing's wrong with them. More like *everything's* right with them. If you know what I mean?" She winks at me. She's fucking talking in riddles now. "They say that a man wearing gray sweats is the equivalent to a woman wearing leggings."

I look at her in her leggings and while they shouldn't be sexy; they fucking are. They show off the curves of her luscious ass and hips, her shapely legs, and I get her meaning.

"Okay, I get it. Maybe we should *both* change?"

She laughs at me, stepping into her closet for a change of clothes, while I change into jeans. The sound of her laugh is something I want to hear every fucking day I'm breathing. I stash the gift I had planned to give her over dinner into my pocket, and we head out for ice cream.

FIFTY-TWO

-kate-

Surprisingly, Oliver lets me pay for our ice cream, which I appreciate. He could have easily stepped in and paid what I'm sure is a negligible amount to him. I love that he gives me the space to feel as though we're equal partners—even though, financially, we're not. After ice cream, we wander down the sidewalk, holding hands, stopping now and then to browse a window display. I treasure these moments with him. We're both very busy; Oliver with his business, and me with my job and volunteering. The time we spend together always feels special.

Oliver's reassurances have knocked out the last of my demons. I no longer need to second-guess our relationship or feel worried. He sees something in me that no other man has before. He values me as a person and what I bring into this relationship and cherishes me in every way, every single day. I mentally watch the last brick in my wall fall away, tumbling, breaking, disappearing. Gone forever.

"Come on. I feel like a coffee." He pulls me into a cozy café and orders us each a decaffeinated coffee made to our preferred specifications. We wait for our order, then situate ourselves in a booth, which allows us to watch people walking by. He directs me to sit first, sliding in next to me—touching every part of my body, from my shoulder to my foot, sending electric currents through me. It's always like this with him. I've never felt anything like it before.

He digs into his pocket and passes me a pink calico pouch. "Happy Valentine's Day, Sunshine." I feel embarrassed—I gave him a cheesy heart-shaped helium balloon for Valentine's this morning. I had no idea what I could possibly get a billionaire that he doesn't already have or can't buy for himself.

"I've had this for a few weeks. I was waiting for the right time to give it to you." He looks down at it, then back up to me. "It's nothing expensive. I thought you might like it." He must have noticed my worry over yet another gift. "Please. Open it."

I smile at him and open the pouch. Out slides three small items, each wrapped in pink tissue paper. I carefully open the first, sucking in a breath when I recognize the rose gold necklace with the rose quartz heart as the one I was admiring when we spent the weekend away. My eyes snap up to his. "How did you know?"

"I saw you discreetly admiring it at the artisan markets. I approached the seller and asked her to contact me when it was finished." He nudges the other two small packages toward me. "She made it a complete set for me. Open the other two parts."

My hands are shaking as I attempt to open the small parcels carefully. As the pieces are revealed, I admire their beauty. Remarkably simple and delicate, yet stunning. Oliver carefully situates the necklace around my neck and closes the clasp, then places the bracelet on my wrist. I carefully remove the earrings I'm already wearing, placing them in the calico pouch for safekeeping, then attach the new earrings to complete the set.

Oliver holds my hair away from my face. "Stunning. Just like you. I knew they belonged on your body when I saw you admiring them."

I wrap my arms around his neck, pulling him toward me. "Thank you. They're divine." I kiss him in gratitude and sit back to admire my bracelet. "I'm never taking these off. It means a lot to me that you went to all the trouble to give them to me."

"It was no trouble at all. Anything that puts a smile on your face is worth the effort." He brushes a lock of hair behind my ear, kissing my lobe. "I always want to put a smile on your face. Every day, if I can."

I'm going to melt into a puddle of goo if he keeps this up. He thinks he's such an asshole, but he's never once shown that side of himself to me. "You know I only need you every day and I'm a happy girl."

I'm going to show him exactly how much I love his thoughtful gesture when we get home. Hmm, *home*. When did I start thinking of my home as our home? But it feels right—a natural progression of our relationship. Maybe I should ask him to *actually* move in with me? It's just, my place doesn't have a heap of space, and remembering what his penthouse is like—enormous and spacious. I feel self-conscious about my home. I know he likes the homeyness of my place, but would he want to live there permanently?

As soon as the front door closes, I back Oliver up against it and drop to my knees, undoing his belt, button, and zipper. He's already hard as granite, and his dick is fighting the constraints of the red boxer briefs I gave him for Christmas. I love that I have this effect on him. A man, powerful in his domain, is at my mercy—little ol' me. It's a heady sensation to feel this powerful. This desired.

"Woah! Slow down, Sunshine. What's going on?" He grasps my hair, pulling my head back until our eyes connect and lock.

"I want to make you feel good. I wanted to show you how much I love your thoughtful and generous spirit."

I pull his dick out of his underwear, pushing them further down his muscular legs, allowing me to tease his balls without obstruction. He looks as though he's about to argue the point when I take the first swipe with my tongue from base to tip, followed by a gentle swirl around the crown. I taste his salty precum as I take as much of his shaft into my mouth as I can. I tighten my grip around the base, coordinating my strokes, to drive him wild.

He's trying to be polite, keeping his strokes shallow—that won't do. I want him to lose control, the way I do when he's working me over with his talented mouth. I double my efforts, increasing the pressure of my hand, while I bring my other hand up to tease his balls again. I moan around his dick—his answering groan spurring me on.

His hips thrust and the hand holding my hair pulls tight in a bid to control my movements. Slowly, but surely, he's letting go. I've lost control of my saliva and it drips out of my mouth. My eyes water from the fullness and the pressure of my hair being pulled—it's exactly what I want from him. I'm getting wetter by the second; my breasts are full and heavy. It won't take much to push me over the edge to ecstasy. My moans and his grunts, together with our heavy breathing, fill the silence of my home as he begins to come undone. He attempts to pull my head away, but I hold on tight to his firm ass, showing I want the complete experience. I want him to come in my mouth. He gives me so much; rarely, does he not meet my needs before his own.

I gently tug at his balls, using my finger to massage his taint, breaking his control. His hot cum squirts down my throat in ribbons, coating the back of my tongue. I work hard to swallow it all down so I can lick his dick clean. His legs give out, and he slides down the front door to the floor, pulling me into his body, and sealing his mouth over mine in a deep kiss full of satisfaction and gratitude.

Nuzzling into the side of my neck, he whispers words of praise and gratitude, while gathering his composure. He awkwardly carries me through to the bedroom, almost tripping over his jeans trapped around his ankles.

Saturday morning seems to come around fast. I wake in a tangled mess of limbs and blankets, snuggled up to my favorite person. Today's the day the kids get to move home. All the work Oliver and Jase did to solve the problem; finding the missing money, organizing a successful gala, putting his work on hold—his generosity was astounding. He was determined to make things right for the kids. I couldn't help but fall in love with him a little more—make that a lot more.

Attempting to extricate myself from the tangle, I wriggle toward the edge of the bed. I don't get far when Oliver pulls me back against his firm chest.

"Mmmm. Where do you think you're going, Sunshine?"

I love that deep raspiness in his voice first thing in the morning. I can't believe this is my life. Every day for the rest of my life, I get to wake up with this man—*hopefully*.

"I was going to the bathroom. It's almost time for me to get up and get ready. It's the big day today."

He tugs me around, positioning me exactly where he wants me. "Not before I get my good morning kiss." I know he won't let me go until I capitulate, so I press forward to peck his lips.

"Uh, uh. Not good enough." I knew it wouldn't be enough, but I have this thing, I prefer to brush my teeth first, even if Oliver doesn't mind morning breath.

He tightens his hand at the back of my head, preventing me from pulling away as he leans forward, taking my mouth in a good morning kiss to end all good morning kisses. His kisses leave me disoriented, and it takes several beats to recover my senses.

"Now you can go to the bathroom." He kindly releases me, allowing me to make my escape before I pee myself.

When I return, he's getting dressed. I know he's still behind with his work and will probably spend his time catching up while I help the kids move home. I step up behind him, wrapping my arms around his sculpted torso and laying my head between his shoulder blades. "Make sure you don't work too hard today. Okay? Remember to stop for lunch, at least."

He looks over his shoulder at me, then grasps my hands and twists around until we're face to face. Tucking a lock of hair behind my ear, he responds, "I love how you worry about me." He reverently cups my face in his large hands. "I didn't know what I was missing until I met you." Leaning forward, he kisses my forehead, then steps back to continue dressing. "I'm coming with you today. I want to help the kids settle back in. I'll catch up on my work next week."

"You don't have to do that. You've already given up so much of your valuable time to help them. Truly. Concentrate on your work. I'll help them over the weekend while you catch up on your folios, or whatever you call them."

"No, I've decided to help. I don't want to miss out on seeing you over the weekend. Work can wait. Now get dressed while I make us breakfast." He smacks my butt as he walks out, making me jump.

I quickly dress in layers, because I know even though it's cold outside, I'll get hot from the physical activity. Roman dropped off a key yesterday, so I'm going to the house first to give it a thorough clean, as well as stock the kitchen with essentials. I'm hoping to get it all done before the kids arrive this afternoon. I bet they're beyond excited to get back into their own place and have their own space again.

There's a knock at my door as we're finishing our breakfast. It's Max, returning my car.

"Hey, Max. Thanks for fixing the tires quickly for me." I feel Oliver at my back.

"No worries." He looks like he wants to say something, but isn't sure how to say it. "Look, I don't know how to tell you this, but your tires were slashed. They didn't go flat by themselves."

What? Who would do something like that? Oliver steps around me.

"How could you tell they were slashed?"

"Well, there was a two-inch incision in each tire. Could only have been made by a knife."

"You're sure?" Oliver's tension ratchets up.

"Yeah, man. You might want to let the cops know." He hands me my car keys and the invoice, but Oliver grabs the invoice quickly.

"Thanks, Max. We'll get on to it. Have you still got my credit card details on file?" Max nods. "Good. Use that to pay for the new tires."

I try to butt in and argue, but Oliver looks at me sternly, shaking his head. "No arguments, Sunshine."

I reluctantly agree. "Okay. Thank you for your help." I turn to Max. "Thanks, Max."

"No problem. See you guys later." He leaves, and Oliver closes the front door, engaging the lock.

"Thanks for paying for my tires, but you don't have to do that." I'm not sure how to feel about my tires being slashed on purpose. "I wonder who would slash my tires? In the school parking lot of all places. Thank goodness whoever did it didn't hurt any of our students."

Oliver's deadly quiet, looking at the closed front door. Then he looks down at me. "I have a suspicion who damaged your tires, and I'm not fucking happy about it." He steps away from me. "Let me make a quick call, okay?"

"Sure." He looks beyond pissed.

The first thing we do when we arrive is open all the windows and doors to let fresh air into the house. Oliver's mood has improved since we left my place and he gets to work outside, cutting the grass and tidying up, while I strip all the beds and replace them with fresh linens. While they're washing, I clean the bathrooms and kitchen, then Oliver comes inside to help vacuum while I dust. The place is looking pretty good.

It's getting close to lunchtime, so we lock the house and drive to the market for what we need, stopping on the way for something to eat. We make quite a team, me and Oliver. It feels fantastic to have him with me. He doesn't seem to mind doing such mundane things. It makes me think about what it would be like to work together to raise a family.

We're unpacking the last of the groceries when the kids come barreling through the door with Roman.

"Hey, wipe your feet. Kate's been working hard to clean up for you guys." As he comes around the doorway, he notices Oliver. "Oh hey, Oliver. I didn't expect to see you here." He reaches out to shake Oliver's hand in that manly kind of way.

The kids crowd around, absorbing me into a group hug of epic proportions, amid a flurry of, 'Missed you, Kate.', 'Thanks, Kate.', and 'You're awesome.' I've missed these guys a heap, and it's fantastic to see them again. To see them happy to be back in their space.

Returning their hugs, I let them know how much I missed them. "Now put your stuff away. We've got a lot of catching up to do."

They take off to their respective rooms to unpack, or maybe a better description would be; to dump their stuff.

"Thanks for getting everything ready for the kids. I couldn't manage to do that *and* keep them out of trouble."

"We were happy to help. I'm relieved they're finally home."

While there's a sunny break in the weather, Oliver takes the boys out for a game of basketball, while the girls and I catch up on all our girlie stuff.

Ivy comes in close to me and whispers, "So, I guess you know who Oliver is now?"

I'm taken aback by her question. "What do you mean?"

"Well, last time he was here, I felt like you didn't know who he was, so I didn't say anything." Her eyes twinkle as a smile grows across her face. "He's Oliver Stone. Only the richest man in America under the age of thirty-five." She lets out a girly squeal.

Ah, I see. She knew who he was because … of course she did. She's always reading business journals and magazines. "So you knew who he was, but didn't tell me. Why not?"

Suddenly, her fingernails are super important and she can't look at me. "Um, I didn't want to ruin anything. You seemed happy, and I figured it wasn't my info to share."

I take her in a big hug. "You're very sweet, Ivy. You're right, I didn't know, but I do now." I pull back, studying her. "It was a shock at first, and I didn't like that he'd kept the information from me. But we've worked it all out now."

"He was mighty kind to me when I asked if I could shadow him at work. I'm not sure if he realized I knew who he was, but he was way cool. He told me I'm welcome to come in any time over school vacation so it doesn't interfere with my schoolwork."

"He thinks with your enthusiasm and drive, you'll be very successful in the corporate world." I have to cover my ears to protect them from the high-pitched squeal she releases.

We hear the boys coming inside and that's our cue to move into the living area.

"Who wants to make cookies?" I call out as we walk into the kitchen. The response is a unanimous 'yes'. We work together to make a couple of different batches, working with the same base recipe.

The time spent with the kids always seems to fly, but today seems to have passed at lightning speed. Before I know it, it's time to leave, allowing the kids to get to bed. Hugs are given freely, filling my heart to the brim with love and joy, because they also included Oliver—even Blake.

Today's the day I get to catch up with Ella and Bob. I'm looking forward to seeing them. It'll be two years at the end of June since I last saw them. I can't believe that much time has passed. Oliver's decided to come along too, as he's interested in helping with the construction. He told me his *CornerStone Foundation* is a major contributor to the work Bob and Ella do with their *Schools for Everyone* project. Why does that not surprise me? He's told me that school was his one constant during his childhood and adolescence and that's why it's important to him to give to Bob and Ella's project.

Oliver's been in and out of court as a witness for the embezzle-ment case over the past few weeks. He's been working late at the office most nights to keep up with his clients. I don't mind, I just miss him when he's not with me, so I'm grateful he came along.

Last Monday, we went to the police about my tires. Oliver told them everything that's been going on with Sonia and I told them about the photographs being left on my doorstep. They're following up to see what they can find, but I'm worried she's become completely unhinged. Oliver's also got his PI, Mike, looking for her, but he hasn't been able to locate her yet.

Walking into the café holding hands with my guy, I see Ella and Bob have already secured a table by the window. Ella notices us first, her face lighting up with a genuine smile. She's out of her chair and moving toward us with her arms open wide, ready to embrace us. Our reunion is full of big smiles and warm embraces as if we're old friends.

Ella holds my hand and then grasps one of Oliver's hands, swinging them between our bodies. "Oh my, look at you two." She looks across at Oliver. "So I guess you found her, huh?"

I look between Ella and Oliver. "Yeah, I did; purely by chance."

"I'm very pleased." She looks at Oliver. "I felt terrible that I couldn't give you Kate's information when you requested it; confidentiality and all that."

"I understood, even though I was frustrated at the time." He looks at me with adoration. "It all worked out how it was supposed to."

"Seeing you two together makes my heart happy." She tugs on our hands. "Come. Sit. Let's chat."

We order coffee and cake. Then Bob and Ella update us on the progress of the last school they worked on, which was the one where Oliver and I initially met.

"Your program was easy to implement. The teachers have moved forward in leaps and bounds. They use what you left for them as a base, and now they build their ideas from that," Bob tells me, with pride clear in his voice.

The update makes me feel proud. The teachers I met with had little confidence in themselves. I spent a lot of time building their self-belief while I was working with them. "They were wonderful when I worked with them. I'm not surprised they've taken what I left and built on it themselves. It makes me tremendously happy to know that."

"So, how is the next project coming along?" Oliver asks.

"Good, good. As you know, Oliver, it's another island community in the Molucca Sea this time. A tsunami came through and the local government is stretched thin with funding. They have an entire community to rebuild, so they contacted us to ask if we would be willing to help rebuild their school."

Oliver nods and my heart breaks for the community. What they must have gone through—the loss, tragedy, and utter devastation.

Bob continues, "At the moment, the teachers are working under a hastily constructed hut, with no resources. We're hoping to start work at the beginning of July. We're in the process of getting the school design finalized and recruiting volunteers to assist with the construction and set up." He looks at Oliver. "Thanks to your foundation, our funding support is strong. We're able to purchase the materials we need to construct the school, as well as the required resources to help the teachers with their program."

Ella takes over from Bob. "The devastation is heartbreaking. The sooner we can get the school up and running, the sooner the community will feel as though they're getting back to normal. As you know, school is more often than not the heart of any small community. Kate, if you could work your magic with the elementary teachers, we'll have another fabulous school supporting the children and the community."

"Of course. I'm excited to be working with you again. I had heaps of fun last time. You can also count on me to help with the construction." I squeeze Oliver's thigh under the table. "Oliver and I will come together. We'll both help with the construction, and then, while I work with the teachers, Oliver will work remotely, so he can help with setting up the classrooms."

We continue to chat about the plans for the new school over coffee and cake for the next hour or so. It gives me such a burst of energy. I'm definitely excited about getting started on this new adventure. The best part is being able to work on this next project alongside Oliver.

FIFTY-THREE

-oliver-

ARRIVING AT WORK ON MONDAY MORNING, I FIND JASE ALREADY HAS my coffee on my desk and my computer booted up, ready to go.

"Morning, boss man." He's more upbeat than usual this morning.

"Morning," I say suspiciously, while he makes himself comfortable in the chair opposite my desk.

"So, I caught up with an old college friend over the weekend. He's a real estate agent now. He works predominantly in the higher end market. You know, for rich guys like yourself." He smirks and I nod, indicating for him to get to the point. I just want to get in touch with Mike to find out what he's got on Sonia. "He's got a sublime property on the books down where the old power station used to be. Remember, it was all redeveloped a few years ago?"

"Yeah, I remember. Properties right on the riverfront."

"That's the one. Well, this property was built across four standard blocks, so it's enormous. House, pool and hot tub, spectacular gardens, a dock with a fire pit, four-car garage, and a smaller home at the back of the property for live-in staff. Apparently, it was built when the development was first undertaken, but it's been sitting empty for the past two years. Never been lived in."

This is interesting. It wouldn't be too far from the office, not too ostentatious for Kate, and space for Margie to come with us. Yeah, whenever I think about asking Kate to move in with me, I know I have to make plans for Margie as well. There's no way Kate would be happy to leave Margie behind. "Sounds promising. Is there anything online I can look at?"

"Uh, yeah. That's why I've already turned on your computer. I've already got the page loaded."

Now his organization this morning makes sense. I wake up the computer to browse the photographs. It's a stunning property. Red brick, timber floors, lots of light, white trims, granite countertops, stainless steel appliances, a stunning double-sided stone fireplace, mudroom, master suite, and six bedrooms, each with their own attached bathroom. I don't think we would have to do much to it— just add furnishings. It screams settled down family life, which is exactly what I want. I can't believe how quickly my thoughts on settling down have changed since having Kate in my life.

I glance across at Jase, who's sitting with a smug smile on his face. "Perfect isn't it?"

I nod, returning his smile as my excitement builds. "It looks pretty damn good. I don't want to live with Kate in the penthouse. It's too cold, and Kate would balk at anything too ostentatious. This is perfect. Not too over the top, but enough room for us to make a family together. Can you set up a time for me to view it in person?"

He rises from his chair. "Sure thing, boss man. I'll get in touch with Simon now."

As he reaches the door, I stop him. "Jase." He turns around with his hand gripping the door handle. "Thanks, man. Be sure you're available for the viewing appointment. I want you with me when I take the first look."

He seems surprised, but nods as he steps out to do my bidding. I'm unsure how he fucking knew I was ready to find a new place for me and Kate—sometimes he knows what I'm ready for before I do.

I take a moment to contact Mike.

"Hey Mike, what have you got for me on Sonia? I want this sorted out as soon as fucking possible."

"I can't locate her; she's disappeared. However, I found CCTV footage from across the road which shows the school parking lot. It clearly shows a blonde-haired woman hanging around Kate's car on the morning of February 14. I believe that's *before* you met with her?"

"Yeah, it was after lunch that I made the mistake of meeting with her."

"Right. Maybe your chat with her wasn't wasted. She hasn't bothered you since then. Am I right?"

"You're right. I haven't heard from her, but she *did* deliver the photographs to Kate's place after our chat."

"That could have been the photographer following through with instructions. It could all be over for all we know."

"Maybe. I would still feel better knowing where she is and what she's up to."

"No problem. I'll keep looking."

"Thanks, Mike. Bye."

I disconnect the call, not feeling satisfied with the conversation. I need a conclusion. I need to know she won't be bothering us. I need to know that Kate's safe.

-kate-

EMMA, HER BOYS, AND I STEP OUT OF THE SCHOOL BUILDING AT THE end of another school day. We stop, chatting next to her car for a few minutes, while she straps her boys into their seats.

"Did I tell you the house next door is up for sale?" Emma asks over her shoulder.

"No. You like your neighbors, don't you?"

"Yeah. I'm going to be sad when they move. They decided they needed something smaller to maintain. I can understand where they're coming from; I'm being selfish. Ever since we moved in, they've always been good to the boys and me."

"You'll be able to visit them and have them over to your place." I nudge her shoulder with a wink. "You never know, maybe some hottie will buy their place and give you some nice eye candy."

Her face lights up. "Ohhh, I like the way you think."

She finishes up with the boys. "Bye boys. Be good for your mom."

"We will." Emma rolls her eyes at me. "Bye, Ms. Summer."

Arriving home, I'm surprised to find Oliver's car already parked in my driveway. It's only four, way too early for him to have finished work for the day. As I quickly collect my things to rush inside, I hope everything's okay.

"Oliver!" I call, as I'm opening the front door.

He comes out of the bedroom, wearing jeans and a t-shirt, looking casual and relaxed, an enormous smile on his handsome face as he steps into me, kissing me chastely. He takes my bags from me, placing them in their designated spaces. Since he's home early and we've got time, maybe now would be a good time to ask him to officially move in with me.

"Is everything okay? You're home early."

Placing his hands on my hips, he pulls me into his body. "Everything's perfect. I wanted to get here before you. I have something I want to show you, but I have a question to ask you first." He takes my hand, leading me to my couch. He sits, positioning me on his lap, then cups my face gently in his warm hands. I'm not sure what's going on, but he looks serious.

"Okay, you've got my undivided attention. What's going on?"

"It's something I've been thinking about for a while now, but I wanted to wait until I was confident we were both on the same page." He takes a deep breath. "I feel we're completely in sync. We fit together seamlessly, and I know I never want to let you go. I'm pretty confident you feel the same way."

I can only nod. My heart rate speeds up to the point I'm worried it's going to explode out of my chest. My palms are clammy, my breaths scarce.

"Hey. Take a breath. It's okay, I'm not proposing." He smiles at me, and I release the breath I was holding. "Yet! I was wondering, Kate, if you would do me the honor of moving in with me?" Oh my gosh, he must be a mind reader. I can't help the bubble of laughter that bursts out of me.

"Oh my gosh, Oliver. I was going to ask you the very same thing. I wasn't sure how you'd feel about moving in here with me, or if we should move into your place. But then I'd have to leave Margie and I'm not comfortable doing that." I'm rambling like an idiot as he attempts to hide his smile.

"Is that a yes, Kate?"

"Yes! That's a huge yes from me." I press forward, planting the biggest kiss on him I can.

"You've made me the happiest man. Now for the second part. I want to take you somewhere. Do you want to get changed before we go?" Judging by his attire, it's going to be casual, so I change into jeans.

As we get closer to the city, he turns toward the river. "I love the river. I don't spend much time here. Occasionally, I'll stroll along the banks on the walkways for an afternoon." I can't remember the last time I actually spent the afternoon doing that.

He smiles at me. "We should definitely do that some time."

I nod in agreement, turning my head back to the window to admire the decadent houses overlooking the banks. It would be out of this world to wake up to a view like that every day. Oliver pulls into a driveway of a breathtaking home. It's an enormous red brick structure, with large windows surrounded by white trim. The garden and surrounds are something from a Pinterest board. Steps lead up to a large porch, which would be perfect for a swing seat, but is currently bare. It seems as though nobody lives here.

"Whose place is this?" I ask Oliver as he opens my door.

He takes my hand, dragging me out of the car. "I don't know the owner's name. It's for sale and I wanted to bring you through to look. Jase's friend from college is the agent selling the property. He brought Jase and me through for a viewing this morning, and I think this would be the perfect place for us." He's studying my face closely, observing my reaction, which is pure shock. My eyes must be as big as they've ever been, and I think I can feel the paving from the driveway scraping my chin.

"You can't be serious. This place is enormous, Oliver. We don't need anything this big. It's only the two of us." My eyes flit between the house and Oliver.

At that moment, a man steps out of the house; he must be the

368 • DEBRA ST JAMES

agent. Oliver takes my hand, almost dragging me toward the house as the agent steps down from the front porch.

"Hey, Simon. Thanks for letting me take another look today. This is my girlfriend, Kate." We all shake hands.

"No problem, Oliver. Welcome, Kate. I hope you like the home. I'll wait out here. Everything's open for you. Take as long as you need and don't hesitate to ask questions about the property."

I manage to find my voice, so I don't seem rude. "Hi, Simon. Nice to meet you."

Oliver's clearly excited as he drags me forward, up the timber steps, onto the wide timber porch. The porch wraps around the house, with white French doors opening onto it from several rooms. From the side porch, I can see we are right on the riverfront.

"Oh, Oliver." I breathe. "Before even going inside, I can tell this home is something else." I've never seen a home like this in real life —it's unbelievable.

"Wait until you see the inside and the rest of the property. You're going to fall in love with it."

He takes me in through the double front doors, which are more glass than timber. I can just imagine walking through these doors after taking our boys to football practice. The floors are a light-colored timber, with white baseboards and trims around the doors and windows. The foyer is roomy and airy with a cupboard for coats, shoes, and umbrellas. I'm giddy thinking of having a life here with Oliver and our very own family.

There's no furniture in the house, making it appear larger than it probably would if it were furnished. The entire home is on the same level, with an attic for additional storage, making it feel homey. The enormous double-sided stone fireplace with gas fire is charming, reminding me of the fireplace at the beach house we stayed in. I can imagine curling up in front of it with a glass of wine and a good book on a cold winter's day, wrapped in Oliver's strong arms. The image is powerful and vivid—stealing my breath.

The walls are all painted the same pale mossy green, which will go with anything and complements the riverfront location perfectly. The to-die-for kitchen faces along the back of the property, complete with a dining area, which has French doors lining the entire wall, opening onto a wooden deck. I don't know where to look, there are too many standout features. I picture nights where Oliver makes us breakfast for dinner; me cooking his favorite risotto—building a life together. My heart feels full to bursting.

As we walk through the home, I can't help but get caught up in Oliver's excitement as he shows me the large walk-in closet, sitting area, and private ensuite in the master suite. It has its own set of doors, exiting onto a private deck with a hot tub, separated from the main deck with privacy screens. He wriggles his eyebrows at me, pulling me into his body. "Imagine what we could get up to in that hot tub." I can't help but giggle and moan at the same time, feeling his hard length pressing into my belly. "We could even forego wearing suits."

"Oh, that sounds divine." I press up to kiss his delicious lips, then step back to look around. The view across the river from the bedroom matches that of the view from the kitchen, dining, and informal living areas.

For as large as the house is, I can imagine a life here with Oliver and our future family. Earnest, loving little boys with Oliver's dark hair and green eyes. As I explore all the rooms, including his and hers offices and an enormous room for a gym, which looks suspiciously like a dance studio; I'm amazed at the amount of thought and planning that was taken during the design process. As I open and close cupboards, taking in every nook and cranny, Oliver quietly observes me. Once I've checked everything over inside, Oliver directs me outside, through the French doors onto the back deck.

"Wow!" It's all I can say as I look out across the property. Apart from the view, the spectacular gardens from the front of the house continue here. A pool is situated beside a fabulous limestone patio with Jasmine growing over the rafters, covering a stunning outdoor grilling area. Further off, there seems to be a small house. I point to it. "What's that place?"

Wrapping his arm around my shoulder, we stroll along the red brick paved path toward it. "It's a smaller home. I thought Margie might like to move with us. She could live there."

Oh, my heart! This man.

I throw myself at him, leaping into his arms, wrapping my legs around his hips. "You are the sweetest man, Oliver Stone. Don't let anyone tell you otherwise!" I kiss his lips through my smile and his. This can't be my life. For real, this only happens in fiction novels.

He carries me the rest of the way, putting me down on a cute front portico. We wander through what could be Margie's home, designed in a similar style to the main house. He then shows me our personal dock and boat shed. Near the dock is a stone fire pit, set in the middle of a red brick paved circle.

I turn to Oliver. "This place is divine, Oliver. I think the original owner thought of absolutely everything when he had this home built." I grasp his face in my hands. "Is this where you would like to live?"

"Only if you're here with me, Kate."

"I would be honored to live here with you, Oliver. But——" He cuts me off with a finger on my lips.

"No buts, Kate. If you think you'll be happy living here with me, that's all I want to hear." He shakes his head in the negative when I try to interrupt. "I know you're going to give me some spiel about not being able to contribute financially to something like this. I don't care. I *can* and I will. Let me do this for us. Please, Kate." He removes his finger, kissing my lips.

"I can sell my place. What's left from repaying the mortgage I'll put toward this house. Please, at least, let me do that. It'll probably only cover the cost of the fire pit, but I would feel better if you let me contribute my meager amount."

He looks at me in that full-on Oliver way and nods sharply. "Okay. I'll let you do that. But then that's the end of talk about money, and who pays for what. Understand?"

He's firm in his statement. All I can do is nod in agreement. I'll just have to contribute in other ways. As we walk back up to the main house, I let out a laugh.

"What's so funny?" he asks.

"I was thinking. I'll probably have to give up work, so I have the time to clean this house. It's so freaking big!"

"I'll have my cleaner come through here once a week, instead of the penthouse. You won't have to worry about any of that."

I don't respond to his flippant comment about a cleaner. I have to accept there are things he can afford to do and will choose to do. I can't fight him on everything to do with money. As long as I maintain the importance of him not spending obscene amounts of money on me. I won't be like his ex, who spent his money on treatments and spa days, unnecessary clothes, and expenses. I need to be certain he knows I'm with him for *him*, and *not* for his money. That *HE* is what's most important to me.

We wander around to the front of the home, and I spot Simon on his phone. When he sees us, he ends the call and walks toward us.

"Hey, guys. What did you think of the property?"

Oliver looks down at me, then looks at Simon with a smile. "Put in the offer. You know my maximum, but let's see if we can get it for the best price possible."

"Sure, sure. I'll get in contact with the seller's agent today. Any questions about the property?" He looks at me. I shake my head in the negative.

After Simon confirms all of Oliver's details, he goes inside to lock up, and we drive to a riverside café for dinner. I can't believe we're going to be moving in together, and into such an outstanding home.

Oliver wants us to work with an interior designer to furnish the home to our liking. He likes the feel of my place, the coziness of it. He says he feels at home there and wants to bring that feeling into this new home. Oliver doesn't want to say anything to Margie about the new house yet, just in case the seller doesn't accept his offer on the property.

Over this last week, Oliver's been busy with work and we've spent our evenings planning for our move into our new home. His offer was accepted on the property, and he's contacted an interior designer to work with us. Tonight, Oliver wants to have Margie over for dinner so we can share our good news and invite her to move into the smaller home on the property.

I've already changed and started dinner when there's a quick rap on my door before it opens; it's Margie. "Hey, Margie. How was your day?" She's getting around a lot better, barely using her cane.

"Hi, Katie-girl. It was okay. I baked a lemon-curd pie for dessert. I haven't baked one of these in years, so I was a little rusty. I think it turned out okay, though."

"It smells delicious. Pop it on the counter and take a seat. Do you want anything to drink?"

"Nah. I'm okay. You keep cooking. I'm a little early, but I thought we could catch up before Oliver arrives. I feel as though I barely see you these days."

Guilt rises. Oliver and I get caught up in our bubble, forgetting about everything else. "I'm sorry Margie. I've neglected—" She cuts me off with a tut and a hard look.

"Don't apologize to me for falling in love and spending time with your fella. That's how it's supposed to be."

We chat, catching up on the happenings in the street, and how Margie's doing with her physical therapy, while I continue preparing dinner. She's looking strong and confident in her movements, which gives me a sense of relief that she's okay. Dinner's almost ready when Oliver arrives home. *Home.* I adore the sound of it.

"How are my girls?" He steps into the kitchen, giving me a semi-chaste kiss in greeting. He then moves to Margie, giving her a hug and kiss on the cheek, which makes her day, judging by the flush of her cheeks.

"We're great. Margie was catching me up on the happenings in the street. How was your day, *Dear?*" It's a bit of a joke between us, now we've officially decided we're living together. As silly as it sounds, it makes me feel even more secure and settled in our relationship.

"It's much better now I'm home with my girls, *Dear*." He winks at us, causing Margie to giggle like a teenager.

Margie and I set the table while Oliver changes and we sit down together for dinner. Oliver waits until there's a natural lull in the conversation, then clears his throat. I'm nervous about Margie's reaction to our news. Oliver takes my hand, looking toward Margie. "Margie, we have some news."

Margie's face lights up, and she places her silverware down. She gestures for Oliver to keep going.

"I've asked Kate to move in with me, and she said 'yes'."

Margie literally squeals in delight. "Oh, I'm supremely happy for both of you. Although I thought you were already living together."

"I guess we were. But we've made it official." He looks at me, and I nod for him to share the next part of our news. "There's more news we would like to share with you, Margie."

"Oh, do tell. Don't keep an old girl in suspense."

"We've bought a house together on the riverfront. Our offer was accepted, and once it's settled and furnished, we'll be moving there."

Margie's joy slips slightly. "That sounds like a lovely spot to settle into your life together. I'll be sad to lose such a wonderful neighbor and friend because you've brightened up my days, Kate. You too, Oliver."

Oliver nudges me to share the next part of our news. "Well, you can't get rid of us that easily, Margie. The property has a place for you. We would be thrilled if you would consider moving with us."

Margie shakes her head, her eyes suspiciously glassy. "Before you say 'no', let us show you the property on the weekend—then you can decide. We truly hope you decide to come with us."

"Oh, you two gorgeous kids. You know how to make an old woman feel wanted, but I don't want to cramp your style."

"You wouldn't be cramping anything. You would have a home of your own; completely separate from us. Wait until you see it. It's truly spectacular. The original owner thought of everything."

"I … I don't know what to say."

"Please say you'll at least consider it, Margie," Oliver implores. "We would love to have you with us."

She's clearly lost for words, her only reply, a gentle nod. She has no family, so we're pretty much it. As we finish dinner and move onto Margie's delicious dessert, Oliver pulls out his laptop to show her the house via the online listing. I can't wait for the weekend when we show Margie around the real thing. We'll also be meeting with the interior designer to walk through how we want the interior decorated.

The rest of the week goes by in a blur of work, spending time with Oliver, and poring over images online to create Pinterest boards for our new home. I don't know if we've got too many different ideas or not enough. We've pinned pictures of the stuff we like that seem to follow a similar theme. We want our new home to be warm and inviting, homely and comfortable. I've never had to think about furnishing and decorating every room in such a large home. I don't want to mess it up, and I don't want it to look like a hodgepodge either. I guess the designer can look at what we've got, and get a feel for the house to help us work it out.

Margie comes with us to the house on Saturday morning, falling in love with the place instantly.

"Are you certain you want an old bird living here with you two?"

"Of course we do, Margie. We love you. We would be crazy to leave you behind." I wrap my arm around her shoulder, giving her a squeeze.

"I'll give you the money from the sale of my house to put toward this place."

"You will do no such thing, Margie. Use the money to go on a vacation or something." Oliver suggests firmly. There's no way he would accept Margie's money.

"You could go on a cruise with Nan. She'll be due to go away again soon." I offer.

Margie smiles cheekily. "That sounds wonderful. But only if you're positive."

"We're one hundred percent positive."

"Okay. I'll move in. I don't know how I can ever thank you enough for this."

"Agreeing to move in is thank you enough." Oliver pulls her in for a hug.

We walk through the property with Gina, showing her the ideas we pinned for each room. She's impressed with our collection of boards for the house.

"You've done all the work for me. These ideas are fantastic and work well with the style of the property and its location. What exactly do you want me to do?"

Oliver responds, "We want you to pull it all together. I'm busy with work, and Kate already has a lot on her plate. Neither of us has the time to source everything we need to make this empty house become the home we want it to be. If you can source everything we need and put it together, so all we have to do is move our personal belongings in. We would be most appreciative."

"No problem. I can do that for you. I can probably access pieces you wouldn't normally be able to find in a furniture store, anyway. With my resources and contacts, this should be a piece of cake. What's your deadline?"

Oliver looks at me, and I shrug my shoulders. I hadn't thought about it. It's not like we have nowhere to live while Gina does her work.

"How about three-to-four-weeks' time? Does that work with your schedule?"

"Absolutely. As I source the larger pieces and soft furnishings, I'll have them stored in the garage. Then once I have everything here, I'll get my team in to put everything in place."

"Sounds good." My head is ping-ponging between Oliver and Gina, attempting to keep up with their conversation.

"I'll email through a contract on Monday, which will need to be approved, signed, and returned at your earliest convenience. Once I have that, I'll move forward. This is going to be a lot of fun."

"Feel free to contact Kate or me with any questions as they arise. I look forward to seeing the end result. Thanks, Gina."

And just like that, Oliver's bought a home and organized to have it completely furnished, ready for us to move in. My head is spinning. I'm not sure I know how to feel about someone else doing all the work of making our house a home. I guess that's how wealthy people do things. It will certainly make my life easier.

After Gina leaves, we wander out to the back deck, looking across the river. The view is stunning and I can imagine weekend barbecues with family and friends. Quiet evenings, drinking a glass of wine, just the two of us. Oliver and I playing with our children on the expansive grassed area, or in the swimming pool. I see it all clearly—as if I'm watching a movie. The future I'd almost given up hoping for. I look up at Oliver and pressing up onto my toes, I kiss his cheek. "Thank you."

Wrapping his arm around my shoulder, he pulls me in tight to his body as our eyes connect. "You don't have to thank me, Sunshine."

"Yeah, I do. You're making sure we have a welcoming and beautiful home, Oliver. I don't want you to think I take anything for granted."

"It's only going to be a beautiful home, because I'll be sharing it with you, Kate. Without you, it's just a big house on the riverfront."

This man slays me with his words. He lost an unthinkable amount as a boy, went through more than he should have growing up, was used and rejected as an adult, and yet he still shows me every day, the wonderful and caring man he grew to be. I've got to be the luckiest woman on this earth.

"Thank you for not giving up on me. I love you, Oliver Stone. Today and for all the days yet to come." I kiss his chest where his heart steadily beats—sure and strong. "Thank you for being mine."

epilogue

FIFTY-FIVE

-kate-

WALKING ONTO THE BACK DECK, MY HANDS FULL OF DISHES TO ADD to the buffet table, I'm especially light, happy, and grateful.

Moving into our new home five weeks ago was a dream come true. Oliver made it easy by hiring Gina to do all the legwork and organization. Then he hired people to pack up and move everything we wanted to keep from my place, Margie's, and his penthouse. All I had to do was wake up in the morning at my place, and then fall asleep that night in our new home. Not that we got a lot of sleep that night—if you know what I mean.

Margie loves her new home. She wakes up every morning and walks down to the dock to enjoy a cup of tea while watching the city come to life across the river. She misses the antics of Pete and Joe from down the street, but I've got a surprise for her today. I invited them to our housewarming party—she's going to be ecstatic.

"Hey, Sunshine. I've loaded all the coolers with drinks, put out all the plates, silverware, glasses, and napkins. Anything else you need me to do before I have a quick shower?"

He's much lighter now. Especially since we received an email from his ex. She apologized for slashing my tires and sending the photographs through. Apparently, she'd already attacked my tires before meeting Oliver, and the photographer was following through on their prearranged plans. She was remorseful for pursuing Oliver and made it clear that she's come to terms with the way things are now. It was such a relief to learn she's moved across the country to live in New York and try her luck at finding love there. Her email seemed genuine and I think it gave Oliver the closure he needed to let his anger toward her go completely.

"Nope. I think we're all good out here. I've got a couple more dishes to bring out. Our guests will start arriving soon, so you'd better scoot."

I press up onto my toes, giving him a chaste kiss. As usual, Oliver takes over and I'm left dizzy and disoriented. His kisses always have that effect on me—I think it will always be that way. He smirks as he wanders off toward the bathroom to shower and change; knowing exactly what he does to me.

Once everything's out on the table and I do a last check, I take five minutes to sit on the back deck, enjoying a cold lemonade before our guests arrive on this perfect spring afternoon. Oliver steps out onto the back deck, wearing jeans and his red Converse, which he bought to match mine. His hair's still wet from his shower and his black t-shirt molds to his muscular torso perfectly. My eyes devour him, the same as they do every time I see him. Now that I know him on such a deep level, I think he's even more attractive than when I first laid eyes on him.

"Stop looking at me like that, Sunshine. We don't have time." He grabs himself a beer out of one of the coolers.

"I don't know about that. You can be pretty creative when you want to be." I wink at him. We've Christened every room in this house—it was a mammoth task, but it had to be done. I think we only have half a dozen more walls to wear in, and then we can start all over again.

I'm torn from my musing when the doorbell sounds. Together, we greet our first guests.

The man at the door takes me by surprise. I've never met him before, but I would recognize his features anywhere. He's an older version of Oliver, not as tall or fit, but definitely Oliver's dad. Oliver invited him to join us this afternoon but wasn't sure if he would make the effort to show. I'm glad he did. For Oliver's sake.

Oliver stops short of the door. "Dad." He takes a moment to recover his equilibrium. "Hey. I'm happy you could make it. Come in, come in."

My family and our friends are pulling up in the driveway, so we step out of the doorway, into the foyer. Oliver quickly introduces me to his dad. "Kate, this is my dad, James Stone. Dad, this is my girlfriend, Kate."

He reaches out his hand to shake mine, but I step straight into his body, wrapping my arms around him in a hug. He's going to have to get used to the fact I'm a hugger. The sooner he learns, the better. He's stiff at first, taking a moment to relax; reminding me of the first time I hugged his son. I whisper in his ear, "It's certainly nice to meet you, Mr. Stone." We pull apart as he echoes my words.

My parents, Toby, Shane, and Nan, are next, and I'm excited to show them our new home. I wouldn't let Mom visit until today because I wanted everyone to see it at the same time. Oliver introduces his dad to my family, and they head off together through the house, toward the back deck to make themselves comfortable.

Margie wanders through in the nick of time to see Pete and Joe arrive. "Oh my goodness, Katie-girl. Why on earth did you invite these two old pains in the ass to your housewarming? They'll probably destroy the joint." She winks at me as she moves forward to greet the two old guys.

I get distracted when I see Emma arrive with her two boys in tow. She's laying down the law because I can see Austin rolling his eyes from here. I made sure to let her know I would have a quiet space, close to the action for Lachlan to escape to if the noise and activity level got to be too much for him. I hug Emma and ruffle Austin's hair. Lachlan rarely makes eye contact, so I say a quiet, 'hi', to which he waves. Emma and Margie hug and move through the house, to the back deck, together with Pete and Joe; stopping on the way, to show Emma and Lachlan the quiet room.

Jase arrives next. I look at Oliver and send him a wink because he plans to give Jase the key to his penthouse today. He doesn't want the place to go to waste. He figured it may as well be a bonus for him. Jase is going to be surprised, but I bet he'll be happy to get out of the shared situation he's been living in for the past four years. He steps in close, greeting me with a kiss to the cheek, to which Oliver growls. I'm sure Jase does that on purpose to wind Oliver up. "Hey guys, nice digs. I'm happy this all worked out for you two." He moves in, giving Oliver a proper greeting with the half-hug, back slap thing they do.

"We have you to thank for the house. We probably wouldn't have even known about it without you and your friend, Simon." Stepping back into his space, I hug him to show my gratitude.

Celia and Marcus, and Ella and Bob are hot on his heels, taking the few steps onto the front porch. It won't be long before Oliver and I begin work on the new school with Ella and Bob. They already know Celia and Marcus through various charity functions. "It's so great that you guys could come this afternoon." Leaning in, I hug each person in turn.

"Thanks for inviting us."

"Go through to the back deck. Help yourselves to food and drinks. We'll be through in a minute."

Marcus holds back for a moment. "I wanted to thank you, Kate, and Margie too, for donating your homes to our New Adult program. It was a great initiative. Just because a child turns eighteen doesn't mean they are automatically self-sufficient. Giving them a place to live while they get on their feet will set them up for life." Oh, that makes me truly happy. It's fantastic that Margie and I could do something to help the young adults leaving *The Parkerville Project*.

"Margie and I were happy to gift you our homes. We didn't need them anymore." My mortgage is the only expense I have these days. Once it's paid for completely, I'll gift the deed to the *Project*.

Roman and the kids are piling out of the people mover. They're our last guests to arrive. The kids are excited to be spending the afternoon with us. They've got their swim gear on, ready to jump into the pool. It's not quite warm enough for me yet, so I won't be going in today. Kids don't seem to notice the cold as much as we do. They high five and fist bump Oliver as they pass, making their way through the house in short order. Oliver steps forward to shake Roman's hand. "Hey, Roman. Thanks for bringing the kids this afternoon. It means a lot to us they could come."

"Wild horses couldn't keep us away. They certainly have plans to make good use of your swimming pool." He laughs as we move together through to the back end of the house, joining all of our guests.

Oliver wraps his arm around my shoulder, pulling me into his body, and kisses the top of my head. I look up at him, and my heart stops at the smile on his face. He looks relaxed, happy, and content to have everyone here in our home celebrating our new start together. This must be unreal for a man who grew up without consistent people in his life. After another squeeze and a quick kiss, and we separate to chat with our guests.

The afternoon is great fun. Between showing our family and friends through our new home and around the property, and laughing at the antics of the kids in the pool, the afternoon is passing quickly. Lachlan even seems to be coping with all the ruckus, with Evelyn's help. She's such a sweetheart; she's been stuck to his side like glue.

-oliver-

I'M FUCKING NERVOUS. I DON'T EVEN GET THIS NERVOUS WHEN I'M meeting a new client or taking a risk on the market. The kids are having fun in the pool and I don't want to disrupt them, but if I don't get this done soon, I'm going to go insane.

I'm so lost in my thoughts that I don't notice Dad come up behind me until he pats me on the back. "You've done well, Son. Your mom would have been very proud of you. After everything you've endured." He's choked up, the guilt written all over his face.

"Thanks, Dad. Finally, I feel like I'm where I belong. It's taken a long fucking time, but I'm there."

"It's a bit of a twist of fate, hey? Kate's family taking you in when you were a boy?"

"Yeah. When I made the connection, it blew me away." I look across at Kate, finding her laughing with Emma. I can't believe how lucky I am. "I'm the luckiest man on the face of the earth to have found Kate, and her family."

"She's a special lady. Beautiful, as well. She reminds me a lot of your mother. You're a very lucky man; make sure you hold on tight to that one, and never let her go."

"Oh, don't worry about that. I plan to keep her."

"Good, good."

Jase sidles up alongside Dad and me. "Kate certainly knows how to put on a good spread of food. I don't think I'll have to eat for at least a couple of days." He rubs his stomach in appreciation.

"She was worried there wouldn't be enough food. She's always looking out for everybody." I rub the back of my neck, pulling the key I've been wanting to give to Jase out of my pocket. Not that he needs a key once security scans his handprint. It's more symbolic than anything else. "Uh, I've got something for you, Jase." I hold the key up to him, motioning for him to take it.

"What's this?"

"The key to my penthouse. I want you to live there. It's about time you moved out of that shared house and my penthouse is sitting empty now." His eyes go wide with surprise. "Security is set to scan your handprint on Monday morning. This key is a backup, in case something goes wrong with the scanner."

"I don't know what to say, Olly. You pay me well and all, but I'm not sure I can afford that kind of rent."

"Consider it a bonus. I don't want any payment. I want the space to be used." I'm unprepared as he embraces me in a solid hug, almost knocking me off balance.

"Thanks, man. I was getting pretty tired of living with a bunch of dudes. It'll be nice to have my own space."

"I only brought my personal belongings with me. The place is still full furnished. You can move in whenever you're ready."

Jase grabs us a couple of beers and we toast his new living arrangement. I probably could have let him move in months ago, I haven't slept in my penthouse for quite some time. Kate was thrilled when I told her I was going to let Jase move into the penthouse. She made sure to put together a welcome gift for him as a surprise when he moves in. I thought letting him live there was enough of a gift, but Kate wanted to make it special.

I catch Roman gathering the kids out of the pool, so I wander over to check they have everything they need to follow through with my plan. Blake's still giving me the evil eye. I'm guessing he's still pissed I'm with Kate and he's not. When I went to speak to Roman and the kids about my plan, he gave me the 'you better not hurt her, or I'll come after you' spiel. He made me feel a little nervous, increasing my respect for the eleven-year-old. The kids are ready to roll, meaning I need to get Kate into position.

I find her giggling with Margie and her nan under the limestone patio. The Jasmine growing over the beams smells divine but not as good as Kate's natural scent.

"Ladies. Would you like to join us on the back deck? I would like to thank everyone for coming this afternoon." Margie already knows my plan; I think almost everyone here knows what I'm about to do. Everyone except Kate. We stroll toward the deck, and it's taking everything I have to keep myself steady and my nerves at bay. Our family and friends are milling around, waiting for us.

I take Kate's hand, guiding her up the steps to the wooden deck. Wrapping my arm around her shoulder, I pull her into my body, and lay a gentle kiss on the top of her head. I'm exceedingly grateful for this woman.

Clearing my throat, I begin. "I would like to thank all of you for sharing in the excitement of our new home by coming out today. Kate and I want you to know we have an open-door policy, and you're all welcome. Any time." Kate smiles up at me, squeezing me around my middle. "I never thought I'd have this. A home, with family and friends to share it with." I kiss the top of Kate's head again, pulling her impossibly closer. "But now I do. It's all thanks to this woman by my side. Who, I hope will choose to stay by my side, until my last breath."

Everyone moves aside to allow the kids to step forward with their poster board signs. Six of her favorite kids in the world, each one holding a sign with a single word:

KATE, WILL YOU PLEASE MARRY ME?

It probably only takes Kate a few seconds to read the signs to realize what the message says, but it feels like a lifetime. When she turns back to me, I'm waiting on one knee, with the ring I chose for her. A 1.5 carat pink Argyle heart-shaped diamond from Western Australia, surrounded by a halo of smaller colorless diamonds, in a rose gold setting. The band is also micro-pavéd with smaller colorless diamonds. The entire ring sparkles like the sun, which was my goal, because she's my personal sunshine. I chose the pink heart-shaped diamond, to match the set I gave her on Valentine's Day.

The blush I love and adore is rising up her neck, her eyes glistening, while her hands cover her chest—as if to prevent her heart from escaping.

"Kate, please do me the honor of becoming my wife. Be my partner, my lover, my best friend, the mother of my children, my future. Let me love you, cherish you, build my life with you." She's already nodding yes. "Let me be the last man to kiss you, share your bed, your body, your heart, your soul, and your mind. Kate, will you marry me?"

She's still nodding, as tears stream down her cheeks.

"I need the words, Sunshine." I smile up at her.

She drops down onto her knees in front of me, wrapping her arms around my neck, pulling me into her. "Yes, Oliver. A thousand times, yes. I'll marry you."

We meet in the middle to seal our promise of forever with a tender kiss. I'm more than aware we have an audience, one that includes Kate's father and brother, but I can't stop myself from taking the kiss I want. Cupping the back of her head, I tilt her face the way I need, allowing me to deepen the kiss. Opening her mouth on a sigh, I slide my tongue in to dance with hers—swallowing her sighs and taking her breath, the kiss lingers for longer than is appropriate. Gentling the kiss, I pull back a fraction, feeling Kate's breath on my lips, as she slowly opens her eyes.

We both smile.

Remembering I've still got the ring, I manage to pull back enough to slide it onto her left hand, where it will remain for the rest of our days.

We both climb to our feet amid cheers from family and friends. Everyone surrounds us in congratulatory hugs.

This is exactly where I want to be for the remainder of my days —building my life with Kate, our families, and the friends we gather along the way.

Would you like to attend Kate and Oliver's wedding and join them on their honeymoon?
RSVP for the Bonus Epilogue:
https://tinyurl.com/lovingsummer-bonusepilogue

Wondering about Toby's story?
You'll find it here:
books2read.com/dsj-2ndchancesummer

Wondering about Emma's story?
You'll find it here:
books2read.com/dsj-stolenkisses

Wondering about Roman's story?
You'll find it here:
books2read.com/dsj-foreverkisses

If you enjoyed reading **_Loving Summer_**, please consider leaving a review at the place you purchased this copy. A few words can really help me out in terms of a new reader making the decision to read or pass on my books. It would only take a couple of minutes of your time, but it would mean the world to me.

bonus extras

[pinterest]

I WENT CRAZY PUTTING TOGETHER A PINTEREST BOARD FOR KATE and Oliver's story. If you're interested, you can check it out here:

https://tinyurl.com/lovingsummer-pinterest

[spotify]

I've also put together a small playlist of the songs mentioned in this story and the bonus epilogue in Spotify. I would recommend waiting until after you've read the bonus epilogue before listening to this playlist. If you're interested, you can check it out here:

https://tinyurl.com/lovingsummer-spotify